"Entertaining." —*Fort Lauderdale Sun-Sentinel*

"Rhys Bowen's wit makes *Death of Riley* more than equal to her award-winning first book, *Murphy's Law*."
—Maan Meyers, aka Martin and Annette Meyers,
authors of the Dutchman series

"A fresh and irrepressible new heroine." —*Romantic Times*

"Bowen nicely blends history and fiction . . . [a] light, romantic mystery." —*Publishers Weekly*

"Bowen's highly detailed picture of New York at the turn of the century is a delight." —*Kirkus Reviews*

MURPHY'S LAW

"History-mystery fans should add Molly to their list of characters to follow." —*Booklist*

"Entertaining." —*Fort Lauderdale Sun-Sentinel*

"[We] look forward to Molly's return." —*Chicago Tribune*

"Irish humor and gritty determination transplanted to New York, but with more charm and optimism than the usual law attributed to Murphy." —Anne Perry, author of *The Whitechapel Conspiracy*

"Bowen tells a phenomenal story, and it will be a real treat to see what fate has in store for Molly and Daniel!"
—*Romantic Times* (Top Pick)

Also by Rhys Bowen

THE MOLLY MURPHY SERIES

In Like Flynn
For the Love of Mike
Death of Riley
Murphy's Law

THE CONSTABLE EVANS MYSTERIES

Evan Blessed
Evan's Gate
Evan Only Knows
Evans to Betsy
Evan Can't Wait
Evan and Elle
Evan Help Us
Evans Above
Evanly Choirs

OH
DANNY
BOY

RHYS BOWEN

St. Martin's Paperbacks

This is a work of fiction. All of the characters, organizations and events portrayed in this novel are either products of the author's imagination or are used fictitiously.

OH DANNY BOY

Copyright © 2006 by Rhys Bowen.
Excerpt from *In Dublin's Fair City* copyright © 2007 by Rhys Bowen.

Cover photograph of NYC street scene courtesy of Library of Congress Prints and Photographics Division. Cover photograph of woman © Bob Osonitch.

Library of Congress Catalog Card Number: 2005054290

ISBN: 0-312-99701-9
EAN: 9780312-99701-4

Printed in the United States of America

St. Martin's Press hardcover edition / March 2006
St. Martin's Paperbacks edition / March 2007

St. Martin's Paperbacks are published by St. Martin's Press, 175 Fifth Avenue, New York, NY 10010.

10 9 8 7 6 5 4 3 2 1

This book is dedicated to my oldest fan,
Marie McCormack, my granddaughters' dear Mimi.

Also a special note of dedication to Denise Lindquist,
who makes a cameo appearance in this
book as a dead prositute.

ACKNOWLEDGMENTS

As always this book would not have happened without the help and encouragement of my agent, Meg Ruley, my editor at St. Martin's, Kelley Ragland, and my brilliant support team at home, Clare, Jane, and John. You are the best.

ONE

New York, August 1902

There was that maniacal laughter again. I looked around, but I couldn't detect where it was coming from. It seemed to be part of the very darkness itself. Black water lapped up at me as I stepped onto the iron lacework of a walkway. I thought I could hear a child's voice calling, "Save me, save me," and I started toward it. But beneath me were other faceless forms, and they held up white arms to me, calling out, "Help us first."

The laughter grew louder until it was overwhelming. I started to run. Water splashed up at my feet and when I looked down at my shoes they were black. That's when I noticed it wasn't water at all. It was blood.

I woke with my heart pounding and sat up, my hands grasping the cool reality of the sheet before I realized I was in my own room. I sat still for a while, conscious of the empty quiet of the house around me, wondering what the dream might mean. It was the third time I had dreamed it this week. The first time I'd put it down to an exotic Mongolian meal at my friends' house across Patchin Place (they were into a nomad phase at the moment), but dreaming the same thing three times must mean more than just plain indigestion.

Back in Ireland dreams were always taken seriously. My mother would have been able to interpret mine for me in a wink, although I rather think her interpretation would be influenced by the fact that I was rude, didn't mind my elders, and was heading for a bad end. But I recall the women sitting around in our cottage over a cup of tea, debating whether dreaming of a black cow meant future wealth or a death in the family. What would they say about an ocean of blood? I shuddered and wrapped my arms around myself.

My life had certainly been in turmoil since I had returned from my assignment on the Hudson, but I couldn't think what could have sparked such a terrifying nightmare. There was my frightening ordeal in the river, of course. That might have prompted me to dream of water. And I had almost lost little Bridie O'Connor to typhoid. She was still far from well and had been sent to a camp for sickly city children in Connecticut, run by the ladies at the settlement house on Sixth Avenue. Was it her voice I had heard in the dream? Had she been calling for me to come to her? Should I have gone to the country to be with her?

I got up and walked across the landing, feeling the cold of the linoleum under my bare feet. I paused at what had been Bridie and Shamey's door, almost expecting to hear the children's regular breathing. But the only sound was the rhythmic ticking of the clock on the mantel downstairs. I shivered suddenly, although it was still midsummer and the night was warm. I went back to bed, but I was afraid to sleep again. It occurred to me that this was the first time in my life that I'd been alone in a building. Normally I would have been proud to be mistress of my own establishment, but at this moment all I felt was overwhelming loneliness. I sat hugging my knees to my chest, staring out of the window at the shadows dancing on the houses across the alleyway. When the first streaks of dawn showed in the sky I got up and made myself a cup of tea, drinking it with one eye on the front window until I saw my neighbor Gus go out to buy their breakfast rolls from the Clement Family Bakery around the corner on Sixth Avenue.

I dearly wanted company at the moment. I knew I was always welcome at their house, but my pride and disgust with my own weakness wouldn't let me barge in on them uninvited at this early hour or tell them about the dream. So I waited until Gus returned, opened my front door with the pretence of shaking out crumbs, then feigned delighted surprise at bumping into her. Of course she invited me in for breakfast, and of course I accepted.

"Look who I just found, Sid dear," Gus called as we went down the hall to their bright and airy kitchen. At this hour it was still cool. The French doors were open, and the sweet scent of honeysuckle competed with the enticing aroma of freshly brewed coffee.

Sid was standing at the stove, dressed this morning in an emerald green silk gentleman's smoking jacket and baggy black pants that looked as if they had come from a harem. The striking effect was completed with her black hair, which she wore straight and chin length, like a child's pageboy bob.

"Molly, my sweet. How good to see you. You're looking pale. Sit down and have some coffee and a hot roll." Sid gave me a beaming smile and started pouring thick, murky liquid into a small cup, then handed it to me. I took a sip, pretending, as always, that I liked my coffee to look and taste like East River sludge. Sid always insisted on Turkish coffee and French croissants in the morning. I'd no objections to the croissants, but I'd never learned to appreciate the coffee.

I sat in the chair that Gus had pulled out for me and accepted the still warm roll from her basket.

"And what were you doing up and about so bright and early this morning?" Gus asked.

"I didn't sleep so well last night." I was willing to confess to that much. "I just needed to get out of the house and breathe good fresh air."

"You're missing those O'Connors, that what's the matter with you," Gus said.

"I most certainly am not," I replied indignantly. "I've spent most of my life looking after someone else's children. I'm glad to be taking a break from them."

The knowing look that passed between Sid and Gus didn't escape me.

"And anyway, they'll be back soon enough when Bridie is

quite recovered and healthy again," I went on. "She's making splendid progress, you know. And in the meantime, I'm doing some serious thinking about my future."

They looked at each other again, this time with amusement.

"Did you hear that, Gus? Serious thinking about her future. Will she be reconsidering the earnest Mr. Singer's proposal, do you think?"

I picked up *The New York Times* that had been lying on the table. "Would you be quiet, you two? Why should you of all people think that any young woman's future would automatically have to be linked to a marriage proposal? I have no intention of accepting any proposals, decent or indecent."

Then I opened the paper and buried myself in the advertisements page, ignoring their chuckles.

"How about Nebraska?" I looked up expectantly from the *The Times* and saw two bewildered faces staring at me.

"Nebraska?" Gus asked.

"Yes, listen to this. 'Schoolteacher needed for one-room schoolhouse. Start August. Must be unmarried, unencumbered, Christian, and of impeccable character. References required. Accommodation provided. Apply to the school board, Spalding, Nebraska.' " I paused and looked up again. My friends were still smiling.

"Dearest Molly, are you suggesting that you should become a schoolmarm in Nebraska?" Sid asked, pushing her bobbed hair back from her face.

"Why not?" I demanded. "Do you not think I'm up to life on the frontier? And where is Nebraska anyway?"

At this they both broke into merry laughter. Gus reached across to me and patted my hand. "You are priceless, my sweet," she said. "Who would make us laugh if we let you escape from our clutches?"

"And why this sudden desire for the frontier, anyway?" Sid looked up from spreading more apricot jam on a croissant.

"Because I've had enough of New York City. Life has become too complicated."

"And you think it would be less complicated having to kill grizzly bears with your Bible on the way to school each morning or having to fight off amorous pioneers in need of a wife?" Sid asked.

I put down the newspaper and sighed. "I don't know. I just want to make a new start somewhere faraway. Never have to see Daniel Sullivan's odious face again. Never have to convince myself that I don't want to marry Jacob Singer, however well behaved and earnest he is."

"One can accomplish both these things without going to Nebraska, I should have thought," Gus said. "If you've finally decided to give up this crazy notion of being a lady investigator, I'm sure we could help you make a new start in the city here. But if you insist on escaping, I'm sure I can come up with some connections in Boston for you, even if my own people don't want to know me anymore."

I looked at Gus's sweet, elfish face, framed in its pile of soft, light brown curls, and finally smiled. "You're really too good to me by half. I don't deserve your friendship. I do nothing but interrupt your breakfast with my whining and complaining."

"Nonsense," Sid said. "Just think how dull and ordinary our lives would be without you."

Since Sid and Gus lead the least ordinary lives I had ever encountered, I had to smile at this. I suppose I should mention that their real names are Elena Goldfarb and Augusta Mary Walcott, of the Boston Walcotts. Both families had cut them off without a penny, but thanks to a generous inheritance from Gus's suffragist great-aunt, they lived a blissfully unconventional existence in Greenwich Village. Gus was attempting to make her mark as a painter, while Sid wrote the occasional left-wing article. Mostly they just had fun, hosting the literary and bohemian set to wild and extravagant parties. They had taken me under their wing when I had been new to the city and treated me as a spoiled younger sister ever since. As I looked at them I realized how I would hate to move away from their company.

"All right," I conceded grouchily, "maybe not Nebraska."

Sid went over to the stove and picked up the coffeepot. "Have another cup of coffee. You'll feel better," she said.

"I haven't finished this one yet," I said hastily.

"So let's see." Gus put down her own cup and stared across at Sid. "What sort of job should we find for her? Bookshop, do you think?"

"Too dreary. Not enough life."

"Ryan could help her get something to do with the theater. She'd like that."

"Ryan is unemployed and seriously short of funds himself at the moment."

"Well, if he will write plays that mock the American theatergoing public, what can he expect?"

I looked from one to the other, amused that I was not being consulted in this discussion.

"You don't understand," I finally cut in. "It's not the change of profession I'm anxious about. It's worrying about whether I'm going to find Daniel Sullivan lurking outside my front door every time I come out. Or Jacob for that matter."

"Jacob doesn't lurk, does he? He doesn't seem the type," Sid said.

"No," I conceded. "He's very well behaved as usual. Waiting patiently for my decision."

"And I don't think we've spotted Daniel lurking recently, have we?" Sid turned to Gus. "Not for the last few days anyway. Maybe he's given up in despair."

"He's still writing to me," I said. "At least a letter a day. I throw them all in the rubbish bin without opening them."

"I call that rather devoted," Gus said.

"Gus! We're talking about Daniel the Deceiver! The man possesses all the worst qualities of the male sex— untrustworthy, flirtatious, and an all-round bounder," Sid said fiercely. "He promises Molly he's broken off his engagement one day, and the next he goes running back to that spoiled Arabella creature as soon as she snaps her fingers. Molly is quite right to ignore him. And Jacob Singer, too. He may profess that he's no longer under the thumb of his family, but I know Jewish families, trust me."

Since she came from one, I did trust her.

"It's not only that," I said. "I don't want to marry just for convenience or security. There is just no spark with Jacob. He's a good man. He'll make some girl a good husband, only not me."

"Quite right," Sid said. "At least we're all in agreement that women don't need to attach themselves to a man to make them happy." She glanced up at Gus with a smile.

I got up and walked across to the French windows. The first fierce rays of summer sun were painting the brick wall behind the tiny square of garden. "I just wish I knew what I wanted," I said at last. "Part of the time I think I must be crazy to try and carry on the detective agency. But at least when I'm on a case I know I'm alive, and it's exciting."

"When you're not fighting for your life, getting yourself shot or drowned, or pushed off bridges," Gus said dryly.

I grinned. "So it's a little too exciting sometimes. But I can't see myself sitting behind a desk all day. Or being a governess to spoiled children, or a companion, for that matter. I can't think of what other job would give me pleasure or prevent me from bumping into Daniel."

"I don't see why you are so worried about bumping into Captain Sullivan," Sid said. "You're not usually a shrinking violet who avoids confrontation or hesitates to speak her mind, Molly. You've faced anarchists and gang members without flinching. Surely you're not afraid of a mere police captain?"

"Not afraid, no." I looked away to avoid meeting her eye. "I just lose all common sense when he's around. I know he'll try to sweet-talk me into forgiving him, and I'm afraid I'll be weak enough to listen to him."

"You're a strong, independent woman, Molly Murphy," Sid said firmly. "Face him, tell him what you think of him, and get it over with."

"You don't know Daniel. He has too much Irish blarney in him. This time I have resolved to be strong. Never seeing him again is the only way of accomplishing this. And I fear that involves leaving the city." I touched Gus's shoulder as I walked across the kitchen. "Thank you for the breakfast. I am quite revived and restored, and I'm off to look up Nebraska on the map."

I let myself out of their front door to the sounds of their renewed laughter. Then I paused, glanced down Patchin Place to make sure that it was devoid of life, before I sprinted across to my own front door opposite. This was no way to live, to be sure.

Silence engulfed me as I closed my front door behind me. No little high voice singing, no Shamey leaping down the stairs yelling, "Molly, I'm starving. Can I have some bread and dripping?"

My friends were right. I was missing the O'Connor children. I had felt myself encumbered by the O'Connors since I arrived in New York, but also responsible for them, since they had essentially saved my life. I had posed as their mother to bring them across from Ireland, when their own mother found that she was dying of consumption and not allowed to travel. Thus I had been able to escape Ireland with the police on my tail. So I could hardly abandon them. And the poor little mites with no mother, too. Seamus and young Shamey had gone to the country to be with Bridie during her recovery, Seamus hoping to find some kind of farmwork to support them.

As I stood lost in thought, there was a plop and the morning post landed on the doormat. I picked up two letters. The first, in Daniel's black, decisive hand, went straight in the rubbish bin. The second a childish scrawl I didn't recognize, liberally dotted with ink blots. I opened it and saw it was from the O'Connors.

Dear Molly,

My pa told me to rite this as he don't rite so good. (Little Shamey had clearly not benefited overmuch from his recent schooling). We're doing fine here. Bridie is up and walking agin. Pa and me is camping out in a farmer's barn and, we're helping him with the

harvest. You shud see me, Molly. I can lift great bales
of hay jest like a man. Pa likes it so good out here, he
says he don't want to go back to the city where there is
sickness and gangs and all. He's trying to get a job all
year on a farm. I wish you'd come out here and join
us, Molly.

Then underneath in an even more illegible scrawl, "It
don't seem the same without you, Molly. I know there's no
question of love between us, but we get along fine, don't we,
and the children already think of you as their mother."

I put down the paper hurriedly on the kitchen table. If I
read this right, I now had three unwanted suitors. I wished I
hadn't left *The Times* over at Number Nine. Nebraska was
sounding better by the minute!

TWO

An hour later I had come to one big decision. I was not going to mope around feeling sorry for myself any longer. Sid was right. All my life I had been a fighter not a coward. I should face Daniel, once and for all. I was going to put last night's dream down to a sluggish liver and get on with my life. Having made this momentous decision, I decided to celebrate. Gus and Sid had been so good to me and I had imposed upon their generosity, giving little in return. So tonight I would cook them a grand dinner, as a thank-you. It would take my mind off things to keep myself occupied.

I wasn't going to try and compete with the exotic fare that they ate, but I decided that I couldn't go wrong with cold chicken and salad for a hot summer night. Chicken was a luxury I could ill afford at the moment, funds not being too plentiful. I hadn't had an assignment since I returned from the mansion on the Hudson, almost a month ago now. And I was still owed my fee for that assignment. But since Daniel Sullivan was the one who owed it to me, I'd rather starve than ask him for it. I suppose my behavior could be construed as childish, but this time I was resolved to be firm.

I sat down to write an invitation to the Misses Goldfarb and Walcott, requesting the honor of their company at Ten Patchin Place for dinner at eight, and delivered it in person to their front door. When they accepted, I headed for a kosher butcher shop on the Bowery where I knew their chickens would be freshly killed and not have been hanging about for days with flies on them. I'd also stop off at the post office on Broadway to see if any mail had come addressed to Paddy Riley, former owner of P. Riley and Associates, from whom I had inherited the detective agency. The occasional commission still came in, and frankly at this moment I needed the work. It had been an expensive business maintaining a house and feeding two hungry youngsters.

On the corner opposite, the tall, strangely Eastern-looking tower of the Jefferson Market Building sent a shaft of black shadow across the early morning sunlight. Even at this hour the sidewalks were beginning to heat up. Smells of rotting vegetables and fruit wafted across to me, as barrows piled with fresher fare crushed them under iron wheels. A couple of policemen came out of the police station that was housed within the same building. I turned and hurried away toward Washington Square. Daniel had been known to emerge from that same police station, and I had unpleasant memories of spending a night in the jail there, having been mistaken for a lady of the night.

On the corner the newsboys were hawking today's newspapers. READ ALL ABOUT IT. THE EAST SIDE RIPPER STRIKES AGAIN.

I had been so intent on reading the advertisements in *The Times* that I had missed the sensational headline. But it screamed out from all the billboards around Fifth Avenue: Another prostitute found murdered. Ripper at work again.

"They ask for it, don't they?" I heard one woman say to another as they picked up a copy of the *Herald*. "If you go into that line of work, you know what to expect."

"Shouldn't be allowed in a respectable city," her companion agreed. "Good riddance I say. I hope he gets the lot of 'em."

I shuddered as I hurried past. So yet another prostitute had been murdered. Four of them this summer, enough that the press now spoke of an East Side Ripper, following in the footsteps of London's notorious mass murderer. Because the victims were prostitutes, there had been little public interest until the most recent murders. Many people agreed with

those women I had overheard—immoral behavior like that
was just asking for retribution.

It was so easy to dismiss crimes like this as happening in
another world. Nothing to do with me, thank God. That was
the general attitude. And yet I had spent a night in a jail cell
with some of those women. They had been kind to me, and
all I felt for them was pity. Those sad young girls with innocent faces hidden under rouge and lipstick could have been
me when I first arrived, penniless, in New York.

I had just reached Broadway and joined the throng of
pedestrians that seemed to populate that street at all hours
when I had a sudden feeling that I was being followed. I
glanced around but saw nobody I recognized. I quickened
my pace but the feeling didn't go away. I suppose you could
say I was born with the Irish sixth sense. Well, it had stood
me in good stead before, and I wasn't about to ignore it now.
Those headlines about the East Side Ripper flashed through
my mind. Ridiculous, I told myself. Those murders were all
done at night, the bodies all dumped on one of the streets
known for their houses of ill repute. I was clearly not that
kind of woman. It was broad daylight, and I was on Broadway. I was quite safe.

Even so, when I saw a chance to dodge between two
streetcars and a dray carrying beer barrels, I took it and continued on the other side of the street. The feeling was
stronger than ever. I stepped under the awning of a greengrocer's shop and stood surveying the crowd. Nobody I recognized. Nobody who looked like an East Side Ripper
either. Just ordinary housewives about their morning shopping before the day's heat became too intense, businessmen
on their way to appointments, children on their way to play.
I noticed a young police constable, his familiar helmet bob-
bing above the crowd, and felt reassured. I could always appeal for help if I really needed to. So I set off again. When I
came to Wannamaker's, the dry goods store on Broadway, I
paused, pretending to examine the hats in the window while
in reality surveying the crowd that passed behind me.

At that moment a hand grabbed my shoulder. I looked

around frantically for the policeman, then found that I was staring up into his face, and it was his hand that held me.

"Holy Mother of God," I exclaimed. "You scared the daylights out of me, Officer. What do you think you are doing? Do I look like a pickpocket to you?"

His angular boyish face flushed with embarrassment. "I'm sorry, ma'am. I believe I know who you are. Miss Murphy, is it not? I was sent to find you by Captain Sullivan."

"By Captain Sullivan?" I blurted out as the crowd parted around us. "Of all the nerve. He daren't face me himself so he sends one of his underlings to do it now, does he?"

"I'm sorry, miss," he repeated again. "But it's important. Captain Sullivan really needs to speak to you, and you haven't answered his letters."

"Of course I haven't answered his letters, and I don't intend to speak to him either. That should be quite obvious by now. He and I have nothing more to say to each other."

"So you won't come with me to speak to him?"

I shook my head. "Absolutely not. You can tell Captain Sullivan that our acquaintanceship is at an end and I have no wish to speak to him again. And if he continues to annoy me, I'll complain about him to his superiors. Is that clear enough for you?"

The young constable's embarrassment grew. "Then I have no alternative, miss. I'm only obeying orders, mark you, but I'm placing you under arrest." With that he clapped a handcuff onto one wrist before I knew what was happening to me.

I stared down at the wrist in horror and indignation. "Jesus, Mary, and Joseph! How dare you! Release me this minute or I'll make the biggest fuss you can imagine."

"I'm really sorry, Miss Murphy, but I've been told to bring you to Captain Sullivan and bring you I will, even if I have to carry you over my shoulder like a sack of potatoes."

"I'd like to see you try," I said. "Now let me out of this contraption at once."

A crowd was gathering around us.

"Do you need any help, Officer?" A distinguished-looking man stepped forward. "Should I summon assistance for you?"

"I think I can handle her, thank you," the constable said, "but she's a feisty one, I'll grant you that. A string of outstanding warrants for her arrest as long as your arm."

"Don't listen to him!" I shouted. "I'm being kidnapped against my will. I'm a respectable woman. I've done nothing wrong."

"If you could just hail that hansom for me, I'd be most grateful," the constable said, wiping the sweat from his brow as I squirmed to break free of him.

The cabby reined in his horse, and I was bundled inside by willing hands.

"The Tombs, as fast as you can," the constable shouted up to the driver, and we took off at a lively trot.

"The Tombs? Have you taken leave of your senses?" I demanded, suddenly feeling frightened. "You're taking me to jail? On what charge? Is this Daniel Sullivan's idea of a joke?"

The constable shook his head. "It's no joke, miss. It's deadly serious, I'm afraid, or the captain wouldn't have had you brought in this way. But he had no alternative. He's in serious trouble, Miss Murphy. He's under arrest and being held in The Tombs pending his trial."

I had been looking out of the hansom, wondering if I had any way of making my escape. Now I spun around to face the constable. "Daniel, under arrest? What has he done?"

"I'm not quite sure of the details, miss. He'll have to tell you himself. I only know that the whole police force has turned against him. There're only a few of us he can trust, me being one of them, and that's why he sent me to fetch you. He needs your help."

"He doesn't deserve my help," I said.

"But you will speak to him, won't you? I don't want to see a fine officer like Captain Sullivan going to jail."

I sighed. "All right. I suppose I'll have to see him." Inside my head a small voice whispered that a stint in jail wouldn't hurt Daniel Sullivan. It would serve him right. But even I couldn't take revenge that far. "But I want this handcuff removed immediately," I added. "I'm not going to be seen entering the city jail in handcuffs. I have a reputation to uphold, you know."

The constable grinned and clicked open the cuff. "Sorry, miss. Captain Sullivan would never have forgiven me if you'd done a bolt on me."

I peered out of the cab as it turned onto Center Street and slowed outside the imposing pillared entry to the city jail, commonly known as The Tombs. The nickname came from the architecture, supposedly copied from an ancient Egyptian tomb. But it carried with it a more sinister connotation these days. People who were sent there for a stint didn't always come out alive. The building was notoriously damp and the crowding led to typhoid, consumption, cholera—those same sicknesses that plagued the tenements and flared up during the heat of summer.

"Here we are, miss." The constable sprang down and offered me his hand.

There had been some major rebuilding going on since I was last here. Scaffolding covered the whole of one wall and the chink of masons' hammers echoed as we emerged from the cab. A cloud of fine dust hung in the air. The papers had reported that the whole edifice was finally subsiding into the mud and in danger of collapsing on the inmates' heads at any moment. Like many New York buildings, it had been constructed over a former stream or pond. Hence the continual complaints about the damp.

I coughed and put my hand to my mouth as I was ushered in through the front door. Inside was noticeably cool and dark after the heat radiating up from the sidewalks. An exchange I couldn't quite hear took place between the constable and the officer sitting at a desk. The latter glanced up at me, nodded, then got to his feet and produced a giant set of keys.

"This way then," he said. "Mind your step." He led us down a long, dark hallway, finally opening a door into a bleak and Spartan room containing a couple of straight-backed chairs, both rather the worse for wear. He turned on a switch and the room was bathed in harsh electric light. The green paint on the brick walls was peeling in places so that the original brick showed through with interesting adornments of mold. It smelled moldy and damp too, with a hint of urine. If the building was being renovated, they clearly hadn't reached this part of it yet.

"Wait here, please," the warder said. "And just ten minutes, mind you, or it's more than my job's worth." He retreated, shutting the door behind us with a hollow clanging finality. The constable offered me a chair. I sat and waited for what seemed like an eternity. Now that I was about to see Daniel again, my heart was pounding so violently that I could hardly breathe. Outside it had been so hot that my thin muslin dress was damp with perspiration. Now I started shivering. In fact, for one horrible moment, I felt that I might faint. Having never worn a corset in my life, I was not prone to swooning and the cold, clammy feeling was alarming. As I leaned back and closed my eyes, I heard distant footsteps echoing on a stone floor. Then a scraping sound as a partition was slid open in the far wall and I found myself staring at Daniel's face through an iron grille.

"Molly!" he exclaimed. "You came. Thank God."

THREE

I pulled the chair up closer to the grille and was shocked at what I saw. He looked haggard and hollow eyed. His normal unruly dark curls hung limply on his forehead. There was a nasty bruise on one cheek.

"I'm sorry to have you hauled in like this," he said, "but you didn't answer my letters."

However shocked I was by his appearance and circumstances, I wasn't about to be unjustly attacked. "Answer your letters? Are you surprised, after the way you behaved?"

"No, I suppose not, but you could at least have let me explain."

"I've listened to too many explanations from you, Daniel Sullivan," I said.

I saw him wince, almost as if I had struck him. I had planned to be cold, reserved, and in complete control, but I had never seen him like this. I was used to the self-assured, cock-of-the-walk Daniel. I heard myself blurting out, "Daniel, in heaven's name—what's happened to you?"

"Good question." He put his hand up to his cheek and attempted a smile. "This was a lucky blow from another inmate who recognized me and took his chance to get even."

"But what were you arrested for? What do they say you've done?"

Daniel leaned closer to the grille. "Would you mind waiting outside, Byrne?" he said to the constable.

"Not at all, sir," the constable said.

"Oh, and thank you for bringing her in. I hope she didn't put up too much of a fight."

"You did warn me, sir. All in all she came quite peacefully."

"Did she now?" He looked at me. Those bright blue eyes that normally flashed alarmingly looked gray and lifeless. "You must be slipping, Molly. I fully expected you'd get in a good kick or two."

The door closed behind me, and I was alone with just an iron grille between Daniel and me.

"I thought it was better to send him away," he said quietly. "He's a good lad, but he could be coerced by the powers that be to repeat our conversation here."

"What on earth have you done, Daniel?" I repeated. The suspense was killing me.

"Caught accepting a bribe from a gang member."

I almost laughed out loud. "Accepting a bribe? Daniel, I thought that was standard practice for the New York police. Isn't that how every policeman manages to squirrel away a hundred thousand dollars from a salary of five hundred a year?"

"Until recently, yes," Daniel said. "But it's the new police commissioner, John Partridge. He was appointed by our new mayor, who you may know is the archenemy of Tammany Hall. So this new fellow, this Partridge, is making a big fuss over reforming the police, stamping out corruption, making New York a city fit for God-fearing people. What he really wants to do is wrest power away from the Irish and put his own cronies in their place. He probably has political ambitions of his own as well."

"So you were caught accepting a bribe, and he wants to make an example of you? Surely jail is a little extreme. I'd have thought a public slap on the wrist would be enough."

"There's more," Daniel said. "I have this friend, a prize-fighter. You probably don't know, but prizefights were banned in the city a year ago. However, there are still plenty of men who enjoy watching a good prizefight and my friend is the best—heavyweight champion of the world at one stage. Now he's down on his luck, finding it hard to make ends meet. So he asked me to help him set up a fight in a place where it wasn't likely to be stopped or raided by the police. There's big money in it, of course. Lots of betting going on. Big money for my friend, too, if he wins." He paused and waited for me to say something. When I remained silent, he went on, "So the police raided my rooms after I was arrested, and they found evidence that I was trying to set up an illegal prizefight. The commissioner decided to throw the book at me as an example to other officers who might want to stray from the straight and narrow. Oh, and apparently I resisted arrest."

"Apparently?"

"Well, I wasn't going to be handcuffed by one of my own junior officers, was I? That will get me another week or so in jail."

I stared at him long and hard. "I don't know why you had me brought here," I said at last. "What do you think I can do?"

"Help me prove my innocence," he said. "Get me out of here and reinstated in my job. You see, Molly, the interesting part of this is that I've never accepted a bribe in my life. I know other policemen have feathered their nests very nicely, but not me. My father was the finest cop in the force, and he never did anything he'd be ashamed of. I was conscious of following in his footsteps, so I've always kept to his standards."

"But you just said they caught you accepting a bribe."

"I thought I was meeting a gang member to be given a list of names of underworld figures who might be interested in sponsoring this prizefight. But when the police opened the envelope, there were five twenty-dollar bills in it, as well as the names of known gangsters. So I can't blame them for thinking it was a payoff."

"You may be innocent of accepting a bribe, but you've just told me that you were setting up an illegal prizefight with the help of a gang. That doesn't sound so innocent to me."

"A prizefight, Molly—what's wrong with that?"

"It's illegal, apparently."

"Good harmless fun. Every man in the world enjoys a

boxing match. The city was shortsighted to ban them. If it takes place, I'll wager half the aldermen and high-ranking police officers will be there in attendance, probably including Mr. Partridge."

I digested this, then continued, "So what about the money in the envelope? You must have some idea who put it there. Was it supposed to be a bribe?"

Daniel shrugged. "I've no idea. I've had a lot of time for thought these past few days and I've come to the conclusion that the whole thing was set up. Why else would the police commissioner just happen to be in the right place, at the right time, to witness me accepting money from a gang member? Why else would they go immediately to search my rooms for more incriminating evidence? They haven't shown me exactly what they found in my rooms, but that could have been planted, too."

"Who would want to defame you?" I asked.

He shrugged. "Again, I've no idea, unless it's Commissioner Partridge himself."

"Why would he want to do that?"

Daniel shrugged. "Maybe he plans to get rid of Irish officers one by one, starting at the top. All I know is that my so-called friends have dropped me like a hot potato. They're all scared they'll be next, you see."

"I still don't know why you called on me, Daniel," I said. "Don't you have all kinds of friends in high places? Your father knows everybody, and they all respect him. And what about your fiancée's family? They're part of the famous Four Hundred, aren't they?"

He looked away. "That's the trouble. I can't let my father know anything about this. The doctors have told him that he has a bad heart and the shock might kill him. I can't take that risk. And as for Arabella—" He looked up suddenly. "Miss Norton and I broke off our engagement."

"You did?" I tried not to sound too interested.

He nodded. "Right after you disappeared from the Flynn place."

"But I heard you," I said. "When she asked about me, you

told her she was making a fuss over nothing. You said I was nothing to you."

"I didn't exactly say that," he said quickly. "And if I did, I didn't mean it. I had to appease her at that moment, Molly. Surely you realize that. I couldn't have told her the truth in front of all those people. It would have mortified her."

"And me? Did you think of how I felt?"

"Molly, the last thing you'd have wanted is for Arabella to make a scene. She's used to having her own way, you know. And she'd never forgive me for humiliating her in public."

"There you are!" I shouted suddenly, loudly enough that the words echoed back from those peeling brick walls and stone floor. "That's it. If you've really broken off your engagement, you have your answer."

"To what?"

"To what? The man's as thick as a plank. You said the whole thing was set up to disgrace you. Well, there you've got it. Arabella didn't like the idea of being made a fool of and being betrayed by you, so she's paying you back."

"Oh, come now. Surely not . . ."

"You told me once before that she'd ruin you if you ran out on her. Well, now she has."

He shook his head violently. "I can't believe that of her. She actually took my request to break off our understanding pretty well, considering. She said she'd suspected for some time that my heart wasn't fully committed to her. Then she did go on to say that if my taste in women didn't aspire any higher than you, then you and I were welcome to each other." For a second I saw the flicker of the old Daniel in his impish grin.

"Then her family wants to punish you for upsetting their precious darling."

He shook his head again. "I think they'd be relieved. They'd hoped for someone with more money and status than me. They are civilized people, Molly. If they'd wanted to pay me back, they could have brought a breach of promise suit against me and attempted to punish me through the courts. I simply cannot believe that they would go to all this trouble to get me thrown in jail. And how would they have contacts with the underworld?"

"They may well have ties to the new commissioner," I said. "Don't they tell you always to start with the most obvious suspect? That's what Paddy Riley told me."

Daniel sighed. "Paddy Riley. I wish he were still here. He'd be able to get to the bottom of this with no trouble at all. He'd know how to pry or bribe the truth out of that gangster."

"But you know I can't do that, Daniel," I said in horror.

"I realize that, and of course I wouldn't want you getting mixed up in that kind of thing."

I remembered, all too clearly, an encounter with Monk Eastman, boss of the Eastman gang, when I had come close to losing my life, or worse. "If you don't want me mixed up in it, then why did you call me here?"

"I want you to take a message to somebody," he said, leaning closer to the grille. There might have been a guard in the cell behind him, listening in on our conversation. It was too dark to see.

"All right. Who?"

He lowered his voice to the merest whisper. "My friend Jack Brady. Have you heard of him? Gentleman Jack, they call him, the Irish sledgehammer. He was a world champion prizefighter once, and he was counting on me to help him make a comeback."

"Why Gentleman Jack? Did he always play by the rules?"

"No, he likes to dress like a dandy, or he did when he was in funds. He'd wear an ascot with a diamond pin at his throat—that kind of thing."

"I see," I said. "And where would I find this Gentleman Jack?"

He leaned even closer so that his lips were almost touching the bars. "He's recently arrived in New York and I have put him up at a boardinghouse around the corner from my place. On the corner of Ninth Avenue and West Twenty-third. Mrs. Collins is the landlady. Tell Jack what's happened to me. He knows what I've been doing on his behalf to set up this fight. He can ask questions in the right places."

"And what would the right places be?"

"Places that he can go and you can't," Daniel said bluntly.

"And what about Arabella Norton?" I demanded. "You may not think she has anything to do with your arrest, but to me she's the logical number-one suspect. Are you planning to send your Gentleman Jack to her first?"

Something like a chuckle escaped from his lips. "I can't see Arabella receiving the likes of Jack Brady."

"Then I'd better go myself."

"I should have thought that would be equally disastrous—even more so," Daniel said. "I don't know what you'd hope to achieve by it, other than the indignity of being thrown out of White Plains."

"I should have thought that was obvious—to find out if she had any part in your arrest."

"And you think she'd tell you if she did?"

"I am a detective, after all," I said. "I'm experienced at asking the right questions."

"You could only ask the right questions if Arabella would agree to talk to you," Daniel said, "and I can't see that happening in a month of Sundays."

"Surely she'd be concerned when she heard what has happened to you. If she's not involved in this plot, she wouldn't want you rotting in this filthy jail."

"She might think I deserve to be taught a lesson."

"So might I, for that matter," I reminded him.

"True enough," he agreed. "But I really don't think you'd get anywhere with Arabella. Just go to Jack and tell him what's happened to me. He's the only one who can help me now."

"You had me hauled in unceremoniously just to tell me to find someone else to help you?" I said. In a way I was relieved that I was being let off this assignment but at the same time stung by his lack of trust in my skills. "Why didn't you have him brought to you if he's the only one who can help?"

"Because he's a well-known face," Daniel said. "If the police got a glimpse of him, he'd be arrested and run out of town. That's why he's undercover at the boardinghouse, living there under the name of John Sykes."

"John Sykes," I echoed. "All right. I suppose I'll do what you ask, since you obviously don't think much of my abilities as an investigator."

"Of course I do," he said. "I'm very impressed with your skills, if you want to know. But I'm not risking putting you in danger. You're not getting yourself mixed up in underworld dealings and that's an order."

I gave him a haughty stare. "It seems to me you're hardly in a position to order anybody around. But don't worry. I still remember my last encounter with a gang. I have no wish to repeat it."

"Good girl," he said. "Of course, there's nothing to stop you from using your brain to help old Jack figure things out. He's not the brightest button in the box."

"You're presuming I'd want to help you," I said. "You haven't exactly deserved my loyalty."

"I realize that," he said. "Molly, I haven't been fair to you before, but this time I've tried to do right by you. I broke off my engagement as I promised, didn't I?"

Until now we had been having a polite and reserved conversation. Suddenly Daniel cracked. He reached for me, grabbing at the bars that separated us. "For God's sake, please don't desert me, Molly. I need you. Help Jack get me out before it's too late. Even if you don't want me as a suitor anymore, then as a friend."

I swallowed hard. "All right," I said. "I'll give it a try."

As if on cue the door behind me opened. "Ten minutes and no more, I said," the warder's voice boomed out. Hands grabbed at Daniel's shoulders. The partition started to close.

"Wait," I called. There were so many facts I needed to know. "Just a minute. Let me talk to him." I tried to shake myself free as I was escorted from the room. The partition slid shut and Daniel was gone.

FOUR

I was led out of The Tombs by the young constable Byrne and stood blinking in the fierce sunlight while the brick dust floated in a haze around us.

"He says you're still his friend." I turned to the constable. "How many friends does he still have?"

"Hard to say, miss," he said. "The problem is that rumors are flying around. Nobody knows what to believe. There's talk that Captain Sullivan is in the pay of a gang. They say he tipped off the gang that a police raid was coming and one of our men copped it. Our boys don't take kindly to being betrayed by one of their own."

I stared at him in horror. "You know very well that Daniel would never do that. He told me he's never even accepted a bribe. This was all arranged to discredit him, Constable Byrne."

Byrne nodded. "Quite possibly."

"By whom? Do you have any ideas at all?"

His young, fresh face flushed red. "I'm only a constable, miss. I do my job, take my orders, and mind my own business. Captain Sullivan was good to me when I first joined the police. Set me straight on a lot of things. So I feel I owe it to him to give him the benefit of the doubt. I'd help him if I could, but I don't see how."

I put my hand on his arm. "Can you tell me the names of more senior officers that Daniel can trust—men who might be able to help him?"

He shook his head. "Like I said, I don't know what goes on among the top brass, miss."

The message was coming through loud and clear. In theory he wanted to help Daniel, but he wasn't going to stick his neck out and lose his own job doing so. I could understand him. A New York policeman was a good, secure job for an Irish person. Tammany Hall and the police were thick as thieves. It wouldn't pay to get on the wrong side of either, and that was just what Daniel had done, apparently.

"Can I ask you to do one thing, Constable Byrne?" I said. "Could you at least keep your ear to the ground? If you hear anything, anything at all that might help Daniel, come and tell me. Daniel gave you my address, didn't he?"

"Yes, miss," he said. "I'll do what I can."

"Then I'll be on my way, if I'm not still under arrest."

He grinned. "No, miss, you're free to go."

"Thank you." I smiled back at him. He might turn out to be the only ally I had among the police.

"One thing, Miss Murphy," he called after me. "How does Captain Sullivan think that you can help him? Do you have friends in high places or what?"

My smile had faded. "I'm an investigator, Constable," I said. "He expects me to prove his innocence."

I didn't wait for his reply as I walked away. It wasn't until I'd gone a block or two, not noticing in which direction I was going, that the full force of those words hit me. Prove his innocence, when by his own admission he was guilty of setting up a prizefight? But surely that kind of crime would only result in a fine? I started to walk faster and faster. I thought about those rumors that Constable Byrne had mentioned—Daniel being in the pay of a gang, tipping off the gang, a fellow officer getting killed. Either Daniel didn't realize how deeply he was in trouble, or he was keeping the worst from me.

I stopped walking when I came to a busy intersection and realized I had walked up Center Street all the way to Canal. I knew what I'd find if I turned right and headed toward the East River. I'd come to Walhalla Hall, locally known as the

Walla Walla, an innocent-enough-looking building but frequented by the Eastman gang. I paused, catching my breath, as a horse-drawn trolley went past, then a dray loaded high with sacks of flour. There was no way I'd want to face those unsavory characters again. I remembered Monk Eastman's comical derby hat perched above that round moon face, the ridiculous pigeon that sat on his shoulder. All in all a harmless-looking figure until you noticed the brass knuckles he always wore and the great brutes lurking as his bodyguards. Then I remembered the Hudson Duster I had had arrested, not realizing who he was. Enough brushes with gangs to last a lifetime. I'd be very happy to stay well clear and let Gentleman Jack have all the dealings with the underworld.

The traffic cleared. I picked up my skirts and hurried across. I was still shaken by Daniel's condition. I couldn't leave him to rot in that cell. I would do everything I could for him. At the very least I would pass on the message to Jack Brady, and then I might just pay a visit to Arabella Norton to verify my own suspicions that she or her family were the ones who had set the dogs on him.

The thought of facing Arabella was only slightly more desirable than a visit to the Eastmans. Our previous brief encounters had not left me with any warm feelings toward her. I don't suppose she had many toward me. I can't say I blamed her. She probably thought that I'd stolen her beau away from her, when that wasn't at all true. It was Daniel who had conveniently kept from me the fact that he was engaged to another woman. As soon as I learned the truth, I had broken off all contact with him. Well, not entirely all contact. That one time on the Hudson River . . . I tried to push it from my mind and headed for the Bowery, resolved to buy my chicken, cook supper, and stay detached.

There was already a long line coming out of the door of Grossman's Kosher Butchers by the time I reached it. The sun shone fiercely on the back of my neck as I waited in line. As I moved into the interior of the shop, the heat was stifling today. The line seemed to be progressing at a snail's pace. The smell of dead flesh, sawdust, and blood made me come over queasy. I shut my eyes and swallowed down bile. That's what happens when you drink Sid's coffee on an empty stomach after a sleepless night, I told myself, and was very glad when my turn came to step up to the counter.

I made my purchase and pushed my way out of the door and into the fresh air. Unfortunately the day was already another scorcher. The air outside was about as warm and stinking as a cesspit. A carthorse had just laid a large pile of manure, and the smell of it competed with the odor of frying chickpeas from a passing pushcart. Trolley bells clanged; children squealed. Although the typhoid epidemic on the Lower East Side had died down, the threat was always there in this heat. Some passersby still held handkerchiefs to their mouths and noses and hurried, heads down.

I made for Washington Square as fast as I could and didn't stop until I was standing under the sweet shade of trees, feeling the cool spray from the fountain floating toward me. Usually I relished the noise and bustle of the city, but I found myself thinking back with longing to the wild coast of county Mayo, where the summer days were never too hot and always tempered with a fresh breeze from the Atlantic Ocean.

I found a place on a bench in the shade and sat there for a while watching small boys climbing into the fountain until they were chased off by a red-faced policeman. I took out my own handkerchief and mopped my forehead. This whole day had been most disturbing so far, first the dream and the sleepless night and then the news about Daniel. It was no wonder that I longed to be somewhere more peaceful and secure.

At last, suitably rested, I deposited the chicken in the meat safe at home and set out to find Gentleman Jack Brady. Usually I covered great distances on foot around the city, having been used to walking miles at home. But I had done enough walking in today's heat. I paid the five cents to ride the Sixth Avenue El up to Twenty-third and then sat patiently on the horse-drawn trolley along Twenty-third out to

Ninth Avenue. It was a pleasant neighborhood of middle-class respectability, unlike either Greenwich Village or the Lower East Side, which were my usual haunts. Housewives were out scrubbing front steps and polishing brass door knockers. Children were playing with tops or jacks on the sidewalks. I passed a little girl, solemnly pushing a doll's carriage, and thought about Bridie. However much I rejoiced in my present lack of responsibility, I really missed her sweet little face.

It was easy enough to find Ma Collins's Boarding House, since the sign was painted in unsteady letters over the front door. I knocked, waited, and the door was opened by a sour-faced woman who seemed to be the epitome of landladies: hair pulled severely from her face, hard eyes, hard mouth, and the look of a perpetual smell under her nose.

"Yes?" she demanded. "If it's one of my boarders you're looking for, I don't allow my gentlemen to receive lady callers."

"I am looking for one of your gentlemen," I said, "but only to give him a message from a friend. I assure you I have no designs on any of your boarders."

"Which one is it?" she asked, still barring the door with her hand resting on the doorpost.

"You have a Mr. John Sykes staying here, I understand," I said. "I'd like a word with him in private, if you have a parlor where we could talk."

"He's not here," she said.

"When do you expect him to return?"

She shrugged. "Your guess is as good as mine. Gone. Done a bunk, if you ask me. Not that I care. Room was paid for a week in advance."

"He's gone, you say? Has he taken his things?"

"Didn't bring much to start with. Just one carpetbag and that's gone."

"And he didn't say where he might be going?"

She shrugged again. "Didn't say a word. Ate his breakfast with the other boarders. I was down in the scullery doing the washing, and when I put the lunchtime meal on the table, he didn't show up. And Millie, who helps me with the beds, said that his stuff had gone."

"Oh dear." I stood staring at her, not sure what to do next. "Do you have any kind of home address for him, anywhere I might find him?"

"What's he done, run out owing you money, or worse?"

"I've never even met the man, but a friend of mine needs to pass him an urgent message, and I agreed to be the messenger, that's all."

"Sorry, I can't help you, miss," she said. "I have to get back to my pie now, or I'll have burned the crust." Then she shut the door. This was a complication Daniel couldn't have foreseen. He had told me that Jack Brady had to lie low because his face would be recognized. Maybe somebody had recognized him, and he'd had to make a swift getaway. So where would he have gone? If he was still waiting for Daniel to set up his fight, he wouldn't have gone far. My next step should be to go to Daniel's rooms and see what I could find there. Maybe I could leave a note for Jack Brady with Daniel's landlady, in case he showed up looking for Daniel.

I walked around the corner to West Twenty-third and the brownstone where Daniel had rooms.

"Why, if it isn't Miss Murphy! How lovely to see you again, my dear," Mrs. O'Shea exclaimed as she opened the door. "It's been a long time since you boarded with us. How have you been faring?"

"Not too badly," I said. "And yourself?"

"Can't complain either, except for this terrible business with the captain. I expect you've heard about it or you wouldn't be here."

I nodded. "I gather the police came to search his rooms."

"They did indeed. Acted as if he was the worst criminal in creation. 'You've got the wrong man,' I told them. 'Captain Sullivan's the finest gentleman on the force,' but they just pushed me out of the way. Louts, the lot of them."

"Did they find anything?"

She shook her head. "They took some papers away, I believe, but they weren't here long. And as for poor Captain Sullivan, I don't even know what's happened to him."

"He's in The Tombs," I said, and nodded as she gasped in horror.

"Holy Mother of God." She crossed herself. "What on earth could he have done to warrant that?"

"Nothing. Someone's out to get him," I said. "They planted evidence. That's why I've come to see if there's anything I can do to help him. I wondered if I could see his rooms? I expect they've taken away anything useful, but it couldn't hurt to look, could it?"

"It certainly couldn't. That poor man. It makes my blood boil after what you told me. Come on in, do. And take a glass of iced tea with me first."

I accepted readily.

"I'm also looking for one of Captain Sullivan's friends," I told her, as she put the glass in front of me at the parlor table. "A big chap, going by the name of John Sykes, I understand. You haven't seen him, have you?"

She nodded. "A man like you describe came here with Captain Sullivan, about a week ago it must have been. A big, burly man, ugly as sin. We just exchanged pleasantries as they went up the stairs."

"So you don't know where I might find him now? He hasn't come by since then?"

She shook her head. "Not that I know of. But he could have come by when I wasn't here. I've been over at my sister's house a lot this week. She's laid up with a confinement—her tenth child, can you believe? I thank the Lord over and over that he let me stop at three."

We nodded in womanly understanding. I rose to my feet. "Well, thank you for the iced tea, Mrs. O'Shea. Most welcome in this hot weather. And if I could go up to Captain Sullivan's apartment?"

"Of course. I'll find you the spare key. I'm just on my way out again, so if I'm not here when you're done, put it in the jar on the hall table."

"I will. Thank you again."

I took the key and climbed the stairs. It was an odd feeling, letting myself into Daniel's apartment. It was a long time since I had been here—a year maybe, but memories flooded back. How much had happened in a year. I stood taking in the unique smell of the place, that combination of pipe tobacco mixed with furniture polish and maybe a hint of grilled chops or steak. A completely manly smell to complement the room. Dark, polished furniture, shelves of books, an easy chair by the fireplace, pipes lined up in a rack on the mantel shelf. It was easy to see that these were bachelor's quarters, with no woman's touch to brighten or soften the tone. I ran my hand fondly over the back of his armchair. I had sat here once and he had perched on the arm beside me and . . . "Stop this at once and get on with things," I said, pushing such thoughts from my mind.

I began with the big oak desk in the window. I felt strange going through Daniel's personal papers and had to remind myself that less friendly eyes than mine had perused them before me. A bundle of letters from his mother, tied with red ribbon, bills all paid on time, nothing useful or incriminating. The living room turned up nothing, so I went on to the bedroom that opened from it. It felt even stranger to be standing in Daniel's bedroom, looking at the neat, burgundy silk eiderdown on his massive mahogany bed. I walked past it and started with the bedside cabinet. When I opened the top drawer I uncovered a snapshot wrapped in a silk handkerchief. I took it out and felt the tears springing to my eyes. It was the picture that Paddy Riley had taken of Daniel and me, strolling in Central Park last summer. How relaxed and content we looked together, with my arm slipped through Daniel's and an absurdly proud smile on my face. What a lot had happened to us since then. I slipped it into my purse, just in case more policemen came to pry.

I searched some more and was gratified to note that there was no portrait of Arabella in evidence, which just shows you of what base thoughts we women are capable. I was going through his chest of drawers, noting how neatly he kept everything folded, in contrast to myself who was messy by nature, when I sensed, rather than saw, a movement behind me. I spun around, but nobody was there.

Too much imagination, I thought, but I felt as tense as a coiled watch spring. I was conscious of being alone in the big house, of being trapped upstairs in a back room with no way out. Cautiously I closed the drawer and turned around. Then I made my way back to the bedroom door. Again, with that sixth sense for danger, I felt a presence behind me. I spun around and this time I was sure that something had moved in the darkened bathroom beyond.

It crossed my mind that I might have surprised a burglar, helping himself to Daniel's things when he was away. Then I reasoned that Mrs. O'Shea was hardly likely to have admitted a burglar. Daniel's windows were shut and the only way in was through the front door and up two flights of stairs. Whoever or whatever it was, I wasn't stupid enough to go and investigate. If someone was in there, I'd try to pretend I hadn't noticed and simply leave. Afterward, I could keep watch to see who emerged.

All would have been fine, except that I glanced back once more just as I was leaving the bedroom. This time I saw him in the mirror. He was standing behind the bathroom door, a huge dark shape with one arm raised and holding some kind of weapon.

FIVE

I turned and fled, blundering in my haste against the wash-stand that stood beside the door. Unfortunately my foot caught against one of the legs of the washstand. It teetered and fell, the china jug breaking as it crashed onto the floor, sloshing water over my feet and legs. I lost my balance and stumbled forward, expecting to feel that blow to the back of my head at any moment. When hands grabbed me, I attempted to struggle to my feet.

"You'll not get away with this, you know!" I shouted. "Mrs. O'Shea is downstairs. I'll scream and she'll come running up here and her big sons with her."

"It's all right, miss. Take it easy. I'm not going to hurt you," said a very deep voice. "Don't be scared. Here, I'll help you up." And I was deposited on my feet.

I turned to look at my attacker.

"You were waiting behind the door to clobber me. I saw you in the mirror," I said.

"I didn't know who it was," the man replied. "I heard someone come in, and I was ready to defend myself in case they were coming for me."

Now I was able to breathe again, I took in the great bulk, the ugly face with its twisted, flattened nose, and I knew who he must be.

"It's Gentleman Jack, isn't it?" I asked. "Daniel sent me to find you. I'm so glad you're here. I'm Molly Murphy, a—a friend of Daniel's."

"Pleased to make your acquaintance, Miss Murphy," he said, in that deep rumble, and extended a huge, meaty hand. The handshake itself couldn't have been more gentle.

"What are you doing here?" I asked. "And how come the landlady doesn't know you're in the house?"

"I've been hiding out," he said. "I thought the police had been tipped off that I was in the neighborhood and were looking for me. Daniel gave me a key in case I needed it. I came to find him, but I don't know where he's gone. He hasn't been home since I got here. I've been waiting for him to come back." He sounded a little like a petulant child.

"He's not likely to do that," I said. "He's in jail."

"In jail? Because of me?"

"Partly," I said and told him what I knew. "So you see," I concluded, "somebody's deliberately trying to get him in trouble."

"Oh, no. That's terrible. I'll go to them and tell them it was all my fault. I was the one who asked him to set up the fight." He had actually started for the door. I grabbed his arm. It was like gripping onto a rock.

"I don't think that would do anybody any good. They'd arrest you too, more than likely."

He must have seen the sense in this, because he changed direction. He went across to the window, moving with surprising grace for one of his size and bulk, pulled back the net curtain, and peered down at the street below.

"So I was right to run the other day. They were looking for me."

"You're lucky the police didn't catch you here," I went on. "They raided the place a few days ago and took away anything they could use against Daniel."

"But why? Why would his pals do that? I thought he was a popular guy."

"I thought so, too," I said. "There is a rumor flying around that Daniel tipped off a gang to a police raid, and one of the officers got killed."

"Daniel would never do that," he said, shaking his big

bony head. "Daniel's the best pal a guy could have. I'd trust him with my life."

"I know," I said, thinking privately that I was glad Daniel had proved trustworthy to somebody. I bent to pick up the pieces of the shattered jug and deposited them into Daniel's rubbish bin. "So we have to get to work, you and I. We have to find out who might have put that money in the envelope and tipped off the commissioner as to where a bribe was being passed."

"How are you going to do that?" he asked.

"I've no idea. Talk to the gang member to start with. Ask him who gave him the envelope."

"Yeah. Right. Okay." He frowned at me. "What envelope?"

"The one that had the money in it."

"Oh yeah. That one. And why were they giving it to Daniel again?"

"I just told you. It was just supposed to be a list of names, not a bribe. Someone put the money in there."

"Who?" he asked.

"That's what we're trying to find out," I said, my temper rising with my voice.

"I'm sorry," he mumbled. "I don't remember things too good these days. They say I got myself clobbered one too many times in the head, and they might just be right. I get these headaches something terrible, and sometimes I see double."

I had heard the term *punch-drunk* before, but I had never seen a living example of it in front of me. Jack Brady's speech was even a trifle slurred and his ugly, misshapen face screwed up in concentration.

"Then why in heaven's name do you want Daniel to set up another fight for you?" I blurted out before I had time to think. "Haven't you been battered enough?"

"I need the money, miss," he said. "I ain't never been good with money. When I had it, I spent it. Once I had a diamond the size of a nickel in my stickpin. That's when they used to call me Gentleman Jack. But I haven't fought in a while and now it's all gone again."

"There are other ways to earn money apart from fighting," I said.

He shook his head. "I ain't never been smart, miss—what did you say your name was?"

"Murphy," I reminded him.

"I ain't never been smart, Miss Murphy. If I hadn't been good with my fists, I'd have wound up as a laborer, sweating my guts out for a dollar a day. When I fight, I'm somebody."

Somebody with an addled head, I thought, but didn't say out loud. Instead I pulled out a chair from Daniel's dining table for him.

"Well, your first job is to help me get Daniel out of jail. Take a seat and let's think this through."

He sat, his big frame too large for the chair, which creaked as he lowered himself onto it. I meanwhile took a dishcloth from Daniel's kitchen and started mopping up the spilled water. Sometimes physical work helps with thinking, I've found.

"Now you and Daniel were planning this fight. How far along in the planning were you?"

"He was getting some guys to put up money and find us a place the police wouldn't raid."

"The list in the envelope was of potential backers for the fight," I said. "So which gang was organizing it?"

He scratched his head, looking like an overgrown monkey at the zoo. "I don't think he ever told me the name of the gang. He just said some guys he knew were going to get it set up."

"He never mentioned the Eastmans, for example?"

"He may have done. The name don't mean nothing to me. I'm not from New York."

"And had you fixed where the fight was going to take place?"

He nodded. "Yeah, I think they got the place fixed. Out on some island."

"Some island?" That certainly narrowed it down—anywhere along the Atlantic Coast.

"An island close to New York City?"

"Oh yeah. Just outside the city, Daniel said."

The only islands I knew about were Blackwell's in the East River, home of a female prison institution; Ellis, home of the immigration depot; and the small rock on which the Statue of Liberty stood. Hardly suitable sites for an illegal boxing match. "Staten Island?" I asked, remembering another name I had heard.

He shook his head. "It wasn't that one."

"Try to think, Jack. You want to get Daniel out of jail, don't you?"

He screwed up his eyes. "Some animal," he said at last. Then a beaming smile transformed his ugly face, making me see that he had once been rather handsome. "Coney Island, that was it."

"Coney Island, of course," I said. As I said the words, I remembered going there once with Daniel, during those blissful days before I found out the truth about Arabella. I wrenched my mind back from a clear image of riding the roller coaster with Daniel's arm holding me tightly around my shoulders. "Now we're getting somewhere. So the fight was going to be on Coney Island. Do you know when?"

He shook his head. "They had to wait until they got enough backers to come up with the money."

Obviously that had been what Daniel had been working on. I got to my feet and went through to the kitchen again to wring out the rag in the sink. "I wonder whether any of the New York gangs have influence as far away as Coney Island?" I said, thinking out loud rather than talking to Jack. He obviously knew no more than I did. "It might have been a member of an entirely different gang that Daniel was meeting that day. We'll have to ask him before we do anything."

"I did meet one guy," Jack said, as I came back into the room. "Daniel took me to meet him. Funny-looking little thing, he was. Comical, you'd say. Crazy about birds. Had a stupid live pigeon sitting on his shoulder."

"Monk Eastman!" I said, feeling a chill of fear shoot through me. "He's not as comical as he looks. He's the head of the Eastman gang. So you met with Monk. That must mean that the Eastmans are at least involved. Do you remember where this meeting took place?"

Jack frowned with concentration again then shook his head. "I don't know my way around the city that well. When I came to fight last time, I stayed at the Astoria. I had money then. I was world champ."

It was like pulling teeth. I was getting more and more tired and frustrated. Suddenly it occurred to me that I hadn't had lunch yet, and it must be well past lunchtime.

I got up. "I don't know about you, but I'm starving," I said. "Does Daniel have any food in the house?"

"He had some but I've eaten most of it," Jack said. He followed me into the kitchen. The pantry shelves were indeed bare. There was a small wedge of cheese under a glass dome, some shriveled onions and carrots, and half a loaf of bread. "It will have to be bread and cheese then," I said.

It was edible, barely, but it stopped the sick feeling of hunger.

"I'll tell Mrs. O'Shea, the landlady, that you're staying here," I said. "Maybe we can ask her to bring in more supplies when she does her own shopping."

"I'd be much obliged, miss. I need to keep my strength up right now if I'm going to fight. I usually have a dozen eggs at a time and steaks the size of a dinner plate."

"I don't know who would be paying for those," I said. "I don't have that kind of money to give you, and I don't know where Daniel keeps his money." I put down the glass of water I had been drinking. "It seems to me the first thing for you to do is to talk to Monk Eastman. He knows you. He's helping set up a fight for you, so you'll be quite safe with him. He has every reason in the world for wanting you alive and well."

"You want me to go out and find this Monk person?" A look of alarm shot across his face. "But what if the police are on the lookout for me?"

"You could put on some kind of disguise, if you're really worried," I said.

"I don't think it's that easy to disguise me," he said

apologetically. Of course I had to agree with him. Stick a beard or false eyebrows on him and he'd be even more conspicuous than he was now. Too bad it wasn't winter, when he could at least have huddled under a cloak and broad-brimmed hat. In summer shirtsleeves everyone in the world would recognize him.

"You'll have to take that chance, Jack," I said. "I can't go looking for Monk Eastman. I tried that once before, and I'm not sure what might have happened to me if the police hadn't broken into the Walla Walla."

"The what?"

"The Walhalla Hall. It's a social club on Canal Street. Locals call it the Walla Walla. It's where the Eastmans are often to be found. I expect we could come up with the money for a hansom cab fare between us. Take a cab right to Walhalla Hall and ask to speak to Monk. They're bound to recognize you, so you won't come to any harm. When you speak to Monk, tell him about Daniel. Find out, if you can, if it was a member of his gang who met with Daniel and who gave him the envelope. Find out if Monk knows anything about the bribe and exactly where Daniel was arrested. See if he has any suspicions of his own as to who might have planted the money. Have you got that?"

"Not exactly, miss. I'm not sure what envelope we're talking about."

"Saints preserve us," I muttered. "I'll write it down for you. You can read out the questions."

"I don't read and write so good, miss," he said.

Not the brightest button in the box, Daniel had said. A definite understatement. Wonderful, I thought. Daniel is putting all his hopes on a man who can't think straight or remember anything for more than a minute. Even if he finds Monk Eastman and asks the right questions, he'd forget the answers by the time he came home. The only alternative was for me to go with him and I was loath to do that.

"I'll write down the questions and you give the piece of paper to Monk," I said. "Then have him write down the answers, or, if he doesn't want to risk doing that, ask him to do what he can to clear Daniel's name. Maybe he'd be prepared to tell the police that Daniel had never been in the pay of the Eastmans or never taken a bribe from him."

Even as I said this, I realized that it was a long shot. From the one encounter between Monk and Daniel that I had witnessed, I had detected little love between them. Monk would probably be delighted that there was one senior police officer less to make his life a misery. Our only hope lay in Gentleman Jack and the fight. Monk would want it to take place; and if he needed Daniel to complete the arrangements for it, he might help spring him from jail.

"Tell Monk you'll not fight unless Daniel is freed," I said to Jack.

"Very good, miss. I'll tell him," Jack said, giving me that strangely ingratiating smile.

I took a piece of notepaper out of Daniel's desk, dipped the pen in the inkwell, and started to write. "I'm putting down a list of all the questions that Monk could maybe answer," I said. "Do your best for Daniel, Jack. If you don't help him now, then nobody else can."

"I'll do my best for him, miss," he said. "I swear it. Should I go now?"

"Better wait until this evening," I said. "Walhalla Hall is usually deserted during the day. Even if Monk isn't there tonight, somebody will know where to find him in the neighborhood." I opened my purse. "Let's see if we can come up with the cab fare there and back."

I had about a dollar in change. Daniel's desk and a jar on his mantelpiece produced another dollar.

"There you are," I said. "Enough to keep you going. And I'll leave a note for Mrs. O'Shea about buying you some groceries, although I don't think you'll get steaks as big as dinner plates. Maybe you should ask Monk to treat you to one of those."

He held out his huge red hand for the change. "Much obliged, miss."

"I have people coming to my house for dinner tonight, or I'd keep you company," I said. "But I have to get home to cook a chicken. So I'll come by tomorrow morning, shall I, and see what you've found out? I'll bring you some chicken if there's any left."

"Much obliged, miss," he repeated. "I'll see you tomorrow morning then."

I wrote the note for Mrs. O'Shea, then added a postscript, reminding her to keep Jack's presence a secret. I felt rather pleased with myself as I let myself out of the house. I had carried out Daniel's commission. With any luck by tomorrow we'd have Daniel free and out of jail.

SIX

On the way home, sitting on a horse-drawn bus that went painfully slowly along Twenty-third, I wondered what else I should be doing to help Daniel. Did I know anybody who could be of use to him or find out who might have tipped off the police commissioner? I didn't exactly move in high circles. I knew Senator Flynn, of course, but this was not the time to approach him for anything. From what I'd heard, he'd left the area and set off personally looking for his son. And after his improper advances to me, he'd only be a last resort anyway.

So who else did I know? Sid and Gus had a wide acquaintanceship, but mostly of a bohemian nature. I doubted that anyone who came to their house knew the commissioner of police, or any high-powered members of the force—at least not socially. Then suddenly it hit me—I did know a member of the Four Hundred. Miss Van Woekem! I had briefly been her companion before I learned of Daniel's engagement and discovered that she was Arabella's godmother. At the very least I could get Arabella's address from her. I still had a sneaking suspicion that Arabella's family could well be behind this whole business.

The more I considered the circumstances, the more I thought that this was likely. On the few occasions I had seen Arabella Norton she had shown herself to be a spoiled darling, used to getting her own way all the time. If she felt that Daniel had humiliated her by breaking off the engagement, then she could definitely have wanted revenge. Daniel thought, somewhat naively, that she wouldn't go to these lengths, but I wasn't so sure. He obviously had no idea what evil thoughts we women were capable of concealing beneath those elegant mounds of curls.

But going to all this trouble—the gang member, the bribe, setting up the meeting with the commissioner. If she had wanted his downfall, then why not attack him through the courts? I could answer that one easily enough. She didn't want to look like a fool. A breach-of-promise suit would expose her to public scrutiny and public pity. And Arabella's public face was very important to her. I resolved to see her as soon as possible. She may have wanted Daniel to lose his job, his status, everything he had worked for, but surely she wouldn't have wished for him to lose his life. And that might very well happen if he had to stay much longer in that damp and dreary place.

Did I have time to fit in a visit to Miss Van Woekem this afternoon, before I had to start preparing my dinner? A portly gentleman sitting across from me was wearing a watch chain. I asked him for the time and found it was now only just after three. Plenty of time then. I was in the right area for a visit to Gramercy Park, but in no condition to pay a call on someone as proper as Miss Van Woekem. I was still wearing my muslin, which had become sweaty and crumpled. I was wearing no hat or gloves. Such things mattered to people like Miss Van Woekem, so I had no alternative than to ride the El all the way home. Once there, I took off my muslin, rinsed it out, splashed cold water over my body, and put on the only other summer dress I possessed. In Ireland it would have been called my Sunday dress, worn only to go to church, but I hadn't done much churchgoing since I arrived in America. No doubt Father O'Reilly at home would say I was going straight to hell. Probably I was.

I combed out my sweaty tangle of curls and tied them back with a white ribbon. A glance in the mirror proved that I was looking halfway respectable as I set out for Miss Van Woekem's house on Gramercy Park. I'd done a lot of walking already today, and my legs felt like lead. So I looked longingly at the trolley that clanged and groaned its way up Broadway, debated on whether to spend five cents on the fare, then made a mad dash across the traffic to swing myself aboard at the last moment. It wouldn't help my cause to arrive at Miss Van Woekem's drenched in perspiration. As I had heard many times when I was sampling the upper-class life on the Hudson, ladies simply don't sweat. It isn't done.

Gramercy Park looked as delightful as I remembered it, cool and countrified, with its leafy park enclosed in a tall, iron railing and its elegant brick homes. I paused to adjust my hat before I mounted the steps to the front door and rang the bell. I was admitted by the same crisply starched maid, who looked at me with the same disapproving stare as the first time she'd admitted me. The look said clearly that I was really of her class and should be entering via the back door if she had her way.

"Wait here," she said. "I'll see if the mistress is receiving visitors."

With that she disappeared into the sitting room. I heard the sharp voice boom out, "Of course I want to see Miss Murphy. You should know that, Matilda. Bring her in."

I passed Matilda with a smile on my face.

"Miss Murphy, what a delightful surprise." The old lady reached out her hand to me. In the year since I'd seen her she had shrunk a little, her face becoming more birdlike with that fierce, prominent beak and those sharp, black eyes. I took the fragile hand.

"How are you, Miss Van Woekem?"

"Bored, as usual, but otherwise well enough. And yourself? When I heard nothing more from you, I began to wonder whether you had returned home to Ireland or left town."

"Nothing of the kind."

"Take a seat, please, do. And Matilda, we'll take coffee and some of Cook's gingerbread."

Matilda shot me another hostile stare as she curtseyed and left the room.

"Now do tell me, Miss Murphy—" Miss Van Woekem

had not let go of my hand. For all its apparent fragility she had a grip like a talon—"are you still pursuing your career as a lady investigator?"

"I am."

"And how is it going? Any juicy cases to report on?"

"I'm afraid not at the moment. I've just returned from a case on the Hudson River."

"So I heard," she said dryly. Well, of course she would have heard. I waited to sense her reaction.

"So Daniel Sullivan finally showed that he has some spunk after all," she said at last. "I was wondering how long he'd allow himself to be led around on a leash by my god-daughter. Quite an unsuitable match. I said so from the very first. But she wouldn't listen, of course. Always been head-strong." She eyed me, head tilted to one side, making her look even more birdlike. "No, you're a far better choice for him, even if you don't have Arabella's money. You're both Irish for one thing. Like should marry like."

"I'm not intending to marry Captain Sullivan," I said.

"You're not? But I thought . . ."

The coffee and cake arrived. The maid placed the tray on the table between us. "Do you want me to stay and pour, madam?" she asked.

"That's all right. Miss Murphy can take care of me," Miss Van Woekem said.

The maid departed with a rustle of starched skirts.

I picked up the coffeepot. "Do you take your coffee with milk in the afternoons?"

"Cream, please. I am still digesting what you just told me," she said. "I had always assumed that you and Captain Sullivan had some sort of understanding, or would have had had he not been committed to my goddaughter. Did I make a mistake on that? I am most surprised. I'm usually a very good observer of human nature."

I poured the coffee and handed her a cup. "No, you weren't wrong. There certainly was—a spark, shall we say—between the captain and myself. But even if I were pre-pared to forgive his past behavior, Captain Sullivan is in no position to marry anybody. He has been arrested and is in prison awaiting trial."

"In prison, you say?" The old lady's reaction made me sure that this was indeed news to her. "On what charge?"

"On a trumped-up charge, Miss Van Woekem. Money slipped into an envelope to make it appear that he was accepting a bribe. And this in full view of the new commissioner."

"Mercy me." Miss Van Woekem put her hand to the cameo at her throat. "In jail for accepting a bribe? From what we hear half the New York police have feathered their nests very nicely in a similar manner."

"But Daniel says he has never accepted a bribe in his life. Someone is out to discredit him."

"Has he retained a good lawyer for himself? He should at least be out on bail."

Good lawyer. Out on bail. Those words echoed in my head. I had little knowledge of the law, but surely this was exactly what Daniel needed right now. I was surprised he hadn't thought of it himself. "All I know is that his fellow officers have turned against him, and he doesn't want his father to know of this because of the father's weak heart. He has asked me to help him clear his name."

Miss Van Woekem stared at me over the coffee cup. "And how, exactly, do you propose to do this?"

"I have no idea," I said. "A matter like this is beyond my sphere of experience. But I thought I'd start off by talking with your goddaughter."

"Arabella? Do you think that's wise? I don't think she'd entirely welcome a visit from you."

"I'm sure she wouldn't," I said, "but I have to know whether this business started with her."

"How do you mean?" Her voice was sharp.

"Whether this might have been intended to pay back Daniel for breaking their engagement."

"Arabella might be a spoiled miss, but she has been brought up properly," Miss Van Woekem said. "She would never even consider such a lowly action. I'm surprised at you, Miss Murphy."

"I'm sorry, Miss Van Woekem," I said. "I meant no disrespect to your family."

"No disrespect? Suggesting that my goddaughter might be involved in planting false evidence to get an innocent man convicted?" She drew herself up, her hand still at her throat. "I'm afraid I have no wish to continue this conversation. Such thoughts are unworthy of you, Miss Murphy."

I rose to my feet. "I am sorry I have upset you, Miss Van Woekem. In the circumstances, I think it may be better if I take my leave of you and go."

Her hand was still on her bosom. "Yes, it may be better before our friendship is irretrievably damaged. Good day to you, Miss Murphy."

SEVEN

As I had suspected, I had no easy task ahead of me. In fact the words "bitten off more than I could chew" came into my mind as I stepped out onto Gramercy Park. I had been ushered out of Miss Van Woekem's by a gloating Matilda, without having managed to glean Arabella's address from her godmother. The old lady's horror and indignation probably confirmed that the Norton family in general was not involved in plotting Daniel's downfall. But that still didn't mean that Arabella couldn't have arranged a secret vendetta of her own. Whatever her godmother might think, Miss Norton certainly had that amount of venom in her, I was sure. Now I'd just have to head blindly for Westchester County and seek out Arabella for myself. I knew from Daniel that she lived in White Plains, but I had no idea exactly how far away it was or whether it was a big town. And I had invited guests for a dinner that was now less than three hours away. So it would just have to wait for tomorrow.

In the meantime I had gleaned one piece of information from Miss Van Woekem that should be shared with Daniel right away. I made my way along Twentieth Street to Broadway and hopped on a returning trolley. It was full and I had to stand, holding onto one of the brass poles. I grasped it firmly, with both hands, knowing what was about to happen in a couple of blocks. Sure enough, as we came toward Union Square, instead of slowing for the sharp curve, we picked up speed. The passengers, including myself, were flung to one side as the trolley negotiated the bend. Hats were knocked off, children screamed. There was also an angry shout from the street as a pedestrian had to leap for his life. I peered out to see the men seated in Brubaker's Biergarten chuckling as usual at this spectacle. It was said they actually took bets on possible fatalities.

After Union Square the trolley continued at a more sedate pace until I alighted outside City Hall and walked down the block to The Tombs. This time gaining entry wasn't so simple. In the company of Constable Byrne, I hadn't noticed the uniformed guards who stood outside the building. Now they stepped out to bar my way as I approached the front door.

"Where do you think you're going, miss?" one asked.

"I need to see Captain Sullivan, who is one of your prisoners at the moment."

"Visitors allowed once a month," the guard growled in a most unfriendly tone, "and today ain't the day."

"I just need to speak to him for a few minutes, like I did earlier today."

"This ain't the Waldorf Hotel." The man scowled at me. "Like I told you, it ain't visiting day. Now beat it. Go on."

"If I could just speak to the sergeant in charge, I'm sure—" I started, but the guard came toward me, looking menacing. "Beat it, I said."

"You don't scare me," I retorted, although in truth he did look rather alarming. "I'm an upright citizen, and I'm not doing anything against the law."

"You'll hop it if you know what's good for you, missy," the other, kindlier guard said. "There's no way you're going to get in through those doors. Why don't you write your sweetheart a message? Prisoners are allowed to receive mail."

"Very well," I said. I crossed the road to City Hall Park and sat on a bench. Then I took out the small gold pencil and notepad I always carried. It had been intended as a dance card for highborn ladies to fill in the evening's contenders. I had bought it for sixty-five cents at a pawnshop and very useful it had become when I needed to take field notes.

"Dear Daniel," I wrote in tiny letters because the cards were small. "They won't let me see you again. Have you hired a good lawyer? If so, why aren't you out on bail? I have met You Know Who and sent him to the right places. More tomorrow. M."

I addressed it to Capt. Daniel Sullivan, currently being held in The Tombs. But when I tried to hand it to one of the guards, I got the same hostile response.

"What do you think we are, your lackeys or a damned messenger service? You'll send your message through the U.S mail like everyone else."

"You two are about as friendly as a couple of gargoyles," I said.

"If you made it worth our while, we might consider it," the unpleasant one said, giving me a knowing look.

The irony didn't escape me. Every other employee of the New York justice system was apparently open to bribes. The one who wasn't now sat in a jail cell. Which made another idea flash through my mind: Was this some kind of payback because Daniel had witnessed another officer taking bribes, maybe had reported him? Another avenue to pursue.

Anyway, I wasn't about to grease the palm of either of these two individuals.

"Don't worry yourselves," I said primly. "I'm sure the postal service will do a splendid job of delivering my message." And I turned my back on them.

So I had no alternative but to purchase an envelope and a stamp, mail the note, and return home in a frustrated mood. The heat may have had something to do with it. Until I came to New York I had never imagined that a city could feel so unpleasant in the summer. The air was as heavy and oppressive as a hot, wet blanket. Sweat ran down into my eyes, and I felt that I didn't even have the energy to put one foot in front of the other and make it home.

When at last I did get home, I poured myself another long glass of lemonade before I had the strength to attack that chicken. In truth I was in no mood for a dinner party. My mind was in a turmoil, and the heat had left me feeling like a wet rag. But I wasn't about to deny my friends their meal. By seven the table was laid; the chicken cooked, chilled, and dismembered, lying on a platter surrounded by lettuce and spring onions. I had even gone the whole hog and purchased a tomato, all splendidly wrapped in foil. I gathered that no smart salad should be without one these days. At the last minute I whipped up mayonnaise. Only just in time. The bell rang and my guests arrived. I had set the table for two guests, but a third figure stood in the shadows at the doorway.

"Molly, dear, how good of you." Gus came in, arms open to give me a kiss on the cheek. "What a treat. Sid was only saying this morning that she felt too lazy to cook and we'd have to have bread and cheese, and then your lovely invitation arrived."

"I hope you don't mind," Sid said, before I could comment on the third figure, "but Ryan dropped in unexpectedly a few minutes ago. He seemed so dejected that we had to bring him with us. There will be enough for one extra, won't there?"

And that Irish rogue of a playwright, Ryan O'Hare, stood staring at me hopefully. What could I say? Of course there would be enough.

"He's going through a terrible time, Molly," Sid said, not letting Ryan speak for himself. "Some despicable person has stolen his idea for a new play and is producing it at Daley Theater this fall. Can you imagine the gall?"

Ryan entered, looking the picture of dejection, although I remembered that he was an actor as well as a playwright. "I feel wounded to the heart, cut to the quick, and all other metaphors that apply." In deference to the heat he was wearing a white cotton peasant shirt, open at the neck, with wide frills at the wrists, and baggy pantaloons. For Ryan this was no more unconventional than usual, but the resemblance to Lord Byron was startling.

"How did he get his hands on your idea, Ryan?" I asked, as the latter deposited himself in my one and only armchair without being invited. "Was it someone you had confided in?" From what I knew of Ryan, he did a lot of confiding.

"Absolutely not," he said. "I hardly know the man. And what I do know of him, I don't like. He has no taste in clothes. He wears tweed, my dear. Never trust a man who wears tweed." He paused and made a dramatic gesture. "He stole it, the blackguard. Or someone stole it and gave it to him." He looked up with sudden interest and waved a finger at me. "You're a detective, Molly. You can find out for me how Ben Archer got his hands on my play. And when we have proof, I'll sue."

"I don't think I can do that, Ryan," I said. For one thing, I had no time at present; for another, Ryan would not be able to pay me for my services; and for a third, I half suspected that Ryan may well have divulged his idea while in his cups. He was known to talk awful rubbish when drunk.

"You won't do it for me, Molly? I am devastated, cut to the quick."

"You're doing an awful lot of cutting to the quick tonight," I said, not able to stifle my smile. "I'd like to help, Ryan, I really would; but I've a big case I'm working on right now, and I've no time. In addition to that I don't think this is something you'd ever be able to prove. Ideas are swapped, shared, and borrowed all the time, aren't they?"

"It's true, Ryan," Sid said. She had perched herself on one of the kitchen chairs. "It's not yours until you've applied for copyright, surely."

"I still want to know," he said sullenly. "I won't rest until I know who betrayed me. There is no way in Hades that a buffoon like Ben Archer could have come up with anything as witty and sophisticated as my play. In fact, there are few in the civilized world who can match my wit and wisdom."

I glanced across at Sid and shared a smile. Modesty was never Ryan's strong point.

"Have you engaged a lawyer, Ryan?" Sid asked. "I should have thought that was the obvious thing to do."

Ryan spread his hands in a dramatically hopeless gesture. "Alas, one needs funds to retain a lawyer. At this moment I am not exactly flush."

"Can't you do anything to help him, Molly?" Gus asked.

"You are an investigator, after all. And what is this big case you're working on? You haven't mentioned it to us. In fact, only this morning you were talking of becoming a school-marm in Nebraska."

"Molly, a schoolmarm in Nebraska? Never!" Ryan said. "I won't allow you to leave civilization for life in the wilderness. You can't dislike our company that much, surely."

"I adore your company, as you very well know," I said. "There seemed to be too many other complications here in New York. Now I fear my complications have only increased. Daniel Sullivan is in jail."

I hadn't meant to tell them. It just slipped out.

"Daniel the Deceiver in jail?" Gus asked. "What on earth has he done? Or has Miss Norton had him rounded up for not paying enough attention to her?"

Which shows that we women all had the same suspicious minds. Their thoughts had also gone immediately to Arabella.

"It's a trumped-up charge," I said. "He was caught accepting what looked like a bribe from a gang member, but he says he never accepts bribes. Someone is out to have him ruined."

Sid's face became grave. "And you are making it your mission to rescue him? Oh no, Molly. No, no, no. Please tell me this is not the big case you've just mentioned. You are not thinking of helping him?"

"I'm afraid I'll have to."

"I don't understand you, Molly," Sid said. "One minute you tell us that he is the most odious man on earth and you never want to see him again, then you go running to his side the moment he summons you. That is how I expect the weaker members of our sex to behave, but not you."

I flushed. "I can't turn my back on him when he needs my help, Sid."

"I should have thought a spell in jail would be good for him. Give him time to mull over his failings." Sid crossed her legs with finality.

"People die in The Tombs." I was conscious of raising my

voice. "The conditions are awful in there, and I'm not going to let him die."

"And what about you, Molly?" Gus asked in her calm, sweet voice. "Surely Daniel Sullivan wouldn't expect you to put your own safety at risk? Gangs, bribes, false evidence—it all sounds highly dangerous and quite beyond your sphere of experience. Your common sense must tell you that you can't get yourself mixed up in this kind of thing."

"Don't worry. I won't be personally involved in that side of it. Daniel has a friend who is going to talk to the gang tonight. By tomorrow I should know more."

Gus reached across and took my hand. "Promise me you won't do anything foolish," she said. "Apart from everything else, there is a maniac at work on the Lower East Side, killing young women and dumping their bodies in the street, in case you've forgotten. There was another one in *The Times* today."

"Prostitutes, Gus, dear," Ryan said, waving a frilled wrist. "Nobody could ever mistake our Molly for one of those."

"If she's snooping in the wrong place at the wrong time they could," Gus said, fixing me with a firm stare. "Leave it to his lawyers and his friends in the police force, Molly."

"But he has no friends in the police force, that's the trouble," I said. "They've all deserted him. There's no one except for a half-addled prizefighter and me." Then, to my horror, I did what I had never done in public. I started to cry. This whole day had been too much for me.

Of course after that they were instantly kind and sweet, fussing over me.

"I'm sorry," I said, hastily collecting myself. "I don't know what came over me. Let's have Ryan pour the wine and sit down to dinner, shall we? I'm sure I'm worrying over nothing and everything will sort itself out just fine."

Unfortunately I didn't believe my own words.

EIGHT

At least I didn't dream the nightmare again that night, but I awoke with a terrible headache. I suspected it must have been the wine I'd served the night before, or maybe it was the prospect of having to face Arabella today. Then I remembered my pathetic performance of the evening before and was mortified. To have sat there in front of my friends, blubbering like the weak females I despised. What on earth was the matter with me? Daniel Sullivan, that was the answer. I was perfectly fine when he wasn't in my life. The moment I got myself mixed up with him again, I became an emotional wreck. Well, no more. I'd go first to hear Gentleman Jack's report on the Eastmans, then I'd pay a call on Arabella Norton. After that I'd make sure that Daniel had a competent lawyer and leave the rest in his hands.

Having taken command of my life once more, I washed, dressed, and headed for Daniel's apartment in Chelsea. The headache still felt like a tight band around my head, but I told myself that I'd feel better the moment I found out that Gentleman Jack had contacted the Eastmans successfully and that they'd be willing to help Daniel. If Monk Eastman wasn't willing to help, I'd no idea what I'd do next, but we'd cross that bridge when we came to it, as my mother was wont to say.

Even at the early hour when I emerged from Patchin Place, the city was already heating up. God knows what it would be like by afternoon. On any other occasion I'd have been looking forward to a jaunt in the leafy, cool country-side. On any other occasion I wouldn't have been meeting Arabella Norton.

I was outside Daniel's house by nine o'clock and rang his bell. Nobody answered. It occurred to me that prizefighters probably kept different hours from my own and that Jack was still lying there in a stupor. So I rang Mrs. O'Shea's bell instead, apologized, and asked to be admitted.

"I had no idea that Captain Sullivan's friend was there," she said, as she escorted me up the stairs. "He must have been quiet as a mouse. Anyway, I got the groceries you asked for and left them in his kitchen, so they should keep the poor man going until the captain returns."

I thanked her and stepped into Daniel's apartment.

"Mr. Brady? Jack?" I called softly. I listened for the sound of breathing, then tiptoed toward the bedroom. The room was unoccupied, nor did it look as if it had been occupied. The bed was made, exactly as it had been the day before. When I went through into the kitchen, the groceries that Mrs. O'Shea had purchased were still lined up in the larder. The remnants of that sorry piece of cheese still sat on the kitchen table. It didn't take a detective to work out that Jack Brady had not been here last night.

New and alarming worries flitted through my head: the police had caught him and locked him up or escorted him out of the city; Monk Eastman had taken a dislike to him, and he'd met with a horrible end in the East River. I told myself I was letting my imagination run away with me. The logical explanation was that he'd spotted policemen near Daniel's house and had been forced to hide out for the night.

I wrote him a note in the simplest terms, hoping his reading skills would enable him to get the gist of it. I told him that I would be back that evening and looked forward to his news. Then I made my way to the Grand Central Station. Soon I was aboard the train to White Plains. It was a pleasant ride. After we crossed the Harlem River into the area called the Bronx, the city gave way to leafy countryside. There were still small farms among the growing number of facto-

ries and houses, and we stopped at neat stations with gingerbread trim. I don't know what I had expected of White
Plains, but it turned out to be a fair-sized town with an air of
prosperity, its own Broadway, and even a few automobiles in
evidence.

I had hoped that the Nortons would occupy the one big
house in the area, but I had underestimated the size of the
town. It seemed to be a considerable community. What's
more, coming into the town, I had noticed several impressive estates. From what I knew of Arabella, I was sure these
were the kinds of places she would live. I asked at the station
but was met with a shrug. So I tried the post office. Here I
had more luck and was told that the Nortons had a fine property a mile or so out of town on the Hartsdale Road. The
clerk suggested that I would be able to hire a hack at the station to take me there.

I didn't have money to waste on hacks, so I set out in the
right direction, hoping that the mile or so didn't turn out to
be five miles or more. It wasn't unpleasant walking after the
town gave way to countryside. While the day was hot and the
flies were a nuisance, it was soft underfoot beside the road
and large oaks spread leafy canopies of shade.

Even so I was dripping with sweat and parched by the
time I came to an imposing brick gateway that had to be the
entrance to the Nortons' estate. I used my handkerchief to
wipe the grime from the journey from my face, adjusted my
bonnet, and hoped that I looked presentable as I walked up
the gravel driveway between rows of tall rhododendron
bushes. At last the house came into sight, a splendid
Grecian-looking affair with a pillared portico, surrounded
by well-manicured lawns.

Until now I had been concentrating on the journey. Now I
was here, and realizing I was about to face my nemesis, I felt
my pulse start to race. This was pure folly. She wouldn't see
me. Of course she wouldn't see me. What on earth had led
me to imagine that she would? And even if she did, she
wouldn't admit to causing Daniel's downfall. Well, it was
too late to go back now, and I've never been one to back

away from confrontation. We Irish seem to love a good mix-up, don't we?

I took a deep breath and marched right up to the front door. It was opened, not by a maid, but by a distinguished old gentleman in tails—an English butler no less. I began to see what a wrench it must have been for Daniel to give up the kind of promise that Arabella offered.

"Miss Molly Murphy to see Miss Norton," I said, and handed him my card. At least I'd learned from Miss Van Woekem how civilized society behaved.

He took the card and invited me to step into the cool of the marble entrance hall.

"I will see if Miss Norton is at home," he said stiffly and walked away.

I waited. The grandfather clock at the foot of the stairs struck eleven. My stomach growled, making me realize that I had only had a cup of tea this morning, having not felt like breakfast. Surely Miss Norton's breeding and good manners would force her to offer me at least a cold drink?

I looked up as the butler's feet tapped on the marble. He came up to me with my card on a silver tray.

"I regret that Miss Norton is not at home," he said. "Should I convey to her that you came to visit?"

"Please do," I said. "What time do you expect her to return? It is a matter of extreme urgency that I speak with her."

"I couldn't say, miss." He looked me straight in the face with the expressionless eyes that only butlers can develop. "I suggest you drop her a note on your return home. Do you have a vehicle waiting?"

"No, I walked," I said. "I enjoy a country stroll."

"I see." He ushered me to the front door. "Good day to you then."

Once again a front door closed on me, leaving me alone and outside. I walked far enough from the house until I had disappeared among the rhododendrons, then I stopped and waited. It was hard to tell with butlers, but I had a shrewd suspicion that Miss Norton was at home and didn't want to see me.

As if to confirm this suspicion, a high laugh floated out through an open upstairs window. Right, my girl, I thought. Molly Murphy doesn't give up that easily. I'll just have to wait for you to show yourself. So I sat in the shade of a large rhododendron and waited. It was not pleasant waiting. Even in the shade it was murderously hot. I had to brush continuously at the flies that tried to land on my face. A couple of bees also investigated me. I must have dozed and woke with a start with no idea what time it was. The shadows had lengthened, indicating it was past midday.

Suddenly I was aware of a dog barking—a shrill yap, yap, yap. That must have been what woke me. Before I could move, the dog itself appeared, a tiny white bundle of fur with pink ribbons tied around its ears. It froze, with those butterflylike ears cocked, then let out a new volley of barks.

"Gyp, naughty boy, come back here immediately," a voice commanded and Arabella Norton herself stepped into view, looking as always all pink and white and frills, like a large china doll. I scrambled hastily to my feet, conscious that my face was red and sweaty, my bonnet was now askew, and that I must look like some tramp in the hedgerow.

"You? What on earth do you think you are doing?" Arabella exclaimed and stooped to sweep up Gyp into her arms as if I might prove to be dangerous. "This is private property. Leave immediately or I'll call the servants."

"Miss Norton—Arabella," I said, resisting the urge to straighten my bonnet and brush myself down. "Please listen to me. Just give me five minutes of your time. It's a matter of great urgency or I wouldn't have come."

She stared at me with cold contempt. "I simply can't think what you could possibly have to say to me, unless you've come to apologize for behaving like a brazen hussy. If that is so, you need not have wasted your time. You have in no way inconvenienced or hurt me by taking Daniel Sullivan off my hands. I see now that Mama was right. He was not of my class, and I should be aiming for better."

She tossed back those perfect corkscrew curls.

A battle was raging within myself. I was all for telling Miss Norton exactly what I thought of her, but I knew that I had to remain calm if I wanted to get anything sensible out of her.

"Believe me, I wouldn't have come to see you if it hadn't been extremely important," I said. "I presume you must have had feelings for Captain Sullivan once; and even though you have parted company now, you would not wish to see him dead."

That worked. She took a step back, startled. "Dead? What do you mean? Daniel's not dead, is he?"

"Not yet," I said. "But he's been arrested. He's in a horrible prison cell where he may well languish and die, if he's not beaten to death by the other inmates."

Those large, blue eyes opened even wider, enhancing the china doll look. "Daniel, arrested? What has he done?"

"It is claimed that he is in cahoots with a gang, that he accepted a bribe. He maintains that he is innocent and that someone is orchestrating his downfall."

Arabella's face remained composed, but she clutched the little dog to her so tightly that it whimpered. Then she stroked its head and shrugged. "I'm very sorry for him, of course, but I don't see why you came to tell me this. Surely he's now your concern, not mine."

"I wondered if you might have any idea who could have planned this," I said carefully, remembering Miss Van Woekem's reaction. "Who wished to ruin him? I thought you might know someone with whom he had crossed swords or who carried a grudge."

She shook her head and the curls danced again. "I know of no such person. Daniel was well liked and respected in our circle. And of his professional life, I'm afraid I know nothing at all. You say he was involved with a gang? There's your answer. The criminal classes are always stabbing one another in the back."

"So you can't think of anybody you know who would be pleased to see Daniel's ruin?" I persisted. I was looking her right in the eye and she returned my stare without blinking. "In spite of our engagement, Daniel and I were never that close. So I'm afraid I can't help you, Miss Murphy."

I opened my purse. "Look, could I give you my card? If anyone comes to mind, anyone at all—any occasion on which he had an altercation and hasty words were said, would you let me know?"

"One has the occasional falling-out, but it rarely leads to sending a friend off to prison," she said. "You Irish always overdramatize everything. I'm sure it's all a misunderstanding, and he'll be out in a couple of days."

I shook my head. "I'm afraid he's in serious trouble, Miss Norton. More serious than even he realizes."

A smile twitched at her lips. "How very vexing for you. All that effort to snare yourself a handsome beau, only to find that he's been taken away from you again."

I bit back the words I wanted to say. "I'd like you to know, Miss Norton," I said as evenly as I was able, "that I broke off all contact with Captain Sullivan the moment I learned about you. I respected your understanding. And even if Captain Sullivan is released from jail, I'm not at all sure I could consider a future relationship with him. He hasn't proved himself exactly reliable so far."

"That's true enough," she said. It was the first time we had agreed on anything.

"But I can't let him languish in jail, even if he deserves it," I added. "I don't believe you would wish that on him either. That's why I'd appreciate any help you could give me."

She was looking at me with interest now. "You're a lady investigator, aren't you?" she said. "Does Daniel expect you to prove his innocence?"

"Yes, he does."

"Then I wish you luck." She brought the little dog's face close to hers and kissed its nose.

"Thank you. I'll need it."

"You Irish are a strange people," she said. "Perhaps you and Daniel deserve each other."

"My card, Miss Norton. I'd be most grateful if you would

take it and think on what I have just told you. If someone wished to punish him, then perhaps the punishment has gone further than they intended. No innocent man deserves to die in jail."

A spasm of concern, or was it annoyance, crossed that perfect complexion; then she shook her head again. "I'm afraid I won't be much use to you or to Captain Sullivan, Miss Murphy. Mama is taking me to Europe in a few days' time. She's hoping I'll meet a duke or a count." Amusement flickered across her face for a moment. "I must play with Gyp now. He's getting restless. You can find your way out, can't you?"

"One last thing," I said, as she put down the little dog and started to walk away. "I understand that Daniel's father is in poor health. Please don't tell him any of this. Daniel doesn't want to worry him."

"Daniel's parents don't exactly move in our social circle," she said. "I think a chance meeting with them is hardly likely."

On the long walk back into town I tried to think charitably about Miss Norton. I knew how I would have reacted if I'd found that my fiancé was keeping company with another woman. And she was a proud person. She could not have enjoyed having to admit that her engagement had ended in failure or having to endure the whispers and pitying glances. A strong motive for wanting to punish Daniel; and yet I had to think that her reaction when I gave her the news was genuine. I had startled her, I was sure. After a life of raising four young brothers, I had become good at knowing when someone was covering up the truth.

But of course that didn't mean that no member of her family was involved in orchestrating Daniel's downfall. Perhaps a doting parent or uncle had taken the law into his own hands to teach Daniel a lesson. I couldn't think how I was going to find that out.

All that way for nothing. By the time I stumbled back into White Plains in the full heat of the afternoon, I was so hot and exhausted that I was almost in tears. After I had fortified myself with a glass of iced tea and a ham roll I felt a little better and made my way to the station to catch the train back to the city. The carriage was full. I sat in one of the few remaining seats and we lurched out of the station. It was fiendishly hot and the air that blew in through the half-open window was like a blast from an oven. No sooner had we left the station than the man opposite me took out a large cigar and lit it, sending noxious smoke in my direction.

I began to feel queasy and closed my eyes as the carriage swayed to and fro. I had never been sick on a train before. I had even crossed the Atlantic in a gale and not succumbed to seasickness. But today the train seemed to be running on square wheels. We were tossed violently from side to side. At last I could stand it no longer. I fought my way down the carriage and out onto the little platform at the back. There I was horribly sick.

As I stood there, feeling clammy all over, a wave of fear passed through me. Had the typhoid epidemic caught up with me after all? Or was it just something I had eaten? I had been poisoned once this summer and had no wish to repeat that experience in a hurry. In the fresh air I began to recover. I wondered if the effects of arsenic poisoning ever lingered. It would be almost a month since—

The world stood still. Almost a month since I had returned from Adare, and during that time I had not been visited by the normal female curse. I wasn't the most worldly or experienced of young women, but even on the remote West Coast of Ireland, I had heard enough whispered tales to know what that meant. The sickness and weakness and emotional state were all explained in horrible clarity. I stood staring out as the countryside rushed past me. I was, to use the vernacular, in the family way.

NINE

I managed to make it home somehow although my mind was in such a state of turmoil that I found it hard to walk or even breathe. I had only felt this way once in my life before, and that was when I had seen Justin Hartley lying dead at my feet and knew that I had to flee from Ireland or be hanged. That terrible feeling of suffocation, of doom, of no way out. Above all I was mortified by my own weakness and seething with anger that fate had dealt me such a cruel blow. One night, one reckless, imprudent occasion, when Daniel and I had been trapped together in a storm and now this—a life in ruins. For that was what it would surely be. Oh, to be sure, Sid and Gus would rally round and maybe even find me a place to hide out during a pregnancy, but in the end I'd be a woman with an illegitimate child that I had no way of supporting.

Daniel would have to marry me. The words came into my head, making me almost laugh at the bitter irony. Daniel was in no position to marry anybody at the moment. I didn't even know that I wanted to marry him, if he were free. There was a big difference between wanting to marry and being forced to marry. And yet society had no tolerance for fallen women. Some of those prostitutes I had met during my night in a jail cell had probably started off as good girls whose lives went wrong in this way.

As I turned the key and opened my front door, the first thing I saw was a letter in Daniel's bold, black script lying

on my doormat. The afternoon post had brought the answer
to the note I had sent him yesterday. I tore it open.

> *Molly—as to retaining a lawyer or posting bail: my
> assets appear to have been frozen until it can be
> proven that they are not linked to gangland payoffs.
> The lawyer they have assigned me is either stupid or in
> the pay of my enemies. He wants me to plead guilty to
> the lesser charge of accepting a bribe and thereby take
> only a short prison sentence and dismissal from the
> police. He doesn't seem to entertain the fact that I
> might be innocent. I am at my wit's end, Molly. You are
> my one candle in this darkness. I'm relying on you.
> Don't let me down.*

I stood there with the letter in my hands, just staring at it.
No hope. That pretty much summed it up. "Holy Mother of
God," I muttered, half exclamation and half prayer. My own
mother had told me on numerous occasions that I'd come to
a bad end. Well, it seemed now that she may have been right.
I could just picture her sitting on that heavenly cloud, rub-
bing her hands and saying, "I told you so." My father, too.
He called me "fast and loose" once for walking home from a
dance with a boy. My hand strayed down to my stomach. It
was hard to believe that a baby might be growing in there.

A new and disturbing thought crept into my head: get rid
of it. I had heard rumors of women who knew how to work
that miracle, but also of girls who had died in the process.
Did I want to take that chance? Sid and Gus were more
worldly than I, and they had a large and varied acquaintanceship. They might know whom to ask. But the more I
thought about it, the more I realized that I couldn't tell Sid
and Gus, at least not yet. Not until I had become used to the
idea myself. And what about Daniel? I thought and felt myself flushing with embarrassment at the thought of facing
him. Shouldn't he know? Didn't he have a right to know? In
any case, I certainly couldn't tell him at this moment. He already had enough worries on his plate.

So the plain truth was that I couldn't tell anyone. It had to remain my secret.

Well, there was no point in standing here, drowning in self-pity. Daniel Sullivan would certainly be no use to me locked in a jail cell. The most sensible course of action right now would be to do what I had been asked and put my own worries on hold until it was done. Hopefully Jack Brady would have returned and read my note. He might even have positive news. I didn't feel like going out again, but I had to do it. Better than being here alone and brooding, in any case.

I made myself a cup of tea and a piece of bread and jam, before setting off for Chelsea. Mrs. O'Shea was home, cooking her husband's dinner. Smells of stew coming from the kitchen nearly had a disastrous effect on my stomach.

She hadn't seen the gentleman all day, she said. And she'd been home most of the day. She had been making her sister a nourishing soup with calves' feet and veal bones. The poor dear was fair worn-out, up all night with the new infant and then taking care of all those lively youngsters all day. She was planning to sleep over there tonight so that her sister could get some rest.

I took the key and fled up the stairs before the smell of that stewing meat made me lose the bread and jam I had just eaten. The apartment was untouched from this morning. Jack had not been back. I sat at Daniel's table and tried to digest this fact. My one ally had gone. He might just be hiding out at a new address and would return to Daniel's as soon as he was able. On the other hand, he might have gone for good. In any case, I couldn't count on his help any longer. I sank my head into my arms and just sat there for a while. Jack Brady might not have been overly endowed with brains, but he had been willing and kind and large enough to be my protector if necessary. Now I had nobody. I had no idea what I was going to do next.

I stared hopelessly at the polished mahogany of Daniel's desk while I tried to calm my racing thoughts. I was strong. I had always been strong. I could get through this somehow. Obviously the first thing to do was to find out what had hap-

pened to Jack Brady. But that would mean going to the Eastmans, and I didn't know whether I was brave enough to do
that. If Jack had met a bad end by visiting Monk Eastman,
then I'd be walking into a lion's den. I needed all the details
that Daniel could give me before I blundered into gangland.
I took a piece of paper from his desk and wrote to him. "I
need details if I'm to help you, Daniel," I wrote. "Where and
when this passing of the bribe took place. The name of the
gang member who handed you the letter. Exactly how the
scene transpired. Who was with the commissioner when you
were arrested? Did he say anything that gave you any hint he
had been summoned to witness your meeting with a gang
member?"

Then I added, "Are there no fellow officers who were
your friends and can still be trusted? I can't believe that
everyone on the force wishes this fate on you. I can't do this
on my own, Daniel."

Then I put the letter in an envelope and sealed it. It was a
strange sensation writing his name on the outside, and I felt
those dratted tears well up in my eyes again.

I wrote another note for Jack, giving him my address and
telling him how to find it. "Come and see me as soon as you
read this," I wrote. "I am most concerned about your safety."

Then I propped it on the table where he couldn't miss it.
But I found that I couldn't leave. He'll be back later, I told
myself. He's waiting until it's dark so that he's not so
conspicuous. I went into the kitchen and noted that Mrs.
O'Shea had brought eggs, as well as a bowl of that broth
she had made for her sister. I could stay and make Jack an
omelet when he returned. Looking at the food made me
feel peckish myself so I had some of that broth, plus a
boiled egg and some bread cut into soldiers to go with it. It
was strangely comforting to be sitting at the table, dipping
fingers of bread into egg yolk, as if I was a small child
again.

But I finished the egg, washed up, and still he didn't
come. Daylight started to fade, and reluctantly I decided that
I would have to leave. Chelsea was one of the safer parts of

the city and Twenty-third was a major street, but no woman was out alone after dark by choice.

A shrill ringing made my heart almost leap out of my mouth. It was coming from the wall in the corner. For a moment I thought it was an electric doorbell, then I saw the telephone hanging there. I had forgotten until now that Daniel owned a telephone, not being used to such a contraption myself. I stood there staring at it while it continued to ring. Should I answer it? What if it was Gentleman Jack, attempting to make contact? I took a deep breath and lifted the receiver with a shaky hand.

"Hello?" I said.

"Have I been given the wrong number?" a brisk woman's voice demanded. I detected a trace of an Irish accent. "It's Captain Sullivan's residence I'm wanting."

"I'm afraid Captain Sullivan isn't here at the moment," I said. "Who is this, please?"

"His mother, of course. More to the point, who are you?"

"I'm—just the maid, cleaning his apartment," I said hastily.

"He lets his maids take important telephone calls, does he?" she said. "You want to watch out that you don't get yourself into trouble, young woman. Please pass on a message to Captain Sullivan that he should call his mother."

"It's not bad news about his father, is it?" I blurted out before I realized this wasn't probably wise.

"Oh, I see that he keeps you informed of his private life, too," she said, and I could detect the disapproval.

"Only that he's been concerned about his father, ma'am. He keeps his landlady informed, and she passes it along to me."

"His father seems to be on the mend, thank the Lord," she said. "No, this is another matter altogether."

"I could take a message for him," I said hopefully.

"That won't be necessary. Just tell him that his mother is expecting his call," she said. That was clearly all I was going to get out of her. It probably wasn't really important, I decided, just a mother wanting to stay in touch with her only son.

"I'll write him a note that you called, Mrs. Sullivan," I said. "He's been working all hours on a case."

"They work him too hard," she said. "Thank you then, Miss—?"

She wanted my name, of course. "You're most welcome," I said, and hung up the phone. I wondered if she had heard about me when Daniel broke off his engagement, whether she actually suspected who I was and was voicing her disapproval. I didn't seem to have too many people on my side at the moment!

As I walked down the stairs I cursed myself for being so stupid—of course I should have remembered he had a phone. He'd given me the number before. But I still wasn't used to such modern conveniences, and it hadn't entered my head to call his address. I could have saved myself another long and hot trip, except that Jack probably wouldn't have answered it, even if he had been there. I wondered where he was, whether he was in hiding or in danger or both.

It had been a long, emotionally draining day and I was never more glad to get home. I had scarcely let myself in and collapsed in my one tattered armchair when there came a loud rapping at the door.

Let it be Jack come to find me. Please, no more bad news, I prayed. I had received enough for a lifetime's supply in the last two days. I opened the door and was relieved to find Sid standing there.

"Thank heavens, you're home," she said, coming in without being invited. "Gus was worried about you, Molly. She knocked on your door several times today to thank you for the dinner last night, but you were never home. She was convinced that you had gone against your word and met a terrible fate with the East Side Ripper."

I managed a bright smile and light tone as I replied, "Nothing could be further from the truth. I've had a pleasant jaunt in the countryside. I took the train to Westchester County."

"To see Bridie?" Her face lit up. "Wonderful. How is she faring?"

"Not to see Bridie, I'm afraid. Her camp is somewhere in the wilds of Connecticut. No, I decided to pay a visit to Miss Norton."

"Molly! What on earth for? That was either brave or foolhardy of you." She looked more amused than horrified. "I'm amazed you've returned unscathed. I should have thought she was the last person on earth you'd want to confront at this moment."

"That's true. It wasn't the most pleasant of encounters. But I needed to know if she or her family had anything to do with Daniel's arrest."

Sid frowned, then nodded. "Oh yes, I see. You suspected that she may have wanted to bring about his downfall out of spite. From what you've told us, she definitely had that in her character. And what did you discover?"

"Not much. I am fairly sure that she herself had nothing to do with getting Daniel arrested. She looked quite shaken when I told her about it. But of course, her father or a relative could have taken the matter into his own hands, unbeknownst to her, and set out to teach Daniel a lesson."

"How would you find that out?"

I shrugged. "I have no idea. The truth is, Sid, that I'm very much an amateur when it comes to detective work. I seem to stumble upon things more by luck than by skill. If only Paddy Riley hadn't been killed, I might have learned true detective skills; but as it is, I just have to muddle through."

"So what will you do now?" she asked.

I had to take a deep breath before I said, "I don't know. I just don't know. But I can't give up for Daniel's sake. I've just written to him again, asking for all the details he can give me. Then I'll proceed from there."

"He can't be much of a gentleman if he gives you details of gangland transactions and expects you to investigate them," Sid snapped. "You're well rid of him, Molly. It was pure infatuation on your part. Put it behind you."

"I gave him my word, Sid," I managed to say, sounding miraculously calm. "I'm going to do what I can."

"All this rushing around in the heat isn't good for you," she said, frowning as she examined me. "You look quite flushed. I hope you haven't yet dined. We were waiting for you to dine with us tonight and you can be the first to hear our big news."

"Big news?" My heart leaped alarmingly.

Her face lit up. "Well, I suppose I shouldn't keep you in suspense. That's not fair, is it? You know that Gus and I have been experimenting with various Eastern lifestyles—"

They're moving to China or Japan, I thought in panic.

"—Well, we've finally made up our minds. We are going to take up Buddhism. From now on every living creature will be sacred to us, and we shall eat no more fish, fowl, or flesh. So Gus has prepared our first vegetarian meal tonight, and we want you to partake of it with us."

I was so relieved I could have wept. "I'd be delighted," I said.

As soon as she had gone, I leaned against the cool wood of the front door, limp with relief. I hadn't realized until now how much I had come to rely on them. They were my only friends in the world. Without them I'd have nobody.

"So tell them the truth," I muttered to myself, but I couldn't. I couldn't force myself to say those words out loud to another living soul because by saying them out loud, I'd make them real.

And now Sid had made me feel guilty about not visiting Bridie. Of course I should have done so. I was the closest to a mother that those children had, and I had become remarkably fond of them. Even as those thoughts passed through my head, another idea sneaked in to join them. I could always marry Seamus. I could never love him but he was a good man, and I already loved his children. They'd like nothing better than to have me as their mother.

"Rubbish," I said out loud, and dismissed the idea as quickly as it had come. I might be desperate, but I still had my pride. I wasn't marrying anyone for convenience.

TEN

Next morning I woke after a good night's sleep. The temperature outside had fallen during the night and sweet, cool breezes wafted in through my open bedroom window. I got up and stood at the window, savoring the cool air on my body through the thin cotton of my nightgown, listening to the sweet chittering of early morning birdsong. I felt refreshed and full of energy. Maybe I had panicked for nothing yesterday, I told myself. Maybe I wasn't in the family way after all. I hadn't always been regular in my monthly cycles, and they did say that shock could delay things. Fighting for my life in the Hudson River would certainly count as shock, wouldn't it?

I even felt hungry. That may have been due to the vegetarian dinner I had been served last night. To tell the truth, I had found it hard to swallow the strange concoction of nuts and greens that Gus had prepared, and I had ended up hiding most of it under a lettuce leaf on my plate. I went downstairs and ate a hearty breakfast, after which I found that my brain was less muddled than yesterday and I was able to think clearly. So I got out my pad and started jotting down notes. What did Paddy always say when attacking a new case? Start with the obvious, that's what he said. Go right to the source, don't skirt around it. That meant I should start with the person who'd put Daniel in jail—with the commissioner of police himself, Mr. John Partridge.

And just how was I going to get an appointment to see

him? On what pretext? I couldn't imagine that he'd welcome me as myself. If I appeared to plead on Daniel's behalf, I might even harm his case. God forbid, he might even suspect I was some kind of gangster's moll. No, this would take some thought and some subterfuge. I got up and paced around the room. A lady reporter come to interview him about his new appointment? Not at all a guaranteed entry. He might well despise them as a breed. A cause—I needed a cause. The commissioner had apparently arrested Daniel because he wanted to wipe out corruption in the Police Department. Very well, I'd be a member of the Ladies Decency League, come to congratulate him on his efforts. It was a risky undertaking. I had no idea if there really was a Ladies Decency League and whether Mr. John Patridge was already well acquainted with them. If he'd thrown the book at Daniel for accepting a bribe, he might well have me arrested for approaching him under false pretences.

"Nothing ventured, nothing gained," I said, more bravely than I felt.

I put on my one respectable business suit. It was too warm for the current weather but it looked efficient. Then I pulled my hair back severely from my face and hid it under a straw boater. The result was not flattering but had the desired effect.

"Better get it over with," I said to the severe young woman in the looking glass and headed out of the door without looking back. I wasn't sure where the commissioner of police was to be found, but I was certain most of the bigwigs had offices in City Hall. He'd either be there or at police headquarters on Mulberry Street. Either way, the folks there would be able to tell me where I could find him.

When I reached the post office on Broadway, I paid the ten cents at the public phone booth and had the operator put in a call to Daniel's number. It rang and rang.

"There is no answer, caller," the operator said, and the line went dead. I hadn't really expected one. I couldn't picture Jack picking up Daniel's telephone, even if he had returned during the night. He'd probably think it too risky to reveal his presence. I was tempted to check in person, but I couldn't spend my entire life going up and down Sixth Avenue on the off chance that he'd come back. He did have my address. He could come looking for me. And I was conscious that time was of the essence. Every day that Daniel remained in jail might put his life in jeopardy.

As I went up the marble steps to that imposing building with its gleaming marble façade and Greek columns, my nerve almost failed me. Molly Murphy, until recently an Irish peasant, was about to worm information out of one of the most powerful men in the city. Men didn't rise to the top in New York City without a certain degree of ruthlessness. If he was as straight and honorable as he claimed to be, then he wouldn't take kindly to my extracting information under false pretences. And if he was the usual sort of New York politician, he wouldn't want me poking into his crooked schemes.

"You have no choice," I told myself firmly and forced one foot in front of the other. There was a young man sitting at a reception desk. He eyed me flirtatiously. I gave him my Queen Victoria stare and told him I was on a most important errand from the Ladies Decency League. His manner changed right away and soon I was heading up a flight of steps to the second floor.

Mr. Partridge had a female secretary who looked even more dowdy and severe than I did. I couldn't possibly speak to the commissioner without an appointment, she said.

"Oh, but I know he'd want to meet with a representative of his staunchest supporters," I said. "The Ladies Decency League is backed by the most influential women in the city. Why only last week Mrs. Astor held a meeting at her mansion on Fifth Avenue." I shut up at that point before I let this ridiculous blarney go too far. But it seemed to have worked because the woman rose to her feet. "I'll see what I can do," she said. "He may just have a minute before his meeting with the mayor."

She returned with a gracious smile on her lips. "The commissioner would be delighted to see you, Miss—?"

"Delaney," I said, uttering the first name that came into my head.

"Miss Delaney to see you, sir," the secretary said, and I was ushered into a most impressive office, complete with a polished mahogany desk big enough to skate on, and walls decorated with citations and photographs of the commissioner shaking hands with President Teddy Roosevelt and President McKinley before him.

"Miss Delaney?" The man behind the desk stubbed out a cigar, then rose and extended a bony hand. He was a big man with heavy jowls and an impressive brush of a moustache. His eyes were hooded, like those of an owl. He was obviously a stickler for convention, as he was dressed in a well-cut suit with a high, starched-collared shirt beneath it, even though most men would be in shirtsleeves or at the very most in a linen blazer in this kind of summer heat. I shook his hand and accepted the chair he offered.

"And what exactly brings you to my office?" he asked pleasantly. "You come from Mrs. Astor, as I understand."

This was going a little too far into the realms of fantasy, even for me. "Not directly from Mrs. Astor," I said. "But our organization, the Ladies Decency League, has dispatched me to congratulate you on the fine job you are doing in restoring decency to our city."

He smiled, a cold, thin-lipped sort of smile that didn't reach his eyes. All in all a very cold fish, I decided, and one whose face didn't betray at all what he was thinking.

"I am doing my best, Miss Delaney," he said. "I am faced with a formidable challenge, as you know only too well. Vice is rampant in our streets. Prostitution, gambling, drunkenness, corruption at all levels—these are blights that threaten to destroy our fine and noble city."

"I couldn't agree with you more, Commissioner," I said. "As for corruption—we know that it is rampant in your very own department, and we are delighted that you are taking such firm measures against it. Are we right in thinking that you had one of your senior officers arrested for receiving a bribe only this week?"

His face registered a flicker of surprise before those eyes became hooded again. "My, my. News does travel fast in this city, doesn't it? How did your organization hear about this?"

"We keep our ears to the ground, Commissioner. One of the reasons I was sent to you today was to congratulate you on this firm and bold action. It sends a message throughout the ranks of the police, as I am sure you mean it to."

"It does indeed." Now he looked pleased with himself. "Corruption must be weeded out from the top down, Miss Delaney. Young officers look up to their captains. We must let them know the high cost of straying from the straight and narrow path."

"Of course we haven't been privy to any details," I said, leaning confidentially forward. "Do we understand that this officer, this captain, was actually in cahoots with the gangs?"

"Of course the case has not come to trial yet, so I'm afraid I'm really not at liberty to discuss it."

"Of course not," I agreed. "But how did you catch him out? Have you already managed to set up a network of spies within the force?"

"Not really," he said. "It was pure luck, actually. I have been conducting walking tours of the most unsavory parts of the city because I believe that displaying my presence sends a powerful sign to the criminals there, also because I wanted to see for myself just what I was up against. I came around a corner, and there was one of my officers actually being passed a bribe by a known gang member. I had him arrested at once, of course. The envelope was opened and dollar bills cascaded to the sidewalk. The gang member took to his heels and left my officer to face the music—which he is now doing."

"Amazing," I said. "So this was all complete happenstance? You just chanced to be in that part of the city at that very moment?"

"Pure coincidence, Miss Delaney." There was something in the way he was looking at me. I couldn't quite read it— was it triumph? Was he gloating? He set the trap to catch

Daniel himself, I thought. I tried to make my brain work. What else could I possibly ask him?

"And he was being passed a bribe in broad daylight," I asked, "or was it under cover of darkness?"

"In broad daylight, can you believe?" The commissioner smiled again at Daniel's supposed stupidity.

"In some back alley, I've no doubt."

"Not at all actually. It wasn't a street where ladies like you would feel safe walking alone, but a broad-enough thoroughfare for the event to be witnessed. Water Street, down by the docks, as a matter of fact."

Firmly in Eastman territory, I thought. Now there was no longer any doubt that Monk Eastman's gang was definitely involved in Daniel's downfall. Not a happy thought because the double cross could have come from them. They may have wanted to set up the prizefight with Gentleman Jack and cut Daniel out at the same time.

The commissioner had risen to his feet again. "So glad to meet you, Miss Delaney. Please give my very best to Mrs. Astor and the ladies of your fine league. Now if you'll excuse me, I can't keep the mayor waiting."

Desperately I tried to come up with more questions. "Just one moment," I said, and he looked back at me in surprise. "We are—thinking of coming up with a league citation to reward noble actions by our public servants," I said, blurting out the first thing that came into my head. "You yourself will be first on the list, in fact. I gather a swank party is being planned."

"I am most honored." He gave a little mock bow.

"I'm sure the ladies will be most impressed to hear about these walks you conduct around the most dangerous parts of the city," I babbled on. "You surely don't walk through those parts alone, do you?"

He smiled again. "I am not foolhardy enough to risk gang members taking a potshot at me. I had an escort of officers who normally patrol that beat and who, I might add, were instrumental in helping me to arrest the errant captain."

"You wouldn't remember any of their names?"

The smile vanished. I had pushed too far. "I administer a force of several thousand men, Miss Delaney. Much as I'd like to be on first-name terms with every constable, that is just not possible. And I'm wondering what interest you could have in knowing their names?"

"Just in case the ladies of the league wish to issue any more citations," I said.

"My officers do their duty no matter what it is," he said. "Now if you'll excuse me, my secretary will show you out." And he was gone. I descended the stairs feeling somewhat pleased with myself. I knew the street where the passing of the envelope took place. I could presumably find out which officers walked that beat, and I knew which gang had to be involved. This latter was not a comforting thought because it meant I would have to pay a visit to Walhalla Hall, whether I liked it or not.

When I was out of sight of City Hall, I took off my hat and shook my hair loose, just in case the commissioner had sent anyone to tail me. Then I hopped on the next passing trolley, anxious to put ground between myself and Mr. Partridge. He wasn't an easy man to read—well, no man would be who had risen through New York City politics to one of the plum jobs—but I had sensed that he was glad about Daniel's downfall. So the next thing to find out would be whether he had crossed swords with Daniel before. I had no idea how I was going to do that. I looked back longingly at the square solid outline of The Tombs. There was no point in asking to see Daniel again, unless I had enough money to bribe my way in. I'd just have to wait and see what his next reply told me.

I jumped off the trolley again at Houston Street, resolved to do some shopping, just in case Gentleman Jack showed up and needed feeding. Houston was in turmoil with pushcarts trying to get through the crush of people, a delivery dray blocking most of the street, and shoppers jostling each other as they tried to squeeze past.

"Move over. Make way. Go on, get out of here." The cries rose up in several languages, presumably all saying the same thing. Then one of the pushcarts gave up the attempt and backed around the dray, and I saw what was holding us all up. A horse had dropped to the ground between its shafts and was in the process of being cut loose by its driver. The load on the cart indicated why the poor beast might have succumbed to heatstroke.

"Get it out of the way and let us through!" a man's voice shouted.

"You come and help drag it yourself!" the driver shouted back. "He's dead as a doornail. He's not going to get up again."

Suddenly the smells became overpowering—the frying chickpeas on one cart, the pickles on another, a string of geese hung up by their necks, and the horse manure scattered liberally over the cobbles. I felt my head whirling around. I backed out of the crowd and sank to the nearest stoop, fighting back nausea. I had to get away from here fast, but I couldn't trust my legs to support me.

When a hand touched my shoulder, I leaped a mile.

"Molly, it is you!" Jacob Singer towered over me, his shadow creating welcome shade. He was wearing his customary worker's cap and Russian-style twill shirt. "Are you all right?" he asked.

"I came over a little faint," I said.

"I'm not surprised, with this heat and the crowd." He lifted me gently to my feet. "Come on. I'll take you to the tearoom around the corner."

I allowed myself to be led, feeling the support of his strong arm around me. He took me into the cool darkness of the tearoom and ordered us glasses of hot tea.

"When you're suffering from heat there is nothing better than hot tea," he said. "It cools the body like no cold drink can."

It came, in tall glasses held within silver frames and with a slice of lemon floating in it. I sipped and felt the nausea subsiding.

"It is good to see you." Jacob was smiling at me. "Have you been keeping well?"

"More or less," I said. "I don't seem to be tolerating the heat this summer."

"Who is?" he replied. "More cases of typhoid last week, you know."

"Little Bridie O'Connor caught it," I said.

"Bridie? I'm so sorry."

"Miraculously she recovered, and she's now out at a camp in the countryside getting her strength back."

"That's good news." He smiled at me again. "You've been constantly on my mind, Molly. You haven't answered my letters."

"No," I said. "I'm sorry. I was out of town for a while and then when I came back, I needed time to think."

"I understand," he said. "And have you had that time?"

I sat there staring at his kind, earnest face, with his round, wire spectacles making him look like an appealing bird, and felt tears welling up in my eyes. Holy Mother, but I certainly couldn't cry in front of him!

"I have and I'm afraid my answer has to be no."

I watched his face fall. "It wouldn't work, Jacob. I couldn't marry you," I said. "I admire you tremendously. I think you're a very fine person, and you've no idea that this is the hardest thing I've ever said."

"Is it still that policeman?"

"In a way." I stared at the steam rising from my glass of tea and couldn't bring myself to meet his eyes.

Two elderly Jewish men with long beards and black homburg hats came in and sat at a table in the corner. I didn't understand the Yiddish, but the looks we were getting were quite plain to read. No young Jewish man should be alone in public with an unmarried girl, especially with a shiksa.

"Now do you see why?" I whispered to Jacob, indicating the men in the corner. "We'd have that for the rest of our lives." It was a good excuse, but I knew very well that, had things been different, I'd say to hell with what other people thought. Jacob nodded with appreciation though. "It is a lot to expect a woman to handle," he said. "Tolerance will never be something my fellow Jews shine at. So I'll accept your decision with regret. But you know where I live, Molly. If I can ever be of help, just let me know." He got to his feet and put a couple of coins down on the table. "I'm late for a meeting. I wish you well. I suggest you stay here until you are completely recovered before venturing out into the sun again."

I watched him walk away. Come back! I longed to shout. You could make this work, a voice whispered in my head. A rapid wedding and he'd never know the truth. But I'd know, and Jacob deserved better. I drained my tea glass, got up, and left the old men staring after me.

ELEVEN

The noon mail delivery brought no note from Daniel. I began to worry that perhaps they wouldn't even let him write messages any longer, or that perhaps his enemies had intercepted any message that could help his cause. I felt as if I were climbing an impossible mountain, staggering forward one step, only to slip back several yards again.

"I can't do this, Daniel!" I shouted into the emptiness of the house. "I don't know how. It's too much to ask of me."

I felt stupid tears of self-pity stinging in my eyes again and wiped them away. I couldn't give up now. It wouldn't only mean Daniel's doom, but my own.

I tried fixing myself some bread, cheese, and radishes, which were normally my favorite foods, but I couldn't seem to swallow and had to push the plate away from me. I knew I'd have to pay a call on Monk Eastman, and I wasn't looking forward to the prospect. But it was the Eastman gang that now provided my only concrete clue. Somebody had either managed to slip that money into the envelope destined for Daniel or had bribed or intimidated the gang member to exchange envelopes. Either that or Monk was also in the conspiracy, which made my going to see him doubly worrying. Added to that, I had sent Gentleman Jack in search of the Eastmans and he hadn't returned.

What I needed was someone to accompany me, someone who could run for help or let the police know if something bad was about to happen. I couldn't think who that person might be. Sid and Gus would not even allow me to go into Eastman territory. Jacob would accompany me if I asked him, but I wasn't going to put his life in danger or mark him as an enemy of the Eastmans when his work was so firmly within their territory.

Then suddenly I had a flash of inspiration. I did know a member of the Eastman gang—or at least, a junior member. Seamus's unpleasant cousin Nuala, with whom I had stayed briefly on my arrival in New York, had three sons. Last time I met them the two oldest had become Junior Eastmans, running messages for the gang and helping with little assignments like knocking over the stalls of those vendors who weren't paying their protection money. Malachy, the oldest boy, had never been the most likeable child and had probably become rotten through and through by now, but I had let him live with me when his family was thrown out of their house. And maybe he felt some kind of gratitude for the way I had taken care of his cousins. On the other hand, maybe he couldn't care a brass fig and would be only too delighted to hand me over to his gang bosses. It was a risk I had to take.

I took care not to make myself too attractive or desirable, thus removing all suggestion of future white slavery. This wasn't hard to do, as it happened. I certainly didn't look like my normal red-cheeked and freckled self. In fact I looked quite pasty faced and hollow eyed. I stuffed my hair under my straw hat and buttoned my costume jacket up to my neck. Then I let myself out of my front door, ready to meet my fate.

Instead I met a strange figure in flowing saffron robes wafting down Patchin Place. It took me a moment to recognize him.

"Holy Mother of God, Ryan. What are you doing?" I blurted out as Ryan O'Hare swept magnificently toward me.

He spread out his arms in blessing. "Our dear friends have convinced me to try out the Buddhist lifestyle," he said. "I saw a picture of a Buddhist monk in a journal, and I thought those robes looked divine. I just had to try them."

"Buddhist monks have to shave their heads," I said, starting to laugh.

"Yes, well there are lengths to which one will not go." He ran his hands through his luxuriant dark curls.

"And I believe monks have to be celibate," I went on.

"You are taking all the fun out of this," he said, wagging a scolding finger at me. "I am merely trying out the lifestyle, not making a lifelong commitment, you know. Eating fruits and nuts and chanting. That's about it, really. Oh, and not stepping on ants. That's about all I can handle. And I must say it is divinely funny to watch people's reactions to my lovely robes. They couldn't take their eyes off me on the trolley."

"I'm sure they couldn't," I said. "They certainly make you look even more gorgeous than usual."

"You are too kind." He blew me a kiss. "But you, on the other hand, dear Molly. Not looking your best, I fear. You have such lovely hair. Why hide it in that manner?"

"Because I'm about to do undercover work, and I have to look prim and severe," I said.

"Ah. The big case." He nodded. "Is this all part of the Save Daniel attempt?"

"It is," I said. "And Ryan—can I ask you to do something for me? Something very secret?"

"You know I adore secrets. What is it?"

"If I don't come home tonight, would you tell Sid and Gus that I went to meet Monk Eastman today? It would probably be too late to do anything, but at least I'd like someone to know."

"My dear child, how utterly foolish of you. I must forbid it."

I shook my head. "I'm not too excited by the prospect myself, Ryan, but I have no choice. There are things I can only find out by talking to the Eastmans. I couldn't tell Sid and Gus because I know they'd do everything they could to stop me."

"And I should, too," Ryan said, stepping in front of me.

"I'll be careful," I said, reaching out to touch his arm.

"I'm going to have Nuala's son Malachy escort me. He's a Junior Eastman, so I should be all right."

Ryan shook his head. "That police captain certainly doesn't deserve everything you are doing for him. I hope he's duly appreciative."

"I hope so too." I looked away. "And what about your own court case?" I asked, steering the conversation away from too dangerous waters.

"Which case was that?"

"The person who stole the script of your play."

"Oh, that." He waved it aside. "The Buddhist lifestyle tells us to forgive our enemies."

"I'm impressed, Ryan."

"And between you and me, I've heard that the play is so dreadful, it won't even run a week. It probably won't even make it through the tryouts in Philadelphia." He gave a wicked smile. "And I've also met a fascinating new friend."

"Also a Buddhist?"

"No. He's a doctor. A European doctor. Very erudite."

"Doesn't sound at all your type."

"You underestimate me, Molly. I can be intellectual if I wish. I have been learning all about the workings of the human brain. Do you know how many circuits there are operating within the brain?"

"No, how many?"

He frowned, then gave that delightful smile. "I've forgotten. A lot. Anyway, the whole thing is too, too fascinating."

"I'm sure it is," I said, "but I must get going. So please, not a word to Sid and Gus unless I don't show up tonight, promise?"

Ryan shook his head. "You need to be taken under the wing of some strong and respectable male and settle down to have babies and darn socks."

"I'll let you know if one presents himself," I said, and hurried away before the conversation became too hard to handle.

I caught the trolley down Broadway to Fulton, then followed that street until the pungent odor of fish announced that I was approaching the fish market and the East River. Last time I had visited Nuala's family, they had lived on the waterfront, in a run-down tenement between sail-making shops and ships' chandlers. There was no guarantee that they were still there, of course. Nuala's husband, Finbar, was better at drinking the profits than earning money at the saloon where he worked, and last time I had heard Nuala had lost her job gutting fish at the market. With income this precarious and three rambunctious boys, they had had to do a bunk in a hurry from several landlords before now.

However, this time it seemed I was in luck.

"Well, would you look what the cat's dropped on the doorstep." Nuala eyed me, hands on her broad hips. "And what could Miss High and Mighty possibly be wantin' with poor folks like us?"

"Sorry to disturb your afternoon sleep, Nuala," I said, as she looked bleary eyed and disheveled, "but I had to come—"

Suddenly her expression changed. "Sweet Mary and Jesus, it's not bad news, is it? You haven't come to tell me that the little one's gone to meet to her maker?"

"The last time I heard, Bridie was well on the mend, and they're all enjoying the fresh air and country living."

"Of course they are," she said, the bitter sneer returning to her face. "Out there living the life of Riley, and did they think to invite their poor, starving relatives to join them? And after the way I took them in when they came here with nothing, too. That's gratitude for you, isn't it?"

"They're not in a position to invite anybody, Nuala," I said. "Bridie's at the camp recovering, and Seamus and son are doing odd jobs for a farmer and sleeping in his barn."

"Then what have you come for?" she demanded. "Showing up on my doorstep, scaring the bejaysus out of me."

"I wondered if I could have a word with your oldest son."

"Malachy? What's he done now?"

"Nothing, as far as I know. I need his help since he knows the area around here so well. I'm willing to pay for it."

That made her eyes open quickly enough. "I couldn't tell

you where he is," she said. "No good, like his father. He's off here and there. Comes home when he feels like it, stays out when he doesn't, and what's more—just between you and me—he's got himself mixed up with some gang."

"Dear me. How terrible for you," I said.

Apparently my sympathy was harder to take than my hostility. She eyed me as if I could be a dangerous animal that might bite. "So what's happened to your fancy man?"

"As I told you more than once, I don't have a fancy man. I run my own detective agency, and I need Malachy's help in a case I'm working on."

"Get away with you," she said, giving a scornful chuckle. "Whoever heard of a lady detective?"

"So you've no idea where I might find him at this time of day?" I asked.

She shrugged. "Like I just said, he comes and goes as he pleases. There's no reasoning with him. He's as tall as I am now, and he tells me I'd better not lay a finger to him if I know what's good for me. He's got friends who will teach me a lesson. They pay him good money, too. Sometimes he gives me some of it, or he'd be out of here on his ear."

"What about your other boys? Are they around?"

"They'll be with their brother, if they're not swimming in the East River," she said. "Malachy's set on leading them into bad ways. There's not a one of them thinks that school is a good idea. If only they'd had a proper father and not a good-for-nothing bag of bones like himself in there." She jerked her head toward the interior of the apartment. "Sleeps his days away and spends his nights on the drink. What kind of man is that, I ask you?"

"Not the greatest," I said.

"But then most of them aren't much better, are they?" She gave me a woman-to-woman knowing wink. "They only want one thing and they're not good for much else, as I expect you've also found out."

"Men are no different from women," I said. "There are some good ones and some rotten ones."

"About time you settled down yourself," she said. "You're

not getting any younger, and I can't say this life is doing much for your looks. Positively peeky you're lookin'."

"I'm on an undercover assignment, Nuala. I have to make myself look as drab as possible."

"Ah," she said. Then she paused and added thoughtfully, "About how much money would there be in this job you've got for Malachy?"

"Depends how helpful he can be to me," I said.

I could see her considering how worth her while it might be to do some active searching for her son. Evidently not worthwhile enough. "You can try O'Leary's Tavern," she said. "I've caught him hanging around there before now. Or ask his brothers. You'll probably find them swimming in the river."

"Thank you," I said. "And if he does come home and I haven't managed to contact him, he knows where I live."

"I'll tell him," she said, and closed the door in my face, friendly as ever.

I saw no sign of the boys on the docks, so I made for O'Leary's Tavern. I had been there before once, when I first stumbled blindly into contact with the Eastman gang. It was on the corner of Division and Market, not far from Monk's headquarters on Orchard Street. I was glad to get the smell of fish out of my nostrils and stopped at a candy store to buy some peppermints to ease my queasiness. Then I continued up James Street and onto Madison, keeping to the shade of the tall buildings until I reached the tavern.

It was now midafternoon. The lunchtime rush was over. The men who had been served a plate of Irish stew for the price of a beer had now gone back to work. As I peered into the deep gloom from the bright sunlight outside, I noticed only one or two motionless figures slumped at the bar. No sign of a lively young'un. At least the scene appeared to be drowsy and not threatening. I plucked up my courage and stepped into the deep shadow of the bar.

One of the figures was instantly awake. "No women," he growled. "She shouldn't be in here."

"Unless she's one of Monk's girls come to offer you her

favors for free," the other man at the counter quipped with a silly, half-drunk laugh.

"Even I can focus well enough to know that she ain't one of Monk's ladies," the first man said. "Go on, girlie. Get yourself out of here. Yer old man's not here; and if he had his wage packet, he's already drunk it."

"I only want to ask a question," I said. "I'm looking for a boy. Young Malachy O'Connor. His family says he hangs around here a lot. Do you have an idea where I might find him?"

"He's out on a job." The bartender's head rose from behind the counter. He stared at me long and hard. "I've seen you before somewhere," he said.

"I imagine that most Irish faces look alike," I said, giving him my sweet, girlish smile and not admitting that I had been asking questions in this very saloon a few months ago. "So you don't know when Malachy O'Connor might show his face again?"

"When he's done with the job, I'd say," the bartender said, and the two men at the bar grinned.

"Could you give him a message from me when you see him?" I asked.

"What kind of message?"

"Tell him Molly could use his help. He knows where I live. Tell him I'll make it worth his while if he helps me."

One of the men roused himself from the bar and moved in my direction. "I'd even help you myself if you make it worth *my* while, darlin'." That stupid grin was still on his face, and he was blowing beery breath at me.

"Thanks all the same, but I'll wait for young Malachy," I said, backing hastily out of reach. "You *will* tell him?"

"I might," the bartender said. "Of course I might very well forget unless you give me a little something to remind me."

It seemed the whole world was in on bribery and corruption except for Daniel.

"And what is it she's wanting Malachy for in the first place, I'd like to know?" The less drunk of the two men at the bar had turned around on his stool to examine me. "She looks like one of those settlement ladies to me. Likely as not she's going to have him carted off to a reform school."

"Nothing like that," I said. "I need his help to meet—certain people who operate around here. People I might not want to meet without . . ."

I stopped talking as the sunlight was blotted from the doorway. Two large bruisers were coming into the saloon.

"What's a dame doin' in here?" one of them asked.

"She's looking for young Malachy."

"What does she want with one of my boys?" another, higher, squeakier voice asked. The two thugs stepped aside and a third figure was silhouetted against the sunlight. I couldn't see his face—but I recognized the shape of the shadow—round head, little derby perched on top of it a couple of sizes too small for him. As he came into the saloon I recognized the rolled-up shirtsleeves on pudgy arms, the bright red suspenders, and the open-necked shirt. A comical figure at first glance until you noticed that the bright metal on his fingers were not rings. I had wanted Malachy to escort me to Monk Eastman. Now I was meeting with Monk himself, here and now, whether I wanted to or not.

TWELVE

O kay, lady. What does youse want with my boy?"
Monk sauntered up to me. I noticed there was no live
pigeon on his shoulder today, but instead he carried a kitten
cradled in the crook of his pudgy arm. The kitten was blissfully asleep. It presented a charming picture, and I had to remind myself that this was a man who routinely ended lives
with a snap of his fingers.

At least I was in a public saloon with the street a few feet
away. I took a deep breath to make myself at least sound
confident. "I wanted to have the chance to speak with you,
Mr. Eastman. I thought that Malachy would know where to
find you."

"Hey, I'm flattered," he said, his beady little eyes not
leaving my face for a second. "It ain't often a young lady
comes chasing after me, is it, boys?"

All the men in the bar chuckled dutifully.

"So what does a nice young lady like youse want with
Monk?" he asked.

I wondered if he remembered meeting me before. On that
occasion his tone hadn't been anything like as friendly; in
fact I had been lucky to escape with my life, my honor, or
both. No sooner had this thought passed through my head
than I saw him frown momentarily.

"I know youse," he said. "Sullivan's bit o' skirt. Right?"

"I'm Captain Sullivan's friend, yes," I said. "It's because
of him that I've come to you. He's in bad trouble, Monk."

"Yeah, I heard about dat. Geeze, dat's too bad." He was grinning. "Don't you just hate it when bad things happen to coppers?"

More chuckling from the ranks.

"I thought you and he were supposed to be working on something together," I said. "You were supposed to be setting up a prizefight for his friend Gentleman Jack Brady."

"Maybe I was."

"And you sent a man to meet Captain Sullivan with a list of names. Well, somebody put money in that envelope of names to make it seem he was accepting a bribe. Somebody arranged it so that the commissioner of police just happened to witness this transaction." I paused before I dared to say the next words. Even so I had trouble keeping my voice even. "So I need to know, Monk—was that on your orders? Did you arrange for Daniel to be caught? I need to know because if you didn't, then someone else is out to get him."

"Me?" He put a pudgy hand to his breast. "Why it's generally known that I love Daniel Sullivan like a brother."

"Cut the blarney," I said, smiling in spite of myself. "I know you and Daniel hate each other's guts, but you were working together. I thought it would be in everyone's interest to set up this fight and make money out of it. I sent Jack Brady to find you and now he's disappeared."

"Gee, dat's too bad," Monk said, his face still in a relaxed grin. "But you don't have to worry yourself about him, girlie. He's been taken care of."

"Then where is he?"

"Didn't no one ever tell you dat curiosity killed the cat?"

"Look, Mr. Eastman—Monk. Daniel Sullivan is in big trouble. It's not just accepting a bribe. They think he's working for you. They're saying he tipped off your people to a police raid where one of the officers was killed. If I don't help him, he's not going to get out of prison alive. So I'm asking you—I'm begging you to be straight with me. All I need to know from you is one thing—did you order the money put in that envelope? Did you tip off the commissioner as to where he'd catch Daniel? If you tell me yes, I'll just get out of here and leave you alone because there's nothing I can do. But at least I'll know."

Monk stepped closer to me until his paunch was a few inches from my own stomach. "Listen, girlie," he said. "Sullivan and I—we shook hands over dis prizefight deal. Monk don't never double-cross no one once he's shook hands."

"So one of your men wouldn't have put the money in that envelope?"

"Let's put it this way." He looked around the room for confirmation of what he was about to say. "If any of my guys went against my wishes, he'd be feeding fishes in the East River by now." He flexed the hand with the brass knuckles on it.

"So which of your men actually delivered the envelope?"

"Bugsy did. I gave the list to him and told him where he'd meet Sullivan. And Bugsy would never double-cross me. I'd swear on dat with my life."

"But somehow money got in the envelope."

Monk shrugged. "It don't make no sense."

"I'm thinking it might be the commissioner himself who was out to get Daniel," I said. "And maybe after your gang, too."

This made Monk chuckle. "In dat case he's wasting his time, ain't he? Don't you know that commissioners are appointed for two years, max? We'll be around long after he's gone."

"He wants to reform the police force and stamp out vice and corruption in the city," I said.

This made all the men in the bar laugh loudly. "Good luck to him, I say," one of the men at the bar commented.

Monk stopped smiling. "If he wanted to reform the police, it wouldn't be Sullivan he went after. Everyone knows Sullivan ain't crooked like some of dem."

"Do you think I could talk to your man Bugsy and find out if anyone had a chance to tamper with that envelope?"

Monk shook his big head. "My boy Bugsy is temporarily out of town, on a visit to his sainted mother, I believe."

I understood this, of course. He'd be wanted for Daniel's trial so had conveniently vanished.

"If you had a chance to ask him yourself, I'd be most grateful," I said. "When he's done visiting his sainted mother, of course."

Monk looked at me and burst out laughing. "I like you." he said. He made a mock gesture with the brass knuckles in the direction of my face. "You ain't like most dames, all tremblin' and twittering when I talks to dem. You got spunk, girlie. Listen, I'll get my boys to keep their ears to the ground. If I hear who might have set up Sullivan, I'll let you know."

"Young Malachy knows where to find me," I said. "I really appreciate this, Monk."

He lifted the sleeping kitten close to his face and rubbed it on his cheek. "Hey, everyone around here will tell you dat Monk Eastman is known for his philanthropy and his kindness to widows and orphans."

His men grinned, but looked away when they did so.

"Thank you again," I said, noticing that I had a straight shot at the door and the sunlight beyond. I didn't wait around, but I took my chance and walked steadily toward the open door. I half expected to feel big hands grabbing my shoulders, but I made it down the steps and out into the sunlight. Then I kept on walking until I had put a block or two between me and the Eastmans. As I walked I was taken over with euphoria. How about that? I had met Monk Eastman and talked with him, person to person, and I had survived.

I made my way home, and this time I was relieved to find a letter from Daniel waiting for me, written on what must be his attorney's stationery as it was headed "J. P. Atkinson, 412 Wall Street, sixth floor, New York." The writing, however, was definitely Daniel's. So were the sentiments.

Molly, I thought I made it perfectly clear to you that you were to keep out of any actual investigation. Jack knows enough to ask the right questions, and he's not going to come to any harm with the gang. You are absolutely forbidden to go to the Eastmans yourself. You should remember what they are like. Monk doesn't take kindly to people poking their noses into his business, especially not women.

I wanted to write back sooner, but it seems they are even depriving me of writing materials now. I'm afraid their aim is to make my life as miserable as possible. I had to demand to see my attorney and finally got some writing paper out of him—about all he is good for, useless specimen of humanity.

You asked if there are any fellow police officers I could trust—there are many I can cite as being straight fellows and true-blue. My own two junior detectives, Quigley and McIver, are both good men, but also ambitious. They may well not want to side themselves with me because of the possible harm to their own careers. I can understand that. I'd probably have acted in a similar fashion.

The one name that does spring to mind is old O'Hallaran. You lodged with him on Twelfth Street. He is one who cannot be bought or bribed and is about as good a Catholic as you'll find. Having said that, he has no power in the department and is marking time until retirement.

I don't know what good any of these men could do you. Frankly, I don't know what good anyone can do me now. It seems I am caught up in a veritable web of lies and deceit.

Take care and don't take any personal risks on my behalf. I think of you every moment. Your Daniel.

I sat at the kitchen table with the letter in front of me for a good long while. Why did someone want Daniel Sullivan in jail? Had he offended someone in a mortally big way for them to want such terrible revenge? If it was only a case of a rivalry within the police department, then his demotion or dismissal would have been enough. No, this was something tinged with venomous hate; someone wanting Daniel's complete destruction.

I should write back to him with questions about his relationship with the commissioner, who was my best bet so far. As I opened the kitchen drawer for notepaper and pen, I was conscious of how much time was being wasted waiting for the delivery of letters. I needed to see Daniel for myself, ask him all the questions I needed to ask, and eliminate suspicions from my own mind. Well, at least I had one thing I hadn't possessed before—his lawyer's name and address. I'd go and bully him into getting me into The Tombs. Maybe I'd even discover whether he was someone's puppet and was dancing to their tune.

I sank my head onto my hands and sat there at the kitchen table with the sun shining in on me. It was good to feel safe for a while. "Just a few moments and then I'll get on with what I have to do next," I murmured to myself. My eyes closed and I fell sound asleep.

The next thing I knew, the kitchen was bathed in rosy twilight, and the clock was chiming eight. My face felt stiff and misshapen from falling asleep against the hard wood of the table. Whatever plans I might have had for the rest of the day, it was now too late. I was also ravenously hungry.

I got up and found some slices of tongue and cold potatoes in the larder. By the third mouthful my stomach rebelled. I had to settle for bread and cheese instead. It seemed that was to be my staple diet at the moment. I managed to get that down. It wouldn't be dark for at least another half hour. Maybe I should pay a visit to Sergeant O'Hallaran when he was likely to be home. I washed my face, brushed my hair, and set out to walk to East Twelfth Street.

Now that the fierce sun had gone down, life was spilling out onto the streets. Men and women sat on their stoops, old ladies fanning themselves, young women with babies on their laps. Children played hopscotch on sidewalks. From open windows came the sounds of the city—babies crying, pianos being played, arguments, laughter. Usually I relished these great affirmations of life around me. Tonight they only reminded me sharply that I was alone. I had no family with whom to fight or laugh. I would come back to an empty house. I really missed the O'Connor children. Then, of course, I remembered what I had been keeping locked away at the back of my mind: I would soon have a family of my own. A picture swam into my mind of a chubby baby with dark curls and Daniel's alarmingly blue eyes, its little head safe against my shoulder as I sang it to sleep with a lullaby. I had not allowed myself to imagine it before, as if not making it real would somehow make it go away. Now I felt a little jolt of excitement in the pit of my gut, and what I supposed was a rush of maternal feeling. I stood there, imagining the feel of its soft warmth against my cheek, and I had to admit that part of me wanted this baby very much.

A ball came bouncing in my direction. I sent it back with a mighty kick.

"Thanks, missus," voices called, and the boys went on with their game. I went on my way, content to have been part of that game for just a moment.

I was still in pensive mood when I knocked on Sergeant O'Hallaran's door. What a lot had happened since I had stood there last. I remembered arriving there over a year ago, as a fresh young immigrant, as Daniel Sullivan's sweetheart. Or at least that was what I had thought at the time. It had taken awhile to find out that his sweetheart was someone quite different from me.

He's brought me nothing but heartache since the moment I met him, I thought.

The door opened and Sergeant O'Hallaran himself was standing there, minus his uniform jacket but in his braces.

"Why, Miss Murphy," he said, a big smile spreading across his face. "What a nice surprise. Come on in, do. What brings you to this neck of the woods? Come back to your old haunts, have you?"

"It's good to see you again, Sergeant," I said, following him into the hallway, which smelled of well-polished wood. I remembered that Mrs. O'Hallaran had been a meticulous housekeeper, if a little too nosy for my taste. "Are you keeping well? And Mrs. O'Hallaran?"

"Can't complain." He smiled at me. "Mrs. O'Hallaran has just popped out to visit a sick neighbor. Was it herself you were wanting to visit?"

"No, it was you I came to see. I need your help, Sergeant. I've come about Daniel."

He turned back to me. "Ah, yes. A bad business. I never thought Daniel would take money from the gangs. He was as straight as his father used to be."

"It was a setup, Sergeant O'Hallaran. The envelope he received was supposed to contain a list of names. Somebody put money in it. Somebody made darned sure that the commissioner was there to witness the transaction."

"You don't say? You'd better come on through."

He ushered me into the unused splendor of the front parlor. I thought that Mrs. O'Hallaran would probably have wanted me in the back parlor or even the kitchen, but I perched on the edge of one of the velvet upholstered chairs.

"So it's up to me to find out who is out for Daniel's blood. I wondered if you had any thoughts on the subject yourself. Daniel says you're one of the few men he trusts completely. Most of his fellow officers seem to have turned against him."

"Well, you can understand why, can't you?" O'Hallaran said, pulling up a chair beside me. "After old Whitey's death in that brawl—men at HQ are saying that it was Daniel who tipped off the gang to the police raid. Our men don't take kindly to being betrayed by one of their own."

"But Daniel swears he had nothing to do with that. He's not in the pay of the Eastmans either. He was trying to help his pal, Jack Brady, by setting up a prizefight for him. And yes, I know it's illegal these days, but that's a far cry from being in Monk Eastman's pocket."

O'Hallaran nodded, digesting this. "Then who's been spreading the rumors?"

"How did you hear?"

"I can't say. You know what rumors are like—like a jar full of moths. Once they escape, they're all over the place."

"Is there anyone you've noticed who seems to take a particular delight in these rumors?"

He shook his head. "Most of the men are real sorry this had to happen to Daniel. He was generally respected, you know. A good captain. Always put his men's welfare first."

"Could someone be jealous of him?"

"It seems a long way to go over a little matter of jealousy. I can't think of anybody he's particularly slighted or upset—other than most of the criminals in the city." He glanced up at me and grinned. "My bet would be on Monk Eastman himself to have planted the money and started the rumors, you know. There's always been little love lost between him and Daniel. In fact, I was surprised when I heard they were in this together."

"It wasn't Monk," I said. "I asked him."

The old sergeant's eyes shot open. "You went looking for Monk Eastman? That was a very foolish thing to do, young lady."

"I didn't have much choice. I sent Jack Brady to ask the questions, and he disappeared. Monk seems to know where he is, but I don't know if he's alive and well or not. So now I'm all that Daniel's got. If I don't find out the truth, nobody will."

"You've got spunk, I'll say that for you," he said. "So it wasn't Monk."

"I'm wondering if it was the police commissioner himself," I ventured. "He seemed so pleased that he'd caught Daniel."

"You went to see him, too?"

I nodded. "Again, I had no choice. He claimed he just happened to be in the area, and it was completely fortuitous that he witnessed the bribe being passed."

"But why would the commissioner want Daniel out of the way?" O'Hallaran asked. "You don't get rid of well-respected officers if you want your department to run smoothly. And it would be the commissioner's own head that would roll if the department doesn't run smoothly."

"Maybe it's a personal grudge. A vendetta we know nothing about."

"Possible, I suppose." He stroked his chin as if half expecting to find a beard there. "Seems to me there are three possibilities—a grudge in his professional life, a grudge in his personal life, or"—he paused and looked up at me—"a case he was working on that somebody didn't want to be solved."

"That's an interesting thought," I said, digesting this new suggestion. "I never asked him what he was working on. But then that wouldn't make sense. If Daniel was taken off a case, another officer would be put in his place and the investigation would go on."

"Daniel was good, Miss Murphy. Better than the average cop. Maybe somebody wants the investigation to drag out until we lose interest."

"Could you find out for me which of your men were accompanying the commissioner when he stumbled upon Daniel accepting the bribe?"

The sergeant nodded. "Yes, I can do that. And if you let me know what Daniel was working on, I can tell you who has been put in to replace him. That doesn't necessarily mean anything. Someone else entirely could be pulling the strings in the background."

"Somebody would really have to be desperate to go to those lengths," I said.

He nodded. "Desperate people do desperate things. Give me your address, Miss Murphy. I'll do what I can for you."

I got to my feet. "I much appreciate it, Sergeant O'Hallaran. To tell you the truth, I've started feeling it's a hopeless case. I have no idea what I'm supposed to be doing and if I don't get Daniel out soon . . ." I had to look away, horrified that I might start crying again.

He put a clumsy hand on my shoulder. "Don't you worry yourself, my dear. I'll do my very best for you and Captain Sullivan. It will all come out right in the end. Truth will out, don't they say?"

I nodded as he escorted me to the front door. It doesn't always come out right in the end, I thought as I walked away. Sometimes there is no justice. Sometimes good people die and villains go free.

THIRTEEN

I could tell, as I climbed the stairs to the legal offices of
J. P. Atkinson, that a top-notch lawyer had not been selected for Daniel. The office was on the fifth floor of a building on the corner of Lower Broadway and Wall Street, the
other floors being taken up by a tailor's shop, a dentist's office (J. BLOGGETT. PAIN-FREE DENTISTRY. WE PULL 'EM—
YOU WALK AWAY SMILING), and various types of small
commerce. There was no elevator. The floors were covered
in worn linoleum, and I was quite out of breath by the time I
reached the top landing.

"I'll see if Mr. Atkinson can see you," a rather slatternly
woman receptionist said, although through the half-open inner door, I could already see that Mr. Atkinson was not with
a client. She went through to the office, a low conversation
took place, then I was ushered in. The inner office was no
more comfortable than the outer one had been. It had the
austerity of a schoolroom.

Mr. Atkinson looked almost painfully young and skinny,
straight out of some college in a suit that could have been
passed down from his big brother. He had a rather fishlike
expression, and the hand that shook mine felt equally cold
and fishlike.

"I understand you have come about Captain Daniel Sullivan? You are a friend of his? Obviously you are concerned.
We all are. But I'm not sure what exactly I can do for you."

I had managed to keep my frustration and fear in check

until now. But everyone has a breaking point, and I've never been known for my even temper at the best of times. His unctuous smile and limp handshake were too much.

"Do for me? More to the point, what are you doing for him?" I shouted. "If he hasn't yet been charged with a crime, then why in heaven's name isn't he out on bail? Why aren't you doing more to prove his innocence?"

He stepped back, eyeing me warily. "I assure you, my dear Miss Murphy, that I am doing everything within my powers. And as to bail—bail would have been granted, except that the captain's assets have been frozen until it can be proven that they are not the proceeds of gang payoffs. All we can hope for is a speedy trial."

"He's already been in jail over a week with no charge. I don't call that speedy. Why aren't you doing something about it?"

He spread his hands in a gesture of futility. "It's summertime. Many of the judges leave the city for the worst of the summer heat. Cases pile up, and we just have to wait our turn."

I noticed that he hadn't invited me to sit. I sat anyway.

"I have to tell you, Miss Murphy," he said, resuming his own place at his desk, "that the captain could make it much easier on himself if he were more cooperative."

"You mean if he pleaded guilty to a lesser offence."

"That is exactly what I mean. Captain Sullivan doesn't seem to realize the severity of the case against him. Accepting a bribe is one thing. Being in the pay of a known gang, betraying fellow officers—they'll throw the book at him for those."

"And what if he is innocent of all the charges against him? What if the money in the envelope was planted and the commissioner deliberately brought to witness the transaction? What if this whole thing were orchestrated with one thing in mind—Daniel Sullivan's ruin?"

"That's what he has tried to tell me."

"Because it's the truth."

He smiled again—that patronizing smile made me want

to punch him in the nose. "You're a pretty young girl and the captain is a good-looking man who has a way with women. Of course you'd believe anything he told you."

"And so should you, if you're being paid to represent him. If you don't start off with the belief that he's innocent, Mr. Atkinson, then who does he have on his side? If you believe he's guilty, then for God's sake find him another lawyer who does believe him."

"You've no doubt heard the phrase 'beggars can't be choosers,' Miss Murphy? I'm doing the best I can with the limited resources given to a court-appointed defense counsel."

"So who hired you? Were you given instructions to try and make Daniel plead guilty?"

"As to who hired me—I'm part of a pool. My name came to the top of the list. I was assigned to his case. And nobody has suggested that I make him plead guilty. I am just trying to get him off as lightly as possible."

"So you don't believe that he could be entirely innocent?"

"That would mean that somebody went to extraordinary trouble—that somebody managed to slip money into an envelope being carried by a gang member, that they managed to bring the commissioner of police himself onto the scene at exactly the right moment—"

"That's exactly what I mean."

"And why would somebody go to all that trouble?"

"You're his lawyer. You're supposed to be looking into it."

He swallowed hard, making a large Adam's apple dance up and down on a scrawny neck. "If somebody was out to destroy him, then it would most likely be the gang members themselves; and you'd never get the truth out of them in a month of Sundays."

"I've already asked the gang in question, and they deny that they had anything to do with it," I said, relishing the look of astonishment in those fishy eyes.

"You went to the Eastman gang?"

"Yes, and I spoke with Monk Eastman himself."

"Good heavens."

"So you see, things can be done. I'm doing my very best,

but I need help. Right now I need to speak with Daniel him-self. They won't let me into the prison again, so you'll have to get me in."

"Impossible. It's hard enough for me to gain entrance."

"They can't deny an uncharged man the right to see his lawyer."

"No, but 'reasonable access,' I believe, is the termin-ology. . . ."

"This is reasonable access. You have new information for him."

"New information?"

"Information that is vital to his case."

"But I—"

"Use your imagination, for God's sake, man," I snapped. "And you'll bring me along as your assistant. You are taking me along to record the whole thing in shorthand—being a very modern sort of office."

"Oh, right. Shorthand. Do you write shorthand?"

"No, but I can give a good imitation."

"I don't really like deception, Miss Murphy. If it came to light that I was smuggling you in, it wouldn't do my career any good."

"Ah, but if you managed to win this case, against all odds, think what that would do to advance your status in the pro-fession." I leaned closer to the desk. "He was the one who got Daniel Sullivan off when nobody else believed he was innocent."

I had tossed out this last thought, but it turned out to be a good one. I saw him digesting the idea.

"You really think you may be able to prove his innocence?"

"I'm doing everything I can," I said, sounding more con-fident than I felt. "But I can't do anything when it takes so long writing letters back and forth. If you can get me in to see Daniel this morning, I can get on with my job."

"Your job? I understood that you were a friend of the captain."

"Who is also an investigator who has worked with the po-lice before," I said, again relishing his astonished look.

"Good God, the police actually use female investigators?"

"When undercover work is needed," I said in a suitably enigmatic way.

"Very well, Miss Murphy." He got up and straightened his tie. "I'll do what you ask. Let's hope it doesn't get both of us and our client into even deeper trouble."

"It won't if you don't let on as to who I really am and what I'm doing there," I said.

I felt more satisfied than I had felt in days as we walked together down the stairs.

It was only later that I experienced a moment of panic as I was ushered into the dark, dank cell and realized I was about to see Daniel face-to-face again. It would be the first time since I had realized my current condition—how could I possibly face him? Would he read from my face that something was wrong or different? My heart was beating so loudly that I put my hand to my chest as if this gesture could calm it.

I heard the sound of footsteps and a voice saying, "Your lawyer to see you, Sullivan. Sit down."

Then the panel slid open. Daniel's face appeared, his hair and expression even wilder than when I'd last seen him. He looked hollow eyed, sallow faced. He was wearing a filthy white shirt that almost matched the ashen gray of his skin.

"What do you want today, Atkinson?" he demanded. "If you've come waving a confession at me again, then you're wasting your time and mine." This tirade was interrupted by a fit of coughing.

"I've come because I was asked to by the young woman I gather is working on your behalf, a Miss Murphy."

"Molly? Has she news for me? She's found out something?"

"She's here herself. You can ask her." Atkinson moved aside so that I was visible to Daniel for the first time through the bars. I saw his face light up and my heart leaped.

"Molly! I can't tell you how good it is to see your face."

"How are you, Daniel?" I asked.

"Not too good. Fighting despair daily. Terrible cough.

What about you? You're looking wonderful. A real sight for sore eyes."

"I'm just fine," I said. "I'm doing everything I can for you, but I don't seem to be getting anywhere, Daniel." I was conscious of Mr. Atkinson, standing to one side, out of Daniel's sight.

"What about Jack? Has he had a chance to talk to the Eastmans?"

"Jack has vanished," I said. "Monk Eastman knows where he is. Whether that's good news or not, I can't tell you."

"Jack has vanished? Gone into hiding presumably. He was awfully jumpy about coming to New York in the first place. Well, that's not good for me." He leaned closer to the grille and wagged a finger in my direction. "And that doesn't mean that you're going to start asking questions yourself. I've already made it very clear to you that I don't want you going anywhere near the Eastmans' territory. You do understand that, don't you?"

"Too late," I said. "I've already spoken with Monk."

"Molly, are you mad?" The words turned into a new fit of coughing. He fought to speak again. "I expressly told you not to. How can you go against my wishes like that?" Those wild eyes glaring at me were quite alarming.

I tried to sound calm. "Somebody had to after Jack disappeared. And don't worry, it turned out just fine. We had an amiable little chat, but he couldn't shed any light at all as to how the money got into the envelope. Just that he didn't order it put there."

"An amiable little chat." Daniel put his hands up to his face. "I'd never have told you anything about this if I thought you were going to take foolish risks. So what else have you done?"

"Saw Arabella, whom I don't think is involved in a plot to ruin you. Also questioned the police commissioner, who might be our leading suspect."

"Mr. Partridge? How in God's name did you manage to see him?"

"Never mind. Undercover work. But I can tell you one

thing—he was very satisfied with himself for having you arrested. So I thought I'd find out if you could think of a reason why."

Daniel shook his head. "He looked satisfied because he's a sanctimonious and pretentious prig. If he believes that I was taking bribes from gang members, he's probably patting himself on the back for ridding the department of a corrupt cop."

"So there was no bad blood between you before this?"

"I hardly know the man. We've never moved in the same circles. I've barely spoken five words to him."

"And you can think of no reason why he'd want your downfall over that of other officers, say?"

Again he frowned, then shook his head. "When he first came on board, he shook hands and said he'd heard fine things about me. Of course, there were rumors that he is the archenemy of Tammany Hall. He may be planning the systematic removal of every Irish cop from the force, starting with me. I did think that at one time."

"But then you'd soon have the rest of the force coming to your defense, once they realized what Mr. Partridge was up to."

"And why go to all this trouble? He could presumably demote me or even fire me for having a hand in the prizefight. Planting money, saying I'm in the pay of a gang—that is more than removing me; that is destroying me."

"You're right," I said. "Somebody is out to do just that. We have to find out who had a compelling reason for setting up the whole nasty little scene. Have you crossed swords with any member of your department recently? Beating out someone for promotion, maybe? Or catching out another officer involved in bribery and corruption?"

He sat silent for a while. "You think it might be a fellow officer?" he said at last.

"Your Sergeant O'Hallaran suggested it. He suggested a grudge in your personal or professional life. So that might mean another officer, or it might be a payback from some criminal you had arrested."

"I can't think of another officer who might have a grudge against me. I've been at captain's rank for over three years. There might have been bad feeling that I made captain before a lot of older men, but surely that would have come to the surface before now. And my men respect me. There's no questioning my ability to do the job. As to catching out a fellow officer accepting a bribe—we have a code of honor among ourselves. How any officer handles his job is up to him. If getting results involves slightly unorthodox methods, then the rest of us would turn a blind eye. I'd never snitch on a fellow officer. It would be more than my life is worth because one day I might need him to back me up in a jam."

"All right. Not a fellow officer then. What about a criminal? Has any big-time criminal gone to the dock recently shouting, 'I'll get you yet, Daniel Sullivan'?"

"Frequently." Daniel managed a grin. "But there's just one thing against that. No criminal with any brains would mess with the Eastmans. He wouldn't be on their territory to start with. And I don't see how he'd get hold of an envelope that came from Monk's hands to Bugsy's."

"This is hopeless, Daniel," I said. "Every turn leads to a brick wall. You must have offended or scared somebody. Sergeant O'Hallaran suggested it might have something to do with a case you were working on. He said you were too good and perhaps somebody wanted an investigation that dragged on forever and ever."

Daniel shook his head. "That doesn't hold water either, because the officers who were working under me on the cases are both first-rate men. They have just as great a chance of solving things swiftly as I would have had."

"So what were you working on?"

"Nothing too thrilling. There was a case of horse doping out at the Brighton Race Track. The favorite dropped dead in the middle of a race. I was just looking into that when I was called to take over the East Side Ripper investigation. No doubt you've read about that in the papers? Somebody bashing in prostitutes' heads and dumping them on East Side streets. Prostitutes get themselves killed all the time, of

course. Normally not much is done about the occasional
dead prostitute; it's considered a hazard of the occupation.
But when the numbers started piling up, the new commissioner said we should put a top man onto it."

"The commissioner chose you for the job?"

"I gathered that he was content that I should take over."

"And from whom did you take over?"

"Quigley and McIver were handling it. I think I mentioned them to you. Both good men. The top brass decided
the widening scope of the case needed a senior officer in
charge. If they weren't too thrilled about having me breathing down their necks, then they didn't show it. Mind you, I'd
not have been too happy if I'd had one of the top brass
foisted on me when I was doing a perfectly good job."

"And what had you found out so far?"

"Not much," he said. "There were four young women,
each of them battered beyond recognition. We tried asking
around to see if any pimps would admit to losing a girl, but
none has so far. Well, I take that back. A prostitute was found
murdered in a similar way a month or so ago. Her body was
dumped under the boardwalk by the Coney Island pier. She
was badly mutilated, but her pimp reported her missing."

"And you think this was the same killer?"

"The modus operandi was definitely similar."

"But the others were all found on Lower East Side streets,
and she was found at Coney Island."

"Correct."

"Maybe the killer killed his first victim out by the ocean
and then found he had a taste for killing prostitutes but didn't
want the long journey each time."

"So then he'd be an East Side resident?" Daniel asked.

"He could reside anywhere in New York City, couldn't
he? He could be from any walk of life. So you're not on his
track yet. He didn't leave any clues at all?"

"Only that he is a man who enjoys risks—the bodies have
turned up on well-traveled streets, and yet nobody has seen
them actually put there. If they came from nearby brothels,

he'd have had to somehow carry the body down the stairs and run the risk of bumping into people at every turn."

"But none of these brothels have reported girls missing, you say?"

"Not when I was arrested. Of course other officers might have made progress since."

"And what about the horse doping? Were you getting close to solving that one?"

"I was inclined to believe it was a rival jockey with a grudge, but again I was only starting the investigation when I was detained against my will."

"So in neither case were you getting close to solving these crimes."

He shook his head. "In the horse-doping case, I was just completing initial investigations. In the East Side Ripper case, I had literally just been ordered to take over."

"So somebody couldn't be afraid you were too closely on his tail."

"No. And besides, if the horse-doping case does turn out to be a disgruntled jockey, he'd hardly have the clout to doctor a letter from a leading gang member and then arrange for a police commissioner to walk a prescribed route at the right time."

"It need not have been the jockey," I said. "Maybe he was suggested to you as a scapegoat."

"It's possible, of course."

"I could continue this investigation for you, couldn't I? I wouldn't be putting myself in danger going out to a racetrack."

"I suppose you could. If you think it would actually do any good."

"And where is the Brighton Race Track?"

"It's one of the Coney Island tracks."

"Coney Island again," I said. "And weren't you trying to set up your prizefight out there?"

"As a matter of fact I was," he said.

"And the first prostitute was found murdered under the boardwalk there. Then is it possible that somebody didn't want you out on Coney Island for some reason?"

He shrugged. "Possible, I suppose, but again I have no idea who. We only selected Coney Island as the site for the prizefight because it's one of those places where the police don't interfere too much. They stay away from the Gut, where pretty much any type of criminal activity abounds."

"The Gut," I said, not liking the sound of it.

"A place where you are not to set foot," he said.

"But the rest of Coney Island must be safe enough for a working girl out enjoying her Sunday. I'd be one of thousands. You wouldn't have to worry about me."

"I do worry about you, all the time," he said. "And I absolutely forbid you to get involved with the East Side Ripper case. Prostitutes on the Lower East Side exist under the watchful eye of the Eastmans. You might have had an amiable chat with Monk once, but that doesn't mean he'll be in a good mood next time, or that he'd take kindly to snooping. You might wind up as one of those working girls in one of Monk's brothels if you're not careful. And I mean it, Molly." He glared at me again with those hollow, bloodshot eyes.

"I'm not stupid, Daniel," I said. "I'll be careful. But what you just said has made something occur to me. The press seems to think that a monstrous serial killer is at work on the Lower East Side—a man who hires prostitutes for the sport of murdering them. What if these girls have been killed by their pimp or protector because they wanted to escape from that lifestyle?"

"Then you're back to Monk Eastman," Daniel said. "He might not control every single prostitute on the Lower East Side, but the pimps pay their protection money to him."

"So he'd know," I said.

"Molly! What have I just been saying to you?" he shouted, and his voice echoed from the bare stone walls.

"What do you expect me to do?" I was shouting, too. "Go home and let you die? Look at you, Daniel. Someone's got to get you out of here, and I don't think *he's* going to do it." I glanced across at Mr. Atkinson, leaning against the wall, watching me warily.

Daniel spread his hands in a gesture of resignation. "Go

and talk to horse trainers if you wish, but you're not poking your nose in the other matter. Do you hear me?" He put his hand to his mouth to stop the coughing. "Besides, as I told you, I had only just been put on that case. I'd discovered nothing of importance. And if you want to know my opinion—I think all this is a waste of time. The cases I was working on can have no relevance to my current plight. The horse-doping case isn't serious enough, and I had barely started the second investigation."

"We can't leave any stone unturned, can we?" I said. "I haven't exactly been successful in the other areas I've searched. I'll go out to Coney Island and snoop around your racetrack. Other than that, I can't really think what to do next. Find out more about Mr. Partridge and his background, I suppose. This is proving very hard, Daniel."

"I know it is. And I can't tell you how much I appreciate everything you are doing for me," he said. "You're a grand girl, Molly Murphy. Without you I don't know what I'd do." He reached out toward me. The bars were narrow enough so that just his fingers poked through.

"Yes, well, somebody's got to take care of you with this mess you've got yourself into." I tried to keep it light; but his fingers, stretching toward me, were imploring me to touch him. He desperately needed warm, human touch, I could see that. I reached out and interlaced his fingers in mine.

"Stay away from the prisoner. You two will get me into trouble," Mr. Atkinson complained, stepping forward to separate us. "I brought Miss Murphy here as a special favor."

"It's about the only thing you've done right so far, Atkinson," Daniel growled.

"Daniel, Mr. Atkinson is doing his best," I said. I had pretty much decided that the best course of action would be to boost the lawyer's confidence and turn him into an ally. "It's not easy, you know. As you can hear, we've encountered one dead end after another."

"If Mr. Atkinson is doing his best, he'll be good enough to move away and let me have a minute alone with my young lady," Daniel said.

"I'll get into trouble for bringing her in here," Atkinson protested. "Please release her and let her step away from the grille."

"Oh, come on, Atkinson, what do you think she's going to do, slip me a cake with a file in it through the bars?" Daniel demanded.

He motioned me to come closer to him. For a second I thought he wanted to kiss me, but as his lips came close to my ear he whispered, "Watch out for Atkinson. I don't trust him. We don't know who he's working for."

Our eyes met and I nodded.

"Good-bye then," I said, pulling away from him.

Reluctantly his fingers released mine.

"Take good care of yourself, Molly," he called after me. "Don't do anything stupid, do you hear me?"

FOURTEEN

When I got home, around midday, having bought veal bones and vegetables to make myself a healthy soup, I found a note on my front door.

"Molly, you have a visitor. We are entertaining her to lunch until you return." It was signed "Augusta." It wasn't very often that Gus used her formal name and I was intrigued enough to brush my hair, wash the grime of the sidewalks from my face, and generally spruce myself up before I presented myself at Number Nine.

"Ah, Molly, you're back. Do come on through. We're having lentil salad in the conservatory." Sid greeted me with an enigmatic smile. "A young lady has called upon you."

We came out into the bright noontime light of the kitchen with its conservatory beyond. A lace cloth had been laid at the wicker table and Gus now sat in one of the wicker chairs. So did another woman with her back to me. At the sound of our voices, she rose to her feet and turned to face me.

It was Arabella Norton. I had never seen her dressed in such a somber manner before. Usually she was all pink and white and frills. Today she was wearing a lilac silk traveling costume, buttoned up to the throat. Her curls were piled up on her head and topped with a jaunty little purple hat with just a wisp of veil at the front and one of those V-tipped peacock feathers sprouting from it. Of course I'm sure the overall effect was delightful, as always, but I was too startled to

take in much. In fact, I couldn't have been much more surprised if Old Nick himself had come to visit.

"Miss Norton," I stammered, "to what do I owe this
honor?"

"You have delightful friends, Miss Murphy," she said.
"They have been entertaining me most engagingly. I am
sorry to drop in on you without any notice, but it is a matter
of some urgency and Mama and I leave for Europe in a
week's time."

"You have news about Daniel?" I blurted out.

"Oh dear, no. I'm sorry," she said. "So Daniel is still in
jail? How terrible for him. I wish I could be of help, but I
can't. I'm afraid I'm here on quite another matter."

"Pull up a chair, Molly. Join us for lunch and then you
and Miss Norton can do your chatting in peace," Gus said.

I had no wish to eat in the presence of Arabella Norton,
but I could hardly refuse Gus's invitation, and Arabella was
halfway through her own meal. So I was forced to sit beside
her at the little table and face a plate of brown lentils and lettuce leaves, which would not have seemed too appetizing at
the best of times. For my stomach, having not eaten for several hours, this was definitely not the best of times. I ate
bread and butter, which I knew I could tolerate, and worked
at hiding the rest under a lettuce leaf again.

Fortunately Sid and Gus were amazing. The way they engaged in polite conversation made me realize that they
moved in the same circles as someone like Arabella. They
knew the right things to say and had sufficient connections
in common that I got through the meal without having to do
more than nod my head.

I refused their offer of Turkish coffee, however.

"I am sure Miss Norton has a thousand and one things to
do if she's leaving for Europe soon," I said. "And I know it
must have been a most pressing matter that brought her to
visit me."

Actually I was all but bursting with curiosity. If Daniel
wasn't involved, what on earth did Arabella want with me? I

led her across to my house and seated her in the one arm-chair, while I put the kettle on for a cup of tea.

"I must apologize for bursting in on you like this, Miss Murphy," she repeated. "How charming your friends are. So intellectual. So cultured. I felt like a philistine country bumpkin beside them. Still, they had the benefit of a Vassar education. Papa wouldn't hear of my going to a women's college. I'm afraid he's of the old school and believes that women learn all they need to know in the kitchen and by observing their mothers."

I had had enough of small talk. My curiosity was now positively bubbling over.

"I don't wish to rush you, Miss Norton, but I can't imagine that you have come to see me on purely a social call. If it's not Daniel that brings you here, then in heaven's name what is it?"

"It is a matter of some delicacy, Miss Murphy," she said, lowering her voice even though we were alone in the house. "Daniel mentioned that you were a lady investigator. Is that really true?"

"Yes, I do run a small detective agency," I said.

"Then I need your help, Miss Murphy. And before you tell me, quite rightly, that I do not deserve your consideration after the way I have treated you, I must tell you that I am not here on my own behalf but on that of my dearest friend."

It raced through my mind that I'd have reacted in the same way if I'd found that my fiancé was courting another woman on the side, but I wasn't going to share that thought with Arabella when I'd just had something like an apology. "I have no time to take on another commission at the moment, Miss Norton," I said. "My entire days are taken up with trying to prove Daniel's innocence. I won't rest until that is accomplished."

"He is lucky that you show him such loyalty and devotion after treating us both so shabbily," she said.

"He has nobody else, Miss Norton. And whatever my feelings are toward him, I couldn't leave him to die in that terrible place."

"I feel exactly the same way about my friend, Miss Murphy. It is because my feelings for her are so strong and because nobody else is prepared to do anything that I feel I have to step in on her behalf. Won't you just hear me out and then decide if there's any way that you can help?"

"Very well," I said. "Tell me what is concerning you."

"Her name is Letitia," Miss Norton said. "Letitia Blackwell. She and I grew up together. Her family has a country home only half a mile from us. We played together as children, and then we became engaged to be married about the same time, too. We were going to be bridesmaids at each other's weddings." She turned her face away from me with her lips pressed together for a second, and for the first time I realized that perhaps she wasn't entirely glad to be rid of Daniel.

"Then three weeks ago something extraordinary happened. She disappeared, leaving a note to say that she had met a penniless young man and they had run away to California together to seek their fortune."

"And what concerns you, Miss Norton? That the young man is penniless? That he is unsuitable? I'm afraid even our dearest friends surprise us with their choices when it comes to matters of the heart."

She shook her head so violently that I was afraid the little hat would come flying off. "No, it's not that at all. If I really believed that Letitia had fallen madly in love, I'd wish her every happiness."

The kettle whistled on the stove, and I went across to make the tea. "You can't expect me to go to California and find her," I said. "I'm afraid that would be too big an undertaking for a small agency like mine, even if I weren't fully occupied with trying to prove Daniel's innocence."

"That's just the point, Miss Murphy. I don't believe she's gone to California at all."

"What do you mean?"

"I mean that none of it makes sense. I know Letitia better than anybody. She's a timid little thing, highly strung, nervous, very dependent. Always wants to please everybody.

And she adores her fiancé. She worships the ground he walks on. She wouldn't suddenly run off with another man without telling anybody. It's just not in her makeup."

I suspected that Arabella was miffed that her supposed best friend had not shared her plans with her. "She probably feared that her friends would stop her if she confided in them," I said tactfully.

"I'm sure she would have told me," Arabella said. "Or at least given me a hint. I was with her several times in the days before she vanished. She was terrible at keeping secrets, and she wore her heart on her sleeve. She would have been bubbling over with happiness and excitement if she were planning such a momentous escape. But as I said, she was timid by nature. I don't think she would have had the nerve to do such a thing."

I placed a teacup beside her. "So where do you think she's really gone?"

"I have no idea. I fear something bad has happened to her."

"What makes you say that?"

"Because of Evangeline," she said. "When we were children we received similar dolls for Christmas one year. Mine was Emily, hers was Evangeline. I loved Emily dearly, but not nearly as much as she loved Evangeline. Evangeline was her constant companion. Even today she keeps that doll on her pillow and sleeps with it beside her at night. I used to tease her about it. 'When you and Carter are married, you'll have to make her sleep in her own bed,' I told her. But she said Carter would just have to get used to dear Evangeline. When I went up to her room after she had run away, Miss Murphy, the doll was still on her pillow."

"Maybe the young man with whom she escaped insisted that they travel light. Maybe she'll send for her doll when they are settled."

She shook her head again. "There are other puzzling elements. The clothes she took. The clothes she didn't take. I realize she might have packed in a hurry and only been allowed to take one small bag with her, but why take a cocktail dress and leave the matching slip? Why leave her sturdy country shoes when she'll be doing so much walking? And why leave a drawer full of undergarments? Surely she'd need those. And her jewelry roll, hidden among the undergarments, was still there. What woman leaves without her jewelry? There were so many little incongruities in the clothing she took and left that made me think that she might not have packed her bag herself."

"If someone else packed it for her, what would be the reason?"

She leaned forward again and her voice was scarcely more than a whisper. "I wondered if she may have been kidnapped or lured away by an unscrupulous man."

"Again, for what reason?"

"Maybe to get his hands on her fortune? Maybe she has met an untimely end. I just don't know. All I have is this uneasy feeling in my stomach. I can't explain it. Perhaps you think I am talking nonsense; everyone else seems to."

"Oh no, Miss Norton. We Irish are firm believers in the power of the sixth sense," I said. "It has stood me in good stead several times in my life."

"Has it?"

"Oh yes. Each time I have sensed imminent danger, it has proved to be real. So tell me the exact circumstances under which Letitia disappeared." I realized as I said it that I should not allow her to go on like this. I had no time for another case, and if I did, the last person I should want to work for was Arabella Norton. But the fact that she had come to me, of all people, for help told me how worried she was. And she had almost apologized. And I knew what it felt like to be worried sick about someone close to me.

"As I said, it was about three weeks ago now. She was supposed to be coming to the city to spend the day with her intended. He was to meet her at the station. She was driven into town to catch the train to the city, but she never arrived. Carter waited and waited for several trains after the one on which she was expected, then telephoned the house to see why she hadn't come as planned. Her parents were away visiting friends for a couple of days, so there were only servants in residence. Finally Carter came up to White Plains to look for her. That's when they found the note on her pillow to say that she had fallen in love with a penniless young man and run away to California with him."

"What happened then?"

"Carter was distraught. Her parents were summoned home. They didn't want the local police called in. They wanted to spare Carter's feelings and their own embarrassment. Letitia's mother was sure that her daughter would contact them in a few days. She was sure Letitia would realize she had made a horrible mistake and beg to come home. But she hasn't. That's what convinced me that something is very wrong. I'm sure she would have written to one of us, her family or me. She was always such a dutiful daughter and wouldn't want to cause her parents grief. Or Carter, either. Even if she had decided not to marry him, she would have been sensitive to his feelings. She would have written to him explaining her actions, I'm sure of it."

"You say he's distraught?"

"Absolutely. Young men make more of an effort than us women to conceal their feelings, but he is walking around in a daze. He even threatened to go to California and challenge the other man to a duel. Carter is normally the most subdued and well mannered of men, so you can see how upset he is. And with good reason. He adored Letitia as much as she adored him."

"So what has been done to find her so far?"

"Discreet inquiries were made at the station and at stations along the route, hoping that somebody might have seen her leave the train before it reached the city. But nobody seemed to remember seeing her."

"So it's possible she never boarded the train in the first place."

"Quite possible, although the chauffeur says that he dropped her at the entrance to the station early that morning. The man at the booking office thinks he remembers her, but he says the young woman was wearing a veil so he never saw her face."

"That sounds as if she didn't want to be recognized," I said.

"I agree."

"Then the most logical assumption was that she really was planning to run away and didn't want to be seen."

"I suppose so. But I still can't believe it. It's all most distressing, Miss Murphy. We don't know which way to turn."

"I understand that feeling well," I said. "It's exactly how I feel about Daniel's case."

"Oh dear, yes. Poor Daniel," she said simply. "Can you not ask his fellow officers to help you? They all adore him."

"Used to adore him. Now they've all turned against him. Someone has spread a rumor that he has betrayed them."

"Then someone is enjoying this," she said, looking up at me suddenly. "You should find out whether anybody has tried to visit him in prison or asked after him."

This was such an insight that I stared at her. "You should be the detective, not I, Miss Norton."

She shrugged and gave me her charming smile. "It's only human nature, isn't it? If I ever played a trick on my little brother, or got him into trouble, I had to make sure I was there to witness his punishment. That was half of the fun. You see, I was not a very nice child, I'm afraid."

"I don't think we're ever nice to little brothers," I agreed. "I had to raise my own three brothers after our mother died. It wasn't an easy task."

"I'm sure it wasn't," she agreed.

For a while I said nothing, savoring the moment. Who would ever have thought that Arabella Norton and I would be sitting companionably in complete agreement. Wonders would never cease!

I decided to make the most of the present climate. "I'm most grateful to you, Miss Norton. And if I might take your suggestion one step further and ask you what might be an impertinent question . . ."

She nodded gravely. "I will answer it if I can."

"The only person who has shown obvious joy at Daniel's imprisonment is Mr. Partridge, the commissioner of police. Do you happen to know him?"

"Mr. John Partridge? My father knows him slightly. He's not one of our close acquaintances, but I have met him. An odious man, I'd say. I didn't like the way he pressed my hand when he shook it. Too familiar by far. Do you think he could have orchestrated Daniel's imprisonment?"

"The thought has crossed my mind more than once."

"But what reason would he have?"

"I wondered—it occurred to me," I began hesitantly—"that he might be doing your family a favor."

"A favor? My family?"

"Teaching Daniel a lesson for betraying you."

"What a horrid thought," she said, her face flushing.

"I apologize. I don't know your family, and I have no wish to insult them."

"To tell you the truth, Miss Murphy, my family was relieved I had broken my engagement. So if Mr. Partridge schemed to have Daniel arrested, it was for reasons of his own."

"Then I can see I'll have to delve into Mr. Partridge's background," I said, "but I thank you, Miss Norton. At least you've given me something to work on and renewed hope that I can save Daniel from that terrible place."

"Is it really so terrible for him?" she asked in a hushed voice. "Surely he's not treated like a common criminal?"

"Very definitely like a common criminal, and among common criminals, too. And of course they all know him and rejoice in his plight. One of them took a swing at him that resulted in an ugly bruise on his cheek. I'm worried that next time it might be a knife."

"Oh, poor Daniel," she said again. "I was angry with him for the way he behaved, and to tell you the truth, my first re-action when you told me the news was secret joy that he was being punished at last. But I truly don't wish him ill. I do hope you can set him free swiftly, Miss Murphy."

To my horror I felt a tear trickling down my cheek. Of all the things that were currently happening to my body, this was the most embarrassing so far. I wiped it away and hoped she hadn't noticed.

"He and I were quite wrong for each other, you know,"

she said, taking a delicate sip from her teacup. "He wasn't my social equal, however much his parents wanted him to be. And it was never a love match. I was a silly girl of seventeen, and Letitia had just become engaged to be married. I couldn't let her outscore me, so I set my cap at Daniel. He was one step more desirable, you see. He was very good-looking, and we made such an attractive couple. But I don't think I'd ever have been happy with him. He was wedded to his profession first. It took all his time and energy. And those times we were together—well, he was somewhat of a cold fish. There was never what you might call passion between us. I hope it's different for you."

I felt the blush flooding my cheeks. "I can't say I've ever found him a cold fish," I said truthfully.

"Do you think you will eventually marry him?"

"I can't even allow myself to think about the future, Miss Norton. The present is so terrifying and overwhelming. All of my energy is directed toward helping him, and I thank you for the wise insight and new hope you have given me."

"I just wish you could give me a similar insight for poor Letitia."

"I wish I could, too. What exactly did you want me to do for you?"

"Find out the truth, I suppose," she said. "Find out where she really went."

"I suggest her parents hire a private investigator in California."

"I had hoped that you'd come to the house and let me show you her room, then you'd see for yourself. And you'd know the right questions to ask people at the station and all that sort of thing."

"I'll try to do that for you as soon as I have time," I said. "I know you must be feeling frustrated that wheels are not being put in motion."

"I am. And I am itching to do more myself, if only I had a direction to follow. So let me ask you, Miss Murphy. Now that you've heard her story—what do you think could have happened to her?"

"I don't know her. If she claims she has run away with a penniless young man, where would she have met him? You know how strictly she was chaperoned at home. You know her interests and at whose houses she was welcome."

"I have already done what I can," she said. "Of course none of our friends entertain penniless young men. I can't even think of any gardeners or grooms or tutors who have recently vanished from the neighborhood. And Letitia is not the type who would go out riding or shopping alone to the kind of places where she could have met young men. She was well chaperoned and was actually afraid to go anywhere alone."

"You mentioned that she might have been abducted by an unscrupulous man. Where would she have met him?"

"I have no idea. Unless—" She paused and looked up suddenly from her teacup. "I hadn't thought of this before, but her mother is one of those ladies who does good works and helps at a settlement house here in the city. Sometimes she took Letitia with her, so it's just possible that the penniless young man or the unscrupulous abductor met her there."

"Yes," I said, "and that is something I can investigate for you."

Her face lit up. "I knew it was a good idea to come here."

"I can't promise anything," I said, "but I have friends who are active at the settlement houses. Do you have Letitia's picture with you?"

"Yes, I do," she said. She opened her purse and produced a framed sepia print. It was of two young girls, sitting side by side on a wicker chair, with a white lapdog between them. One of them was an enchantingly dimpled Arabella Norton, the other a paler, less vibrant girl, her light hair held back from her face with a big black bow, and then cascading over her shoulders. She looked exactly like Mr. Tenniel's illustrations in *Alice in Wonderland,* which used to be my most treasured possession.

"That was taken about five years ago now when we were leaving Miss Marchbank's Academy," Arabella said. "But I don't think we've changed much. Except that Letitia now wears her hair up."

"It's strikingly fair," I said. "You'd expect people to remember if they'd seen her."

"Yes, her hair is her finest feature," Arabella said. "When she wears it up, it's like a great golden halo. Everyone says she looks like those old pictures of saints."

"I wonder how she communicated with this man," I said. "Have you asked her family whether she received any mail recently?"

"They are all completely in the dark. Letitia was not a girl with a wide social circle, and her friends were all in the neighborhood. I'm sure her family would have noticed if she'd received letters from someone whose name they didn't recognize."

"You know what I'm wondering, Miss Norton," I said. "You're saying she was a quiet, mousy type of girl. When you were together, everyone would pay attention to you, would they not?"

"I'm afraid they would." She couldn't resist a little smile at this thought.

"Then might this not be an action to draw attention to herself? Maybe she wanted her fiancé to pay her more attention; she wanted to seem more glamorous and exciting. Don't you think it's possible that she staged this dramatic event and is now hiding out at a friend's house or at a hotel in the city waiting for a triumphant return?"

"Oh," Arabella put her hand to her mouth, "I never thought of that, but you could be right. That might be in Letitia's nature."

"I could show her picture at suitable hotels in the city."

"Yes. That would be wonderful of you."

"How soon do you sail for Europe?"

"Next Monday. I come to the city again on Thursday to pick up my new wardrobe from the dressmaker. I'll be staying with my godmother, Miss Van Woekem, so you know where to find me."

"That doesn't give me much time, considering the effort I have to put into Daniel's case."

She lifted her purse from her lap. "I should pay you a retainer in advance. Isn't that what's normally done in these circumstances?"

"Please don't, Miss Norton." I put up my hand to stop her. "I shouldn't feel right. I really can't tell you how much time I'll be able to devote to your cause or what possible chance of success I'd have. All I can say is that I'll do my best, but it's not easy rushing all over the city in this summer heat."

All the time we had been speaking, I had felt increasingly unwell. Now my stomach was churning dangerously. I took a hurried gulp of tea in the hope that the warm liquid would calm my insides, but it seemed to have the opposite effect.

"If you will excuse me, Miss Norton, but I have to rush to another appointment," I said and helped her to her feet. "I am honored at your trust in me. I hope I will succeed."

"If you do succeed, I will be in your eternal debt," she said, grasping my hand fervently. "I simply can't sail for Europe not knowing the truth about her. It will spoil my entire vacation."

I tried to extricate myself from her grasp politely. With a supreme effort of will I shepherded her to the front door and thanked her for coming.

"You have my telephone number on my card, don't you? And you know Miss Van Woekem's address."

"I'll do my best, I promise, Miss Norton."

"You are really so sweet, Miss Murphy. I'm sorry I misjudged you." She took my hands into her own.

"And I you." I managed the reply and received a light brush of a kiss on my cheek. The moment the door was closed, I fled to the privy and was horribly ill.

FIFTEEN

When I had finally finished vomiting, I leaned against the cold stone of the privy wall until the dizziness passed. There was no question now about my current condition. The panic I had managed to hold at bay returned. How could I hope to get anything done if I was going to be so hopelessly frail and ill all the time? Women at home in Ireland were always having babies and never seemed incapacitated like this. I recalled my own mother, who must have gone through five or six pregnancies. Some of them had resulted in miscarriages, three of them in my brothers. But she had done her normal work around the house until the day of her confinement.

I stood there, hugging my arms to myself, finding it hard to breathe as the panic threatened to overwhelm me. I was at a crossroads of my life. I couldn't handle all this alone. However loath I was to do it, I should tell Sid and Gus the truth. I made up my mind to go and tell them later that afternoon, after I'd had a rest and felt somewhat restored. I took off my dress, sponged myself down with cold water, and lay on my bed. A refreshing breeze was coming in through the window. It was peaceful and calm. I tried to sleep, but my brain was still racing.

I worried what might happen if my condition worsened and I was confined to bed. I had to be strong and well enough to complete the task set for me. Getting Daniel out of jail had to be my priority for all our sakes. I sat up and tried to think clearly. At least Arabella had given me a new direction to explore. Someone who was delighting in Daniel's downfall. Someone who had come to the prison to see for himself. It was so obvious now she had mentioned it that I felt ashamed of myself. I wasn't really much use as a detective, was I? This spurred me into getting back to work. I went downstairs again and took out pen and paper. Find out who has come to the prison asking after Daniel or wanting to visit him, I wrote. Go out to Coney Island. Find out about the horse doping at the racetrack. Meet the officers who have taken over the cases from Daniel. Find out if they have discovered any more about the East Side Ripper.

And, of course, now I had extra work to keep me occupied if I could spare a moment from Daniel's case. I had imprudently told Arabella that I would show her friend's picture at the settlement houses and at the sort of hotels where a young girl would stay alone. Just how was I going to find the time and energy to do that?

It was all so overwhelming that I sat there, staring at the paper, and for once wished myself back home in Ireland. Oh, to be sure, every day was a hard, physical grind, with lots of laundry and cooking and beating rugs and sweeping up mud. But I had been safe there. I knew what to expect of every day. Then I reminded myself of the reason I had been forced to flee to America. I hadn't been safe at all.

"It's no use sitting here sniveling like a weak ninny," I told myself, sounding suspiciously like my mother.

I stared at the list again. The next day was Sunday. Half of lower Manhattan would be spending it at Coney Island. Maybe I should, too. I didn't think I'd be able to persuade Mr. Atkinson to take me to Daniel again soon, so I wrote two letters. One was to Daniel himself, one to the lawyer, both asking the same questions: Who had come to visit Daniel? Who had asked after him? I planned to go and ask those same questions of the desk sergeant at The Tombs. I also realized that I should follow up on Daniel's suggestion and see if I could find out who was really employing Mr. Atkinson. That would mean finding a time to talk with his secretary when her boss wasn't in the office, or, even more ideally, having a chance to go through his books when neither of them was there.

There was no point in trying this on a Saturday afternoon. A lawyer's office would probably close early if they worked at all on Saturday afternoons. Half day Saturday had become all the rage, I gathered. I'd just have to wait until Monday. I put my two letters into envelopes, found stamps for them, and went out, hoping to make the last collection of the afternoon, as there was no post on Sundays. As I passed Sid and Gus's house I felt a pang of guilt. I was just putting off the evil hour when I would have to tell them the truth. I had been making all kinds of excuses for delay. I don't know why I was so afraid to tell them. After all, they were the least judgmental people I had ever met. They didn't care two figs for the rules of society. They would probably throw themselves instantly into the role of adoring aunts. But I knew they would somehow think less of me, and I was already ashamed of my own weakness.

Still, it had to be done. They would be hurt if they found out later that I had kept such an enormous secret from them. And God knows I needed support right now. I would do it tonight, as soon as I returned from my errands, as soon as I had thought out the words to say. . . .

As always on Saturday afternoons, the town was in festive mood. Those people who only worked half days on Saturday were out shopping. Two children skipped by me, a few paces ahead of their parents, each clutching an orange. The parents smiled fondly at their excitement. As they came to Sixth Avenue, the husband took his wife's arm to help her across the road, and I noticed that she was to have another child soon. I hurried past them. It seemed that everywhere I looked, fate was mocking me.

I was just fishing for my key to open my front door on my return home when the door opposite opened and Sid stood there, hands on hips. "And where have you been, you sly creature?" she demanded. For a moment I thought she was serious until I saw the twinkle in her eyes. "Gus and I have been absolutely dying to hear about the demon Arabella's visit. We waited patiently until we were sure she must have departed, and then we found that you had slipped out without telling us a thing, leaving us in the most horrible suspense. So put that basket inside and then come straight over. That's an order, by the way, because we have more guests. And you'd have never forgiven yourself if you had missed them."

"You have other guests? My, but you have had a busy day." Privately my brain was racing, wondering who could possibly have turned up now, possibly looking for me. After Arabella Norton, all things were possible.

Sid hovered behind me while I put the basket of groceries on my kitchen table, then escorted me across Patchin Place as if I might be about to do a bunk.

Gus met us in the hall. "You've found her! Well-done, Sid."

"I gather you have more guests?" I asked.

"I know. What a thrilling day. Miss Norton, of all people. You could have knocked us down with a feather when she told us her name. Of course we wanted to protect you, in case she had come with evil intent, but she said she bore you no malice and had come asking for your help."

"Yes, she wants me to find her friend who has vanished," I said.

"Maybe Sid and I could help you," Gus said, her face lighting up in that delightfully elfish way. "We seem to know a lot of people in common with Miss Norton, don't we, Sid?"

"We do seem to," Sid agreed. "Just give us our assignment, and we'll be at your beck and call."

"That would be a godsend," I said. "I didn't know where I was going to find the time to fit in Miss Norton."

"You know we're always dying to play at investigators and to keep an eye on you when you get yourself involved in dangerous missions," Gus said. "Come on through and you can give us our briefing."

"I thought you said you had guests."

"They'll want to hear, too," she said. She leaned close and whispered. "Ryan has brought his new friend to meet us."

"Is he still in Buddhist monk's robes?" I paused, as she led me through the house and out to the conservatory.

"No, he is very properly dressed like an English gentleman—or should one say an Irish gentleman?"

"Definitely the latter, if you don't want a crack on the head with a shillelagh."

She chuckled. "Look who we found, Ryan, dearest," she announced, as we came upon two men relaxing in wicker chairs. The glass doors were open onto the garden. A large jug of some kind of punch stood on the wicker table next to a vase of roses. It presented a wonderfully rural scene in the middle of the city.

The two gentlemen rose to their feet.

"Molly, I was quite desolate when we tapped on your door and nobody was home." Ryan came around the table to plant a kiss on my cheek. "I have told Fritz so much about my adorable friends that he insisted on meeting you. So let me introduce you: Miss Murphy, this is my dear new friend Fritz Birnbaum, Dr. Fritz Birnbaum, lately of Vienna."

I took in the neatly trimmed blond beard, the pale face, the light eyes, the immaculate dress. The doctor and I both reacted at the same time.

"Dr. Birnbaum!" I exclaimed at the same moment that he said, "Miss Gaffney."

"Miss Gaffney?" Ryan demanded.

"You two have already met. How splendid," Sid said. "Have some punch."

"Dr. Birnbaum and I met at Adare, Senator Flynn's house on the Hudson River," I said. "Unfortunately at a most difficult time."

"Indeed yes. Poor Mrs. Flynn. I feel so responsible. I wish I could have done something to save her." His English was fluent, although delivered with a pronounced German accent.

"We all wish that, Dr. Birnbaum," I replied.

"But you—you were her cousin, were you not?"

"Not really," I said. "As you have been told, my real name

is Molly Murphy. I am a private investigator. I was sent to the Flynn mansion to pose as the senator's cousin."

"*Gott im Himmel!* So foul play was suspected from the first?"

"There was such a web of lies and deceit at that place that it was hard to tell what was suspected," I said tactfully. "Now I just pray that the Flynn family finally finds some peace."

"I join you in your prayer," Dr. Birnbaum said.

"Let's have no more talk of gloomy things." Ryan waved an elegant hand between us. "Today is for happiness and goodwill among friends."

"So you already know that Dr. Birnbaum is a real-life alienist, Molly?" Sid asked.

"Yes. He was brought to Adare to treat Theresa Flynn."

"He has been giving us the most exciting insights into the mind of the East Side Ripper," Gus said. "Positively spine tingling."

"Really?" I tried not to sound too interested. "And what conclusions has Dr. Birnbaum come to? Can you tell us what kind of person the killer is, Doctor?"

"Not the kind of person you might think, Miss Murphy. I did research in Vienna with my mentor, Professor Freud. Mass murderers are rarely obviously depraved and violent people. They are often models of the virtuous life. They are professional men, pillars of the community."

"Pillars of the community? Hiring prostitutes?" Gus said in surprise.

"Perhaps he did not hire the women for the normal purpose, but lured them away with the intention of stamping out vice and punishing them for their sins," Sid said.

Birnbaum nodded. "That is indeed a possibility, Miss Goldfarb. But I'm inclined to think that such crimes of passion are driven by baser motives. You'd be surprised, Miss Walcott, how many supposedly virtuous men are married to a socially correct wife but get their pleasures elsewhere."

"I suppose so," Gus said. "But most men don't end up by making killing a part of their pleasure."

"They often lead lives where all emotional outlets have to be suppressed. But inside this fire rages. The first time the killing is accidental, but it gives them such a rush of excitement that they have to duplicate the feeling. And the need to kill becomes more and more intense, just like a drug."

"But surely it would take a base and violent man to disfigure a woman in the way described in the newspapers?" Sid asked.

"There are several reasons for wanting to disfigure a victim," Dr. Birnbaum said, gravely stroking at his neat, blond beard. "I'm afraid this is not a suitable topic for mixed company, however. I have no wish to make the ladies swoon."

This produced merry laughter from Sid and Gus.

"I am delighted to tell you, Dr. Birnbaum, that you are looking at three ladies who have never swooned in their lives. What's more, Miss Murphy has conducted undercover assignments in the most depraved quarters of the city. So please continue."

"Very well." The doctor took a sip of punch before continuing. "In my experience the murderer disfigures his victim for two reasons: first, when she is still alive, because he is essentially ashamed of what he is about to do and doesn't want her to look at him. If he dehumanizes her, somehow it makes her easier to kill. Second, when she is already dead, so that the corpse cannot be identified."

"Interesting," I said, "and which do you think it is in this case?"

"I haven't been privy to enough details yet," he said. "I only learned of this case last week and immediately went to offer my services to the police. I am meeting with the officers in charge of the investigation on Monday. Then I hope to find out more."

I made a mental note of that. If at all possible, I wanted to come along to that meeting. I'd have to think how to broach the subject.

"How will you be able to tell whether the victims were alive or dead in this case?" Sid was asking.

"A lot will depend on the amount of blood. If the victim

was already dead then the heart would have stopped pumping. Even several cruel blows to the face would not produce much blood. If she were still alive, I am afraid to say that the face would be a bloody mess."

"Oh dear," Gus put her hand to her mouth, "perhaps I am not as strong as I thought I was. I find this most disturbing. I think I shall go and water the flowers in the garden."

"We will talk of it no further, Gus dearest," Ryan said. "Let us instead discuss my new play, which Fritz is helping me to write."

"You're writing another new play, Ryan?" I asked.

"Yes, and I'm telling nobody about it except my most trusted friends. I'm not risking another idea being stolen. This one will be a black comedy with lots of gothic elements—hands coming out of mirrors, trapdoors opening to swallow victims—all the stuff that the audience loves. And the central character is an evil doctor, thanks to dear Fritz here, who has told me of one of his case histories."

"A real case history? Do tell us, Dr. Birnbaum," Sid said.

"Yes. It was my first encounter with a real-live mass murderer," he said, staring at us in that intense way of his. "A doctor. A pillar of the community. First, he poisoned his shrewish wife and got away with it. The next time he married for money and dispatched her as well. Then he enjoyed the power of being able to kill at will. He started using his medical knowledge to finish off his patients. He would appear at the bedside and act the concerned and loving doctor who had done all he could. Families would thank him for his trouble and give him lavish gifts."

"And how was he finally caught?"

"Too cocky. And rather annoyed that nobody suspected him. He took greater and greater risks until finally he was caught red-handed administering a lethal dose of morphine."

"Fascinating," Gus said.

"Isn't it, just." Ryan beamed at us. "And I will duplicate the evil doctor on stage, with a few touches of my own added in. Maybe I will even play the character myself. I've always secretly fantasized about being truly evil."

"You will never cease to surprise us, Ryan." Sid glanced at Gus and me with a smile.

"I sincerely hope not. The moment I cease to surprise I shall become ordinary and boring like the rest of the world. When that happens there will be nothing for it but to jump off the Brooklyn Bridge and end it all."

"The dramatic dramatist," Dr. Birnbaum said, with a wink at me.

"And our little conversation is giving me more ideas as we speak." Ryan dismissed his observation. "I was thinking perhaps my evil doctor will lure young women to his boudoir with the intention of killing them. Prostitutes are more exciting than patients, don't you agree? Far more mobile, in any case."

"That's not nice, Ryan," I found myself blurting out. "How can you possibly want to write about this when it's really happening in this city? Those girls might be on the lowest rung of the ladder, but they were somebody's daughter and sister and once they had hopes and dreams beyond their present station."

"There speaks the voice of passion," Birnbaum said, applauding. "Well said, Miss Murphy."

"I didn't realize you were such a crusader, Molly," Sid said.

"I suppose I feel strongly because I could have ended up as one of those girls. When I first arrived here I had nowhere to go and no chance for employment. If I had fallen in with the wrong people, rather than the bible-toting ladies from the hostel, who knows what might have happened to me?"

"Knowing you, you'd have given the pimp a black eye, and he would have found you more trouble than you were worth," Ryan commented, making us all laugh and breaking the spell of gloom. "I've just come up with a marvelous idea, children. No, don't look at me like that. No more suggestions of black comedy. Why don't we take a picnic to Central Park this evening? The march king, Mr. Sousa, is giving a free concert tonight, and you know how I adore brass bands. It brings out the military in me."

"The military in you?" Sid burst out laughing. "When did you ever have military inclinations, Ryan?"

"When I see all those splendid red uniforms and those awfully tall chaps wearing them."

The banter continued. For once I wasn't anxious to join them. I'd be worrying about whether I'd be taken ill and how I would feel trapped in a great crush of people on a hot night. "I don't think I'll join you, if you don't mind," I said.

"Of course you must come. It will be no fun without you," Ryan said.

"Yes, Molly. We insist." Sid wagged a finger at me. "You're not allowed to even think of working on a Saturday evening."

"I'm not feeling too well," I ventured.

"Then good music and good company are just what you need to revive you," Ryan said. "Think how heavenly it will be, stretched out under the stars, sipping champagne and eating oysters."

"I thought you'd become a Buddhist, Ryan," I said. "And oysters are certainly living creatures when you swallow them."

"Oh dear, Molly, you are right. What was I thinking?" Ryan put his hand to his face in a mock expression of horror. "Let me amend. Sipping champagne and eating a nice ripe French cheese with crusty bread. One is allowed to eat cheese, is one not?"

"I believe cheese is allowed," Sid answered, smiling.

"Then what are we waiting for? Let us make haste to the deli before they close. Now which wineshop keeps champagne on ice?"

"For someone who hasn't worked for a couple of months, you seem remarkably flush," I said.

Ryan had the grace to blush. "One's friends are so generous," he said. "And dear Fritz does so like his champagne."

As usual Ryan had latched onto a new friend with the money to keep him in the style to which he'd become accustomed. As the others rushed around the house in a frenzy of

excitement, I was caught up in it. How long since I had
shared a picnic with friends or listened to a good band? It
would be good for me and help me to forget my present worries for a while.

Miraculously I survived the evening well. I even enjoyed
the ripe cheese and crusty bread that Ryan had promised,
followed by such sinful items as grapes and figs. The champagne, sipped slowly, also seemed to have a calmative effect
on my stomach, so that I lay back against my pillows, content for once, watching the stars come out over the city sky-
line. It wasn't until we were walking back to the park
entrance amid the crush of people that I remembered I had a
mission. I fell into place beside Dr. Birnbaum.

"I wonder if there is any way that you could take me with
you when you visit the police officers on Monday," I said in
a low voice.

"My dear Miss Murphy!" He looked startled. "I don't
think that would be at all proper. The most unpleasant sub-
jects will be discussed."

"It's for a case I'm working on," I said. "Details of this
East Side Ripper might turn out to be important to getting—
my client—out of jail. I promise I won't interfere. Could I
not be your assistant, or one of your students from the university in Vienna?"

"I suppose . . . if it were that important to you," he looked
at me long and hard. "You are working on a case that involves the East Side Ripper? Surely that is no job for a
woman to be tackling."

"A dear friend is in jail, falsely accused," I said. "I'm doing everything I can to get him released."

"He is suspected of being the Ripper?" Birnbaum eyed
me warily.

"No, he was the police officer in charge of that case. It
has been suggested that perhaps somebody wanted to make
sure the case was not solved quickly."

"Fascinating." He nodded. "But could you not speak with
his fellow officers yourself, whenever you wished, rather
than this pretence?"

I shook my head. "Someone has spread false rumors about him. His fellow officers have turned against him. And those who haven't, don't wish to risk their own careers by speaking out. This is a perfect chance for me, Dr. Birnbaum. If you take me with you, I promise I won't do anything stupid or let you down in any way."

"I'm sure you wouldn't, Miss Murphy. I was impressed by you when I met you at Senator Flynn's. It is against my better judgment, but I'm prepared, on this occasion, to call you my assistant."

"Thank you!" I beamed at him. "I'm tempted to give you a hug, but I don't want people getting the wrong idea."

"I hope you'll feel just as grateful after what might be a harrowing experience."

"I hope so, too," I said.

We reached the entrance to the park and the crowd streamed away in all directions, making for omnibuses and trolleys. Ryan and Birnbaum were perfect hosts and insisted on taking us home in a cab and escorting us to our front doors. Thus the evening ended without sharing my secret with Sid and Gus. And the more I thought about it, the less keen I was on making this confession. First, I'd prove Daniel innocent and set him free, then I'd be able to make decisions about my future.

SIXTEEN

The next day was Sunday. I woke to the sound of church bells and lay listening to the evocative sound, which reminded me so sharply of home. It had been a long time since I'd attended church. Would it be wicked of me to go now and pray for a miracle? If anyone needed prayers at the moment it was myself, and Daniel, of course. I dressed and headed to Saint Joseph's on Sixth Avenue, a stone's throw away. I'd passed it many times but I regret to say that I'd never set foot inside. Now I entered into the cool, incense-laden darkness and found a mass in progress. The murmur of the priest's voice seemed to blend with the smoke from the incense, giving the interior a hazy, unreal quality. Fractured light from stained-glass windows fell in colored stripes on the floor. I knelt in an empty back pew and tried to pray. It had been so long. The familiar childhood prayers came back to me. I muttered an Our Father and a Hail Mary, but they didn't seem enough somehow. Did I really believe in any of this?—that was the question.

"If you're up there, God, and you can really hear me, I need your help right now," I muttered.

The priest had stepped to the lectern. "The wages of sin is death," he proclaimed.

I stood up, as if he had struck me. Why hadn't I realized this before? I had sinned. I was being punished. Simple as that. I fled from the church without looking back.

Coney Island was my destination for the day. I would

concentrate on my assignment and keep more disturbing thoughts at bay. I boarded a crowded tram across the Brooklyn Bridge and it was only when I was standing on the platform of the Brooklyn, Flatbush, and Coney Island Railroad that I realized what I might be in for. I had been out to the seashore once or twice before, but never on a weekend. It seemed that most of the population of Manhattan had the same idea. The platform was a seething mass of humanity. When the train finally arrived, I was swept aboard with everyone else. I wasn't lucky enough to get a seat and was packed like a sardine between a bony child sucking a lollypop and a large Italian lady who smelled strongly of unwashed body and garlic. I closed my eyes, tried to shut off my sense of smell, and pictured myself running along the cliffs at home with the fresh tang of seaweed in my nostrils.

It was only by grim determination that I made it as far as the terminal stop at Brighton Beach. I caught a glimpse of the ocean as I stood at the top of the ironwork steps. People poured from the station in a great tide. I stood to one side as they swept past me and I tried to get my bearings. They were obviously headed for the beach and the amusement parks. Now I heard shrieks competing with hurdy-gurdy music, confirming in which direction the beach and amusement parks lay. Within minutes the crowd had disappeared, leaving a young, sad-faced rail employee to sweep up their litter before the next invasion.

"Excuse me, sir," I said—although he was younger than I and didn't deserve the title—"in which direction is the racetrack?"

He gave me a quick once-over glance. "There's no racing today, lady," he said. "Too hot for the horses."

"But where would the racetrack be if I wanted to take a look at it?"

He sniffed, went to wipe his nose on the back of his sleeve, and thought better of it. "There's three of 'em," he said. "Sheepshead's over dat way, Gravesend's in the other direction, and Brighton's just across de Gut on de other side of the railway."

Brighton—I thought that was the name Daniel had mentioned.

"So the Brighton track is close by?"

"Yeah, like I said. Under the railroad. Across the Gut."

Daniel had warned me against the Gut, and it definitely sounded unsavory, but it was broad daylight, after all. I thanked the young man, who touched his cap to me and looked expectantly at my purse, as if he thought he might be paid for giving such vital information. Instead he got a smile as I hurried under the iron supports of the elevated track.

I found the Gut easily enough and saw why Daniel had warned me. Saloons were doing a lively trade, even at this hour on a Sunday morning. Obviously the police didn't enforce Sunday temperance out here. Half-dressed girls, sprawled on porches and in doorways, gave me scornful glances while their pimps sat playing dice or spitting gobs of chewing tobacco. One or two eyed me appraisingly. I gave them my haughtiest stare in response and hurried past.

Tucked in between the brothels and the saloons were cheap boardinghouses and various types of cafes and food stalls. I picked up my skirts to avoid the filth that lay beneath my feet and hurried past. Soon I was in a more respectable neighborhood. I caught sight of a grand gothic structure, made my way to it, and found myself at the gateway to the Brighton racetrack. These imposing main gates were closed, but I walked around the side of the track, behind the pavilion, until I came to more modest wooden gates. One of these swung open to the touch and I found myself in a stable area behind the main pavilion. One or two horses' heads appeared over stable doors, but the area had a deserted air about it.

I was about to give up and admit defeat when I heard the sound of boots on cobbles and a stable hand came around a corner, carrying a light little saddle. He almost dropped it when he saw me standing there.

"Whatta you doin' in here?" he demanded. "This area ain't open to the public. Go on. Beat it."

"I just need a couple of minutes of your time," I said. "It's about the horse that dropped dead a few weeks ago at one of the tracks here. There was a big scandal."

"What's it to you?"

Hurriedly I weighed plausible excuses. "I'm a reporter," I said. "I'm writing an article on horse doping."

He stared at me blankly. "I don't know nothing about it. Go on, beat it."

"Where do you think I might find somebody who can answer my questions?" I asked. "My newspaper editor will be angry if we can't run the story in tomorrow's edition."

"You're a bit late, ain't ya?" He gave me a sneer. "Half the reporters in the world have already been here. And the police has been investigating."

"But they haven't found out the truth behind it, have they?" I asked, giving what I hoped was a smug and secretive smile. "We might just have a new angle on the case."

"Yeah?"

"I'm not at liberty to say any more. But I was sent to get the inside scoop from people who work here at the track."

"It'd be more than my job's worth to tell you what I think. We've been told to keep our mouths shut—especially to reporters."

"Very well," I said. "I'll just have to look for someone else. But there might be money in it, if my editor thinks I've come back with a good story. Of course your name need never be mentioned."

He looked up sharply. "How much money?"

Again I was amazed at how easily the whole world could apparently be bribed, except for Daniel, of course.

"I can't promise anything, but my editor has been known to be generous. I tell you what—if he gives me a bonus, you'll get your cut. And that's a promise."

"All right," he said. "Name's Jerry. Jerry Jameson. And yours is?"

He was holding out his hand. My brain resorted to the last alias I had used to Police Commissioner Partridge. "It's Miss Delaney. Mary Delaney." I shook his hand. His fingers felt as callused and rough as old tree bark. "So, Mr. Jameson, you really know nothing about the horse doping? Didn't it take place at this very track, and you work with the horses here?"

He half met my gaze. "Didn't say I didn't know nothing," he muttered. "We all knew about it."

"And you do think it was doping, don't you? The horse didn't die of natural causes."

He sniffed. "Of course it was doping. That horse was fit as a fiddle. I rubbed him down after his exercise that morning. Ballyhoo Bay—lovely colt he was. Three to two on favorite. And he was ridden by Ted Sloan. Best in the business, Ted is. Those other owners knew they didn't stand a chance against him."

"So you reckon it was one of the other owners who doped the horse?" I asked.

He shrugged. "Who can say? It's quiet in here now, but on race days it's crazy. Owners and trainers and jockeys and the press all milling around. It wouldn't have been too hard to slip into Ballyhoo's stall and doctor his mash. And even if anyone knows who's behind it, nobody's going to talk, are they? We all want to keep our jobs."

I tried another tack. "Someone suggested that it might have been a disgruntled jockey, getting his own back."

The stable hand sucked through his teeth. "Billy Hughes, you mean. Well, he was scheduled to ride Ballyhoo until the owner changed his mind and had Ted Sloan brought in. I heard the owner had a lot of money on his horse and wanted to make sure that it didn't lose."

"So do you think it's possible that Billy Hughes was the one who doctored the horse's food? He could have moved around without drawing attention to himself."

"And he did a bunk right afterward, too," the man agreed. "They say he's gone out to race at Santa Anita in California."

Another person who had supposedly fled to California, I noted. Did he count as a penniless young man? I'd have to check whether Letitia had ever visited a racetrack.

"So is this the kind of thing you might have expected of Billy Hughes?"

He thought for a moment before answering. "He carried a grudge, all right," he said, "but he sure loved his horses. I can't see him wanting to kill one of the loveliest animals that ever lived. And if word ever got out that he did it, he'd never work in racing again. Too big a risk to take, if you ask me. And for what? One less good horse to ride."

"And what about the jockey who rode Ballyhoo—Ted Sloan you said? Where's he to be found?"

"He may be out of the hospital by now," the man said. "He broke his leg when the horse fell on him. He's recuperating out in the Hamptons at the owner's estate, so I hear."

"If it wasn't Billy Hughes, but a rival owner, wanting to make sure that his own horse won, who would come to mind then?" I asked.

He gave me a sideways look. "It was a syndicate that won. A bunch of city gents who had a horse brought over from Ireland. Pride of Killarney, the horse is called. Not a bad little runner, but I don't think he's got what it takes to be a champion. Now old Ballyhoo, he'd won the Brighton Derby once before, and the Futurity Stakes. Made Mr. Whitney a tidy sum over the last couple of years. You should talk to him about this. He's hopping mad, I can tell you. He's hired his own investigators to look into it."

"You say the police are also looking into it."

"The police." He sniffed. "If it's anything to do with the Morningstar Syndicate, then they've got the police in their pocket. Those guys have all got connections."

"So do you happen to know who is part of this syndicate?"

He shook his head. "Don't ask me. I know most of the owners because they come down to the track and follow their horses like they were their children. I've no time for syndicates who just use their horses to make money and couldn't care a damn what happens to them—pardon the language, lady."

I nodded my forgiveness. "Was it obvious that this Pride of Killarney would win if the favorite was eliminated?"

"Nah. Lucky winner, if you ask me. Old Sultan's Dream was taken out too fast, and he didn't have the stamina to keep going in that heat. Otherwise I'd have backed him to win."

"Do you have any suspicions yourself?"

"Me? Not really. To tell you the truth, I can't think who would want to harm old Ballyhoo. Everyone loved him. He had a real sweet nature and it was pure poetry to watch him run. I used to think it was a privilege just to rub him down. He'd never turn and give you a nip, not like some of them."

It didn't seem as if we were getting anywhere, and I wasn't sure what to ask next.

"They didn't find any kind of incriminating evidence, then?"

He shook his head. "The police went through the whole place and found nothing. If you ask me, Billy Hughes was angry with the owner for bringing in another jockey to replace him. He probably never meant to hurt Ballyhoo, just slow him down so that he'd lose. When the horse keeled over and died, Billy hoofed it to California."

This seemed quite logical to me as well.

"Well, thank you for your help, Mr. Jameson. I'll make sure you get a copy of the article if my editor runs it, and if there's any money forthcoming, I'll make sure you get your cut." A wave of guilt swept over me as I said this. I'd had my mouth washed out with soap enough times for lesser fibs as a child. But then I reminded myself that Daniel's life was at stake. My life, too, in a way. Besides, as the church had reminded me, I was already damned to hell, so one more lie wouldn't matter.

SEVENTEEN

I left the stable yard with no clear idea what I should be doing next. If a disgruntled jockey had already fled to California, he wouldn't be interested in trying to stop an investigation. Those influential businessmen in the syndicate might have more interest, but as Jerry Jameson pointed out, their horse only won by luck. There was no clear second favorite. So what now? Back to New York, I supposed.

As I passed along the fence beside the racetrack, I glanced inside and saw movement. It wasn't a horse trotting around the track, but a person—a big, gangling man, dressed in a singlet and what looked like white long johns, lurching along with large, ungainly strides. Then the surprise turned to astonishment as he came closer, and I realized that I recognized him. It was Gentleman Jack Brady. I ran up to the fence and yelled his name as he trotted past me. He started, looked up, and his battered face broke into a smile as he recognized me. He came up to the fence.

"I know you. It's Daniel's friend, isn't it? I met you at his place."

"Yes, you did, right before I sent you on a mission and you disappeared," I said severely, anger now replacing the worry I had felt for him. "I've been worried sick about you. Why didn't you contact me again? Why didn't you come back?"

"Monk said I wasn't to tell no one where I was." He gave me a sheepish grin. "I went to see him, and I thought the police were following me. Monk said I should get out of town, for my own safety, so he had me brought out here. He's set me up in a nice hotel room, and he's got a trainer for me to work with and everything."

"So the fight is going ahead?"

"All arranged," he said, looking around, although we were the only two within hearing. "Some Casino, next week. Tell Daniel. He'll be pleased."

"Daniel isn't pleased about very much at the moment," I said. "He's still in jail and things don't look good for him."

"Oh, jeez. That's right. I forgot he was in trouble, poor guy. Is there anything I can do?"

Since he had clearly forgotten that he had been sent to question Monk the last time, I saw little point in assigning him another mission. But it was worth a long shot, I supposed. "If you come across a man called Bugsy, one of Monk's men," I said, "ask him about the envelope. Ask him who gave it to him and who might have had a chance to slip money inside."

"What envelope?" His gorilla face was wrinkled into a frown.

"The one that got Daniel arrested," I said. "Better still, if you see Bugsy, tell him to contact me—it's Molly Murphy, Ten Patchin Place. Can you remember that? Here, let me write it down for you. Tell him it's very important. Daniel's life may depend on it." I printed the words carefully onto a page in the notebook I always carried and handed it to him. "Bugsy. Can you remember that?"

"I'll try, miss. I'll really try."

I wasn't too optimistic but I smiled at him. "I'm glad to see you're safe and well, Jack. And if you win this fight, for heaven's sake, get out of the boxing business or your brain will be more addled than a plate of scrambled eggs."

"You're right, miss. I should get out. It's just a question of making the money last. I never was good with money."

"Then buy yourself a little property. Settle down. Raise chickens."

He laughed. "Chickens? Can you see me with chickens?

If I picked up a chicken with this hand, I'd squash the life out of it in one second." The smile faded. "I wouldn't mean to, of course, but when you've got big hands like mine, and all this strength . . ."

He left the end of the sentence hanging in the air.

"So where can I find you if I need you?" I asked.

"Right here. Brighton Beach Hotel. See those turrets down by the beach? Real swank place where all the snobs stay. Monk's taking care of it for me."

"Monk must have a lot of money invested in this fight."

"Oh yeah. He stands to do real good out of it, if I win."

"Then I'd better let you get back to your training. I don't think he'd be too happy with you if you didn't win."

"That's right. I've got three times more around the track if I'm to get down to my fighting weight," he said. "Nice seeing you again, Miss—"

"Murphy," I said. "Nice seeing you too, Jack. Take care of yourself."

"Come out and see the fight," he said. "I'll get you a free ticket, if you like."

"That's kind of you," I said, although I didn't think I'd want to watch two men beating each other to a bloody pulp.

Jack waved a big hand and loped off again around the track. I went on my way. I decided that since I was here on Coney Island I should take a look at the site where the prize-fight would take place. Some casino, Jack had said. And a stroll in the sea air might do me good.

I headed toward the beach, passing the grand turrets of the Brighton Beach Hotel, sitting right beside the board-walk. Fashionable ladies with parasols strolled the grounds beside men in straw boaters and striped blazers. It was the height of elegance and I wondered what they made of Jack Brady, lurching among them in his fighter's training outfit. Sudden screams behind me made me turn in the other direction, just in time to see a carful of people come hurtling down from a high trestle on the roller coaster. I had once rid-den that contraption with Daniel in the happy days before I knew about Arabella. The thrill of the speed, the sense of his closeness, his arm around mine, came rushing back to haunt me. I shut my eyes and marched toward the boardwalk.

It was hard to walk at any pace along the boardwalk, even though it was a wide thoroughfare. Today it was chock-a-block with people—families, mothers pushing prams, fathers with toddlers on their shoulders, old couples, sweethearts, all out for a day's fun. I felt like a salmon, swimming upstream. And beyond the boardwalk the beach was a seething mass of humanity. The crowd spilled from the beach and into the ocean, where a sea of heads bobbed at the edge of the waves. If people did this to escape the crush of the city, I couldn't see much point in it myself. My mind went back to the ocean at home in Ireland—deserted beaches, strands of seaweed, waves crashing, gulls circling overhead, and that salty tang that made you feel good to be alive.

I continued along the boardwalk, past one amusement after another—the giant Ferris wheel, the Flip Flap coaster that hurtled its riders in a complete loop, the waterslide with its boats rushing down a steep ramp to hit the water with a mighty splash.

Cooking smells wafted up to me.

"Get your red hots here," a man was yelling and holding up something that looked like a sausage in a bun. The pungent smell of onions reminded me that I hadn't eaten for a while and that disaster could strike at any moment. I stepped into one of the little shacks that were dotted along the boardwalk and downed a glass of lemonade and a cheese sandwich. Suitably fortified, I came out and resumed my quest for a casino, until suddenly I realized that I could go no farther today. I just wasn't up to tackling the heat, the smells, and the crowds any longer. I'd come back on a working day, when I could have the place to myself.

I looked around and realized that I was near the ornate iron pier extending into the ocean. Beside it was a bathing pavilion, and squeals came from inside its walls as the bathers negotiated the waves. As I observed the structure of the pier and the pavilion, built out over the waves, I remembered that the first of the prostitutes had been found murdered at this very site. This was something else I should investigate, only not now. I'd have little luck finding prostitutes and their pimps working at this time of day. I'd have to come back at night sometime, and I was uneasy about coming out here at night and alone.

I made my way down the steps from the boardwalk, through the crowded amusement park, until I came to a busy street, stretching away to my right. It was boarded with planks and crammed full of amusement arcades, food booths, dance halls, beer halls, and God knows what kinds of vice. A sign on a post proclaimed it to be THE BOWERY, but it was not as savory as the real street with that name. My ears were assailed by the competing sounds of all kinds of music and shouting touts, luring people to their particular attraction. "Roll up, roll up. Three balls for a nickel. Have a go at Aunt Sally. Hit a coconut, win a prize. All the wonders of the Orient. Belly dancers straight from the harem of the sheik."

I felt repelled but yet attracted at the same time. So did half the population of Manhattan by the look of it. The crowd surged down this Bowery, and I allowed myself to be swept along with them. We passed the entrance to the Streets of Cairo Pavilion, where the mysteries of the Orient would be revealed. Outside an Oriental archway, a man in a turban stood holding a real camel while a young girl, wearing precious little, gyrated to the tune of a wailing flute. A little farther and there was a fire-eater, standing outside a bunting-draped passageway. The sign proclaimed it as AMERICA'S PREMIER FREAK SHOW. The tout was a midget, dressed as a king, standing on a barrel. "Come inside, ladies and gentlemen, and see the freaks too amazing, too grotesque, even for P. T. Barnum. See the amazing snake woman. Yes, she's half woman, half python. See the world's smallest horse, only twenty inches high. See the horrendous human tree. Instead of limbs, he has branches; instead of skin, he has bark. And the world-famous mule boy. He was born with the face of a mule and the body of a human!"

I wonder how people can be taken in by that, I thought, shuddering with revulsion, but a portion of the crowd was already lining up and paying good money to go inside. I allowed myself to be swept onward past the India Pavilion, where a live elephant stood at an arched gateway. I'd never actually seen a real elephant before and just stood and stared until the crowd swept me along once more. Then more dancing girls, this time straight from the Moulin Rouge in Paris. The picture outside showed a girl dressed in corsets, fishnet stockings, and not much else, kicking up legs in a most unnatural fashion.

I felt safe walking along the real Bowery, but I didn't feel entirely safe here, even though I was among so many people. I felt myself being watched from dark alleyways between booths where unsavory types loitered. I clutched my purse to me and decided I'd come far enough. Those seething, sweaty crowds, squealing children, and blaring music were all too much for me. I knew I had to get out of there or faint. The search for the casino would have to wait for another day. I pushed through the crowd and made my way back to the relative civilization of Surf Avenue and an elevated train station. I had a carriage to myself on the train back to the city.

EIGHTEEN

Monday morning's post brought no message from Daniel or from his attorney. I dressed in my business suit, even though the day promised to be too hot for it. If I were to pose as Dr. Birnbaum's assistant, I wanted to look the part of a bluestocking. So my hair was wrestled into a bun and tucked beneath my hat again. I wished I owned a pair of a bluestocking's round wire spectacles to complete the picture. I wasn't sure what I hoped to learn or accomplish by going with Dr. Birnbaum to visit the police officers, but at least it would give me the opportunity to see who had taken over Daniel's case and hopefully find out what they had learned so far. Maybe I would get a feeling for whether these men might be sensitive to Daniel's cause—or the opposite.

Dr. Birnbaum was waiting for me at the corner of Canal and Mulberry. He was dressed today in a dark suit and homburg hat and looked every inch the somber physician.

"Miss Murphy." He clicked his heels in that European way and gave me a polite bow. "I have serious reservations about what we are about to do. For one thing it goes against the ethics of my profession, and for another I am concerned that you will hear things never intended for a woman's ears."

"Are there no women medical students at your hospitals, Doctor?" I asked.

"One or two, yes. But I have always considered it a strange choice of profession for a woman."

"I consider it a very natural profession for a woman," I

said. "Do women not spend their entire lives taking care of others? Is it not part of our very nature to want to heal and help?"

"Put that way, yes." He nodded agreement. "But our profession has its seamy side—the blood, the infections, the operations, gangrene—one would not want one's sister to experience sights that I have seen. And today's discussion—a man who has repeatedly molested and mutilated young women . . ."

"I'll handle it," I said. "I have to handle it. If my friend dies in jail, it would be my fault."

"Then he's lucky to have such a noble and devoted friend as yourself," Birnbaum said.

Damned right he's lucky. The phrase went through my head even though I didn't utter it out loud. Ladies, after all, never swear. We walked side by side up Mulberry Street. Tenement windows were open because of the heat. Bed linens were airing, babies crying, neighbors shouting to each other across the street, while below pushcart vendors called out their wares. It was the usual cacophony of noise. I hardly noticed it anymore, but I saw Dr. Birnbaum wince.

"The conditions here in the slums are deplorable," he said in a low voice. "Such crowding can only lead to disease and violence. When you put too many rats together in the same cage, they start to eat each other."

I looked up at him. "So are you suggesting that our mass murderer might be from these streets himself? Not necessarily an outsider who hired the streetwalkers and then lured them to their deaths?"

He looked surprised at my suggestion. "All things are possible," he said, "although the murderer would need some privacy and time to kill and disfigure his victims. That would make an attack on these streets almost impossible. You see for yourself that there is much activity here. And in such crowded quarters it is necessary to sleep in shifts. I suspect that someone is awake and alert for most hours of the night." He paused as we had reached the square brick building that housed police headquarters. "We shall know more when we meet the officers. Until then, idle speculation is pointless."

As we entered through the main doors and stood in the foyer, I was assaulted by my memories, some pleasant, some not so—Daniel questioning me here when I was still a suspect in the murder on Ellis Island, my first meeting with Arabella in Daniel's office, Daniel giving me a good ticking off after my first encounter with Monk Eastman—Daniel's presence was so much a part of the very walls of this place, I half expected to see him come running down the stairs as I looked up.

Instead a very different young man was coming to meet us. He was tall, immaculately dressed in a summer suit, light brown hair parted in the middle, a pleasant, well-bred face. You'd never have taken him for a policeman in a month of Sundays. He was hurrying down the stairs with an expression of worried concentration on his face. A few paces behind him was a second man, more like Daniel in his appearance. He was good-looking in a dark, brooding sort of way, rather like drawings I had seen of the romantic poets. He was dressed in an official dark blue police uniform, which made him look rather dashing.

"Dr. Birnbaum?" The first of the officers held out his hand, even before he reached us. "How good of you to come. I am Detective Quigley. This is my fellow detective Jock McIver. We have been assigned together to this wretched case, in the hope that we can put a stop to it before there is flat-out panic on the Lower East Side. So any help or insight that you can give us will be much appreciated. However, I'm afraid that something rather pressing has come up. A fifth body was discovered on Elizabeth Street early this morning. McIver and I are actually on our way to the morgue. Will you accompany us? Your opinion on what you see will be most valuable."

Dr. Birnbaum gave an embarrassed cough and half turned to me. "I hope you don't mind, but I have brought my assistant with me, to help me by taking notes. Miss—"

"Fraulein Rottmeier," I said, having given some thought to a name this time, then imitating the doctor in the curt little bow. "I study in Vienna with Dr. Birnbaum."

Detective McIver was looking at me with half-amused interest. "A lady doctor," he commented, as if I was a strange specimen.

Quigley shook his head sadly. "I regret, fraulein, that I couldn't possibly allow a young lady to accompany us to the morgue, however qualified she is. What she would see there would be too disturbing."

"I assure you I am not of delicate disposition," I said, in an accent as close to Birnbaum's as I could muster. I had practiced before the mirror the previous night.

"No matter. Even bringing in an outside doctor is likely to cause raised eyebrows," Quigley continued. "I apologize, fraulein, but I'm sure Dr. Birnbaum will give you a detailed account later. Now, if you will excuse us, we have a carriage waiting."

He nodded in his refined, serious manner. McIver was still eyeing me with not entirely wholesome interest. So these were the two men that Daniel had mentioned. Both of them good cops who were also ambitious and might not want to jeopardize their careers by sticking their necks out on his behalf. I was furious that I wouldn't be present to observe and ask the occasional question, although in a way I was relieved that I was not going with them to the morgue. I wasn't at all sure my insides would hold up to what I might see there.

"This latest victim follows the pattern of the others?" Birnbaum fell into step beside Quigley as they made for the front door.

"So we are to understand. We were both off duty last night and unfortunately the body had been removed to the morgue by the time we were called in."

"The only difference is that this one was still alive," McIver added, lowering his voice as if he didn't want me to hear.

"Still alive? But she was mutilated like the others?"

"So we understand," McIver went on. "The constable

who found her noticed she was still breathing and had her rushed to the nearest hospital."

"And was she able to speak—to name her killer?"

"Unfortunately no," McIver muttered. "She muttered some word and then died. Mercifully, of course."

They emerged onto the street and Quigley snapped his fingers at a waiting black police carriage.

"I will report back to you later, fraulein," Dr. Birnbaum said, turning back to me.

"Very well, Doctor."

He clicked his heels, bowed, and climbed into the waiting vehicle. I watched them go, seething with frustration. Yet another occasion on which my sex had barred me from participating. The two detectives had not even bothered to ask if I was a fully qualified doctor, and I don't think it would have made any difference if I had been. I was not to be allowed to join in their men's world.

I left police headquarters and began to wander aimlessly up Mulberry Street. I didn't even know where Dr. Birnbaum was staying. I would just have to wait until he reported back to me—and patience wasn't one of my stronger virtues, if indeed I possessed any virtues at all. Then it occurred to me that I could, at least, take a look for myself at the scene of the crime. If the body had been whisked away to a local hospital, then evidence might have been left behind where she had lain.

I changed course and set off down Broome Street for Elizabeth. It was only when I actually reached Elizabeth Street and wondered whether to turn left or right that I stopped to ask myself what I was doing. I wasn't a police officer, investigating a crime. I was grasping at the thinnest of straws, hoping somehow, somewhere to find the link between Daniel Sullivan and the man who had plotted his downfall.

Elizabeth Street was relatively quiet, compared to the hustle and bustle of Mulberry and Canal. I knew that this street was known as a den of vice, and I supposed that most members of that profession slept in late. Even so, there were the usual housewives, shaking out linens from upper windows, and children playing hopscotch on the sidewalk, giving the scene an air of respectability and even tranquility. Nothing seemed to be happening to the north, toward Houston. So I turned to the south, back to Canal. I couldn't see any unusual police presence, only an ordinary constable standing on the corner, swinging his baton and looking around with disinterest.

I was going to approach him, then thought better of it. He wasn't likely to direct a thrill seeker to the scene of the crime, was he? So I made a careful inspection of the street, looking for goodness knows what, and came upon a woman down on her hands and knees among the filth, clearly looking for something.

"Can I help you?" I asked. "Have you lost something?"

She looked up at me. She wasn't young anymore, even though she still had a trim figure, with sharp features made even sharper by wire-rimmed spectacles. Her hair was pulled tightly back into a bun, and she was wearing a severe, high-necked, dark blue costume.

"Thank you. I don't need any help," she said, and her voice was more pleasant than her appearance.

I pretended to move on, then stood watching her from the shadows as she went back to work. After a while she lifted something with tweezers and dropped it into a small paper bag. Then, to my delight, she took out a tape measure and laid it across the street. That was enough for me. I went back to her.

"Forgive me for asking, but this is where the young woman was found this morning, isn't it?"

"It's no concern of yours," she said. "Just run along and let me get on with my work."

"Are you a relative of the poor girl?" I asked. "Such a terrible, tragic thing to have happened."

She eyed me appraisingly. "What are you, a reporter?"

"No, an investigator," I said.

"Looking into a criminal case? That's the business of the police."

"You appear to be doing some investigating yourself," I suggested.

"That's because I'm a member of the police force myself."

You could have knocked me down with a feather. I stared at her in surprise and delight. "A woman? In the New York police?"

"Officially I'm a matron," she said.

"Oh, I see." I had come across such matrons when I spent a night in a police shelter once.

"But now they use me in undercover work," she continued. "It just happened that I was assigned to patrol this area last night. We've had people constantly on the alert since the second girl was killed."

"Then you saw—" I began excitedly.

She shook her head. "That's just it. I didn't see a thing. I was on this very street several times. I'm so angry with myself. How could I have missed seeing the body dumped here?"

"When do you think it was put here?"

She frowned. "I heard a church clock chiming five as I turned onto Elizabeth Street. I walked down to Canal and turned right. By five-thirty the woman had been found and I was two streets away. I might even have seen the carriage as it passed with her in it. I could just kick myself. So near— what a chance that would have been for us women."

I squatted beside her, since she remained on her knees. "You say a carriage. What makes you think the girl was not brought down from a room in a nearby brothel and merely left outside the door?"

"Because I have asked at nearby brothels and none of them reports missing one of their girls." She looked a trifle smugly at me. "And because of this"—she drew an outline with her finger above the surface of the street—"the poor young woman lay approximately here; and if you'll look about a foot away, there's the clear imprint of a wheel in that patch of manure, and over there, a matching wheel imprint. Now that wheelbase is too wide to be a hansom cab; the wheel too delicate to be a draught wagon. Hence we're dealing with some kind of carriage. He drove here, opened the door, pushed her out, then drove on."

I stared at her in admiration. I had stumbled blindly through most of the cases I had investigated, coming to the right conclusion more through luck than skill. Here I was watching a trained, skilled detective at work. It reminded me how much of an amateur I was. But of course I wasn't going to let her know that.

"I've done some undercover work for the police myself," I said.

"Really?" She sounded skeptical.

"I was the one who went to the Flynn mansion and found out the truth about Senator Flynn's kidnapped son."

"Is that so? Who sent you?"

"Captain Sullivan."

Her face became stony again. "Ah yes, Captain Sullivan. You'll probably have heard. He's no longer with the police. He left in disgrace."

"Because somebody plotted his disgrace," I said, angrily. "He's innocent of the charges against him. He has never accepted a bribe, nor worked in the pay of a gang. Never."

"I wish I could believe that," she said.

"It's all lies! Someone has been spreading false rumors. Circumstantial evidence."

"Not all circumstantial," she said, and her voice was now ice cold. "My husband was one of the officers sent to raid a meeting between two rival gangs that was going to get ugly. But someone had tipped the gangs off. They were waiting for our men. My husband was beaten up and later died of his wounds."

Without thinking I put a hand on her shoulder. "I'm so terribly sorry," I said, "but it wasn't Daniel who tipped off the gang, I swear that. He swears it, and I believe him. I'm doing everything I can to prove his innocence."

"You're a relative, are you?" she asked.

"Just a friend."

She nodded with the understanding that always exists between us women and rose to her feet. She was a big woman, maybe five foot six or seven. Tall, angular, bony. Certainly not what you'd ever call a beauty. "Well, Miss—?"

"Murphy," I said, giving my real name for once. "Molly Murphy."

"Well, Miss Murphy," she went on, "I don't know how you think that poking around at the scene of a sordid crime can help prove Captain Sullivan's innocence."

"Because there has to be a reason somebody wanted him disgraced and arrested. The details of his arrest were so well plotted. Money was slipped into an envelope delivered by a gang member, and the police commissioner just happened to arrive on the scene at exactly the right moment to witness this handing over of a bribe."

"It sounds almost too well plotted to be true to me," she said. "Did it ever occur to you that he may just be guilty? Men aren't always straight with us women. He may not have wanted to diminish himself in your eyes."

"Oh, I know all about Daniel Sullivan's failings. But he's never out-and-out lied to me, and I believe him this time. He'd never want to send me on a wild-goose chase if he didn't believe I could come to the truth. What would be the point in it?"

She looked at me, long and hard, then she nodded. "And you think that this series of crimes is somehow linked to Captain Sullivan?"

I shook my head. "Not really, but I'm leaving no stone unturned. Someone has a motive for wanting him off the force and out of the way. He can't think what that motive might be, but someone must have a grudge against him, or somebody must have been worried he was coming too close to solving a case. At the time of his arrest he was lead officer in a horse-doping scandal out at Coney Island, and he had just been put in charge of this case. Hence my interest." I paused, looked at her, then put my hand up to my mouth as I realized it might have gotten me into trouble yet again. I've never known when to shut up. "I don't know why I'm telling you all this. You'll probably go straight back to police head-quarters, report what I've told you, and thus make somebody aware that I'm snooping around."

"Not me, my dear," she said. "Contrary to popular belief, we women can hold our tongues when necessary, and one thing we can do very well is stick together. I shouldn't like you. I shouldn't trust what you say. But I do." She held out her hand. "The name's Goodwin, Sabella Goodwin."

"I'm pleased to meet you, Mrs. Goodwin," I said. "You don't know how pleased I am to meet you. And if there's anything I can do to help you, I'd be only too happy to assist."

"Get away with you. I've been around enough Irish blarney in my life," she said, but she was smiling.

NINETEEN

I'd better let you get back to your work," I said, noticing that a group of children had gathered to watch us. "If we're not careful they'll spoil any clues you might have picked up. May I ask what you put in a bag?"

"A cigar butt," she said. "It may just be coincidental, but then it might have been discarded at the same time as the body. Cigar butts don't usually last long on these streets. Those last shreds of tobacco are too precious to waste. The urchins would have pounced on it. And that's about all I've got to go on." She sighed. "Too bad they rushed her to the morgue this time. I hope the detectives managed to have photographs taken."

"They rushed her to the hospital, not the morgue," I said.

"The hospital?"

"Because she was still alive."

"Saints preserve us. Still alive? But I understood she was another victim of the Ripper. I saw the last of those poor girls and there was no way . . ."

"She died soon afterward," I said.

"Thank God." She paused and looked up at me. "And how did you manage to find out this?"

"Like I told you, I'm an investigator." I smiled.

"All right, Miss Investigator," she said, "see what you make of the crime scene."

I looked down. It seemed to be a normal patch of New York street. Not too clean, with rotting vegetables, scraps of paper, and horse manure in the usual quantities. In fact, I saw nothing unusual until . . .

"Oh yes," I said. "You can see she lay here. Those are blood spots on that cabbage leaf."

Mrs. Goodwin nodded and picked up the leaf with tweezers, putting it into another paper bag. "But not much blood," she commented. "Which confirms she was dumped here after being assaulted somewhere else and found almost immediately."

The nosy youngsters had closed in on us.

"What's youse doin'?" one of the braver boys asked.

"It's where that lady copped it this morning," a girl said.

"That weren't no lady. That was one of the girls," the boy retorted.

I looked up at the child. She was a skinny little thing with hollow cheeks and a much-patched dirty muslin dress. "Did you see the lady lying here?"

She nodded, suddenly worried that she might have said too much or somehow be in trouble. "Yeah. It was horrible. Her face was all bashed in."

"I saw her too," a small boy ventured. "There was blood all over."

"How did she get here?" I asked. "Any of you see the body put on the street?"

Heads shook.

"My ma heard the noise going on outside, and we all went to the window and saw the police wagon and all. And my ma told us not to go down, but we came down here anyway and they were just picking her up and putting her in the back of the wagon. I didn't really want to watch, but I did."

I glanced at Mrs. Goodwin. "We should question the people who live in these tenements. Someone must have been awake between five and five-thirty and seen something."

"Someone should question the local inhabitants, but not you or me," she said. "This is a police investigation."

"You're with the police. You told me."

She looked just slightly embarrassed. "Yes, but I'm not officially assigned to this case. In truth they only use me for undercover observation where a male officer would be too obvious. They've yet to trust me with a real detective's work."

"Then this is a good chance to prove yourself," I said. "Look, they've nobody out here. What harm can there be in asking a few discreet questions before the men show up? And you've already nabbed the cigar butt."

She grinned. We were fellow conspirators. "I like your style," she said. "As I said, I've already checked the official brothels on the street to see if any girls are missing, so you take that tenement and I'll take this one. Then we'll work our way down to the end of the block. The vehicle came up from Canal, because the wheel tracks are on this side of the street. The man wouldn't want to risk causing any kind of traffic holdup."

"Right you are," I said. "I'll tackle this place then."

"And I the one directly opposite. Report back here."

And off I went, followed, like the Pied Piper, by a string of inquisitive children. "So who lives here?" I asked, and room by room, I made my way through the house. Many of the apartments only had windows that looked out to the back of the building, or worse, to the air well in the middle of the building. That meant another window or a brick wall, literally two feet away. I heard they had just passed a new law saying that tenements had to have better ventilation and an inside toilet, but I couldn't see City Hall making anyone tear down existing buildings or correcting these pitiful air ducts.

At last I came to the apartment where the skinny child lived, whose name I had by now found out was Kitty. Her mother was home, stirring a huge pot of laundry over a gas ring with a big wooden spoon. Her sleeves were rolled up and her forearms red and raw from the soda in the washing tub. She scowled as the children spilled into the room, sweeping me in with them.

"What in the world—" she began, but they twittered around her like sparrows.

"Mah, she's come about the body. You know, the woman what had her face bashed about?"

"I'm sorry to disturb you, Mrs . . ." I said, when I could get a word in edgewise, "but we're wondering if anyone in this apartment was up and around at five this morning, which was when the poor girl was dumped on the street."

"Up and around?" she glared at me, her lip curled up scornfully. "With a man who has to be at his shift digging the subway by six, and a couple of girls off to the sewing shops, I don't know where we'd be if I wasn't up and around by five."

"So was it possible you might have seen something from your front window? You have a good view of the street."

"Oh sure. And I've the time to sit behind my lace curtains, sipping my morning coffee, and peeking out at the world, haven't I? It's like a zoo in here, in the mornings. Crazy. The man's yelling for his boots and his breakfast at the same time. Me father wants something else, and the girls want their lunch pails. No, I can safely say that I didn't look out of the window. Not until we heard the commotion."

"And what happened then?"

"The kids rushed to the window, and the police had arrived and they were in the process of carting her off to the morgue, I suppose. Several of them were lifting her into the back of a Black Maria and off they went."

"But you didn't hear or see any carriage come down the street before that. A carriage, not a hansom cab."

"Carriage, you say?" She sniffed. "Can't say you see too many carriages down this street. If a gentleman wants a visit to one of the houses here, he comes incognito, on his own two feet, or in a cab at best. It's not likely he'd have his coachman drop him off." She sneered again. "And if he can afford a coachman, then there are better and cleaner houses up around Forty-second Street, so I hear. And even fancier ones on Fifth Avenue itself."

This, of course, was true. I thanked her. "And if anyone does remember anything about this morning, any of your neighbors saw a carriage stop, or a man behaving suspiciously, then here's my card. One of the children can find me, I expect, and there will be a tip for him."

"What are you, a lady detective?" she asked.

"Something of the kind. Helping the police to stop these horrible killings."

"About time. I worry for my own daughters. Fifteen and seventeen they are; and if they were coming home on a dark night, who's to say the brute might not mistake them for that kind of woman?"

"Who's to say indeed?" We nodded at each other with understanding. "You wouldn't catch me walking here alone and in the dark."

"What's all this commotion? Can't a man have a moment's peace anywhere?" a rasping voice demanded and an old man came into the room. He was bent over like a shepherd's crook. "Who's she?" he demanded. "Not the rent collector again?"

"She's been asking questions about the streetwalker who copped it today."

"What for?"

"Lady detective, apparently."

I looked at him. He stared back with bloodshot, tired eyes.

"You didn't happen to see anything yourself, did you?" I asked. "This morning, around five?"

"I was sleeping like a babe, up on the roof," he said. "I always takes a cot up on the roof in this weather. Can't sleep, packed in like sardines down here. They'd all sleep better too, but she won't let the kids up on the roof, just in case something happens."

"Up on the roof?" I asked. "And you didn't hear any of the commotion when they found the girl?"

"Oh yes, when they found her. Shouts and whistles and horses galloping up."

"But you weren't woken by galloping hooves earlier? A carriage, maybe?"

He shook his head. "Galloping hooves? This ain't the Wild West, lady." His skinny body shook with silent mirth. "The brewer's dray and the occasional hansom cab. Black Maria whenever they decide to raid one of the houses or one of the clients gets a little too lively. That's about it."

"So a carriage and pair might have woken you?"

"Might have. Didn't."

"To tell you the truth," his daughter said, stepping back into the conversation, "you could have knocked me down with a feather when the kids said there was a body down there because the police have been camped out on that corner since the first body was found on the street. How your carriage got past the police, I don't know."

"Neither do I," I said, resolving to find out which officers had been assigned to the corner this morning and whether they might have been dozing on duty and not wanting to admit it. Mrs. Goodwin had similar thoughts when I met her to compare notes. "These young men are not all as dedicated as we'd like them to be. But I was here myself this morning. That's what baffles me."

"Could she possibly have been thrown from an upstairs window or a roof?" I suggested. "The tire tracks might be just coincidental."

She looked up at the rooftops, considering. "I suppose it's possible."

"Then she could have been brought over rooftops from another street altogether."

She nodded, glancing up and then down. "If she was dropped from a height, the body will show signs of considerable bruising, especially if she was, as you say, still alive. And it would be a miracle if the fall didn't kill her outright."

"We'll never know unless we see the body for ourselves," I said.

She looked at me, half excited, half doubtful. "Are you suggesting that we go to the morgue and take a look?"

"You are a police officer, after all," I said. "Look how you found that cigar butt. What's to say there's not something else they've overlooked."

She shook her head. "Did anyone ever tell you that you were trouble?" she demanded.

"Constantly. Since I was born." I grinned, and she returned the smile.

"Well, come on then. No point in hanging about," she said, and set off at a lively pace toward Canal Street.

TWENTY

As I hurried to keep up with Mrs. Goodwin, a thought struck me. "Wait," I called, grabbing at her blue serge sleeve.

"You've lost your stomach for the morgue after all?" she asked, turning back to me.

"It's not that. It's just that the two detectives in charge of the case might still be there. They took an alienist with them but wouldn't let me come along. So I don't think they'd take it too kindly if I turned up while they were there."

She gave me a suspicious frown. "And how, in heaven's name, did you think they'd invite you to join their little party?"

"Because I know the doctor in question. He was willing to let me accompany him as his assistant. He understood how important this is to me. But the snooty one of the pair, Detective Quigley, absolutely said no. No women allowed."

"I understand that this is important to you, but what did you really hope to gain by going to the morgue? What do you think the sight of a dead body can tell you?"

I sighed. "I wish I knew. Maybe I'm chasing at straws. But someone worked very hard to bring about Daniel Sullivan's disgrace. Someone must have had a very good reason. So I'm thinking that either it was Police Commissioner Partridge himself who wanted Daniel out of the way, or somebody who didn't want a particular case solved. He was only working on two cases, remember. It could be something to do with the doping at the horse track, but then even if a doping scandal came to light, it wouldn't be the end of the world. However, we've just seen carriage tracks and a cigar butt on Elizabeth Street. What if we're dealing with an important man who doesn't want to be unmasked? A man of substance who has this unnatural bent to murder prostitutes?"

She stared at me, long and hard. "Why don't we go and have a cup of coffee first, and then you can tell me how far you've got. Maybe I've a way to help."

We had just turned onto Canal when I espied a young man coming toward us, his derby hat set at a jaunty angle above an innocent and angelic face. At first glance he looked like a well-dressed bank clerk on his day off, but I knew better. I had met him once before, to my cost. He went by the name of Kid Twist, and he was Monk Eastman's right-hand man and enforcer. But encountering him in broad daylight, in the middle of a busy street, was too good a chance to turn down.

I nudged Mrs. Goodwin. "Wait a moment. We have to talk to that man. Maybe he can help us."

"Do you know who that is?" She clutched at me and held me back.

"Of course. It's Kid Twist. I've had dealings with him before. But who would know better about missing prostitutes in the area? And what can happen to us here in the midst of this crowd?"

Her face was a mask of hate. "It's not just that. The Eastmans killed my husband—they and their cronies. They beat him to death. I won't rest until they are all behind bars or dead themselves."

"I can understand you'd feel that way," I said. "Believe me, I'd want justice too, if it had happened to my man, but I can't let this chance slip through my hands. You wait over here, if you don't want to have to face him. I'll be quite safe, and you can keep an eye on me, in case he tries anything."

She let me go, reluctantly. I dodged between delivery wagons and ran to catch up with him. "Kid. Mr. Twist. Wait a second," I called.

He turned around, eyed me suspiciously. "I've seen your face before," he said. "Whatta you want?"

"I need to talk to you for a moment. It's about these prostitutes. Another one was found dead this morning."

"Yeah. Dat was too tragic. What about it?"

"I just wondered—well, I know you work with Monk Eastman, and I know he controls most of what goes on around here."

"He's very active in the community, sure," he said with heavy sarcasm.

"So those girls? Did they work for him? Do you know who they were?"

"I didn't hear about no girls going missing," he said.

"And if they came from one of the houses around here, you would have heard?"

"Yeah, I'd have heard."

"And what if they weren't from one of the brothels, if they were real streetwalkers who took men to one of the cheap hotels?"

He stared at me, as if seeing me for the first time. "Nice girls like you ain't supposed to know about things like dat. It ain't good for you."

"I'm an investigator, Kid. I know about many things that aren't good for me."

He eyed me warily. "Investigating what? Who's killing whores? What for—some kind of newspaper story?"

"Something like that," I said. I didn't think he'd be overly helpful about saving Daniel's skin. "And I imagine you'd want this case solved as quickly as possible, too. It can't be too healthy for Monk to have his territory crawling with police day and night."

He looked at me in surprise, then he grinned. "You can say that again."

"Okay. So if they were real streetwalkers, not part of a brothel, would Monk have heard when one of them disappeared?"

"There ain't much that gets by Monk on his own turf. All

the girls have their protector, and dose guys pay their protection money to Monk. So do dose hotels you're talking about. Yeah, he'd have heard."

"So I'm wondering"—I took a deep breath—"and I'm not accusing you of anything, you understand. Just curious. If a girl wasn't behaving properly, if she wanted to escape from that kind of life, might somebody make sure that she didn't?"

His eyes narrowed. "You're asking me whether Monk would order to have a girl killed because she didn't do what she was told?"

"That's exactly what I'm wondering," I said.

He laughed. "Dat's not how it works. Dose girls, they're our assets. We want them alive, well, and working."

"If they were trying to run away?"

"Where would they run to? When they land up here, it's at the bottom of the heap. There's nowhere left to run. And if they needed teaching a lesson, one of the boys would slap them around a bit, without damaging the assets, you understand." He paused then said thoughtfully, "And if she don't listen good after that, then maybe she'd wind up floating in the East River. But I don't know nobody who would be dumb enough to dump a body in full view on the street. What's the sense in it?"

He was right. What was the sense in it? The only answer was that the killer was getting an added thrill from knowing he was baffling the police. Maybe he had been close by and watching. . . . I felt my skin prickle when I remembered that we had been into those tenement buildings. Had he been watching us then? Still there was no point in asking the children if they'd seen a strange gentleman on the street. There must be a steady procession of them, night after night.

"Listen, Mr. Twist," I said, "if the Eastmans find out anything about these girls, would you let me know? The sooner we catch this man, the better for all of us. Young Malachy knows where I live. You can send a message with him."

His eyes narrowed. "You working with da cops?"

"Not at all. You could say I'm working in competition with the cops."

"Then you better watch your own skin, girl. Cops around here don't take kindly to having their toes stepped on."

"I'll be careful. So will you tell me like I asked?"

He nodded. "All right. Monk certainly ain't too thrilled about having the police in his backyard."

I gave him my most winning smile. "Thank you. I really appreciate our little talk."

"My pleasure, ma'am." He tipped his bowler.

I almost skipped back across the street.

"Well, that's taken care of," I said, trying not to look too pleased with myself. "The Eastman gang knows nothing about these girls."

"So he tells you," Sabella Goodwin snapped. "They're a bunch of low-down, dirty scum, the lot of 'em. They'd swear on the body of their grandmother and look you full in the face and lie."

I put my hand on her arm. "Look, I can understand how you feel about them. I'm no champion of them myself. I almost got kidnapped by them once. God knows where I'd be now if the police hadn't raided at that moment. But they are the ideal ones to help us if we want to solve this."

We started to walk toward the Bowery.

"Monk Eastman has a finger in every kind of criminal pie in the Lower East Side," I continued. "If one of his girls had wound up dead, he'd want to know who did it, wouldn't he? Someone would be messing with his assets, as Kid Twist so nicely put it. So I wanted to find out if they were Monk's girls."

"And are they?"

"That's the odd thing. Kid says they haven't heard of any girls going missing, which must mean they're brought in from somewhere else."

"Another part of the city, you mean?"

"Daniel says the first dead girl who fit this pattern of killing was found under the boardwalk at Coney Island. So maybe our killer preys on Coney Island prostitutes but now finds it more exciting to dump them on city streets."

"This is something we should share with the detectives in charge," Sabella Goodwin said.

"I'm sure they must have thought of it themselves and wouldn't take kindly to being told how to conduct their case by a couple of women."

She grinned. "Quigley wouldn't, that's for sure. Conceited young fellow. He's planning to go to the top in a hurry."

And might have found Daniel stood in his way? The thought flashed across my mind.

"What about McIver?"

"He'd like to go all the way to the top on Quigley's coat-tails, I reckon," she said. "He's certainly bright enough, but lazy. Quigley's meticulous, by the book. McIver's the opposite—any means to get to the end. It will get him into trouble one day."

We continued along the sidewalk in silence. I was thinking about two ambitious young men, one of them prepared to take risks to get what he wanted. They had both been handed this plum assignment when Daniel was arrested. Did either of them want promotion badly enough that they were prepared to go to extreme lengths for it? And if either of those detectives had set up Daniel's betrayal, then these dead girls were of no use to me at all. I didn't really need to go to the morgue.

Because, to tell the truth, I was having serious second thoughts about what lay ahead. I had seen a few dead bodies in my lifetime. I hadn't enjoyed those experiences and they had been but fleeting glances—and my stomach had been more stable in those days. To see a body laid out on a marble slab, its face badly disfigured, was something I might not be able to handle. What if I fainted or threw up in front of Sabella Goodwin and the doctor at the morgue?

As we sat at the coffee shop under the El station I tried to come up with a plausible excuse to get me out of what lay ahead. Before I could think of anything, however, Sabella

Goodwin smiled at me. "I'm so glad you've agreed to come to the morgue with me, because I have to confess—I'd never have summoned the nerve to go there alone."

As I didn't answer she went on. "I can't tell you how glad I am to have found an ally. I've been trying to make those men in the police department see that we women are just as capable of carrying through an investigation as they are. We may not be strong enough to chase after crooks and arrest them, but we can do the legwork as well as any man."

"And I'd like to see any man chase after crooks if he had to wear corsets and long skirts," I said, and she laughed.

"We'll show them, Molly. We'll go to that morgue and solve their case for them."

It looked as if I was going to the morgue, whether I wanted to or not.

TWENTY-ONE

The city morgue is on the grounds of Bellevue Hospital beside the East River. We hopped off the train at Twenty-third Street and walked up First Avenue. At first glance the hospital didn't live up to its name. Several dreary brick buildings, chimneys belching smoke, provided more of an aspect of dark satanic mills than the beautiful vista promised in the name. Of course, I might have seen it through a prejudiced eye at this moment, because, in truth, my reluctance had grown with every step. Now my knees were positively trembling, and worse still, my stomach had started to churn. I had hoped that the coffee and bun I had just eaten would have calmed my insides for the next hour. Now the bun lay like a lead weight, refusing to be digested. I took a deep breath and attempted to pull myself together. I was going to do this. It was clear that Sabella Goodwin already admired me and thought of me as a kindred spirit. My pride wasn't going to let that image be shattered if I could help it.

We found the main gate in the high brick wall, more prisonlike than hospital, and were directed toward the morgue with several curious and pitying glances. I expect they thought we'd come to claim the body of a dear one.

"Ah, here we are," Sabella said, and I noticed that her voice didn't sound too confident either.

"Why don't you go ahead and find out if the detectives

have left?" I suggested. "I don't want to cause a scene and spoil your chances by being here."

"All right." She nodded briskly. I gave a sigh of relief as she pushed open the front doors and went inside. Anything to buy a few more minutes. I even eyed the path back to the main gate. Crisply starched nurses were hurrying in pairs, patients were being pushed in wheelchairs with rugs over their knees, although the day was hot. I could just melt among them, get out, and go home. Sabella Goodwin didn't even know where I lived. I firmly dismissed the little voice whispering in my head. I had always despised weak women. I was not about to become one of them.

I turned back as Sabella Goodwin pushed open the door. "It's all right. They've gone," she said. "I showed my police badge to the clerk and asked if my fellow officers were still here. He was clearly surprised and told me I'd just missed them, but the doctor was about to do the autopsy if I wanted to go in. So we've been given permission. Come on. Let's go."

"Excellent," I managed to say, and followed her into the gloomy interior.

There was an overwhelming smell pervading the place, sweet and cloying to the nostrils. It wasn't the usual hospital smell, that mixture of strong disinfectant and death. I learned later that it was formaldehyde, in which body parts were preserved. My stomach lurched alarmingly. I reached for a handkerchief and put it to my nose.

"It's not very pleasant, is it?" Mrs. Goodwin agreed, but she didn't seem unduly distressed. In fact, she pushed open the swing doors with great confidence. I followed. We found ourselves in a big, well-lit room, dominated by three marble-topped tables. On one of them something lay, covered with a white sheet. I was so glad that the body was not fully exposed that I gave a sigh of relief. The doctor appeared from a side room, washing his hands. He was a jolly-looking man with big mustaches and a red face.

"Who have we here?" he asked. "This is the autopsy room, I'm afraid. You've taken a wrong turn."

"No, we came to find you," Mrs. Goodwin said. She produced the badge again. "Sabella Goodwin, New York Police. I understand my colleagues have already been here this morning; but I'm also investigating this case, and I wanted to take a look for myself. This is my assistant, Miss Murphy."

"A woman police officer; now I've seen everything," the doctor said.

"They even have women doctors, so I'm told," she said sweetly.

"Quite right." He chuckled. "And some of them do a damned fine job. I'm Dr. Hartman. Now, what can I do for you, Mrs. Goodwin?"

"The body that was brought in today. We'd like to take a look. I understand you haven't done an autopsy yet?"

"No, only the most preliminary of findings," Dr. Hartman said. "Cause of death strangulation and then trauma to the face with a blunt instrument as an afterthought."

"But she lived through all this," Mrs. Goodwin said. "She was alive when she was found."

"So I heard. Died as she was being admitted to the hospital."

"And that was here?" I asked, not remembering to keep quiet and let the police officer do the talking.

He shook his head. "No, that would have been Saint Vincent's. Closest hospital to where she was found."

"So you don't know if she said anything before she died?" I asked.

"I'm afraid my job is to cut up the bodies after they're dead. My patients rarely speak to me." He gave a macabre grin. "You'd like to see the body? I'll keep the face covered. Not a pretty sight and it won't help you in your investigation. Not even recognizable as a face anymore, just a bloody mess. Whoever did it did a very thorough job."

He pulled back the sheet.

"She hasn't been here long. As you can see, we haven't even got her cleaned up and prepped yet. Your fellow officers wanted to make a full note of her clothing and measurements to see if she matches any of your Bertillon records."

"Bertillon? What is that?" I blurted out before I remembered that I was supposed to be attached to a police officer myself.

Mrs. Goodwin turned back to me. "It's a system of identification based on a set of standard measurements. It's fairly new and proving to be very useful. We take photographs and measurements when we book a criminal, and those cards are kept on file. Every person has a unique set of measurements. So if she has ever been arrested before, we're likely to have her on file."

As she talked I was staring at what I could see of the body. She was still wearing a tawdry blue satin skirt, which was slit all the way to the knee on one side, and above it a black-boned corset, liberally decorated with black lace. The sheet still lay over her face, exposing a swollen neck discolored with black-and-yellow bruising. I swallowed hard, repulsed, yet fascinated, by what I saw. Such a frail little thing. Dark curls escaped from below the sheet, lying over one white shoulder. A slim hand lay at her side. I stared at that hand and then shook my head.

"There's something strange here," I said.

They both looked at me. "Look at her hand," I said. "Her fingernails are so clean. And you say you haven't washed her yet. She doesn't smell."

They continued to stare at me. "Look," I said. "I've been in a jail cell with a group of prostitutes like this one. They're not so careful about their personal habits. One thing I noticed was dirty fingernails, some of them bitten. And they mask their body smells with cheap perfumes—ashes of roses or lily of the valley."

"Maybe this girl comes from a higher-class establishment," the doctor suggested. "Not all prostitutes live in squalor, as I'm sure you know."

"In which case, why is she dressed like this? These are clothes you'd expect to see on a streetwalker in the worst part of town. No man going to a high-class brothel would want his young lady to look like this."

"She's right, you know," Mrs. Goodwin agreed. "She is

very clean, yet her clothes are a disgrace. Look at them,
about to fall apart."

"Then I'd say she was a good girl fallen on hard times,"
the doctor said. "Some of them try to keep up their old standards for as long as they can. I've seen it often enough before. The girl gets herself into trouble, has the baby or an
abortion, and there's nowhere left for her to go but on the
streets. Tragic really—the number of them who kill themselves in despair."

The smell had been getting to me. Now suddenly the
room started to sway around. I clutched at the edge of the
table and everything went black.

Someone was calling to me from the other end of a long,
dark tunnel. Then I felt my head shoved forward and recoiled as a sharp smell was placed under my nose. I opened
my eyes. I was sitting on a bench in the hallway of the
morgue. Mrs. Goodwin was sitting beside me, holding a bottle of smelling salts.

"Don't worry about it. It happens to the best of us," she
said. "I fainted the first time I saw a dead body. Ashamed
of myself afterward, but it's a natural reaction. And that
smell, too."

I nodded gratefully.

"The doctor is conducting a preliminary autopsy now,"
she said. "He'll let us know his findings."

"What is there more to find?" I asked. "We know how she
died."

"I expect he'd want to know whether she was pregnant, for
one thing," Mrs. Goodwin said. "Now we've seen how well
cared for she is, we have to assume she's new to the game,
which means someone might have reported her missing."

"Yes, I see," I said. I hugged my arms to me.

"Probably tried to run away from her pimp, poor soul,"
she went on. "He might have killed her himself."

"And left her in full view on the street?" I shook my head.
The smelling salts had cleared my head. "No, if he'd killed
her, he'd have done the same as the Eastmans. He'd have

dumped her quietly in the East River, not left her for the police to find."

"Then she was just picked up by the wrong man," Mrs. Goodwin said. "Well, we've some chance of finding out who she was. We don't know what her face looked like, but Quigley and McIver took Bertillon measurements and we know she has pretty dark hair and fine bones. I just hope we catch this fiend before he gets his hands on any more girls."

My brain, at least, was now fully recovered. "I wonder if the detectives went to the hospital?" I asked. "If she was still alive, she might have been able to say something that could help us."

"I doubt it," Mrs. Goodwin said, "but it's worth a visit, just as soon as we're done here."

"Aren't we done here?" My heart sank. There was no way I wanted to go back into that room again, especially if the autopsy was being conducted at this moment. I had no wish to add vomiting to my list of embarrassments.

Mrs. Goodwin clearly had no such squeamishness. "Oh, I'd like to know for my own curiosity whether she was in the family way. And maybe what kind of instrument was used to disfigure her. I have a feeling that those two young men really won't put themselves out too much to solve this. It's the general consensus among policemen that prostitutes are disposable, that they ask for what they get. I, on the other hand, feel that a society should be judged by the way it treats its most vulnerable members. In fact—" She broke off as the door opened and Dr. Hartman came out. We both rose to our feet.

"The young lady has quite recovered, I see," he said, smiling genially at me.

"Yes, thank you. I must apologize for my amateurish behavior."

"Nonsense. Half the first-year medical students faint, and most of them are men, too."

"Your autopsy is surely not completed?" Mrs. Goodwin asked.

"No, but I'd like you to contact the two detectives who

were here this morning. They should come back right away. I've found something that completely changes the complexion of this case."

He looked almost shaken. I found that my own knees were trembling.

"As I said, I have completed the most preliminary of investigations. I was looking for signs of"—he paused and coughed discreetly—"recent sexual activity."

"And was there?" Mrs. Goodwin asked.

"There was an obvious attempt at it," he said, still looking most uncomfortable to be discussing such a subject with women, "but the attempt was not wholly successful."

"What do you mean?"

"I mean, dear lady, that this young girl was still technically a virgin."

TWENTY-TWO

T he full implications of this statement didn't hit me until we were leaving Bellevue Hospital after Mrs. Goodwin had put through a telephone call to summon back Detectives Quigley and McIver. She was walking rather fast, and I had to break into a trot to keep up with her. I gathered she didn't want to be anywhere in sight when the detectives showed up again. I suspected that she had exceeded her authority by a mile, but I wasn't going to let her lose face by suggesting this. Besides, she was now my partner in crime, and I admired her pluck.

"That girl never was a prostitute then," I blurted out, somewhat naively, as I'm sure the fact had dawned on her immediately.

"Someone dressed her up to make us think that she was, and then dumped her on a street known to be frequented by streetwalkers. What a cruel and horrible trick. Why, I wonder?"

"The man is clearly deranged," I said. "He enjoys killing young girls. I wonder if the others really were prostitutes?"

"The doctor is applying for an exhumation order," she said. "We may know more when they dig up the bodies of the other girls."

"Will there be enough—left?" I asked, skirting around this distasteful subject.

"Enough to go on. Hair and height and body build. The last one was scarcely a week ago, so the body should still be pretty much intact. The others will be less well preserved, but they can match hair samples these days. If the others turn out to be young girls with no ties to prostitution, then they must have families and friends. Someone will be missing them."

"Unless he preys on young girls who have run away from home or come alone as immigrants to the New World," I said. "When I first arrived here, I knew nobody. Not a single person would have missed me if I had been taken off by a stranger. Maybe he promises work to new arrivals, a safe place to stay?"

She sighed. "That's possible. But there have been five of them so far. Surely just one will have made a friend, someone who might come forward if we put a notice in the newspapers."

"If they read English," I said. "But there's one thing I'm thinking—that first girl who was killed this way. The one who was found under the boardwalk at Coney Island. I understood she was indeed a real prostitute, identified by her pimp. One of her fellow streetwalkers might even have seen the man she went with that night."

"So you think we should go out to Coney Island and inquire?" she asked.

"Definitely."

"I'm supposed to report into the station by noon," she said. "And then I'm ready to go home and fall asleep. I've been on duty all night."

"I could do it," I said.

She shook her head. "No, I don't want you going out there alone. In the police force we always work in pairs. Safer that way. We have plenty to do in the meantime— placing that advertisement in the papers and seeing if any girls have been reported missing. That's something I can do before I go home."

I sighed. "We still seem so much in the dark. What we are really looking for is a depraved monster who preys on young girls. How will we ever find him in a city this size?"

"He'll make one slip. They always get too cocky in the

end or annoyed that the police are too slow. He's dumping those bodies on the street to taunt us. One day he'll dump a body where someone will see."

"I don't want to wait for that day," I said. "It will mean more girls have to suffer this fate. Do you feel too tired to go on to Saint Vincent's Hospital? Maybe she did say something—anything to give us a clue."

She nodded. "All right. We've just got time if I'm to report in by noon. I don't want them panicking and sending out search parties for me." She almost sprinted for the El station. I had to admire her stamina. She had been on duty all night, and she was still going strong. Myself, I was already flagging under the heat of the day, and I was at least ten years her junior. I struggled to keep pace with her as she leaped aboard a departing train. The carriage was jam-packed and we had to stand, swaying in rhythm as the carriage creaked and groaned its way down First Avenue, blowing noxious smoke in through open windows. Of course we'd have to be traveling on one of the lines that hadn't been electrified yet.

By sheer force of will I managed to keep going until we reached Saint Vincent's Hospital. I knew my way around that somber place well enough. Bridie had almost died from typhoid here, and I had visited her every day. A pang of longing for her and her brother swept over me.

Sabella Goodwin strode purposefully down the tiled hallway until she reached the stone-faced, white-coifed nun in charge of the admitting desk.

"I am a police officer and I need to question somebody about the young woman brought here earlier today. The young victim who subsequently died," she said in a voice that echoed from the tiled walls. Even the admitting sister was impressed by it.

"I'll find the sister who was on duty," she said, and dispatched a junior nurse. "A tragic business." She shook her head so that the starched veil rattled. "The sisters who tried to care for her were quite distressed about it. We had to relieve them from duty for a while. And believe me, we see everything here."

We stood and waited while the life of the hospital went on around us. I leaned against the cool tile of the wall for support. I certainly wasn't going to faint again. At last there was a neat tap of feet along the corridor and a young, fresh-faced sister appeared. She looked about as white and pale as her veil and uniform.

"I'm Sister Mary Margaret," she said. "You wanted to know about that unfortunate woman who was brought to us."

"We do, Sister," Mrs. Goodwin sounded brisk and efficient. "It can't have been a pleasant experience for you."

"It was awful," the young nun said. "I've never seen anything like it. Neither had Sister Rose. She's been crying all morning."

"We were wondering," Mrs. Goodwin said carefully, "if the young woman was at all conscious, and if she might have said anything."

"We didn't think she could be conscious when we first saw her," Sister Mary Margaret said. "If you'd seen what was left of her poor face . . . We were sure she must be dead, but then Sister Rose felt a pulse and we were just moving her onto a gurney when she made a sound. Of course she could hardly speak, but I took her hand and put my ear close to her. 'What did you want to tell me, my darlin'?' I asked her. She just moaned and then she said what sounded like 'Tree. Tree.' Then there was a gurgle in her throat and blessedly she died." The sister paused to cross herself. Mechanically my hand followed hers.

"Tree?" Mrs. Goodwin asked. "What could that mean?"

"We were wondering if perhaps she was an immigrant and that was the way she pronounced three."

"Meaning there were three men in on this?"

The sister sighed. "I've no idea what she meant. Maybe she was trying to give her address so that we could notify her family. I really can't tell you. But I do know it's affected me deeply. I've been on my knees in chapel most of the morning, praying for her poor, departed soul."

"We'll let you get back there then, Sister," Mrs. Goodwin said gently. "Thank you for taking the time to see us."

She led us out of the building, and not a minute too soon. Another second and I would have vomited on those spotless tiles. I made it outside but had to hold onto a lamppost while the world swung around. "I'm really sorry," I said. "I had no idea this would upset me so. I live only a couple of streets away. I should probably go home and let you get to your work."

She put an arm around my shoulder. "Come on. I'll take you home."

"That's really not necessary. You have to report in to your police station," I tried, but she was adamant. I was escorted back to Patchin Place. She waited until I'd turned the key in the lock then came inside with me. "What you need is a cup of chamomile tea," she said.

"I'm afraid I don't have chamomile," I said. "It's not something I'm familiar with. I've just ordinary tea like we drink at home."

"That will be better than nothing." She started bustling around my kitchen, filling the kettle and lighting the gas with a spill. "Sit down. Unbutton your jacket, get some air to yourself."

I did as she commanded. "I didn't think I'd be so affected by this," I said. "I thought I was strong."

Her eyes narrowed as she looked at me. "I've taken care of enough young women in my life to recognize the signs," she said. "I presume that's why you're so anxious to rescue Daniel Sullivan?"

I felt myself blushing scarlet. "I don't know what you mean," I said.

"Oh, come on now. I wasn't born yesterday," she said. "And you're not the first girl it's happened to either. It seems to me that young Sullivan has a lot to answer for—to you and to me. Maybe he'd be better off rotting in jail. It would teach him a lesson."

"Oh no," I said. "I can't let that happen to him. How would you have felt if it was your husband who had been falsely implicated and faced a lifetime in jail?"

"I suppose I'd have done what I could for him, the way

you are. And I can see that your life will be a whole lot worse if you don't prove his innocence."

I swallowed hard so that I didn't cry in front of her. "But I don't seem to be getting anywhere. This case we're working on—what on earth can it have to do with wanting Daniel in jail? The sort of depraved man who is doing these terrible things—how would he have known about Daniel's meeting with the Eastmans? How would he have steered the commissioner to the right spot at the right moment?"

"You'd be surprised what depraved men look like by daylight," she said. "He could be anybody, someone you know; someone I know. But I agree. If Captain Sullivan is telling the truth, then it would have to be someone with inside knowledge of the workings of the Police Department."

"Someone who might be jealous of Daniel, who might want his position?" I asked. "What about Quigley and McIver? They took over the case from him. And you said they are both ambitious young men."

"Yes, but removing Captain Sullivan wouldn't really enhance their own chances of promotion that much. I can think of several men who could be made captain before them."

"And if removing Daniel from this case would give them a chance at glory? Saving the world from the East Side Ripper?"

She shook her head again. "Hardly the case I'd have chosen. Not at all sure that we'll ever catch the killer. Of course things look a little more hopeful now that we know this girl was only dressed up to look like a prostitute and may be missed from her home. But Quigley and McIver didn't know that until now. Besides, I've worked with them enough to know they're both straight. Quigley comes from an old family and abides by those rules. Old family honor and all that. McIver— well, he's more devious, but I'd trust him." She considered this for a moment, then nodded. "Yes, I'd trust him well enough."

"Which leaves me back at square one," I said. "I've no idea what to do next."

"Drink your tea and take a rest," she said. "I have to go, but I'll get that advertisement put into the papers and let's see if anyone comes forward to report a missing girl. And in the meantime . . ." She was halfway to my front door when she turned and looked hard at me for a long moment before saying, "You don't have to go through with this if you don't want to, you know."

"What do you mean?" I asked cautiously.

"Exactly what I say. There are ways . . . to end it . . . if that's what you'd want."

"But isn't that very risky?"

"Of course it's always a risk, but no greater risk than trying to survive on your own in this world with a child."

She came over to where I was sitting at the kitchen table and bent her head close to mine. "Look, I know a woman," she said in a low voice. "I've sent other girls to her before. She knows what she's doing. She'll want paying, but I'll have a word with her. I've done her favors before now—got her out of a couple of arrest warrants."

"You know a woman," I echoed, parrot fashion. "But I couldn't."

"It's that blasted Catholicism drummed into your head, I suppose. Don't tell me the Catholic Church is going to support your child for you?"

"It's not that," I said. "I'm afraid I'm already damned as far as the Catholic Church is concerned. It's just that I can't afford to be idle and recuperating right now. I've so much work to do."

"I told you. This woman knows what she's doing. You'll be back on your feet in no time at all, and feeling a lot better than you have been today, I'll guarantee. Think about it. I'll try to speak to her and let you know tomorrow if we can work out something between us."

"Thank you," I stammered. I rose to my feet. "I—I'm very glad I met you."

"And I you."

"I think we were meant to be in on this together," I said. "If we find out who framed Daniel, then maybe we'll also find out who brought about your husband's death."

"Maybe." She gave a sad smile. Then she brightened up, waved, and was out of my front door.

TWENTY-THREE

As I closed the door behind her, I noticed two notes stuck in my letter box. I recognized Daniel's angry black script on one of them, but the other was in a small, meticulous, unfamiliar hand. Of course I tore open Daniel's note first.

> *You ask whether anybody has been to see me in jail? Apart from that damned fool lawyer and yourself, the answer is no. The days and nights seem interminable. I understand from the guard who brings me my food that my date in court might be soon. But one small mercy— the food has improved, and they are emptying the buckets in our cells more frequently as rumor has it that the commissioner of police will be inspecting this week. You can bet he can't wait to see me in this condition.*
>
> *I know you are doing everything you can. I just pray for a miracle. I think of you every waking moment.*
>
> *Daniel*

I looked at it, then carefully folded the letter back into its envelope. So the commissioner of police was planning to visit The Tombs, was he? It might just be coincidence. On the other hand, maybe my first instincts had been right after all, and he was the one who had orchestrated Daniel's betrayal himself. What could have been easier than having those dollar bills hidden in his own fist, ready to scatter as the letter was opened?

So I might have been wasting valuable time looking into a series of sordid murders when my investigations should have gone in quite a different direction. Daniel himself knew of no particular reason why Mr. Partridge should want him out of the way, but that didn't mean that one didn't exist. Had that man of moral rectitude something he wished to keep hidden? It seemed that my next task should be to look into Mr. Partridge's life and affairs. I had no idea how I might do that, but maybe Sabella Goodwin could help me get started when I next saw her. She was in a position to nose around at police headquarters and pick up on any rumors.

Then I remembered what else would happen when I next saw her. She'd bring me news of a woman who might be able to end my current predicament. I felt hot and clammy all over, just at the thought of it. She was right about that Irish upbringing. If ever there were mortal sins, that was surely one of them.

I opened the second note, with some trepidation. Most letters these days did not seem to be bringing me good news. I saw from the neat signature that this one was from Dr. Birnbaum.

My dear Miss Murphy:

In truth I was much relieved that you were not allowed to accompany me to the morgue this morning. The sight of the young girl was most distressing, even to a hardened medical man like myself. I am sure you would not have been able to endure it, and it would have left a lasting impression of horror on your delicate psyche. And in truth, not much was gained from my visit or my discussion with the two detectives.

They are deeply baffled by a man who can apparently drop girls on crowded streets under the very eyes of the police. Of course, they did point out to me that they had only just been assigned this case when Captain Sullivan was removed from his post, so have little to go on.

*All I could tell from viewing the corpse was that she
was killed by a man of considerable strength and bru-
tality. The thumb marks on her neck were impressive as
was the force of the blows to her face. So we are dealing with a man who is not only powerful but enjoys
taking tremendous risks. He probably realizes that his
desire to kill is now out of control. Sooner or later it
will drive him to take one risk too many.*

*I don't know if this helps you at all in your own
quest. I fear not. We have so little to go on. We could be
looking for any man in the Greater New York area.*

I regret that I can't be of more assistance to you,

Your faithful servant,
Frederick Birnbaum, Doctor of Medicine

I had to smile at such a correct and perfectly executed
missive and found myself wondering what he and the flam-
boyant Ryan could possibly have in common. Then the smile
faded. Another dead end, it would appear. I had learned
nothing new from his note—or had I? It struck me that the
two officers in question claimed they had just taken over the
case from Daniel. But I seemed to remember it was the other
way around—hadn't Daniel been assigned to the case over
them? So why make this false claim to Dr. Birnbaum?

I could come up with a perfectly good answer, of
course—they were ambitious, according to Mrs. Goodwin.
They didn't want to lose face by admitting how little they
had achieved so far. Or Birnbaum, not being a native English
speaker, might just have misunderstood. Besides, I couldn't
see Quigley and McIver scheming to have Daniel removed
from this case just so that they could get all the glory for
themselves. As Mrs. Goodwin had commented, it was a devilish puzzle with no guarantee of a successful outcome.

So far my bet was on John Partridge. Men who rise to po-
sitions of power often have shady secrets in their past, secrets they'd rather didn't come out. If John Partridge had

such a secret and Daniel had inadvertently stumbled upon it, then the commissioner might feel himself threatened. But since Daniel had no idea himself what he could have done to antagonize Mr. Partridge, I wasn't sure how I could unearth any deep, dark secrets in Partridge's past. Still, I had to try. Who might possibly know details of Mr. Partridge's past life and indiscretions? Nobody in my circle of friends. Then it occurred to me—newspapers! They loved to dig up dirt on political figures, didn't they? A visit to the archives at *The Times* or the *Herald* might at least set me in the right direction. At the very least they'd have his biography on file.

I changed into my cooler and less-constricting summer muslin, then departed on the hunt again. Another hot and muggy day, with thunder threatening over New Jersey. Flies and mosquitoes hummed around me, and I wished I had been like the fashionable ladies and bought myself a hat with a veil. I decided that the *Herald* was closer and by claiming to be from the Ladies Decency League again, sent by Mrs. Astor, I had the stern-faced woman in archives promising to search out all references to John Partridge for me. She even promised them by the next day.

By the time I came out of the Herald Building, those storm clouds had grown into impressive thunderheads. The first fat drops were spattering onto the hot granite blocks of the street. I had thought of doing a thousand and one other things, including visiting some of those hotels in search of Letitia, but now, without an umbrella, I made directly for home.

I was halfway down Patchin Place when the heavens opened and in the few short steps to my front door, I was soaked to the skin. I hung my dress to dry, made myself a cup of tea, and was overcome with weariness. I lay on my bed, listening to the rumble of thunder, getting closer by the minute. I should be making plans, I told myself. Instead, in spite of the flashes and crashes outside my window, I fell deeply asleep.

I awoke to another loud rumble. It was dark as night outside and apparently the storm was still going on. Then I realized that the noise I was hearing came from my front door and not the sky. I scrambled into my skirt and shirtwaist as my muslin was still soaking wet and ran down the stairs. Outside, the rain was still coming down heavily but under a large, black umbrella stood Sid and Gus.

"Oh, you're home. We're so glad," Sid said, already stepping in through the front door and shaking out the umbrella behind her. "Did you get caught out in this awful storm? We did. Soaked to the skin, both of us. I made Gus take a bath so that she didn't catch cold."

"I'm fine," Gus said. "I'm not really a delicate little flower, you know. I'm quite hardy, in spite of appearances."

"Would you like a glass of lemonade or some tea?" I asked.

"Thank you, but we've just had coffee," Gus said. "You know Sid can't exist for long without her Turkish. We came to tell you what a fun and jolly day we've had."

"Doing what?"

"Playing at sleuths." Sid beamed, pulling out a chair at my kitchen table. "Finding out about the missing Letitia as we promised we would. Molly, now I see why the profession is so attractive to you. I felt like such a conspirator, slinking around and asking clever questions."

"Did you find out anything?" I asked, my heart sinking a little at the thought of Sid and Gus acting the part of sleuths.

"Nothing really important, I regret," Sid said. "We found out that when Miss Blackwell comes to town with her mother, she always stays at the Brevoort, just a stone's throw from us."

"The Brevoort," I echoed. A nice-enough hotel, but not on the level of the Plaza or the Astoria, where I am sure Arabella would have stayed. That presumably meant that Letitia was not as rich as Arabella's family. Which, in turn, meant that no young man would be trying to get his hands on her fortune.

"But we couldn't find any hotel where Miss Blackwell registered alone recently," Gus said. "Of course, she might have used an assumed name, but we did describe her from the photograph."

"We thought that maybe Mrs. Blackwell stayed at the Brevoort because it is within easy reach of the settlement house and the Lower East Side," Sid said. "One can walk the distance with sturdy shoes on. They speak very highly of Mrs. Blackwell there, by the way. One of their most devoted patrons and workers."

"And what about Letitia?" I asked.

"She comes quite regularly with her mother," Sid said, "and once or twice with her fiancé. The comment was that they made a lovely couple and seemed quite enraptured with each other."

"The settlement workers were expecting her to come and help them the day she disappeared," Gus said. "They were planning an outing for the children to Coney Island the next day. Miss Blackwell was supposed to be one of the chaperons, and there was to be a final planning meeting that day. They were annoyed when she didn't arrive."

An outing to Coney Island? Until this moment I hadn't seen any connection between Letitia and the murdered girls, but at the mention of the name, I felt my skin prickle. Letitia had been scheduled to go to Coney Island—but not until the next day. Letitia hadn't actually gone there. Everything seemed to revolve around that place—and yet how could the murder of a prostitute, a prizefight, a doped horse, and a children's outing be linked? It had to be one of those strange coincidences that haunt us in our lives—or maybe it was my Irish temperament seeing portents where there were none.

"What is it, Molly?" Gus asked.

"Nothing. It just startled me that an outing to Coney Island was planned. Everything I do seems to be somehow linked to that place. And yet I can see no connections."

"It's a big, bustling place," Sid said. "New Yorkers practically live there during the summer months, so it's no wonder you hear it mentioned so often."

Of course she was right, and I was overreacting again. After all, what possible connection could there be between the patrician Letitia and some murdered prostitutes? Then the chilling thought came to me—one of the girls had not been a prostitute, had she? Letitia's Coney Island connection did need to be investigated after all.

"So tell me, at the settlement house, was there any hint of a young man who might have been interested in Letitia?"

"As a matter of fact there was," Sid said. She was still looking very pleased with herself. "He's a divinity student who volunteers there from time to time. I was told that he seemed quite smitten with Miss Blackwell and awfully anxious to help her."

"And was she smitten with him?"

"That wasn't mentioned. In fact, her devotion to her fiancé was stressed."

"Has he been seen there since that day?"

"Apparently he has gone home to his family for the summer. They live in Newport, Rhode Island."

"You have his name?"

"We do," Sid said. "You see what wonderfully efficient sleuths we are."

"And since my family has numerous acquaintances in Newport, it should be easy enough to find his address," Gus added. "You'll just have to make us partners in your firm, Molly."

"In fact, we're all ready to go out to Newport and interrogate the suspect," Sid said.

"Oh, I'm sure that won't be necessary," I said hastily, imagining the stir it would cause if Sid and Gus started interrogating.

"You've done marvelously," I added. "And you've saved me precious time when I have not a moment to spare."

"So you're no closer to rescuing Daniel?"

I sighed. "I wish I could say yes, but that's just not so. I have leads, I have theories, but nothing that's a clear indication of the path I should follow."

"What about the murdered prostitutes?" Sid asked. "Did Dr. Birnbaum actually take you along with him to the morgue?"

"The officers in charge wouldn't let him," I said. I had been going to tell them of my adventure with Sabella Goodwin when Gus said firmly, "And quite right, too. What good could possibly come from going to a place like that?"

"And it can have no bearing on Daniel's case, Molly," Sid added.

"I'm inclined to agree with you," I said. "My latest theory is that the commissioner of police himself is the one I should be investigating. He is the only one who could have arranged with ease to come upon Daniel at exactly the incriminating moment. And he plans to visit The Tombs this week. Arabella suggested the guilty party would want to gloat over his victim."

"Do you have any idea what Daniel might have done to upset the police commissioner? I'd have thought they should be on the same side," Gus said.

"Daniel himself has no idea," I said. "I'm going to the *Herald* tomorrow to look through old newspaper articles. Maybe some sordid aspect of Mr. Partridge's past will come to light." I sank my head into my arms. "I wish Paddy Riley hadn't been killed. I could have learned so much from him. I'm a hopeless detective, you know. I just stumble upon things, more by luck than by skill."

"I know this case means a lot to you, Molly, but Sid and I feel you've been overdoing it lately," Gus said with concern. "You're not looking well. Why can't you rest for a couple of days? You'll feel so much better."

I should tell them the truth now. I tried to form the words in my head, but I couldn't. Then it occurred to me that by tomorrow Mrs. Goodwin might have set up an appointment for me with a certain lady. Whether I would have the nerve to keep that appointment, I really couldn't say.

"I'll take a rest soon, I promise you," I said.

TWENTY-FOUR

The next morning I woke to gray skies and steady, un-relenting rain. Hardly the sort of day to be out and about. Not that I felt much like being out and about anyway. My day started with a bout of sickness that left me feeling hollow and frail. And I didn't want to miss Mrs. Goodwin's visit. I hoped she'd stop by on her way home after her night shift. I felt excited and anxious at the same time, as if I was waiting for the results of an important examination. Don't get your hopes up, I told myself. Perhaps the woman will want too much money. Perhaps she'll refuse to see me. And if she agreed? My heart started racing at the thought of it. Was there any sin worse in the universe than killing your own child? And yet what sort of life would it be for the both of us? How could I go through with this on my own?

By midday Mrs. Goodwin still had not appeared. The rain had subsided to a light drizzle, and I paced impatiently. At last I could stand it no longer. If she hadn't come by now, then surely she had gone home after her long night vigil and was now sleeping. I wouldn't be likely to see her before this evening. I should go to the *Herald* and see what the fearsome Miss Pritchard had uncovered for me.

I was just turning onto Sixth Avenue when I saw a young policeman heading my way with purposeful strides and recognized him as Constable Byrne. Hope surged that he had come to escort me to Daniel again. He tipped his helmet as he approached me.

"Miss Murphy," he said, "I've been asked to deliver this note to you."

"Is it from Captain Sullivan?" I asked.

"I'm afraid it isn't. It's from one of our matrons. She apologized for not coming herself, but she was exhausted after a night in the rain and felt that she had to get some rest if she wasn't to come down with a dreadful chill."

He handed me the envelope.

"Thank you," I said. "I appreciate it. So you haven't had a chance to see Captain Sullivan again?"

"No, miss."

"And you've heard nothing? What are they saying about him at headquarters?"

"Nothing, miss. They're saying nothing. It's as if he never existed."

"And what about this investigation that Quigley and McIver are leading? Is there any talk at the station about that? Any hunches? Any suspects?"

He grinned. "If there are, miss, they don't share them with me. I'm just a constable on the beat. But I was assigned to that patrol myself the other day. Dreary work standing on a street corner and nothing happening."

"You didn't see any suspicious vehicles then?"

"What kind of vehicles?"

"Carriages? Large and presumably enclosed carriages?"

"Oh no, miss. Nothing like that. In fact, the only vehicles to pass me during one twelve-hour shift were delivery drays, a couple of hansoms, and one automobile. That was about it. Why do you ask?"

"Just curious," I said and declined to go into details. Maybe it would be better if nobody at police headquarters knew I was following this case.

He shifted uneasily from foot to foot. "Well, I best be getting back then, miss. I've work to do."

"Of course you have, Constable. Thank you again."

He nodded, then turned on his heel. I couldn't help wondering if I should have tipped him. But since I was currently more of a pauper than he, it seemed a strange thought. The moment he was gone, I tore open the envelope.

My dear Miss Murphy,

I must apologize for not delivering this in person, but I am soaked to the skin after a night of observation on the Lower East Side and can only think of getting home to dry clothes and a warm bed. Another fruitless night, I'm afraid. But at least no more bodies. The advertisement should have run in this morning's papers, so we'll see what turns up.

And on the other matter we discussed. My friend's name is Mrs. Rose Butler. I told her about you and she says she'd be delighted for you to pay her a call this evening, around eight, if that is convenient. She wouldn't want you going home alone in the dark and would expect you to stay the night at least. You'll find her a most competent and organized person. Her address is 231 Allen Street.

I do hope you take her up on her kind invitation. You'll find the visit most worthwhile. But I should warn you to be on your guard throughout the Lower East Side after dark. Detective Quigley's latest theory is that the murderer may ride around in his carriage or wagon or even automobile, looking for likely girls to snatch off the streets. He may then take them to a house nearby or may even pull into a convenient alleyway and assault them there, in the vehicle. So please be alert, and at the first sign of danger run, scream, and draw attention to yourself.

Believe me when I say that I wish you all the best and that your health should improve in the near future.

I remain yours truly,
Sabella Goodwin

I noted the clever way the letter was phrased so that there was nothing incriminating in it. So Mrs. Goodwin suspected that other eyes might read her letter, did she? That was interesting. I found myself trembling. "Mrs. Rose Butler, 231 Allen Street." I said the words out loud, like a chant, over and over. And she was prepared to see me tonight, if I dared to go through with it. My hand strayed involuntarily to my stomach. Eight o'clock, I thought. That gave me almost eight hours to think about it. All the more reason to throw myself into my work so fully that I didn't have time to think.

I climbed the steps to the El station and headed back to Herald Square. Today I had taken rather more trouble with my appearance, wearing my business suit and tying my hair back with a black bow. The lady in archives seemed to approve, and she nodded at me in almost kindly fashion.

"I have located a good sampling of material for you on the commissioner. What a fine man. I'm glad he is to be honored."

She indicated that I should sit at a long, mahogany table, then produced a box of typewritten sheets, yellowed newspaper clippings, photographs, and etchings. I sat under one of the ceiling lamps and started to work my way through. Mr. Partridge, it seemed, had led an exemplary life. He had been commended for his hard work and devotion to duty by Theodore Roosevelt, when the latter had been commissioner of police himself. He had served in various other boring city departments—ways and means and public works—nothing glamorous and certainly nothing controversial. A short biography detailed his background as son of an Episcopal minister, his education at Princeton, his time as a lawyer, his marriage to a highly suitable young woman, and the birth of four daughters.

I started to flip through the pictures. There were photographs of Mr. Partridge shaking hands with Teddy Roosevelt, with the mayor, with the chief of police upon his appointment. Then I found myself looking at a photograph that made my pulse quicken. The headline stated: CITY BUSINESSMEN WELCOME IRISH CHAMPION TO NEW YORK. And several smiling men stood around a handsome racehorse. At last I had my link. Mr. Partridge was part of the syndicate that owned the winning horse that day at Brighton Race Track.

For a moment I was jubilant. I've got you now, John Partridge, I thought. Then I found myself rethinking things. So John Partridge was part owner of a horse that had won on that fateful day. Didn't that just make it a lucky coincidence? The man I had spoken to at the racetrack hadn't thought that any horse had a clear chance of winning with the favorite removed. And even if the worst had happened, even if Mr. Partridge's syndicate had been responsible for doping the favorite, they would have made sure that they could not be directly connected to the crime. They were, after all, powerful city businessmen. Such men have underlings to do their dirty work. And even if Daniel had discovered that Partridge was part of the syndicate, was it really so damning?

I started to write these thoughts in a letter to Daniel, then thought better of it. It was quite possible that all his mail would be read by unfriendly eyes. I certainly didn't want to make things worse for him. I'd have to approach his lawyer and see if we could arrange another visit to The Tombs. And I still hadn't found out if someone was paying his lawyer to lose the case. . . . Once again I felt overwhelmed by everything that lay ahead of me. Even if I proved that Mr. Partridge was privy to horse doping, I couldn't prove that he had planted the money on Daniel himself. It wouldn't release Daniel from prison.

It looked as if I had no choice but to go through with tonight's appointment after all.

TWENTY-FIVE

I arrived home by three o'clock. That left five more hours to brood. I looked out of my upstairs window across the street to Number Nine. I longed to have company, but I knew I couldn't. Sid and Gus were so perceptive of my moods. They would ask me what was wrong, and I might well break down and tell them. Not that they would judge me, but I couldn't do it. So I penned a note to Mr. Atkinson, the lawyer, requesting a chance to meet with Daniel as soon as possible to report on newly surfaced information that might help his case. If Atkinson was a spy for someone, then that might just cause a stir.

There was no sign of Sid or Gus all afternoon. I half hoped that Mrs. Goodwin would stop by in person. God knows I could have used a friendly face and a chat because I was definitely going through last-minute jitters about what lay ahead of me. Seven-thirty came at last and I set out. I had packed a nightgown, hairbrush, and face flannel in a bag, just as if I was going for a visit to a friend. I had also brought my checkbook with me. I had no idea how much she would want or how much I could really afford. There was still some of Paddy Riley's money left, but it was dwindling fast with the lease on the house, at least through October, and no money coming in. I also had no idea whether I would actually have the nerve to go through with it when I reached Mrs. Butler's house.

It was still raining and I held an umbrella over me as I

splashed through puddles along Fourth Street to First Avenue. I knew that First turned into Allen Street on the other side of Houston. I suppose I could have taken a horse-drawn bus to get me across town, but they were generally slower than walking. Besides, the cold water splashing up around my ankles kept me tied to reality at this moment when everything else felt decidedly unreal. I don't think I had ever felt more alone, not even when I fled from Ireland. Not even when I was thrown out of Nuala's house after I first arrived in Manhattan.

As I crossed from West to East, the streets became more crowded, and as I turned south on First, it became positively clogged with humanity. The street itself under the El was lined with pushcarts trying to avoid the worst of the rain, and the pedestrians were channeled along a narrow path between storefronts and carts, accosted from both sides by merchants shouting their wares. At any other time I would have enjoyed the lively scene. Now the crowd was just an added nuisance through which I had to negotiate.

I should have taken the El after all because it was a long way down Allen Street. I crossed Rivington, then Delancey. At Rivington I looked longingly toward the East River to where Jacob lived. How long ago it seemed that I had hurried down to his studio by the river and he had welcomed me with a glass of tea. Then life had been safe and relatively uncomplicated. If only I had felt differently about him. What a pity I wasn't willing to settle for security over love.

Still, there was no point in brooding over what might have been. I was trapped in the present, and there was no way out but through 231 Allen Street. It was a tall tenement like any other, rising five or six floors high. The ground floor was occupied by a tailor shop. Gaslights were on and someone was still working. I went in and asked for Mrs. Butler. From the way the man looked at me, I guessed he knew what Mrs. Butler did as a profession.

"Fourth Floor, at the front." He almost spat out the words.

This is how you would be treated every day of your life with an illegitimate child, I reminded myself and started to climb the stairs. There were raised voices on the second floor—a woman and man yelling at each other in what sounded like Italian. If I could hear so easily through this closed door, what would happen if I cried out later? I hadn't thought about the pain that might be involved. Now I did. I had seen women in childbirth screaming and crying and imploring the Blessed Virgin to take them out of their misery. I hesitated and took the next flight more slowly. I couldn't turn back now, could I? After all, Mrs. Goodwin was risking her own career by getting involved on my behalf with something so horribly illegal.

I took a couple of deep breaths to pluck up courage, climbed the last flight of stairs, and knocked on the door. The woman who opened it could have been anybody's maiden aunt. She was slight, refined looking, dressed in a gray dress with wider skirts than are fashionable nowadays. Her hair was matching gray, and she wore a light net over it. She would seem, to anybody she met, to be a gentlewoman who had known better days and now possibly eked out a living as a seamstress.

"Mrs. Butler?" I asked.

"Miss Murphy?" She smiled. "Come in, dear. I'm expecting you. I've made some iced tea."

The door closed behind us.

"It was brave of you to come." She motioned to a Queen Anne–style armchair. The furniture was old and shabby but had been good once. I sat. She poured iced tea into a tall glass and handed it to me. "Now before we go any further, I must make sure that your condition is what you think it is. No sense in going to a lot of trouble for nothing, is there?" She smiled sweetly. I sipped iced tea.

"Now, what makes you think that you are having a baby? You have had a recent—encounter with a young man?"

I nodded.

"And you've missed your monthly, have you?"

I nodded again.

"Any other symptoms?"

"I'm horribly sick all the time, and dizzy, and I passed out."

"And your breasts—are they tender?"

I put my hand to one and realized that it did feel tender to the touch.

"Oh dear," she said. "Then I don't think there's much doubt. I'll double-check before I do the operation, of course, but I think we can safely say that we are sure." She took a drink from her own glass. "And there's no chance the young man can marry you? I always think of this as a last resort, seeing that it's not without its own risks. I haven't lost a girl for many years, you understand, but there is always the risk of bleeding and infection."

"The young man is in no position to marry me at the moment," I said. "He is in jail. He may be there for a while."

"Oh dear. That's not good. Still, you're better off not being saddled to a criminal type. Trust me. Mr. Butler was the same—always into some illegal scheme or other. Always hoping to get rich quick, and of course he never did."

"What happened to him?"

"Same as your sweetheart, my dear. Twenty years in Sing Sing and me constantly running away from his creditors. We had a nice house once. Still, you didn't come here to hear my problems. Now this is my usual procedure on such occasions. I've found it works successfully for most girls: a good-sized glass of gin to start with. That not only makes you less anxious, but it will dull the pain later—and it can help get things started. It's not for nothing that it's known as Mother's Ruin." The smile this time was quite wicked. "And when the gin starts to work, a hot bath, hot as you can take it, plus a mixture of my own that seems to work wonders with starting contractions. Then I go in and open things up. Not very pleasant but it will be all over by morning and you can go home. All right?"

I nodded again. It was hard to speak.

"And my friend Mrs. Goodwin told me your financial circumstances, so shall we just say twenty dollars will take care of my fee? I never ask a girl to pay beyond her means."

"That's good of you."

"Don't worry. I make up for it with the society ladies."

Again there was that wicked smile. "I make them pay through the nose for my silence."

I got out my checkbook. She looked horrified, and then she laughed. "Oh no, honey. Cash only, I'm afraid. I wouldn't be stupid enough to leave a trail for the police to follow. I have no wish to join my husband behind bars."

"I didn't bring cash. I can go to the bank and withdraw the money in the morning."

"Of course you can. You're a friend of Mrs. Goodwin. I trust you. So let's get started, shall we? No sense in waiting and brooding about it too long, I always say."

She opened an ornate mahogany cabinet and took out a gin bottle. Then she poured a generous tumblerful.

"Get that down you," she said. "You'll feel better. You know what they say, don't you? Lots and lots, no tiny tots."

I gave a nervous laugh at the double meaning. She watched me as I swallowed the gin. I had never drunk spirits apart from a brandy when I had been taken ill once. It was like firewater. I coughed and my eyes streamed.

"Small sips," she said. "Don't try to knock it back at once if you aren't a hardened drinker."

I sipped, coughed, and sipped some more. It was not un- pleasant tasting but strange—like no flavor I had encoun- tered before. By the time I had finished, I was already feeling the first effects. Mrs. Butler got to her feet. "I'll leave you for a while until it really starts working. You won't want to sit and make polite conversation at a time like this. I've a copy of *Ladies' Home Journal* for you to read, and I'll go and make sure the water is hot for your bath."

She slipped through the door beside the liquor cabinet. I opened the magazine and tried to make my mind concen- trate. There were articles on using oatmeal and cucumber to freshen the complexion, one on cleaning brassware, and a full-page drawing of a Gibson Girl. My head started to feel strange. The Gibson Girl was blurring. I turned a page and found myself looking at the "Good Mother's Guide to Rais- ing Healthy Children." The picture showed a young woman bouncing a chubby baby on her knee. The baby had big dark eyes, a mass of unruly dark curls, and was screaming with delight.

Suddenly I flung down the magazine and got to my feet. What was I thinking? It had nothing to do with my Irish Catholic upbringing or with hellfire. It didn't matter that my life ahead looked bleak or that I had no way to provide for a child. It wasn't even that I was scared. This was my baby we were talking about—mine and Daniel's. If it lived it would look just like that chubby darling on the page, and I was about to kill it before it ever had a chance to laugh or be cuddled or to know what life was about. My heart was hammering so hard that I could scarcely move. I tiptoed across the room and picked up my purse from the table and my umbrella from the stand. I made it to the front door. I held my breath as it opened. I slipped out and closed it silently behind me. Then I positively ran down the stairs and out into the night.

The rain had picked up again as I came out onto the street. That glass of gin was already starting to affect me and I clutched at railings, trying to get my balance. When I closed my eyes, the world swung around. This was terrible. I was already showing signs of being drunk, and I had to make it home somehow. I certainly didn't want to appear drunk on the El, to say nothing of running the risk of falling off the platform! And I didn't have enough money in my purse to cover a cab fare, so I'd just have to walk. At least walking in the rain would help sober me up.

My driving wish was to get away from Allen Street as quickly as possible, which wasn't easy, given that my feet didn't want to obey me. I turned left onto the first cross street and struck out in the direction of the Bowery. I'd gone a couple of blocks when it really hit me what I had just done.

"You've burned your bridges now, my girl," I said to myself severely. "Letting your stupid heart rule your head again. Now what do you think you're going to do?"

"Muddle through as always," came the reply. I reached the Bowery and decided to keep on going to Broadway, where I could catch the trolley, if I was in any condition to climb aboard. As I approached the next intersection, I came upon a commotion. A crowd was gathered, half in the street, half on the sidewalk.

"Now move along, move along," I heard a voice shouting and saw a policeman trying to disperse them.

An ambulance came galloping up, bell clanging, from the direction of Broadway.

"Did anyone see what happened?" a voice was shouting. I looked at the speaker and saw that it was Detective Quigley. Then I glanced up at the building on the corner and saw the street name. Elizabeth Street. It must be another victim. In spite of my unsteadiness, I wormed my way into the crowd. A woman's body, dressed all in black, was lying huddled in the gutter, while water and debris from the storm sloshed around it.

"It came so fast, it was all over in a second," a woman said. "I barely had a chance to pull my little girl out of the way."

"What kind of vehicle was it?" Quigley asked.

"I just heard the racket as it came around the corner, and I saw those galloping hooves," the woman said. "He was driving like a madman. The poor thing stood no chance. I believe it almost came up on the sidewalk."

"Maybe it was a runaway horse," someone else suggested.

"It was almost as if it was coming after her," a man commented.

"I heard the scream and saw this big black shape disappearing into the night," someone else ventured.

"No signs or anything on the wagon?" Quigley asked. "Nothing to give away what it was? A private carriage, do you think?"

"Could have been," the first woman answered. "I tell you, I was more concerned about my little girl. It missed her by inches."

"Make way, now," a voice commanded, and the ambulance boys pushed through the crowd, carrying a collapsible stretcher.

"What happened?" one of them asked, squatting cautiously beside the body.

"She was run down by a wagon," someone volunteered. "It came right at her and didn't stop."

"Is she still alive or is this another morgue job?"

"I felt a pulse," Quigley said. "Get her to the hospital, as quick as you can, for God's sake."

"Easy now, Bert. She could have any number of broken bones," the first ambulance man said. They bent to lift the frail form from the street. I didn't want to see if her face was disfigured like the rest, but I couldn't stop myself from looking. She was wearing a black bonnet and as they turned her around her arm flopped over like a rag doll's. I gasped in horror. It was Mrs. Goodwin.

"Come along. Step back, please. Let them through. Go on. Go to your homes." A constable forced the crowd back, his billy club in his hand.

The stretcher was put into the back of the ambulance. The doors closed and it galloped off into the night.

TWENTY-SIX

I must follow it, I thought, and broke into a shambling run.
My legs refused to obey me. I tripped, fell, and the smell
of dog and refuse came up to meet me. As I sat there, with
the world swaying violently, I realized that I was in no state
to go to any hospital. They certainly wouldn't let me see
Sabella Goodwin, and I ran the risk of being arrested for in-
toxication. I had no wish to spend a night in a Jefferson Market jail cell ever again. I just prayed she was still alive, and
that someone was with her if she imparted a dying message.
Because she must have discovered something that made the
East Side Ripper scared enough to take the appalling risk of
running her down on a city street, with other people as witnesses. At least now we knew that the theory about the large,
dark vehicle had been correct. Maybe she had spotted such a
vehicle earlier and gone to investigate. Perhaps she could
now identify it.

Somehow I made it home. I let myself into my house and
crawled up to bed. I felt terrible—not just because of the effect of the gin, but because I had lost a woman I had come to
admire enormously. More than that—my one ally had been
taken from me. How could I possibly go on with this investigation alone? Then all at once I sat up in bed. It wasn't my
case, was it? Nothing we had discovered pointed to any connection between the East Side Ripper and Daniel's imprisonment. He admitted he had just been assigned to take over
with little to go on. And now with John Partridge's link to

the racing syndicate, I even had a motive for him to have plotted Daniel's arrest. So it didn't matter if I was off the Ripper investigation. I felt relief but also annoyance. I didn't like to leave things half-finished. Still, there wasn't much I could do about it anymore. Quigley and McIver were hardly likely to share their findings with me.

About an hour after I'd gone to bed I woke from a half doze to a bad attack of cramps. I lay, hugging my knees to me as my insides were wracked with pain. At first I wondered if it was something I had eaten until I remembered the gin. Mrs. Butler had made me drink it for this very purpose. Mother's Ruin, she had called it and given me a significant wink. I got up and paced around, hugging my arms to my stomach. Did this mean I was going to lose the baby, after all? I knew now with complete certainty that I didn't want that to happen.

Please no, I prayed silently.

I went downstairs and made myself a cup of tea, then sat at the kitchen table, sipping the hot liquid and hoping for the cramps to subside. After a while they did seem to lessen in strength. I crawled back to bed and lay curled up in a ball. Eventually I must have drifted off to sleep.

When I awoke bright sun was streaming in through my bedroom window. Birds were chirping. I sat up and realized I had survived the night. The cramps had gone. My baby was still there. I felt like a new person. I had literally been given a new lease on life. I jumped up and almost ran down the stairs. I snatched a quick breakfast before making my way to Saint Vincent's Hospital.

The sister at the reception desk was not the same one I had met before. She looked at me with horror.

"Visiting hours are posted on the wall over there," she said. "We certainly don't allow strangers tramping all over the hospital at seven in the morning."

"But this is important. A lady was brought in here last night by ambulance. Mrs. Goodwin."

"Ah yes, a terrible accident."

"It was no accident, she was run down," I said. "She's a police matron, and she was on an important case."

"And what is your interest in this?" she asked starchily. "Are you some kind of reporter?"

"I'm—" I was about to say I was on the case with her, then I changed my mind. "I'm her sister," I said. "I got word that she had been struck by a runaway horse, but they couldn't tell me any more."

She looked at me with those piercing nun's eyes that have made any number of young children blurt out sins. "Her sister, are you? I understand that she survived the night but remains unconscious."

"Is there any chance I could see her? It might bring her back to consciousness to hear my voice."

As I said this I was stricken with conscience. We had never discussed Mrs. Goodwin's family situation. It was very possible that she had children who should be at her bedside, not a woman she hardly knew. Their voices might bring her back to the world of the living. Mine certainly wouldn't.

It was of no matter. The sister shook her head. "She's allowed no visitors until further notice. Doctor's orders. Absolute peace and quiet, that's what he said. I told the same to the policemen who came last night."

"If I come back at visiting time, I'll be allowed to see her then?" I asked.

"If she is allowed visitors and has regained consciousness."

She made a motion to go back to her paperwork. I still hovered, reluctant to take no for an answer. She was still alive, that was good news. "And which ward is she in?"

Those eyes were fixed on me again in an innocent stare, but she understood all right. She was thinking that I'd find my way there the moment her back was turned, which had obviously been my intention. "She's under observation at the moment. I can't say which ward she'll be transferred to if and when she awakes."

I stood looking down the long, white-tiled hallway. Nuns floated up and down it in pairs, gliding almost like ghosts.

There were too many of them for me to slip past unnoticed. I'll have to find myself a nun's outfit, I thought, as I admitted defeat. I remembered Paddy Riley's complete wardrobe of disguises. I needed to start my own.

Back home I experimented with bedsheets and my one good tablecloth, but I couldn't come up with anything that looked like a believable Sister of Charity. If only they wore simple veils, like the nuns at Saint Finbar's at home, I might have gotten away with it. Now all I could do was wait.

The midday post brought a letter from J. Atkinson, attorney at law. He assured me that Daniel's case was progressing nicely. However, if I had come up with new information that might be pertinent to the case, would I please drop him a note to share it with him. He didn't think an interview with Daniel himself could be arranged at this time without jeopardizing his own position and responsibility.

"Damn you," I muttered. Not words I'd have said out loud to anyone, but they felt good in my own kitchen. If he really was working for Daniel's enemy, wouldn't he just love me to deliver everything I'd found out so that he could report it to his boss. If I'd found out anything important, it would then be suppressed. If I had found out anything important, my own life could be in jeopardy.

Wait a second, I thought. Such drama! What had I found out? Not much, except that Mr. Partridge might have been part of the racehorse-doping scandal and he was visiting The Tombs in the near future. Interesting facts, but to be shared with Daniel alone. I wasn't sure how I was going to do that, if Atkinson wouldn't get me into The Tombs, and it wasn't visiting day until the end of the month.

The other interesting fact to be shared with Daniel was that someone had tried to kill Mrs. Goodwin and might well have succeeded. That was surely important, but the police were already onto it, questioning witnesses even as I arrived on the scene.

I did my household chores, which had been neglected for the past week, hung out a line of laundry in the backyard, and had some of my homemade soup. I felt better today and had an appetite. One small blessing to be enjoyed. Then the moment I had washed up, I went back to Saint Vincent's. I was going to get in to see Mrs. Goodwin this afternoon by hook or by crook.

On my way I stopped off at the Jefferson Market and bought a bunch of roses. As I approached the hospital, I saw two policemen emerging and recognized one of them. His face lit up in recognition when he saw me. "Why, Miss Murphy. What a lucky coincidence. I've been wanting to contact you for the past few days, but the wife had mislaid your new address."

"Have you been to see Mrs. Goodwin?" I asked. "Is there any news on her condition?"

"You know Mrs. Goodwin, do you?"

"I do. She's a friend."

"And a fine woman," he said, his big face a mask of grief. "Her late husband Whitey and I started on the force at the same time. What a tragic accident."

I nodded and thought it wiser to feign ignorance of the true circumstances.

"And how is her condition?" I asked.

"I'm told she's holding her own but still hasn't regained consciousness, I'm afraid."

"I'm on my way to visit her now," I said. "Do you think they'll let me in?"

"You can tell them that Sergeant O'Hallaran gave you permission, if you think it will help," he said. "There's a constable stationed at her door."

"I appreciate it. I tried to see her this morning, but they wouldn't let me."

"They want her to have complete peace and quiet," he said, "so they're forbidding most visitors. Now tell me, is there any news on Captain Sullivan?"

"Nothing good," I said, conscious of the other policeman standing beside him and not wanting any snippets of gossip to get back to headquarters. "I'm still praying."

"You wanted to know who was assigned to take over the cases Captain Sullivan was working on," he said.

"I've found out some of it for myself," I said. "Detectives Quigley and McIver are in charge of the East Side Ripper case. They were in charge of it before Captain Sullivan was ordered to take over, so I gather. And about the other case—the racehorse-doping—"

"The same pair," he said. "They were Sullivan's protégés. He thought highly of them. Young officers with a bright future. I've no doubt they'll do a fine job on both cases—as good as the captain himself could have done."

"And the men assigned to escort the police commissioner that day he saw Daniel?"

"Officers whose normal beats were in that area. McCaffrey, Doyle were with him for the first part and then Jones and Honeywell took over."

"And who designed the route?"

"I understand the commissioner just wandered where he wanted. He asked to see the Eastman headquarters and Walhalla Hall and where the bodies of the murdered girls had been found. That's about it."

And somehow he knew when Bugsy was going to meet Daniel, I thought. Or somebody knew. Or somebody had bribed one of those four men. At least I had four new names to check out now, something new to work on.

"Thank you, Sergeant," I said. "I'd better get in to see Mrs. Goodwin now."

"If she comes to, tell her we were here. O'Hallaran and Hendricks and we're wishing her all the best," he said.

"I will."

The other officer nodded to me. O'Hallaran waved and they continued on their way, while I went into the hospital.

"Visiting hours are not for another twenty minutes," said the same woman at the reception desk, "and if you've come to see Mrs. Goodwin, I'm afraid . . ."

"Sergeant O'Hallaran said that he has given me permission to be with her," I said, trying not to look triumphant.

"I see." She sniffed her disapproval. "She's in Mercy Ward. That's up the stairs and along to the end of the hallway."

I climbed the stairs and made my way past one ward after

another until I came to the end. I saw immediately which room Mrs. Goodwin was in. A young constable stood outside the door. I repeated the message from Sergeant O'Hallaran and added that I was her sister for emphasis. I wasn't going to risk being turned away this time.

"She has someone with her right now," he said, "but I suppose it's all right for you to go in if you're her sister."

He opened the door for me. It was a big ward, but the area close to the door had been curtained off with screens so that Mrs. Goodwin was in a private tent. As I came in a man was standing by the bed, leaning over the patient. He straightened up as he heard me approaching and turned around. It was Detective Quigley.

"What are you doing in here? They were told no visitors." He frowned as he tried to place me and couldn't right away.

"I'm a particular friend of Mrs. Goodwin's," I said, not daring to use the sister lie with him, "and Sergeant O'Hallaran said he was sure it would be all right and might do her good to see me."

"Very well." He was not looking pleased. "Although as you can see, she's still unconscious. I've been with her most of the morning, hoping she'd regain consciousness and be able to tell us something. When you came in, she groaned in her sleep, and I thought she was trying to mutter a word."

"It's really tragic," I said. "I admire her greatly."

I moved past him until I was standing beside the bed. Sabella Goodwin lay, pale and white as the sheets around her. There was a bandage around her head and ugly bruises along one side of her face. It was hard to tell if she was alive or dead.

I perched on the edge of her bed and took her hand. "Sabella—Mrs. Goodwin? It's Molly. Molly Murphy, your partner in crime. I need you to get well quickly." I said it brightly although her hand felt cold and limp, as if she was already dead.

"Just a minute," Quigley said sharply. "I remember now. Last time I saw you was with that German doctor. He introduced you as fraulein something. You're not German. What's the big idea?"

I tried to do some pretty fast thinking, wondering how much he should be told, seeing that we were essentially on the same team. "I'm sorry," I said. "I attached myself to Dr. Birnbaum that morning against his will, because I was—interested in this particular case. My friend Mrs. Goodwin told me about it, and I was trying to do what I could to help."

"Why?" He eyed me coldly. "Mere curiosity?"

Should I tell him the truth about Daniel? After all, Daniel had been his mentor until recently. I decided against it, not knowing what unfriendly ears were waiting back at police headquarters, or even whether Quigley himself was secretly glad that Daniel was out of the way.

I decided on another lie. "I'm—something of a student of psychology myself. I was trying to give Mrs. Goodwin some insights that might help her with the case. I had discussed it with Dr. Birnbaum."

"Mrs. Goodwin's assignment was limited to patrolling the streets and keeping an eye open for suspicious activity," he said. "She is not a detective. Neither are you. Whatever she has been doing has already almost cost her her life. And who knows if your bumbling amateurism has already hindered the investigation? I suggest you both stay out of our way and leave the work to trained professionals."

I wasn't sure how to answer that but was spared by the arrival of a sister.

"What's going on in here?" she demanded. "I thought I heard raised voices. My orders were that this patient was to be kept absolutely quiet. No visitors at all. I'm not sure who you are, but be off with you."

"I am the police officer in charge of the case Mrs. Goodwin was working on," Quigley said frostily. "It is important that I speak with her as soon as she wakes."

"She's not likely to wake for some time," the sister said. "She was in a lot of pain last night and is heavily sedated with morphine."

"Was she badly injured?" I asked.

"And who might you be?"

"A close friend," I said. I couldn't go back to the sister lie with Quigley standing there. "One who was supposed to meet her last night and came upon her too late."

"Well, she's not out of the woods yet," the sister said, looking more kindly at me than she had at Quigley, "but she's been extremely lucky. Apart from the head wound, which was fortunately only superficial, she's got a couple of cracked ribs, some horrible bruising, but it seems she managed to avoid the horse's hooves, which would surely have been fatal. With any luck she'll be up and walking in a few days, praise the good Lord."

"Oh, that is good news," I said.

"But only if she gets her rest. Now out, both of you."

"You'll let me know when she regains consciousness?" Quigley asked. "It is very important to the case we're working on."

"I'll let you know when she's well enough to talk," the sister said. She attempted to drive us out before her as if we were a flock of ducks.

I hesitated. "I brought her some flowers," I said. "Would there be some kind of vase somewhere to put them in?"

"How lovely." She leaned toward the roses and sniffed. "Reminds me of my girlhood. My father always grew yellow roses. Yes, there should be some jam jars in a cupboard. Go to the next ward and ask one of the sisters. Tell her Sister Mercy sent you."

I thanked her and soon had my jam jar filled with water. Not the most attractive vase in the world, but it suited quite fine. It also gave me an excuse to go back into the room to put them on the bedside table. There was no sign of Sister Mercy, and I was just putting the jar down when Mrs. Goodwin gave a little sigh. I turned to her, and her eyes were open.

"You're awake, that's wonderful," I said.

She stared at me, trying to place me, and I feared she might have lost all memory of who I was.

Then she gave a faint smile. "Molly Murphy. What are you doing here?"

"I came to see you," I said. "How are you feeling?"

"Just fine until the morphine wears off," she said. "Before

that I felt as if a herd of elephants had been dancing all over me. I was almost run over, wasn't I?"

"You certainly were. The nurse says you were very lucky. You've got away with a couple of cracked ribs. The horse's hooves must have missed you entirely."

"Luckily I heard it coming, and I was able to fling myself aside at the last moment," she said. "I think some part of the carriage or the shafts must have struck me in the side."

"Were you able to see what kind of carriage it was?"

"It all happened so fast," she said, "and it was dark and raining. And the vehicle itself was dark. That's all I remember."

"Was someone deliberately trying to run you down, do you think?"

"Oh, absolutely. The horse was at a full gallop and coming straight for me. The funny thing was that just before it happened one of the local urchins came and told me there was something odd in the gutter on the corner of Elizabeth Street, and that I should come and take a look at it. I found it where he said. It looked like a piece of red satin, halfway down a drain. I was just bending down to examine it when the horse came flying at me."

"So you were lured there, and the man was waiting for you?"

"It seems that way."

"Why? What had you discovered since we parted?"

"I'm darned if I know," she said. She closed her eyes and sighed. "Maybe it will come to me, but as of now, I can't think of anything. Of course my head's still fuzzy with that morphine."

"Do you think you could find the child again, and we could discover who sent him?"

Sister Mercy appeared in the doorway. "I thought I sent you home," she said severely to me.

"I was just putting the flowers on her bedside table when she woke up," I said. "Isn't that wonderful news?"

"It certainly is. However, if you want her to make a speedy recovery, you'll leave her to rest in peace."

"I will," I said. "I'm just going. Is there anything I can do for you?"

"You could fetch my mail for me," she said, after a moment's thought. "We may have had a reply to my advertisement by now."

"I'll do that right away," I said. "What is your address?"

"It's 429 East Seventh, just past Tompkins Square. It's a brownstone with two bay trees in pots outside."

"That's easy enough," I said. "Do you have the key?"

"There's one in my purse, wherever that is." She tried to look around, then sank back with a sigh of pain. "Why don't you ask my neighbor for the spare? Mrs. Oliver. At 431. She keeps a spare, just in case."

"All right. And what else can I do for you? Are there any family members you'd like me to contact—anyone who should know you're in the hospital?"

She shook her head sadly. "No one at all, my dear. I have a sister in Ohio, but apart from that, nobody anymore. My husband was killed, as you know, and I lost my only child to diphtheria."

She gave me a questioning glance and I could tell what she was asking. Was I still pregnant?

"I did visit your friend Mrs. Butler last night," I said, "but I changed my mind."

"Ah." She closed her eyes and grimaced. "The painkiller is wearing off, I see. I feel literally as if I was kicked by a mule."

"I'll send for the doctor," Sister Mercy said. "He'll give you another dose, and I know he plans to strap your ribs today, which will help with the breathing."

"I'll be back tomorrow then," I said, touching her hand gently. "Is there anything I can bring you? Some grapes? Oranges?"

She patted my hand. "You just take care of yourself," she said. "Stay away from the Lower East Side."

"I will."

"Promise me you won't go there alone."

"Very well. I promise."

As I left I heard Sister Mercy saying, "A nice young friend you've got there, Mrs. Goodwin. A real saintly girl."

If she only knew, I thought, with a grim smile.

TWENTY-SEVEN

I decided to wait until the afternoon mail delivery before I
went to Mrs. Goodwin's house. I'd have liked to question
the constables who escorted Mr. Partridge on that fateful
day, but I had promised Mrs. Goodwin I wouldn't go to that
part of town alone. Given her current precarious condition, I
couldn't break a promise right now. Besides, I suspected that
Mr. Partridge had chosen the route with one purpose in
mind. And now he was planning a visit to The Tombs—was
that just to gloat over Daniel, or did he have a more sinister
purpose in mind there, too?

I looked up at the clock on the mantel. I didn't really have
time to visit Mr. Atkinson and convince him to take me to
The Tombs today if I wanted to be at Mrs. Goodwin's house
in time for the afternoon mail. I'd have to leave that for tomorrow morning. A stiff breeze was blowing off the Hudson, and I retrieved my line of dry laundry before starting
the long walk across town, past Cooper Union to Tompkins
Square. The rain, followed by the breeze, had brought the
temperature down and the walk was not at all unpleasant. It
gave me time to think. I've always found walking was great
for putting my thoughts in order.

I was anxious to see if any answers to the advertisement
had come in the mail yet. If the dead girl we saw yesterday
was not a prostitute, then it was possible that some of the
others weren't, either. If so, where did this monstrous killer
meet the girls and persuade them to go with him? I decided

Detective Quigley's theory was a good one—he trolled the streets in his carriage, looking for likely victims. Maybe he offered them a ride; maybe he simply grabbed them off the street. If we received letters from one particular part of the city, we'd be able to start hunting him down in earnest.

Mrs. Goodwin's house was in a pleasant, established neighborhood, just beyond a square with a green and leafy park in it. The front steps were well scrubbed, the brass door knockers well polished. The children who played hopscotch or whipped their tops on the sidewalks were well cared for. I got the key from the neighbor, who was most upset to hear about Mrs. Goodwin's accident.

"That poor dear woman has devoted her life to the service of others, and look where it's gotten her," she said. "And her man before her, too. He was one of the best, and he was struck down in his prime."

She handed over the key with no difficulty, and I was about to put it into the lock when the door swung open. This was strange, and I hesitated for a moment. There was no sign of forced entry around the lock, however, so I decided there had to be a reasonable explanation. Either Mrs. Goodwin herself had left in such a hurry that she hadn't quite closed the door and today's strong wind had blown it open again, or she had another friend or neighbor who had been entrusted with the key.

"Hello?" I called, standing in the narrow front hall. "Is anyone there?"

I stood listening but heard no kind of movement. I went on into the house, leaving the front door open, just in case. There was no mail of any kind on the front door mat, which was disappointing. I suppose I should have left again straightaway, but my curiosity got the better of me. I went down the hall into a meticulously scrubbed kitchen, complete with a row of gleaming copper pans hanging over the stove. I then conducted a brief tour of the front parlor, with its furniture covered in dust sheets, then the back parlor, which she obviously used for day-to-day living. The furniture in here was well-worn, and over the mantelpiece there was a framed photograph of a man in police uniform. I stood looking at it for a moment. Her husband had been taken from her, but she still carried on his work. That was noble enough. What was even more noble was that she had become my friend. She had every reason to hate Daniel as the man supposedly responsible for her husband's death, and thus to hate me, working to secure Daniel's release; but somehow she had believed me enough to trust me. Not only that—she had gone out of her way to help me.

I glanced around the room, and my gaze alighted on a piece of paper, sticking out from under the armchair. It was so unlike Mrs. Goodwin to leave anything untidily that I bent to pick it up. It was a new envelope. I decided to return it to the oak secretary nearby. When I opened the front of the secretary I gasped. The papers inside it were in complete disarray. Somebody had gone through her papers and then stuffed them back anyhow.

I froze, suddenly realizing the implication of this. He or she could be in the house at this minute, going through the rooms upstairs. I crept back to the front door.

"I'll be going then," I called out loudly and closed the front door behind me. Then I went as far as the street corner, stood out of sight, and waited. And waited. After a while nobody had appeared. I was tempted to go back and see if anyone had been through the upstairs rooms, but I was also a little hesitant to do so. Then I saw the mailman, coming up the street from the other direction. So the mail here was delivered later than I had anticipated. There might still be a letter for us today. My desire to see what the mail was bringing overcame my reluctance to go back to the house. I had just plucked up courage to go back inside when I noticed a constable coming toward me from around Tompkins Square. I ran over to him.

"You know Mrs. Goodwin who lives on this street?"

"I should say so. Old Whitey was a good mate of mine."

"Did you hear she's in the hospital, run down by a horse and wagon?"

"I heard, at the station this morning. Do you know how she's doing?"

"Better than we could have hoped. She's regained consciousness and is alert and talking."

"Well, that is good news, miss." He beamed at me, pausing to take out a handkerchief and wipe sweat from his round face before giving every intention of continuing his beat.

I put a hand on his arm to detain him. "Mrs. Goodwin has just sent me to her house to pick up the mail and there are signs that somebody has been in there, poking around in her desk. I didn't go upstairs, in case somebody was still up there. I don't think they are, but the police should know."

"Somebody broke in?"

"No, there was no sign of a break-in, but the front door was open."

"You don't say. Don't you worry, miss. I'll keep an eye on the place in the future," he said.

"No, it's more than that, Constable. Mrs. Goodwin was working on the East Side Ripper case. I think the detectives in charge of that case should know, Officers Quigley and McIver. Do you know them?"

"Quigley and McIver? Stationed at headquarters, no doubt."

I nodded. The mailman had now reached Mrs. Goodwin's front door, and I watched him push something through the mail slot.

"I'm going back to that house now to collect the mail that's just been delivered," I said. "Could I ask you to take a look and make sure nobody is hiding upstairs?"

"Very good, miss," he said, but he didn't look at all happy about it.

"I'm sure there's nobody there," I said. "I left the house at least half an hour ago and nobody has come out since; but just in case, I'd rather have a big, strong constable with a club along with me."

He accompanied me down the street, trying to appear confident and resolute, his hand grasped on his billy club. I opened the front door, picked up the letter that was lying on the mat, and let him into the house. Then I followed him up the stairs.

"There's no sign anyone's been up here, miss," he said, having checked both bedrooms and the large wardrobe. "Maybe you imagined it."

"Oh no," I said. "Someone has rifled through her desk, all right. Come and take a look for yourself. The officers in charge should know about it."

"Very good, miss," he said. "I'll pass along the word."

I let him out again, not entirely convinced he'd take this seriously. I suspected he put it down to female hysteria. I was dying to take a look at that letter. I shot the bolt across the front door, just in case, then carried it through to the kitchen. It was simply addressed to "MG" at her address. The postmark was Queens. I turned it over in my hands a couple of times, knowing full well that it wasn't addressed to me and I should wait until Mrs. Goodwin herself opened it. Then finally curiosity got the better of me. If it was a letter we were hoping for, then Mrs. Goodwin would want to know about it as soon as possible. If not, then there was no rush to deliver it to her. I ripped it open.

It was written in a rounded, rather childish hand, but neatly, with no blots.

Dear Sir or Madam:

I saw your notice in today's Herald. *My sister, Denise Lindquist (we call her by her nickname, Dilly), has been gone for over a month. Everyone says she ran off with a boy, but I don't believe it. Dilly's a good girl and hardworking at the button factory, and she wouldn't just run off with a boy like that.*

But she did tell me a secret before she went and made me promise I wouldn't tell nobody—she said she got a note from a boy asking her to meet him at Coney Island. She was very excited. I never had a secret tryst with a boy before, she said. Then she never came home. My

*mother and father are from Sweden. They are real strict
with us and don't let us go with no boys. Now they say
she is a no-good girl, and we don't talk about her no
more. I went to the police, but they don't seem to care.*

*Yours truly,
Kristina (Krissy) Lindquist*

I stared at it with growing excitement. She had gone to
meet a boy at Coney Island. It had to be connected with the
disappearance of the other girls. I had learned something
else important too—she had gone to meet a boy. We were
dealing with a young man, attractive enough to make girls
want to take risks to meet him.

I wanted to show this to Mrs. Goodwin straightaway, but I
knew I had no hope of making it past the platoon of guard
nuns once more this evening. I'd just have to be patient and
wait until morning. By that time the morning post would
have arrived as well, maybe bringing us more letters. I was
just putting the letter back into its envelope when I heard a
noise at the front door. I stood in the kitchen doorway and
saw the door handle start to turn. Of course the bolt held the
door firm. The door handle then jiggled, and the door was
shoved with considerable strength.

My heart was racing. If he found that he couldn't get in
through the front door, would he just go away or try to break
in? I went and looked out of the kitchen window. Breaking
in through the rear of the house would be almost impossible. There was a tiny square of yard, fenced off from other
yards and with the wall of another house at the rear. So he
could hardly climb in that way. I had to make sure I got out
safely and went to find that constable again. I decided I'd
bluff it out.

"There's someone at the front door, I think, Bessie," I
called in my best Irish accent. "Would you go and see who
it is?"

Then I crept into the front parlor and peered through the
lace curtains. There was nobody to be seen. Now the horri-

ble truth dawned on me that he might be crouched down by those potted bay trees, out of my line of vision from this window, waiting for me to come out. I stayed safely out of sight behind the curtains and waited. Then I spied a welcome sight—the constable was making his rounds again, coming along the other side of the street. I unbolted the front door, glanced in both directions, saw nobody, then ran to intercept him.

"He was here again," I gasped.

"Who was, miss?"

"The man who broke into Mrs. Goodwin's house. He tried to get in at the front door, but I'd bolted it from the inside."

"A man, miss? Can you describe him?"

"I didn't see him," I said impatiently. "I looked out through the window, but I didn't see him."

"I've been standing on that corner over there for the past fifteen minutes and haven't seen any men on the street. Are you sure about this?"

"Yes, I'm very sure. The door handle jiggled," I said. "Then he shoved the door hard, trying to force it open. He must have escaped while you were making your rounds."

"Maybe," he said.

Another idea struck me. "Have there been any vehicles passing on the street?"

He frowned. "Not recently. There was a delivery on the square earlier. And the butcher's boy came by on his bicycle."

Bicycle, I thought. Somebody could make a hasty getaway on a bicycle.

"Any other bicycles?"

"Not that I noticed," he said. "Look, miss, I think you're getting a bit overexcited about this—possibly because you're upset about your friend's accident. Why don't you go home and have a nice lie down and a cool drink."

There was nothing more to be done today, so I accepted his suggestion. "You will keep an eye on the place, and you will report it to the right people?"

"I've already done so, miss," he said. "So don't you worry. Nobody's going to break into the house again."

I collected the letter and locked the front door. Of course I couldn't bolt it from the outside, but it was the best I could do. Besides, he'd already been through Sabella's papers. I couldn't think of anything else in the house that might be of interest to him. So why had he come back this afternoon? Had he come back because he knew I was there? This wasn't likely. How would he know I had any connection with Mrs. Goodwin or that I'd be sent to pick up her mail? Then I took this one stage further: Was the mail the reason he had come? He had seen the advertisement in the newspapers and wanted to make sure the letters that could incriminate him never got to Mrs. Goodwin. Possibly there had been letters in an earlier post that were now in his possession.

I made a resolve to come back early tomorrow morning in time to intercept the first post of the day before I went to see Mrs. Goodwin in the hospital. One thing I was sure of was that we were on the right track. Something we were doing had definitely gotten him rattled.

TWENTY-EIGHT

As I walked home along Seventh Street, I sensed that I was being followed. I turned around, but saw nothing but housewives returning home with their shopping, children playing, fathers coming home from work. But the feeling didn't go away until I reached the busy area of the university with its noisy throngs of students. I crossed Washington Square and looked back at the entrance to Patchin Place before I walked up to my front door and let myself in.

I had scarcely sat down at my kitchen table when there was a thunderous knock at my front door that set my heart racing again.

"Who is it?" I called.

"Who else would it be?" came Sid's voice.

I opened the door and saw them both standing there, beaming at me.

"Why the secrecy?" Sid asked.

"Because I thought I was being followed home," I said. "No matter. My vivid Irish imagination, I expect."

"Come over to us for dinner," Gus said. "Then we can keep an eye out for suspicious individuals skulking in the alley. We're getting really good at it, Molly. We're turning out to be brilliant detectives."

"You'll never guess where we've been today," Sid burst out as she took my hand and led me out of my house. "Go on. Ask us."

"Where have you been today?" I asked, with sinking heart.

"To Newport, Rhode Island, to track down the mysterious young man who had a pash on Letitia Blackwell."

"You went all the way to Rhode Island?"

"It wasn't that far. A couple of hours by train," Sid said. "And a pleasant journey at that along the ocean."

"And you managed to locate the young man?"

Sid pushed open their front door and dragged me inside. "Absolutely," she said. "Gus was amazing. She knows everybody, you know. We only had to stroll along the seafront for five minutes before she had located an old friend from Boston. Five minutes after that we had heard all the gossip about what was going on in each of the cottages."

"Cottages?" I asked, confused.

Sid laughed. "That's what they call them—their cottages. The fact that all the houses have at least twenty-five bedrooms doesn't strike them as absurd. Newport is where the rich and famous spend their summers."

We went through the kitchen and out to the conservatory at the back. There was a jug of lemonade and glasses waiting on the wicker table. Sid motioned me to sit.

"So what about the boy you were hunting? Don't tell me he's among the rich and famous?" I asked, as she handed me a glass of lemonade.

Gus looked pleased with herself. "Not a Vanderbilt, but the house is pretty impressive, wouldn't you say, Sid?"

"Definitely not a pauper," Sid agreed. "And his mother actually went to finishing school with Gus's mother, so of course we were invited in for lunch."

"And you met him?"

"No, because apparently he's volunteering at a camp for poor city children out on a lake somewhere. His name is Harold Robertson, by the way. He's the despair of his industrialist father because he shows no interest in going into the family business and only wants to do good. He's studying divinity and works among the poor in his spare time. She showed us a picture of him—chubby and adorable, like an overgrown choirboy."

"Did you find out anything about Letitia?"

Gus nodded. "He had told his mother about this wonderful girl who came to help out at the settlement house, and he said what a pity it was that she was engaged to someone else because she'd be the sort of wife a minister should have."

"But the mother had never met her," Sid added. "She said he arrived home quite disgruntled on the day when Letitia must have gone missing. He said they were supposed to go out to Coney Island together to plan the children's outing for the next day, but Letitia never showed up."

"And he's now at a camp by a lake for the summer?" I asked.

"So we gather," Sid said.

"Far from New York?"

"In the wilds, I believe," Gus said. "Harold's mother said it was horribly primitive, and she couldn't understand what made him do it as she'd brought him up to expect the best."

"Why do you ask, Molly?" Sid asked, with her usual great perception.

"Because Letitia is not the first girl to disappear after a planned trip to Coney Island. I know of another girl who went there to meet a boy and never came back."

"You don't think—you can't possibly think that Harold Robertson . . ." Gus exclaimed.

"I've never met Harold Robertson, so I don't know what to believe. I'm trying to piece together a jigsaw puzzle, and so far I've remarkably few pieces. Now I have a name, a missing girl, and a planned trip to Coney Island. They all fit very nicely."

"So you think he could have lured Letitia to Coney Island and then what? Killed her? Hid the body?" Sid was looking at me, her expression half horror, half excitement.

"Possibly not hid the body," I said.

"What do you mean?"

"I mean that we've found out that at least one of those

dead prostitutes killed by the East Side Ripper was not a prostitute at all. She was just dressed up to look like one. So maybe the others weren't either."

"That is incredible," Gus said. "But Molly, what are you doing looking into the East Side Ripper murders? Please don't tell me it is a case you are trying to tackle."

"It may have some connection to Daniel's false imprisonment," I said. "I'm beginning to think it doesn't, but I've been helping a woman police officer who is involved."

"A woman police officer? Are there such beings?"

"There are and she is wonderful," I said. "She started off as a matron, but now she is used on undercover assignments."

Sid thumped Gus on the back. "There you are, Gus. Our next career move."

"Hold it," I said, laughing. "She's very smart, but she's not having an easy time of it. The male officers resent her and don't trust her, and right now she's in the hospital, having been deliberately run down by a horse and carriage."

"So you are taking over while she's out of commission?" Sid asked.

"Not really. Just helping out," I said. "She made me promise that I wouldn't go alone to the Lower East Side."

"Thank heavens for that," Gus said. "So do tell us—do you have any suspects in mind? Do you think it's a pillar of the community, as Dr. Birnbaum suggested?"

"I think it's someone who is clever and likes taking risks," I said.

"Do you really think it's possible it could be Harold Robertson?" Sid asked. "He's certainly a pillar."

"We should find out exactly where that camp is, and then we can determine if he could get to Coney Island and back with ease," Gus said.

"But why Coney Island?" Sid asked. "If he wants to lure girls to their deaths, why not Central Park? Why not the Palisades on the other side of the Hudson? I should have thought that Coney was the last place where one could get a girl alone and be able to kill her. It's absolutely seething with humanity at this time of year."

"He could take her to a hotel room," Gus suggested. "There are plenty of cheap hotels in the Brighton Beach area."

"But what respectable girl would go to a cheap hotel room with a strange man?" I asked. "Certainly not Letitia Blackwell."

"She's right," Sid agreed. "This is an enigma."

"I suggest we eat." Gus got up and headed for the kitchen. "You'll join us, of course, Molly."

Visions of Gus's latest attempts at vegetarian cooking floated before my eyes, but I couldn't find a polite way to refuse. "Thank you, I'd love to," I said.

"We're having pork chops," Gus called back from the ice chest.

"Pork chops? I thought you had become Buddhists."

Sid grinned. "We decided we weren't the meditating types. After we went out sleuthing for you that day, we agreed that we are women of action, and women of action need good red meat to sustain them."

"Ryan will be disappointed," I said, "after he's invested in those saffron robes."

TWENTY-NINE

The pork chops must not have agreed with me because I had the dream again, the first time for a couple of weeks. This time it was more nebulous, with the laughter, the water, the blood, all blending together into a deep feeling of dread that had me waking, drenched in sweat. I went downstairs and saw from the clock that it was four-thirty. Hardly worth going back to sleep, even if I could.

Instead I got up, washed, dressed, and made my way over to Mrs. Goodwin's house by first light. I wanted to make sure that I got my hands on any letters that came in the morning mail. Seventh Street was quiet and deserted. Unfortunately there was no sign of a policeman as I stood outside the Goodwin home and put my key in the door. Was I being stupid, going into a house where there had recently been a prowler, and maybe a dangerous prowler at that? But I had to have that mail. I opened the front door and stood in the hallway, waiting for my sense of danger to sound out a warning. No alarm went off in my head. I left the door ajar as I went to the back parlor and checked the desk again. Nothing had been moved since last night.

I was just closing the desk when I heard a noise. Someone was coming down the hall. I froze, looked for somewhere to hide, and found nothing. Before I could do anything more sensible than grab the letter opener, a man came into the doorway. He started when he saw me.

"What are you doing here?" he demanded.

I recognized him then.

"Detective McIver," I gasped. "You gave me an awful shock."

"Likewise," he said. "Now do you mind telling me what you're doing here?"

"Mrs. Goodwin gave me her key," I said. "She wanted me to come and pick up her mail for her."

He was still eyeing me suspiciously. "That's odd because I have Mrs. Goodwin's key in my possession," he said. "And why would the mail be anywhere other than on the doormat?"

"Ah," I said. "Well, I can answer both of those. She told me to collect the key from her neighbor, which I did. But I found her front door open, so I came in and saw that someone had been at her desk. That's when I alerted the police that someone had broken in and asked the constable to tell you and Detective Quigley. I thought the break-in here might have something to do with the case you're working on and the reason that Mrs. Goodwin was run down, you see."

"Yes, I do see." The scowl eased a little. "I'm sorry if I frightened you. I came to check on the place on my way to work this morning and found the front door open. Naturally I suspected . . ."

"That I was a burglar," I finished for him.

"And who exactly are you?" he asked. "The last time we met, you were introduced as Dr. Birnbaum's assistant, but you are clearly not German or Austrian, unless they now speak with an Irish brogue."

"No, that was a piece of subterfuge, I'm afraid. I'm a friend of Mrs. Goodwin," I said, deciding not to mention my connection to Daniel, "as well as of Dr. Birnbaum. I was particularly interested in this case; and then, of course, there was Mrs. Goodwin's tragic accident, so I'm doing what I can to help her."

"Very commendable," he said. There was no smile in his eyes. "And who exactly are you?"

"My name is—" What name had I given to Quigley? My real one? Delaney? All the lies were coming back to haunt me. I opted for the truth. "Murphy," I said. "Molly Murphy. You can ask Mrs. Goodwin to vouch for me."

"If she's well enough," he said. "She took a turn for the worse last night."

"She did?"

"Yes, she was unconscious again when I stopped by this morning."

"Oh no, and they said she was doing so well."

"Head wounds are funny things," he said. "And broken ribs can penetrate the lung or even damage the heart."

"I'll go to see her if they'll let me," I said, "after I've collected her morning mail."

He stared at me, went to say something, then realized I wasn't about to move and he couldn't throw me out.

"Very well," he said. "I'll leave you to it, then. Please make sure you lock the door after you when you go. We don't want any more break-ins, do we?"

"Absolutely not," I said. "And I'm so glad to see you're taking this seriously. I'm very concerned for Mrs. Goodwin's welfare. I suspect she may have stumbled upon some connection with the East Side Ripper without knowing it, and he is now trying to get her out of the way."

"You could be right," he said. "But if you are, then heed the warning yourself. This is a man who doesn't play games. Winding up with your face bashed in is not the most pleasant way to exit this life."

He gave me a long, hard stare before turning on his heel and leaving me alone in the hall. A few minutes later the morning post fell onto the mat. There were four more letters about missing girls. Three of them didn't seem to have any relevance to the case. One was an emigrant from Germany who was supposed to have come through Ellis Island, then taken the train to her family in Albany but had never arrived. One had clearly run off with a young man her family did not want her to marry. One was from a young man wanting to be reunited with a former sweetheart. But the fourth was from an Italian, a Signor Rosetti. His daughter Rosa had not come home from work in a garment factory last week. He was out of his mind with worry. He had spoken to her friends and all he could establish was that she seemed excited when she left work and hurried off, as if she had somewhere special to go. He had been to the police, but they hadn't seemed very interested. He enclosed a snapshot. It was of a group of four laughing girls, each with luxurious dark hair around her shoulders, standing at the edge of the ocean. On the back he had written: "My daughters. Rosa is on the right."

I remembered that impressive dark hair falling out from under the sheet at the morgue. This could well be the victim we had seen. I imagined that poor father, still living in hope, not knowing that his daughter was lying on a marble slab, having died in such horrible circumstances.

I put the letters into my purse, let myself out, and locked the door carefully behind me. Then I made my way straight to Saint Vincent's Hospital. The same sister I had encountered on the first occasion was on duty today.

"You again." She gave me that withering stare. "I thought I told you yesterday that she wasn't allowed visitors yet."

I leaned closer. "Look, Sister," I said in a low voice, "this is a police matter of great importance. You know that Mrs. Goodwin is a member of the New York police force, don't you? And you've heard of the East Side Ripper?"

"I should say so," the nun answered. "That poor girl was brought in here only a few days ago."

"Exactly," I said. "Well, Mrs. Goodwin was working on that very case when she was run down. I was helping her, although I'm not officially with the police. I have some letters with me that Mrs. Goodwin must see as soon as possible. So if you don't let me see her, you'll just be hindering us in solving this case, and the Ripper will claim more victims. Is that what you want?"

She looked surprised. I remember the nuns in school looking the same way when I sauced them back. Then she nodded. "Very well," she said. "You can go up, but it's up to Sister Mercy whether she lets you see her patient or not."

"Thank you," I said. "And don't worry. I want the best for Mrs. Goodwin as much as you do. I'll not put her in any harm."

With that I went up the stairs and along the hall to Mercy Ward. There was no constable outside this morning, but I pushed the door open to see Sister Mercy herself sitting at the patient's bedside like a watchdog. She sprang up instantly.

"I don't know how you sneaked up here, but there's no point in it," she said. "The poor dear is unconscious again."

I looked down at Mrs. Goodwin's white, tranquil face on the pillow.

"What happened?" I asked.

"I can't tell you that. She was doing so well yesterday evening, talking about getting up and trying to walk, she was. And then suddenly we couldn't rouse her. We called the doctor, and he was mystified too."

"Is it possible she was drugged?" I asked.

"By whom?" she demanded. "You can see how strict we are about letting in visitors. And the medicines are all kept in a locked cabinet in the orderly room."

"What about the morphine she was given for her pain? Was any of that left lying around?"

"Lying around?" she demanded. "We are very strict about the keys to the drug cabinet."

"But the doctor who examined her couldn't come up with an explanation for her sudden relapse into unconsciousness?"

"Head wounds are funny things sometimes," she said, echoing McIver's sentiments.

I continued to observe the patient. Her breathing was steady and regular. There wasn't anything I could do until she woke up.

"I'll come back later," I said. "Hopefully she'll have regained consciousness by then. If she wakes, tell her that Molly has some news for her. And in the meantime . . ." I paused, giving her what I hoped was a meaningful glance, "you'll keep a good eye on her, won't you?"

"She won't be out of my sight," Sister Mercy said, and I realized that she might have had the same sort of suspicions as myself. I felt better knowing I was leaving Mrs. Goodwin in good hands. I certainly had plenty to occupy me until she awoke, not the least of which was my duty to Daniel. I needed to warn him about Mr. Partridge's visit and to let him know what I had found. I also just needed to see him again, to make sure he was all right.

THIRTY

I came out of the hospital and boarded the Sixth Avenue El down to the end of the line at Rector Street, then walked back up Broadway a couple of short blocks to where J. P. Atkinson, attorney at law, had his offices. I was determined to force that insipid man to take me to see Daniel, or else. By the time I had climbed those stairs to the fifth floor, I was feeling horribly dizzy and had to lean against the peeling paint of the stairwell before I collected myself sufficiently to go in. I knocked, entered, and found, to my disappointment, that he wasn't there. The woman secretary looked annoyed at being disturbed, and I got the feeling she might have been taking forty winks.

"Do you know when he'll be back?" I asked.

She shrugged. "I really couldn't say. May I take a message?"

"Do you know where he's gone? I'd really like to speak to him today."

"I think he had an appointment with a client at the jail," she said.

"The Tombs?"

"No, the Plaza Hotel—what do you think?"

"Thank you, you've been most helpful," I said, only half sarcastically. "I'll see if I can track him down there."

I came down the stairs and swung aboard a trolley that was going up Broadway. It was only after I had done this that I reminded myself that I probably shouldn't be behaving in this way, given my current condition. Then I promptly forgot and hopped off again, while the thing was still moving, at City Hall.

More work had been done on The Tombs in my absence. It appeared that the building was being demolished around the inmates.

"I'm here to give a message to Mr. Atkinson, the lawyer," I said before the constables could stop me from entering and swept past them. I said the same thing to the sergeant at the front desk, stressing that it was vitally important to his client that I speak to him right away. I didn't know if that client was Daniel or not, but at least it would guarantee that Mr. Atkinson would speak to me.

"Wait here," the sergeant said and indicated a chair by the desk. I sat and waited, listening to the annoying tap, tapping of the men working outside. At last I heard echoing feet coming down a passageway and the sergeant appeared again, followed by an anxious-looking Mr. Atkinson.

"Miss Murphy!" he exclaimed. "What on earth are you doing here?"

"Tracking you down, Mr. Atkinson. I told you before that I had important information for Captain Sullivan. I'd like to give him that information."

"And I told you that you could share it with me, and I'd be happy to pass it along if it was relevant."

"And if you chose not to, he wouldn't get it," I said. I was aware of the desk sergeant listening with interest. "I have the strongest feeling, Mr. Atkinson, that you have Daniel Sullivan already tried and convicted in your head. You're only going to go through the motions of a fair trial."

"That's just not fair, Miss Murphy," he said. "I assure you I am doing my best in a very difficult case."

"I'd love to know who assigned you to this case," I said.

'I told you we have a rotation of defense attorneys," he said. "My name came to the top of the list. Pure luck."

"Pure bad luck for Daniel then."

"I assure you, Miss Murphy, that he could have done far worse. Some court-appointed lawyers have no interest in anything other than collecting their fee."

"But you have? Can you truly tell me that you are working with all your might to get Daniel Sullivan freed, even though you believe him to be guilty?" I demanded.

He went to say something then broke off as there was a commotion at the front entrance. The doors swung open, the sergeant leaped to attention, and Commissioner John Partridge entered, followed by a retinue of lackeys.

"Welcome, sir. The governor is expecting you. I'll let him know you've arrived," the sergeant said and scurried off down a corridor.

Partridge looked around in a bored sort of way. I held my breath, just praying that he wouldn't remember me. Then he said, "Hello, Atkinson. How are you?"

"Well, sir, thank you. And yourself?"

"Can't complain, although New York is devilish uncomfortable in this heat, isn't it? I can't think why you and I stick to duty before pleasure and don't head off to the seashore like sensible folks."

"Some of us can't afford to, sir," Atkinson said, with a rueful smile.

"And this young lady is already familiar to me," Mr. Partridge said, his gaze now fastening on me. "A Miss—"

"Murphy, sir," Atkinson said.

"Murphy? Now that's interesting," The police commissioner was frowning. "I seem to remember the last time we met it was Delaney, wasn't it? You were part of some ladies' league with Mrs. Astor."

"That's right," I said.

"Fascinating." Partridge's eyes had narrowed, making him look like a large bird of prey. "I happened to dine with the Astors the very next evening, and she had never heard of you."

"I didn't say I was her friend. Just a junior worker in her cause," I added quickly.

"Or your cause," he finished. "Never heard of any Ladies Decency League or whatever you call yourselves. So now

I'm really curious to know what your true motive was then, and what you're doing here now. What are you—one of these scandal-mongering newspaper reporters?"

"She's a *friend* of Mr. Sullivan," Atkinson said, before I could answer. He put the kind of stress on the word "friend" that would normally be accompanied with a wink between gentlemen.

I chose to ignore him. "That's quite correct," I said. "I am Captain Sullivan's friend, one of the few who haven't deserted him or been scared off from helping him. And I am working with all my might to prove his innocence because nobody else seems interested in doing so."

There, I had said it. I had thrown down the gauntlet, however unwise this was.

Partridge continued to frown. "Then you have set yourself a daunting task, Miss—uh—Murphy, and one that seems doomed to failure. Because, unfortunately, his crime was committed in the presence of witnesses. Myself and two stalwart police officers were on the scene to witness his interaction with a known gang member and to intercept the money changing hands. I don't see how you intend to prove that we didn't witness what we did."

I faced him, looking him straight in the eye. "Oh, I believe you did witness it exactly as you said. But Daniel was meeting this gang member in good faith. He was supposed to be receiving a list of names, not a bribe. He believes, as I do, that the whole scene was orchestrated by somebody intent on his downfall. You were brought to the spot at the right moment. Money was somehow secreted in the envelope."

The commissioner chuckled. "And how did that happen? Or was it Monk Eastman himself who wanted Sullivan out of the way?"

"No, it wasn't," I said. "Trust me. I've already spoken to Monk about it. Somebody either intimidated the gang member or managed to exchange the envelope somehow."

"Has this gang member himself been questioned?" Partridge turned to Atkinson, who shook his head. "He seems to have skipped town, sir."

"Very wise, considering." Partridge chuckled again.

"Or very useful to somebody," I said. "Somebody who wants to make sure he keeps his mouth shut. Somebody who wants to make sure there is no witness for the defense."

"And who might this mythical somebody be?" he asked. "Have you managed to unearth a conspiracy against Mr. Sullivan?"

"I'm working on it," I said. "It would appear that one or two people might have a motive to want him out of the way, but not to want his complete and utter ruin. That would take someone with the most horrible grudge and hatred in his heart."

At that moment the prison governor appeared. "My dear Commissioner," he began, opening his arms expansively. "What a singular honor for us. You've come to see how the building is progressing? Excellent. You'll be pleased with the new wing that is almost completed."

Hands were shaken. Pleasantries were exchanged. I stepped out of the way, thinking it might be prudent to make myself scarce at this moment. The party was about to move off when Partridge turned to Mr. Atkinson. "You're here to see Sullivan today, are you?"

"No sir, another client, just brought in."

"And Miss Murphy was here for what reason?"

"She wanted to see Sullivan. I have discouraged these visits. It gives the prisoner false hopes and can even interfere with any case we might be able to present."

"Quite right," Partridge said. He turned to me. "My advice to you, little lady, is to go home and leave this to the professionals. Atkinson is doing what he can."

"If only Sullivan would cooperate, I could work to get him the lightest sentence possible," Atkinson said. "But he is being stubborn. He still won't admit to any guilt."

"And no more should he," I exclaimed before I realized that I should probably be playing the helpless female at this point.

"She claims she has new information for Sullivan but

she's unwilling to share it," Atkinson said, sounding rather like the model pupil, telling tales to the schoolmaster.

"Why don't we all pay a visit to Sullivan right now," Partridge said amiably. "Then I can get a feel for myself as to whether his defense has merit and whether the conspiracy you suggest is in any way possible."

"I think you already know the answer to that," I said, "and I would not upset Daniel even further by exposing him to his accuser and a lawyer who has no interest in setting him free!"

I went to sweep past them in a dignified exit. But Mr. Partridge grabbed my arm. "I admire your bravery and your loyalty," he said, "but I don't think you realize you are playing with fire. Go home and read your Sherlock Holmes stories, because in real life young women who dabble in affairs beyond their scope have an unfortunate habit of winding up dead."

He released my arm. "Now, Governor, let's go and see this new building of yours." And he was gone.

I came out of the building alone and stood with the particles of brick dust flying around me, trying to calm my racing thoughts. Had that been a direct threat, or was he just warning a young girl as any avuncular figure would? I had no way of knowing. What's more, I was furious with myself. He had been right. I had probably put Daniel's whole case in jeopardy by revealing my hand like that. Now he knew I was working to prove Daniel's innocence he could do any number of things, like rush through the trial, or transfer the prisoner. It didn't need to be anything too obvious, but a cell with the right amount of damp and mold, or a cellmate who was already infected with consumption, would do the trick quite easily.

I wasn't going to let that happen. I brushed the dust from my shoulders and sleeves and stepped out into full sunlight. At least I hadn't revealed the information I had come to give Daniel. If Partridge were the guilty one, that would be on his mind. He'd be asking himself how much I had found out. Which wasn't too good for my own health and safety.

THIRTY-ONE

I spent the rest of the morning at Mrs. Goodwin's bedside while she slept on, breathing steadily but not stirring. Fear gripped me that she might stay asleep forever and then quietly slip away into death.

"You've got to wake up," I said out loud, "because I can't do this on my own. We've letters from the families of two girls now, and I'm sure one of them is the latest victim that we saw at the morgue. So it's up to you to get well quickly and help prevent any more deaths."

I was all too aware that I was wasting my time by talking to an unconscious person, but it made me feel better—less alone, anyway. Because in truth I felt horribly alone at this moment. It had nothing to do with my own safety. It was thinking about Daniel and the very real possibility that he might be in prison for years. On the way back to Saint Vincent's I had been forced to face the reality that I might never be able to prove his innocence. If it came down to a confrontation, me against the police commissioner, what jury would be persuaded to believe me?

I also was forced to admit that I still loved him. I had kept those feelings in check, ever since I found out that he was engaged to another woman. Now the feelings came to the fore with a vengeance. He did have his faults, he had treated me shabbily, but I still loved him in spite of everything. It's one of the failings we women have. Our hearts rule our heads all too often.

I dragged myself out of this wallowing in introspection and self-pity. It certainly wouldn't help Daniel or Mrs. Goodwin if I wasn't strong and alert right now, and it wasn't getting me anywhere either.

"Now, about these girls," I said to the sleeping Mrs. Goodwin. "Someone should go out and talk to their families. Maybe one of them has left a note from the boy, hidden away somewhere. At least we can find out if the girls have any identifying marks or ways of knowing who they are for sure."

"The exhumation," said a weak voice beside me. Mrs. Goodwin was looking at me. "What day is it?"

"It's Thursday," I said.

"And the exhumation is set for Friday morning." She sighed as if it was still an effort to talk. She tried to sit up, groaned, and flopped back to the pillow. "You'll have to go. I'll be in no condition to."

"How can I go to an exhumation?" I blurted out, my mind presenting me with pictures of partly consumed flesh and maggots. "They surely won't let me be present."

"You mustn't let them see you," she said. "You should appear to be a mourner, come to deliver your respects to another grave site. Keep well away, disguise yourself beneath a big hat, and watch who comes to observe. The notice about the exhumation should have made it to the press by now. Someone might be interested to see what we dig up."

"You mean the Ripper himself might come?"

"It's possible. In my experience, killers show a fascination with their own cases. I've heard of men volunteering to help look for missing girls whom they've actually murdered and buried. I suppose it gives them an added thrill to know they are one step ahead of the police."

"Then I'll do it," I said, "although I hate to leave you here. You gave us all a nasty shock last night, lapsing back into unconsciousness. Was there any warning you were feeling worse?"

She shook her head. "I wasn't aware of feeling worse. I certainly feel groggy, so I presume I've been asleep for a while."

"Unconscious," I said. "They couldn't wake you earlier."

"Curious." She closed her eyes again.

"You didn't feel anything while you were dozing?" I asked. "A prick, perhaps?"

Her expression became instantly alert. "Are you suggesting that somebody gave me an injection? Somebody wanted to make sure I stayed asleep?"

"And didn't wake up, I believe," I said. "I've no idea how this person could have slipped in past the guard here, but our killer has shown himself to be the most resourceful of men."

"He certainly has," she said. "But I take your warning seriously. I will ask to be moved to my own house right away, with a police guard."

"Will you be able to manage at home?"

"I'll hire a nurse."

"Good idea," I said. "I'll come and sit with you as much as I can."

She patted my hand. "You're a good girl," she said. "And I'm sorry it didn't work out with my friend the other evening."

"My choice," I said. "Probably a foolish one."

She gave a tired smile. "We all have to follow our own hearts. It may turn out all right in the end for you."

"At least I'm not an invalid myself when you need me," I said. "I can go to that exhumation. I can even go and question the families."

She tried to prop herself up again. "Ah yes, the letters about the girls. You have them with you?"

I produced them from my purse. She read them in silence, then she nodded. "I'd say the one from the Italian father could well be the girl we saw on Monday, don't you agree?"

"I do," I said. "And you'll note that other one—the Swedish girl, Dilly Lindquist. She had a secret meeting with a boy at Coney Island."

She nodded. "Yes, we have to go out there as soon as possible. You feel that Coney Island is significant, don't you?"

"We know that the first girl to be murdered was a prostitute at Coney Island and her body was found under the boardwalk there. Now we have proof that a second girl went to meet someone at Coney Island and never came back. But that's not all. I've also been asked to trace a missing heiress who supposedly ran away with a penniless young man. It probably has nothing to do with this case, I realize, but it's interesting that she was supposed to go to Coney Island on the day she disappeared. With a young man who was not her fiancé."

Sabella Goodwin frowned. "And do we know this young man's name?"

"Oh yes. My associates have visited his mother. He is from a good family, summering in Newport, Rhode Island."

"Close enough to make the train journey," she said, "and rich enough to hire a carriage when needed. We must pass this information on to the detectives."

"He is supposedly away for the summer, helping out at a camp for city children in the wilds of New England," I said. "Nobody has verified this yet, or exactly where the camp is. It might be within reach of a train station and the city."

"Good work," she said. "It all fits very nicely. Son of a rich family. Not quite comfortable with girls, or not quite right in the head. Shielded by his family. Yes, I think our detectives should question him as soon as possible. Write down all your information on him, and I'll give it to them next time I see them."

I was loath to do this, but I couldn't quite determine why. I suppose that until then it was our case—mine and Sabella Goodwin's—and I didn't want simply to hand it over to two supercilious young men, who clearly had no regard for me or my skills.

"I could go and check him out myself first," I said.

"You'll do no such thing," she retorted. "If this charming young man is indeed our East Side Ripper, he is devious and cunning, and very good at killing. I certainly don't want you to wind up as his next victim."

"He wouldn't have to know that I have anything to do with this case," I said. "I'm merely investigating the disappearance of a Miss Blackwell."

Sabella shook her head firmly. "If he's killed her, do you think you wouldn't be next? And at a camp in the wilderness, you don't think he'd have ample opportunity?"

She did have a point. "Very well. I'll write down the information for you. But I'm going to stay with you until you are safely moved to your own home and have a nurse installed. Shall we ring for Sister now and see if we can arrange this?"

Mrs. Goodwin looked at me and laughed. "You're a very forceful young woman, do you know that?" she said. "I've always been told that I was aggressive for a woman, but you take the cake."

I smiled, too. "It comes from having to fend for myself in New York. If I don't stand up for me, nobody else will."

"That's why you have to behave sensibly and not take too many risks," she said. "If you have nobody watching out for you, you're very vulnerable. And I don't think I'll be well enough to be your bodyguard for some time yet."

"Don't worry. I'll take care of myself," I said. "I've no wish to wind up as the Ripper's next victim."

Surprisingly, Sister Mercy thought that moving Mrs. Goodwin to her own home was a good idea.

"More chance for peace and quiet," she said. But she looked at me as she said it, and I read her thoughts.

By that evening Sabella was installed in her home with the next-door neighbor, who had supplied me with the key, fussing over her and making chicken soup. She was going to stay the night, and a real nurse was to arrive in the morning. What's more the constable I had spoken to earlier was assigned to keep an eye on the house. I went home feeling much relieved and tried to get a good night's sleep before my own ordeal the next day.

I was up when the first touches of dawn streaked the eastern sky and made my way to Hart Island, where I was told the potter's field was located. Mrs. Goodwin had warned me that the exhumation would be done early in the morning, and it would be quite a long journey. I don't think she had any idea how long and arduous the journey would be, though. I'm sure she'd never done it herself. I doubt if many people had.

It turned out that Hart Island was in the middle of a piece of water called Long Island Sound, halfway between the Bronx and Long Island. It could only be reached from another island called City Island, and that was in the middle of godforsaken marshes. The journey involved taking the elevated railway to the Harlem River and then picking up a ferryboat that took a circuitous route through a narrow channel called Hell Gate, into Long Island Sound.

It was a misty morning and I was quite chilled when the ferry finally reached City Island. I don't know why it was called by that name because anything less like a city I've never seen. We docked at a quaint waterfront community of boatbuilders and seafarers that looked as if it belonged to another age. The harbor was already a hive of activity at this early hour. Sounds of hammering rang out from a boat shed. A tugboat tooted a warning as it left port. I asked about a ferry to Hart Island and was given strange looks. Only the government boat goes over there, I was told. In fact, it had already gone in that direction this very morning. And it was just a great big cemetery—a sorry place, unmarked graves of those who were too poor to pay for a decent, honest burial or those whose remains had never been identified.

"I know what it is, sir," I told the boatman who had given me this information, "but I have a special reason for being there today. I understand they are to exhume some bodies and I've a terrible fear that one of them might be my own dear sister. So if you could think of any way I might get there?" I looked appealing, grief stricken, and helpless.

"I reckon Old Tom could run you over—couldn't you, Tom?" One of the men turned to a leathery old sea dog sitting on the harbor wall, puffing at his pipe.

"If she makes it worth my while," Tom said grumpily.

"Oh come on, have a heart," another of the men entreated. "She wants to know if they're digging up her lost sister. You can do that much for her, can't you?"

"I'm quite willing to pay," I said, as Mrs. Goodwin had given me money for the fare. "And I assure you it would mean a lot to me."

Old Tom got up, spat onto the cobbles, and inclined his head in my direction. "Come on, then," he said. "While the tide is favorable."

He helped me to climb down from the jetty into a rowboat. We cast off and slipped silently out of the harbor. As soon as the township was left behind we entered an unreal world. In the city the early morning sky had been clear and promising. On the voyage to City Island we had encountered patches of mist, which had grown thicker as the coastline became uninhabited marshland. Now we entered a world enveloped in mist. It rose, curling like smoke from mudflats, and hovered over the skiff. There was no sound except for the gentle lapping of waves and the rhythmic splash and creak of the oars. I had no idea where we were going or how close the island was. After a while even the mudflats vanished so that all that was visible was a few feet of water on either side of us. It was like entering a dream, and the thought crossed my mind that it was the River Styx, and I was being ferried to an afterlife.

Which in a way it was, of course. All those corpses had made this same journey to a final resting place. I sat, gripping the side of the boat, my head full of uneasy thoughts. I feared that we'd run into a rock or a bigger boat, or we'd get lost and find ourselves out at sea. I also feared what I'd see once we reached Hart Island. I was glad that Old Tom wasn't the talkative sort. His face was impassive as he pulled on the oars, and we moved smoothly over a glassy surface. At least there aren't waves, I thought. One thing to be thankful for, because I was definitely feeling queasy.

The journey seemed to go on forever. I lost all sense of time. Every now and then the mist parted to reveal a blue sky above, then closed in again. Once a cormorant rose flapping right in front of us, making my heart leap into my throat. Old Tom glanced up then and shot me a withering look before he went back to the business of rowing.

At last we were passing more marshes; reedy mudflats, a patch of sandy beach, and a wooden jetty appeared from the mist in front of us. A large motor vessel was already moored there. Old Tom jumped out easily in spite of his advanced years, and tied up the boat before helping me out.

"You will wait for me, won't you?" I asked, my nerve almost failing me.

"Don't worry. Old Tom will be here," he said, in an almost kindly fashion.

I picked my way along the rickety jetty and passed what must have been a caretaker's shack, looming out of the mist. I was expecting to see headstones, crosses, something to tell me that I was in a cemetery, but it wasn't until my foot hit against something hard that I spotted the small metal number plate and realized I was already walking on the dead. I recoiled in horror. In Ireland it was regarded as terribly bad luck to step on a grave. But they were all around me. It was scarcely possible to walk forward without stepping on them. I made my way forward, searching for a path.

Then the mist lifted a little and I saw what looked to be one large, rolling meadow before me. There were a few stunted trees, bent by the force of the wind, but apart from that, nothing. No sign of other people, anyway. I realized with annoyance that they might have already exhumed the bodies and departed. I wasn't sure what to do next. Then I heard a strange rhythmic clanking sound. It was coming my way, getting louder and louder. I made for the nearest tree and attempted to hide behind it. A line of men came into view, walking one close behind the other. Then I saw the striped uniforms and realized that the clanking I had heard was the chains of the leg irons that bound them together. A convict chain gang.

Of course that sight really alarmed me. Was there also a prison on this island or had Old Tom made a mistake and deposited me on a prison island instead? Not a happy thought. Then I heard voices and saw figures motioning behind a far clump of trees. The chain gang headed toward them, breaking into an ungainly trot when urged on by their overseer.

When they were far enough ahead and their forms blended into the mist, I followed them.

On this occasion the mist was my ally. I could get quite close to the group without being observed and found a vantage point behind some kind of prickly shrub. I could hear voices now. Commands being given.

"This is the first site. Start digging here."

"Come on, lads. Jump to it. Grab your shovels."

Then the sounds of spades digging into earth, spades hitting something hard, and exclamations and grunts as a coffin was lifted. I could make out the shape of it as it was laid on the grass. Then the group moved off and the process was repeated. I crept to another stunted tree and flattened myself against it. I could see the party more clearly now. The man in the dark suit and top hat was probably the coroner. There were several policemen in full dress uniform. I thought I recognized McIver standing beside an older man wearing a captain's uniform. A couple of young constables brought up a rear guard, watching with disinterest as the convicts dug and grunted as they raised another coffin. This one must have been the most recently buried as there were sounds of coughing and retching and some of the men produced handkerchiefs to hold over their faces. McIver and the captain backed away as the coffin was dumped on the ground with a dull thud.

It suddenly struck me that they were not about to open the coffins here. They would be shipped back to the morgue and examined there. I wondered for a moment why I had gone to all this trouble, until I remembered why Mrs. Goodwin had wanted me here. It was in case the killer himself showed up to watch.

A sudden gust of cold mist wrapped around me, making me conscious that I was standing all alone behind this stunted tree, cut off from any help should a hand suddenly come around my mouth. I spun around, scanning the mist-swept island nervously. What was that dark shape? Had something moved beside that hump of rock? When a seagull skimmed overhead and screeched, my heart nearly stopped.

A third body was exhumed, then a fourth. The mist was starting to clear now, revealing a rocky shoreline and then shining blue water. It was also about to reveal my hiding place. I realized that Old Tom and I could find ourselves in trouble if we were spotted on the island. I made my way back to the jetty as quickly as possible, keeping to the places where the mist was still thick. I was out of breath as I climbed down to the rowboat and obviously disturbed Tom's forty winks.

"Back so soon?" he asked. "See all you wanted to?"

"It was a waste of time," I said. "The coffins are still sealed. They'll be taking them back to the morgue before they open them. I'll just have to find a way to take a peek there."

"You might not like what you'll see," Tom said. "I've seen corpses in my time. The sea washes them up, you know. It's a sight that would turn a grown man's stomach."

"I know," I said, "but I have to know the truth."

He nodded. "Yeah. I suppose the truth is better than not knowing, one way or the other."

With that he pulled away from the dock and started to row. We were halfway back to City Island when we heard the deep chug-chug of an approaching motor and the big government launch sped past us, rocking our tiny craft with its wake.

THIRTY-TWO

By the time I returned to the city, all traces of mist had vanished and the sun scorched down on me as I sat on the ferry deck. I was glad to disembark and catch the train back to Mrs. Goodwin's house. She was already looking much better after a good night's sleep, and she was very interested to hear that a strange police captain had been part of the group.

"That sounds like Captain Paxton from your description," she said. "Dear me. Quigley and McIver aren't going to be at all pleased that he's been put in charge of the case over them. He's one of the old school of policemen. Worry everything like a terrier until you shake something loose. He'll make their lives hell, I can tell you."

"Is he likely to solve the case, do you think?"

"He stands as good a chance as anyone," she said. "He doesn't have Captain Sullivan's brain or intuition, but he's a solid investigator. My husband thought highly of him. They were old pals."

"Well, that's good news, isn't it?" I said. "Maybe he'll be happy to fill us in on the progress of the investigation."

She snorted. "Absolutely not. Quite the contrary, in fact. He was vehemently opposed to women on the force in any capacity and became quite apoplectic when there was a suggestion of using me undercover. To him women belong in the home, doing their sewing and raising children. His own wife is a poor browbeaten creature who does just that. And she has eleven children." She raised her eyes in despair. "I asked her once if she'd never heard of birth control, and she said her husband wouldn't countenance such a thing."

"There are plenty of women like her who are under their husband's thumb," I said. "If I do marry, I'll not let that happen to me."

She smiled then. "I can believe that."

"So what next?" I asked. "Do you really want to turn all our information over to this Captain Paxton and go back to our sewing?"

"Much as it grieves me, I suppose we'll have to," she said. "I'm in no fit state to do more investigating, and I wouldn't want to be in your shoes if Captain Paxton found you snooping around."

"At least we should be sure of our facts before we turn them over," I said. "We don't know yet that those missing girls really are the ones they've just dug up. It could be coincidence. They could have run away from home for any number of reasons."

"So what do you suggest?" she asked.

"I'm thinking I ought to go to the morgue, much as I don't relish that task," I said. "We have to find out the truth. If we can positively identify just one of the girls then we'll know we are on the right track. And we should also contact their families. We need to get a complete description and to know if the girls have any distinguishing marks that would help us identify them."

"Yes, we certainly need to do that," she said. "Now, let's see again, where did they live?"

"One in Brooklyn, one in Queens," I said. "Both convenient for Coney Island."

She gave me her knowing look. "You want to go to Coney Island, don't you?"

"I really think it's the key to everything," I said. "I think we're looking for a young man who preys on impressionable young girls at Coney Island. But I've no idea how he contacts them, or where he finds them, and I've really no idea how we'd start looking in that kind of crowded place."

"Maybe I'll be feeling strong enough in a few days to go there," Mrs. Goodwin said.

"Don't be silly. That's the last place you should go," I said. "You'd get pushed and jostled and you might damage your ribs even worse."

"I'm a tough old bird," she said. "And I believe you can rent bath chairs on the boardwalk. You could push me around in a bath chair."

I laughed. "I'd like to see that."

She chuckled, too, then put her hand to her side. "I'm on the mend, but I've a way to go yet," she said. "I'm going to have to rely on you for a while."

"I'll go to the morgue later today," I said. "I don't want to risk getting there when it's swarming with police."

"And what do you hope to find?"

"I'm not sure," I said. "Confirmation that those other girls weren't prostitutes either, and just maybe . . ." I let the rest of the sentence hang. I couldn't tell her what my suspicion was at this stage because it was too fanciful.

I left Mrs. Goodwin in the capable hands of a nurse. On my way out I muttered a warning that she was never to be left alone with anyone, and that no strange men were to be admitted on any pretext. The nurse nodded and flexed a beefy arm. "Don't worry. Nobody gets past me."

I went home for lunch. I wasn't sure whether I should write to Daniel again. I knew he must be longing to hear from me, but I couldn't tell him any of the things I wanted to. I couldn't even give him any hopeful news. But it had been a couple of days now without a letter from me. So I sat down and wrote a bright, cheerful note, telling him how hard I was working on his behalf, and how I felt I was getting somewhere at last. This was quite untrue, but I had to keep somebody's spirits up, didn't I? My own were pretty much in the dumps.

It was late afternoon when I set out again for Bellevue Hospital and the morgue. I had left it as late as I dared, because I was dreading what would happen next. I had fainted at the smell of formaldehyde and the sight of a body under a sheet. How much worse would four decomposing bodies be?

They probably won't let me in anyway, I told myself to give me courage. I'll ask the doctor for a description of his findings and then I can go home. This reassured me a little until the high brick wall around the hospital grounds came into sight. It was all I could do to put one foot in front of the other and force myself in through that gate. I walked around the morgue twice, trying to see in through the windows and to spot if the police were still in evidence. Then I took a deep breath, got my handkerchief at the ready, and pushed open the front door.

The marble-floored entry hall was deserted, but the smell was stronger than ever—sweeter, more cloying. Instantly my stomach lurched, and I swallowed back bile. I was not going to disgrace myself again. I went over to the double doors that led into the autopsy room, put my ear to them, and listened. I could hear sounds of low voices inside. Did that mean that the police officers were still here? I had no wish to face an angry Detective McIver or Quigley, or that new captain either. I just wished I could see what was going on. There was no keyhole, but I put my eye to the crack in the door. I got a glimpse of a white coat moving. No sign of blue uniforms.

Then suddenly the white coat was growing larger, coming toward me. I leaped back and flattened myself against the wall as the door was flung open and a young man appeared.

"Tell them I'm ready for the next one," a voice called from the autopsy room, "and go and get yourself a cup of coffee. You look as if you're going to pass out on me."

"I'm all right, sir, honestly," the young man called back. He had an earnest schoolboy's face with round wire glasses, and he did look decidedly green. I wondered if he'd chosen the right profession. Maybe this was a required element of medical training. He passed by without noticing me and pushed open another door down the hall. I had recognized the first voice as that of the same doctor we had seen before.

I mustered my full courage and stepped into the autopsy room before the door swung closed on me.

The first thing that assailed me was the smell, so overpowering that my eyes started to water and I could feel myself retching. Like rotting meat on a summer's day but far, far worse. I put my handkerchief to my nose but even the eau de cologne on it did little to help. There were two bodies lying under sheets on marble slabs and one—my stomach lurched alarmingly—was lying fully exposed. I tried not to look, looked anyway and a little cry escaped from my lips. The doctor spun around.

"My dear young woman, what are you doing here? This is no place for you. Out with you."

"I agree with you completely, but Mrs. Goodwin sent me," I said. "I need to talk to you urgently, if you could spare one minute."

"I'd be glad of a minute's fresh air," he said. He crossed the room and wiped his hands on his apron, like a butcher, before opening the door for me. The warm summer air had never felt better as we came outside.

"Now, what is it?" he asked. "I only have a moment before my student brings me the next body, if he doesn't keel over in the process." He smiled at me.

As rapidly as I could, I told him about the letters we had received from relatives of missing girls.

"So you want to discover whether your missing girls could be the ones lying on my slabs here?" he asked gravely.

"Can you tell for sure whether these girls were real streetwalkers or not?" I asked. Somehow I couldn't make myself use the word "prostitute" in the presence of a man. "Streetwalkers" was hard enough.

"If you are asking me whether any of these girls was still a virgin, the answer is that I can't tell for certain," he said. "You understand that it's summer. Decomposition sets in rapidly. The soft tissues don't last long."

I stared out across the green lawn, trying to stay calm and detached and not let the image of what I had just seen creep back into my mind.

"I went back over the notes from the past autopsies and it would appear that there had been recent sexual activity in each case. Which might have meant the predator was successful in his attempt on those occasions." He looked up at me. "And you say the missing girls were of Italian and Swedish background?"

I nodded.

"One of the young ladies I have just examined had the most lovely fair hair," he said. "She could be your Swedish girl."

"Lovely fair hair?" I asked.

"Oh yes. Luxuriant hair, almost white blond. I got quite a shock when we opened the coffin. It was covering her, draped over her shoulders like a cloak."

I found I was trembling. "And is it possible to identify someone by their hair?"

"Oh yes," he said. "If the family has kept some hair in a locket, we can examine and compare the hairs under a microscope and make a good match."

"Would it be possible for me to take some strands of that hair for comparison?" I asked.

He looked at me oddly. "Why would you be doing this?" he asked. "Isn't this a job for the police? They were all here today, you know. They've already taken hair samples as well as Bertillon measurements."

"Mrs. Goodwin plans to turn everything over to her superiors as soon as she's completed her part in the investigation," I said, "but there are a few things she wants to complete first."

"Then why isn't she here herself? Don't tell me she couldn't take it, when you were the one who fainted?"

"She met with an accident," I said. "She was run down by a horse and carriage."

"Dear me," he said. "That's unfortunate. But she survived all right?"

"Fortunately yes. But she's still confined to her bed, so I'm trying to do what I can to help her."

The doctor shook his head. "I could release a strand of

hair to Mrs. Goodwin, because she's official, but you're not. You could find yourself accused of hampering an official police investigation, you know."

"I don't mean to hamper anything, just to speed things along," I said. "The official detectives on the team are not about to listen to a pair of women, even if we are on the right track. And I'm only asking for a couple of snippings of hair."

He laughed then. "Well, I suppose we can do that much for you. Wait here. You won't want to come inside again, I'm sure."

I waited and he returned with an envelope, which he handed me solemnly. "There," he said. "I will be keeping hair samples from the other girls on file, should Mrs. Goodwin need those at a later date."

I thanked him and made a grateful retreat, clutching my precious hair sample.

As soon as I returned home, I paid a visit to Sid and Gus to see if they had Dr. Birnbaum's address. Surely he would have a microscope and be able to compare hair samples for me. I was suitably vague about why I needed to speak to him. I really didn't want to reveal the thoughts going through my head until they proved definite one way or the other. But I had a clear picture in my head—two girls at Miss Marchbank's academy, sitting side by side. One of them pale and delicate looking, but with the most beautiful fair hair cascading over her shoulders.

THIRTY-THREE

It turned out that Dr. Birnbaum was lodging at the Hotel Lafayette, on University Place, the very same place where Ryan O'Hare himself had rooms. Well, that explained how they had met! I was glad it was a short walk as I had been up since before dawn and had already put in a full day's work. My feet flagged on the hot sidewalks, and I looked longingly at the fountain in Washington Square, from which came delighted squeals of small boys splashing merrily. The sound of their voices brought back a whole string of happier memories—Bridie and Shamey had played in that same fountain until they were detected by me and brought home in disgrace. Now I wondered when I would see them again.

Lost in thought, I almost walked right past the Hotel Lafayette, until I glanced up and saw the striped awning over its dining room window, giving it a gay continental appearance. The clerk inside confirmed that Dr. Birnbaum was indeed staying there, and could probably be found in his room at the moment. I was deemed respectable-looking enough to go up as they didn't seem to have a room-to-room telephone system. The doctor's room was on the top floor of three, overlooking University Place. I heard the sound of laughter as I tapped on the door. It was opened by none other than Ryan, dressed, for him, in ordinary city attire—white tailored shirt, light trousers, no frills, no Buddhist robes.

"Molly, what a delightful surprise," he said. "We were expecting some German friends of Fritz's but you'll do equally well. Come on in."

He ushered me into a comfortable suite with plush armchairs, table, and writing desk at one end, a bedroom area at the other. It was meticulously neat, with no clutter other than a pile of books. Dr. Birnbaum was sitting at the desk. He got up in a hurry as I came in and looked rather awkward at finding me there—possibly because he was entertaining Ryan in his rooms.

"Miss Murphy," he said, clicking his heels and bowing. "To what do we owe this honor?"

"I have a favor to ask, Dr. Birnbaum. It's about the case we've been discussing. The murdered girls."

He eyed me warily. "I hope you don't wish to be my assistant again. That was rather embarrassing for me."

"Don't worry," I said. "I'll not embarrass you again. You've kept abreast of what is happening, have you?"

"Ah yes. I read that they plan to exhume the other girls who were murdered."

"They did so today. I was present."

"And how did you manage this feat? I can't picture those two officers inviting you along for the ride."

"They didn't even know I was there." I caught Ryan's eye, and we exchanged a grin.

"*Gott im Himmel,* you never fail to astonish me, Miss Murphy." Dr. Birnbaum mopped his brow with his handkerchief. "Please do be seated. Ryan, will you please pour our guest a glass of wine?"

I took the armchair offered.

"No wine for me, thank you," I said, as Ryan picked up the bottle, shrugged, and poured himself a glass. "I'll not detain you for more than a moment. You have probably also heard that these girls might not have been prostitutes at all, but ordinary, respectable young women dressed up to give the appearance of that kind of person."

"Extraordinary," he said. "Our killer has gone to a lot of trouble. And why, I ask myself? If he wanted to abduct young women and kill them, why not do so and hide their bodies? Bury them under the floorboards, drop them into a lake, dig graves for them in a forest. The chances of their ever being found would have been slight. So why advertise them and go through all this pretense?"

"Maybe because prostitutes don't matter?" I suggested. "If the murdered girls are thought to be ladies of the night, then nobody will care too much who is killing them. Perhaps this is what the killer thinks."

"Didn't I tell you she was a bright girl, Fritz?" Ryan asked. "The flower of Irish womanhood."

I decided he had already attacked that wine bottle before my arrival. He was at that expansive stage of drunkenness we Irish go through. Morbidity would come next.

Dr. Birnbaum stroked his blond beard reflectively. "Possible. Although there is something here that I can't quite grasp. Something is not true to type, or at least to any type that I have come across. A brutish man who violates a girl and then kills her so violently and yet displays all the characteristics of a mind cunning enough to have baffled the police until now. He's reckless enough to take extreme risks, yet well behaved in his daily life so that he is not suspected. It is almost as if we're dealing with two people. This kind of split personality is most fascinating to me. I can't wait to meet him."

"And I can't wait to catch him," I said. "It makes me sick to think of those poor girls, imagining they were about to meet an admirer, only to be lured to their deaths."

"An admirer, what is this?" he demanded.

I told him everything Mrs. Goodwin and I had found so far.

"Going to meet a boy?" He looked perplexed. "I find it hard to believe that we are dealing with a boy here. A young man kills in the heat of passion. He would then be likely to panic and try to hide the body at all costs. These deaths are coldly calculated and the whole execution of the plot carried through to perfection. No, I do not think we are dealing with a boy."

"Then how were the girls lured to their deaths? At least two of them took risks to meet with a young man. He must have been attractive and exciting enough for them to risk their parents' wrath."

Dr. Birnbaum shook his head. "I can't answer that. But what did you want me to do for you?"

"I wondered if you would be able to match up hair samples for me? I have obtained a strand of hair from one of the dead girls. I hope to obtain hair from the girl's home, from a locket or a hairbrush, and I wondered if you would have the means to examine it under a microscope."

"I always travel with a microscope," he said. "It is not the biggest or best model, however. I could give you a preliminary answer, but to make a detailed analysis, we would have to go to a good laboratory. I am sure the police must have this facility. Why not take the hair to them?"

"I intend to," I said, "but I would like to confirm my suspicions first."

"Very well," he said. "Did you bring the hair sample with you?"

"No, it's still at my house. Now I know that you will do this for me, I'll try to obtain a hair from the girl's home. I'll do that in the morning."

"In the meantime, I have no wish to rush you or to appear discourteous," Birnbaum said, "but we expect the arrival of some friends from Freiburg University any minute and we go to dine with them tonight."

I got up. "I'll be on my way, then," I said. "And I thank you for your help."

Ryan remained sprawled in the chair, eyeing his wineglass, as Dr. Birnbaum ushered me out.

I was exceedingly weary as I came out onto University Place, but I made a supreme effort and dragged myself across to Broadway to catch the trolley car north to Gramercy Park, where I hoped to find Arabella Norton. I wasn't looking forward to sharing my suspicion with her, but it had to be done. The sooner we arrived at the truth, the better.

As I stood outside Miss Van Woekem's house on that lovely square, the first thing I heard was the sound of voices and laughter. Then I saw movement behind the lace curtains and realized some sort of large function was taking place. Hardly the right time to disturb Arabella. So it was a case of the trolley back home again, a quiet supper, and an early night. I slept peacefully and was disturbed by no strange dreams.

In the morning I repeated the trip to Miss Van Woekem's. Knowing a little of the behavior of girls from Arabella's background, I suspected that breakfast for her would never be before nine at the earliest. So I timed my arrival for ten, hoping to fit in between breakfast and leaving for the first shopping expedition of the day or fitting at the dressmaker. I was in luck. I requested to speak to Miss Norton, presented my card—although the maid knew full well who I was—and was shown into the drawing room. Arabella was sitting at her aunt's desk writing letters. She jumped up when she saw me.

"Miss Murphy. You have news for me?"

"I may, Miss Norton," I replied, "although I fear it will not be the news you want to hear."

"Bad news? The worst?"

"I may be wrong. Let us hope so."

She motioned to the sofa. "Please forgive my lack of manners. Do sit down. May I call the maid to bring you some coffee?"

I had to admit that ladies of Arabella's class were exceedingly well trained in manners. I declined her offer, knowing that she was dying to hear the news.

"You've read of the string of murders they call the East Side Ripper attacks?"

"Yes, but they are all—ladies of low morals." She flushed at the mention of them.

"Not all," I said. "Some of them have proved to be ordinary working girls, whom the killer has dressed and painted to look like"—I spared her sensibilities—"such ladies."

"But surely this can have nothing to do with Letitia? She wouldn't have been anywhere frequented by—such girls. By her clothing and her manner she would never have been mistaken for a common girl."

"I would agree with you, except for one thing, Miss Norton. One of the bodies possessed the most impressive head of pale blond hair. Now I do realize that one of the girls reported missing by her family is from Swedish descent and may also have such magnificent hair, but I thought the coincidence too striking to ignore."

"But how—where could Letitia ever have been mingling with common people?"

"As to that, you said yourself that she helps her mother at a settlement house. The strange thing is that all these girls had something in common. They had all just been to Coney Island."

Arabella gave a relieved laugh then. "There you are, then. Letitia would never have been to such a low-down place. We talked of it once and both agreed that it could hold no attraction for us."

"But she was due to go there the day she disappeared. She was to plan an outing for the settlement house children the next day."

"But she never arrived in the city. Her fiancé waited for her for hours."

"What if she had taken an earlier train? What if she had somehow missed her fiancé at the station and gone to Coney Island that day to meet her doom."

"Don't." She put a hand to her mouth. "What you suggest is too horrible. You say you've seen the body? Did it—did it look at all like her?"

"I can't tell you that," I said. I was about to mention the face, but stopped myself quickly. "And in truth I didn't see the body. I was too much of a coward. But the body had been buried in the ground for some time. Her hair is the only way we have of identifying her."

"You can identify her by her hair?"

"If we can find one of Letitia's hairs at her home, a doctor will try to match the two samples under a microscope."

"Amazing," she said. "I am sure Letitia's family will be able to find any number of her hairs. A locket, maybe, or the hats she wore, or even a comb she left behind. I'll telephone them today and have the hairs sent down by train. With any luck we'll know, for sure, before I depart for Europe on Monday."

"It would be unfortunate for you, if you had to leave with such terrible news hanging over you," I said.

"But better than not knowing."

I nodded.

"And what news on Daniel?" she asked. "You are still working on his behalf? Is he out of that horrible jail yet?"

"I'm afraid not. I have made some progress, but I don't think it's going to get us anywhere."

"You've found the person who was out to discredit Daniel?"

"I think I have, but it's no use," I said. "It's the police commissioner himself, the one on whose evidence they will convict Daniel."

"What reason does he have to hate Daniel so?"

"He may be involved in a horse-doping scandal that Daniel was investigating."

"But surely such a minor scandal wouldn't make anyone go to such lengths," she said.

"He prides himself on his moral rectitude. Perhaps he couldn't bear that any hint of scandal should tarnish his reputation."

"Then why not just have Daniel removed from the case and put another officer in his place—one who wasn't so competent?"

She had a good point there.

"I don't know," I said. "I really don't know. All I know is that time passes, and I can see no way of securing Daniel's release."

"But why is he in prison if he hasn't even been tried yet?" Arabella asked. "I don't know much about these things, but couldn't he just pay them bail and they'd let him go?"

"That's the problem," I said. "Because he has been accused of having ties to a gang, his assets have been frozen. He doesn't want to ask friends or family because he doesn't want word to get to his father, who is quite ill."

"Daniel does have his noble side then, after all," she said, "but in this case it's rather silly of him, isn't it?"

"I don't think he'd ever forgive himself if his father had a heart attack because of him. It wasn't too bad when there was hope of setting him free in the near future, but the longer this drags on, the more it seems that . . ." To my horror tears started trickling down my cheeks. I turned away but not quickly enough.

Arabella came over to me and put her hand awkwardly on my shoulder. "My dear Miss Murphy, please do not distress yourself. I'm sure everything will be all right. The truth will come out. They won't let an innocent man languish in jail."

"But they will," I said. "Who will believe me? Who will believe Daniel against the word of a powerful man like the commissioner of police?"

At that moment the door opened and Miss Van Woekem came in.

"Molly Murphy!" she exclaimed. "What on earth are you doing here?" She took one look at my tear-stained cheeks as I quickly tried to wipe away the tears with a handkerchief. "Although I hardly think it was wise to come here with my goddaughter in residence, knowing your sentiments about each other. I hope you two haven't been at each other's throats."

"Oh, but Godmother, that's all in the past," Arabella exclaimed. "Miss Murphy and I are now the dearest of friends. She came because she had news for me in a quest of mine."

"And Miss Norton was comforting me when I became distressed."

Miss Van Woekem looked from Arabella to me. "Wonders will never cease," she said. "And what is this quest of yours, child?"

"It's—" Arabella looked at me for inspiration.

"Miss Norton wanted me to locate a friend of hers. I appear to have done so." I nodded to Arabella. "I really should be going. There is much I need to accomplish, as I'm sure you do, too. Please excuse me if I rush away, Miss Van Woekem." I bowed to her and made for the front door.

"I'll make that telephone call today and attempt to supply you with what you need," Arabella called after me.

"I must say the Irish are an emotional race. Now what was all that about?" I heard Miss Van Woekem saying as I closed the door behind me.

THIRTY-FOUR

I went to visit Mrs. Goodwin on my return, stopping off to buy a bunch of grapes at a greengrocer's. Her neighbor let me in. She was clearly enjoying herself, having established herself as queen of the household, bossing around the nurse and Mrs. Goodwin.

"I've made her a junket," she said, ready to give me my instructions, too, "and I've some calf's-foot jelly cooling and a poultice all ready for her ribs."

"I keep telling her a poultice isn't going to help with a cracked bone, but she won't listen to me," the nurse said.

The two women glared at each other. I stepped between them.

"Thank you so much. What a lucky lady Mrs. Goodwin is to have such a kind neighbor as yourself," I said. "Why don't you go home and have a rest. You must be worn-out."

"Well, I have been on my feet all day," the neighbor conceded and left.

"Odious woman," the nurse muttered. "Comes in here, bossing me around as if I was the hired help. And bossing the poor invalid, too."

"How is she?" I asked.

"Go upstairs and see for yourself," she said.

I climbed the stairs and found the supposed invalid sitting in a chair beside her bed.

"Well, this is good news," I said. "I've brought you some grapes."

She smiled. "It was a case of get well or have to suffer those two women going at it hammer and tongs," she said. "Getting well seemed the safer option."

"Are you sure you're not rushing things?"

"Well, my side feels as if a mule kicked it, and my head aches when I try to stand up, but other than that I'm right as rain," she said. "And I can't abide wasting time lying in bed. Now, tell me everything. I was worried when you didn't return yesterday evening."

"I wanted to set things in motion as quickly as I could," I said, and recounted my visits to the morgue and Dr. Birnbaum. "But I don't want to give Letitia Blackwell's family grief for nothing, so I'd really like to have the hair samples examined before we hand this information over to that police captain."

"And I'd really like to interview the families involved before the police get at them," Sabella Goodwin said.

"I don't see how I can do that for you," I said. "You told me yourself that I would get in terrible trouble if I went prying without proper authority, and you won't be well enough for a while yet."

"Don't be so sure of that."

"How can you think that you'd be able to take trams and trains and be jostled by crowds?" I said. "You'd be risking even greater damage to yourself."

"Not necessarily," she said. "It just happens that my late husband's brother runs a small garage and repair shop in Brooklyn. And he happens to own an automobile of sorts. I've never seen it actually run, but it would be better than trying to fight the crowds or hoping a cab will turn up."

"But even an automobile won't spare your sore ribs," I said. "I really think you should put your own health first at this moment."

"I am putting myself first," she said. "If we can present all the facts to Captain Paxton, one step ahead of those arrogant young men, then my superiors will have to take me seriously. It won't hurt your reputation as a detective either." She held up her hand as I went to speak again. "And frankly

I'd rather put up with a bit of bone shaking in an automobile than listening to those two women all day. I thought we might take a trip out to Brooklyn tomorrow and see if Bert can spare the time to run us around. Are you up for it?"

She gave me a determined, defiant stare. "I'm up for it whenever you are," I said.

"Good. Then that's settled."

So it seemed to be. I must say I was anxious to speak to the girls' families and see if they could give us any hints to the identification of the young man who might have lured two girls to their deaths. Of course maybe I was jumping to conclusions here. Maybe each girl was grabbed or lured away by the Ripper before they ever got to their assignation—snatched up into a passing carriage, maybe. In which case we had little hope of tracking him down, unless history repeated itself and this time there were witnesses.

Arabella Norton was swift to act and by that evening a parcel had been delivered to my door. It contained a silver locket that encased a strand of golden hair. I delivered it to Dr. Birnbaum and entreated him to go to work on it as soon as possible.

It felt as if we were poised on the brink of finding out one way or the other. However, if my suspicions were confirmed, it would bring no relief but only heartbreak. It was not an enviable task that lay ahead of me and I lay in bed wondering why I felt compelled to see it through. I wasn't a police matron, hoping to make my mark as a detective. And I'd be no nearer to releasing Daniel. Yet I knew that Mrs. Goodwin was counting on me. She needed me more than ever in her current condition. Of my own current condition I chose not to think.

Early on Saturday morning I arrived at Mrs. Goodwin's house and found a cab waiting for us.

"I decided I would be foolish to risk my ribs on the tram over the Brooklyn Bridge," she said.

"But a cab, isn't that an awful expense?" I blurted out.

"I shall present the bill to my superiors at the same time as I give them the benefits of my investigation," she said, looking a trifle smug. "When they see what we have accomplished, I don't think they will dare turn me down. And it's not as if I have access to police vehicles like my male colleagues."

"Quite right," I said. This woman never failed to impress me. She would be my model from now on.

The cabby and I assisted Mrs. Goodwin to board and seated her with pillows in her back before we set off. There was brisk traffic across the bridge to Brooklyn. The half-day Saturday laws were beginning to take effect, meaning that many city workers were probably headed to the nearest beach to escape the heat. That beach would be Coney Island. I wondered how soon Mrs. Goodwin would be well enough to go there with me. I was anxious enough to go there, but not alone!

We crossed into Brooklyn and the cab deposited us on a street of wood-framed row houses and various small businesses. The brother-in-law's house was at the end of the row, and the shed beside it sported an impressive sign: GOODWIN'S MOTOR SHOP. AUTOMOBILES REPAIRED.

We knocked and Mr. Goodwin himself appeared at the door—a big, ruddy man with arms like tree trunks, dressed only in an undershirt, with a hairy chest clearly visible.

"Sabella—well, I never. What a surprise to see you. Come in, do. Marge will be pleased." He went to enfold her in a bear hug, but she blocked his advance.

"I've come to ask a favor, Bert," she said, "and I'd like to introduce my young friend and helper, Miss Murphy. Molly, may I present Albert Goodwin."

"Pleased to meet you, I'm sure." He shook hands with awkward embarrassment at the formality. "Now come on in. What is it I can do for you, Bella, my dear?"

Bella explained her accident and our mission, then we had a pleasant cup of coffee in their little kitchen while Bert prepared the automobile. It was nothing like the sleek models that I had ridden in a couple of times before; in fact I suspected that it was partly homemade—not much more than a box on wheels. Bert had to crank it up several times, but at last it popped and banged and then chugged away merrily.

He helped me into the backseat, Sabella into the front beside him, and we were off. Even though the ride was smoother than a horse and trap, I could see it was an ordeal for Mrs. Goodwin, although she'd never admit it.

Fortunately the first address was not too far away, on a small side street just off Flushing Avenue. It was obvious as soon as we came to a halt that we were in an Italian neighborhood—the smells, the sounds, the very exuberance of life. Italians don't talk to each other—they yell, they laugh, they fight, and all with the maximum of arm gestures and flashing eyes. The children played equally loudly. A street musician was singing a haunting Italian song in a rich, pure voice. Our automobile caused much interest. The children stopped playing to swarm around it. Bert leaped out and drove them off before they could damage his precious vehicle or burn themselves on the hot hood.

We asked for the Rosettis' residence and were escorted to it by a mass of dark heads. The man who opened the door looked as if he hadn't slept in a few nights. Mrs. Goodwin showed him her badge, and we were ushered inside. A large woman, dressed head to toe in black, appeared from the kitchen.

"They've come from the police, Mama," the man said in broken English.

"They bring news? News of my Rosa?" she asked.

"Not yet, I'm afraid," Mrs. Goodwin said. "But we'd like to ask your daughters some questions, to see if they can shed any more light—" she stopped, realizing she was going beyond his English skills—"if they can tell us anything we don't know."

"Bene." He nodded. "Our young ones are here. Lucia come home from the factory soon. Gina! Sophia!" he boomed. "Mama, go get the girls."

The wife disappeared and immediately two young girls came rushing into the room.

"What is it, Papa?" they asked and stood there looking shyly at us.

"They want to ask questions about Rosa," he said. "Answer them good. Tell them everything you know."

"We don't know nothing, Papa. I told you that already," the older one answered. "If we could do something to find Rosa, we would."

Mrs. Goodwin produced the letter. "You say that she went to work at the factory that day and never came home?" she asked the father.

"*Si*. That's right."

"Do your other daughters work at the same factory? Didn't anyone see her leave?"

"Her sister work there with her, but she's been staying late. They're trying to start a union, and my Lucia wants to be part of it. She is very"—he slapped himself on the chest—"my Lucia. Strong. With fire. Big heart."

"So nobody saw Rosa leave that evening?"

"Another girl say she was in a hurry, and she look excited. But she didn't tell anyone where she goes."

"Did she have a young man?"

"Young man?" he boomed out the words. "She was sixteen years old. No boys. Too young. That's what we tell her. We find her a nice Italian boy when the right time comes."

He looked up at his wife, who was still hovering in the doorway, and she nodded.

Mrs. Goodwin glanced at me before saying, "Mr. Rosetti, would it be possible to talk to your daughters alone, without you and your wife in the room? They may be too shy to speak in front of you, but Rosa may have confided something to them. Something she didn't want you to know."

"My Rosa, she tell her mama and papa everything," he said angrily.

"Sometimes even the best girls don't tell their parents everything," I said quietly. "You do want us to find out what happened to Rosa, don't you?"

"You want I should go?" he demanded.

"If it helps to find Rosa," Mrs. Goodwin said.

He gave a large, expressive shrug. "*Bene*. I go. Anything to bring my Rosa home to me. Come, Mama."

The door closed behind them.

"Now girls," Mrs. Goodwin said, "we need to know if your sister told you anything that she kept secret from your parents. Did she have a secret admirer? Did she give any hint that she was planning to meet a boy?"

"Oh no, signora," the older girl said. "She wouldn't do that. Papa would never allow it. When we go out, he makes us all go together and watch over each other."

"Like this photograph at the beach?" She produced the picture.

They smiled. "*Si, signora.*"

"Was this taken at Coney Island?" I asked.

"*Si.*" They nodded again, their eyes smiling with the memory.

"Do you go there often?"

"When there is money to spare. It's only a nickel on the train and Mama packs us a lunch so we don't have to buy food. Sometimes Lucia treats us to a ride or a show. Sometimes we just walk around and watch the people."

"And did Rosa ever meet a boy during one of these outings?" I asked.

"No. Never," the older one said.

"But she did get that note," the younger one reminded her.

"What note?" Mrs. Goodwin asked quickly.

The younger girl gave her sister a half-frightened glance then said boldly, "Last time we went. Rosa laughs and says some boy slipped a note into her pocket. He said he liked her and wanted to meet her alone."

"Did you see the boy?" Mrs. Goodwin asked.

"No, and neither did Rosa. She just found the note in her pocket. It would be easy for someone to put the note there without her noticing because the crowd is so thick that it's hard to move."

"Where was this exactly?" I asked.

"On the Bowery. You know where that is? It's like a street

in the middle of the fun fair. Lucia had made overtime money and she treated. She told us we could choose what we wanted to do. So we went to the freak show, cos we'd never seen it before and we had a good laugh there."

The older sister took over. "Then Rosa said she wanted to visit the Cairo Pavilion and maybe be snatched up by a sheik and taken to his harem. We all laughed. Rosa was naughty sometimes. She said wild things. Have you ever been there? They have real camels and belly dancers and fire-eaters—oh my, it's wonderful. It's like being in another world."

"And did she keep the note? Do you still have it?" Mrs. Goodwin asked.

"Oh no. Lucia made her throw it into the nearest rubbish bin. Rosa made a fuss and said Lucia was being a spoilsport and no boy had ever said nice things to her in a note; but Lucia grabbed it, crumpled it up, and tossed it into the bin. 'You know what Papa would say about that, don't you?' she said."

"And she never heard from the boy again?"

"Never. Lucia made us go straight home after that. She was mad at Rosa."

"How long was this before she disappeared?"

The girls wrinkled their foreheads. "Four days," the little one said. "It was the weekend before she vanished."

"Mrs. Goodwin got to her feet. "I'm going to ask your father if I can look through her things. She might have a secret hiding place for letters and treasures."

The girls looked at each other and laughed. "We share a chest of drawers, all four of us," the younger one said. "There is no place to be secret in our room."

"Nevertheless, I'd like to see for myself." Sabella was firm.

Papa Rosetti led us upstairs and we went through the room carefully. The girls owned nothing more than a change of underclothes, a few pairs of well-darned stockings, missals, rosaries, and a few treasures like a lace handkerchief or a cheap broach.

"Tell me, Signor Rosetti," Mrs. Goodwin said carefully, "does Rosa have any special ways to identify her—a mole perhaps or a scar? Anything unusual?"

His face went ashen gray. "You think something bad has happened to her."

"We're not sure yet. But just in case."

"No," he said. "She has nothing wrong with her. She is a beautiful girl. Full of life. Everyone loves Rosa."

At that moment the oldest girl, Lucia, burst in.

"They have news about Rosa?" she asked, her face bright with hope.

"Not yet," Mrs. Goodwin said. "We think her disappearance may be linked to that of some other girls. We hear that your sister received a note from a boy while you were all at Coney Island."

"Oh that?" Lucia shook her head. "It was just a bit of nonsense that goes on in places like that. Boys come there alone and tease girls. That's what boys do. Anyway, I made Rosa throw the note away."

"So you don't think she could have gone back later to meet him alone?"

"How could she? I crumpled the note myself. I threw it into the bin. It was gone."

"She could have memorized the important parts of the message first?" Mrs. Goodwin suggested.

"I don't think so." Lucia looked perplexed. "That is—I don't know how long she'd been reading it before she showed it to us." Then she shook her head violently. "But she wouldn't do a thing like that. She knows what Papa would say. She wouldn't do that. She wouldn't."

But I got the feeling that Lucia was not sure of this at all. Rosa, the fun-loving, naughty daughter, might very well have disobeyed Papa.

THIRTY-FIVE

The whole family escorted us to the front door. Papa shook our hands earnestly. "We thank you for all you do to find our dear daughter," he said. "If you bring her back to us, we will be your servants forever."

We tried to smile as we went back to Bert, standing guard beside his auto.

"At least we've established that she received a note on Coney Island," I said as he got the automobile started again and then we edged our way, with much horn honking, past the inquisitive children and back onto Flushing Avenue. "We now know that two girls received notes from a boy saying that he liked them. It's a pity we don't know whether Rosa's note suggested a time and place they could meet again. Or where that place was."

"That's true." Sabella Goodwin nodded. "Maybe the other family will be able to show us the note their girl received."

The day had heated up rapidly and the sun beat down on the front seat, sparing me in the back, where there was a rudimentary canopy that looked as if it came from an old carriage.

"I wished we'd thought of bringing a parasol," Mrs. Goodwin said. She looked hot and uncomfortable, and I guessed that her side was hurting her. But she refused my suggestion to stop for a cool drink or an ice cream.

"Let's get it over with," she said. I realized it was not her own discomfort she wanted to end, it was the difficult meeting with another family, for whom the ultimate news could only be even worse.

We headed north along Fifty-eighth Street into Queens. The Lindquist family had an apartment over a baker's shop and the delicious smell of baking lingered in the warm air. We went up the stairs beside the shop, and the door was opened by a round-faced young woman with light blue eyes and light hair.

"Are you, by any chance, Krissy Lindquist?" Mrs. Goodwin asked.

"Ya." The girl looked worried.

"You wrote me a letter about your sister."

"You have news for me?"

"Not yet. I wanted to ask you some questions about your sister," Mrs. Goodwin said. "I wondered if we could talk."

The girl glanced nervously into the interior of her apartment, then closed the door quietly. "Downstairs. On the street. Maybe safer," she said, and led us down.

We stood under the awning outside the baker's shop.

"Now, Krissy," Mrs. Goodwin began. "You said your sister received a note from a boy. Did she show it to you?"

"No," Krissy said. "I think she maybe made it up. She don't always speak quite truthful." Her accent was foreign with definite overtones of someone who has learned English on the streets of New York.

"And did she tell you anything about this boy she was going to meet?"

"No. Nothing. I ask her lots of questions, but she acts all mysterious. Very pleased with herself because I never had a boy want to meet me, and I'm older than her."

"Had you been to Coney Island with her before she got the note?"

"No. She went. Not me. I was supposed to go too, but I got sick right before it. She said it was wonderful, like a dreamland. I was annoyed because I couldn't go, so I didn't ask her too much about it."

"But you think she met the boy there?"

Krissy shook her head. "I don't know. She could have

met him anywhere, but Coney Island would be a safe place to arrange a secret meeting, wouldn't it, because there are so many people. It's like you're invisible. Nobody to report home to my pa."

"Do you have a picture of Denise?"

She glanced up the stairs. "Wait here. I bring you one."

She came down again soon after, a little out of breath, and handed us a photograph. It was a portrait, taken in a studio, and it showed a pretty, plump girl with her hair braided in a rather unflattering way across her head. But the hair was light brown at best, and the girl I had seen on the morgue table had been much smaller.

"It's not her," I said, without thinking.

"You've found someone?" Krissy asked.

"Yes, a girl's body," Mrs. Goodwin said quickly, "but it's not your sister."

"Then there is still hope." She put her hands together in prayer. "I tell you, lady, I feared the worst news. Dilly would never run off and leave me and Mama and Papa worrying about her. She was a good daughter and a good sister. So I really thought something very bad had happened. You read about it in the newspapers, don't you—bad things happening to girls?"

Mrs. Goodwin touched her arm. "I can't guarantee that something bad hasn't happened to your sister, Krissy. Tell me—one thing the police will want to know. Did she have any distinguishing marks on her?" As Krissy looked puzzled she went on, "Anything we could recognize her by? A mole? A broken tooth? A scar?"

"Well," Krissy said, "she lost the top of a finger once. It got slammed in a carriage door when she was little. You hardly notice it now, but she has no nail on the finger." She pointed to her right hand.

"Thank you. That's most helpful," Mrs. Goodwin said. "May we take the photograph with us?"

"If you bring it back to me," she said. "It's all I've got now. My parents won't even talk about her. They won't even listen."

At that very moment loud footsteps stomped down the uncarpeted stairs and a big, fair-haired man appeared. His shirtsleeves were rolled up and he wore red suspenders.

"What's this?" he demanded and broke into a flood of Swedish.

His daughter answered him. As she spoke he glared at us.

"Go. Be gone," he said, gesturing in a threatening manner. "Tell them." And more Swedish came out.

Krissy looked at him imploringly. "But Papa."

"Tell them!" he roared.

"He says he don't want his daughter back no more, even if you find her. He don't want to know. His daughter is no good. Ruined." A tear escaped from the corner of her eye. "But please don't believe him. Please go on searching for her. I beg you."

"Don't worry." Mrs. Goodwin gave her a reassuring smile. "We will do our best, I promise you."

We made our exit with Papa Lindquist watching us go, hands on hips and glaring.

"I fear we have just left two families whose hearts are destined to be broken," she commented as the automobile got up speed and a warm wind blew in our faces.

Bert's wife, Marge, insisted that we stay for a meal with them.

"You're lucky you came today and not tomorrow," she said as we helped her clear away the dishes. "You'd have got no sense out of him then. He'd be busy tuning and polishing that ridiculous motor vehicle so that it made it all the way to Coney Island."

"Coney Island? You like to spend the day at the beach?" I asked politely, trying not to sound too interested.

He laughed. "Can't stand it. Can't stand crowds either, but I love a good fight. There's a boxing match going to take place out there tomorrow evening. I reckon half of New York is going. I'll be going early to get a good seat."

"A lot of silly men watching two other men beat each other to a pulp," Marge muttered to us. "You wouldn't catch me there for all the tea in China."

"It's no place for a woman," Bert Goodwin replied. "But men need their sport. It was a stupid law that tried to shut it down." He looked at his sister-in-law. "Your husband enjoyed a good fight, Bella. He liked nothing more."

"I know he did. And I'm quite partial to one myself," she said unexpectedly. "In fact I wouldn't mind coming with you tomorrow."

Bert Goodwin laughed. "You never cease to surprise me, Bella. Come if you want to, but I warn you it will be rough."

"Do you think that's wise?" I whispered to her. "You'll get jostled and bumped in that crowd."

"But it's too good a chance to turn down," she muttered back to me. "And I'm sure we'll be quite safe with Bert to escort us," she said in a louder voice.

"Quite safe? I reckon you will be, especially with half the New York Police Department out there."

"Trying to stop the fight?" I asked.

He threw back his head and laughed even louder. "Trying to stop it? Betting on it, my dear. There's nothing a cop likes better than a good brawl. Am I right, Bella?"

"I can't disagree with you," Mrs. Goodwin said. "I'm sure half the department will be there. Whitey always was."

"But your little friend here surely won't want to go, too?" Marge Goodwin looked at me as an ally in the midst of all this barbarism. "She can stay here and keep me company."

"Oh no," I lied. "I love a good boxing match. I used to watch them all the time with my brothers in Ireland."

"There you are, Marge," Bert said. "You heard her. But I'm warning the both of you—if I take you with me, don't go changing your minds and come begging me to take you home in the middle of the fight because I'm not budging until it's over, even if it goes on all night."

"Wouldn't dream of it," I said.

"Right, then I'll expect you back here by six tomorrow evening. The fight starts at eight-thirty and I'm allowing plenty of time for the crowds."

"Thank you kindly, Bert," Mrs. Goodwin said.

"Why don't they stay with us tonight, rather than going

all that way back to the city?" Marge Goodwin said. "It's a while since we've had Bella to talk to. I'll make us a good Italian spaghetti tonight."

"Very kind of you," Mrs. Goodwin said. "We accept, don't we, Molly?"

I could hardly refuse. "Very kind," I echoed.

Later when we were up in their guest room, I accosted her. "Are you sure you know what you're doing? By rights you should still be in your sickbed. Even riding in that auto today was painful for you, I could see it."

"You learn to be tough in the police force," she said. "And who knows when we'd ever get a chance like this again? We'll have Bert to escort us, and, as he said, half the New York police will be on hand, if we should get into trouble."

"That's what I don't understand," I said. "I understood that one of the reasons for Daniel's arrest was that he was setting up an illegal prizefight. Now you tell me that most of his fellow officers will be attending it?"

"Officially it's against the law, if you wanted an excuse to arrest somebody," she said. "But nobody's going to stop that fight tomorrow night. I can guarantee you that. Too much money riding on it."

"So the betting is a big part of it, is it?"

"Oh yes, indeed. There will be plenty of men who go, not to watch the fight particularly, but to wager large amounts of money. And heaven help their favorite boxer if he doesn't win. He'll have to make a hasty getaway."

I thought of Gentleman Jack and wondered how many times he'd had to make that hasty getaway. There was a lot for him riding on this fight, too. Tomorrow would be an important day for all of us.

THIRTY-SIX

We passed a pleasant enough Sunday morning. Bert and Marge went to church, but Bella declined for herself and me, saying she didn't feel up to sitting on a hard bench for a long sermon. I thought this was a poor excuse for one who was about to sit through a twenty-something-round boxing match, but it was accepted with good grace.

"Now let's get down to strategy," she said when we had the house to ourselves. "What is it we hope to accomplish on Coney Island?"

"For one thing we want to talk to the pimp of the first prostitute whose body was found under the boardwalk," I said, "and maybe some of her fellow workers. One of them might be able to give a description of the man with whom she was last seen."

"And apart from that?"

"I'm not sure," I said. "If two young girls were given notes by a strange boy, then maybe I'd better make myself available and unaccompanied. You or Bert can keep a safe distance behind me and watch."

"You're making yourself the bait?"

"If you put it that way. But I'll be quite safe, because I'll be aware, and you'll be watching."

"Coney Island is a big place," she said. "It's a long shot."

"It might pay off," I said. "If it doesn't, we present our findings to Captain Paxton."

She nodded. "And he'll solve the case and get all the

glory and I'll go back to being assigned to the women's dormitory, and picking up fleas into the bargain."

It was early evening and the world was bathed in rosy twilight when Bert wheeled out the automobile. True to Marge's prediction, he had polished it until it gleamed. He cranked it up and we were off.

"Is the fight going to be at the Athletic Club as usual?" Bella asked.

"Out at Norton's Point, you mean?" Bert shook his head. "They can't hold it there. That would be the obvious place, and it would be shut down before it started."

"But I thought you said half the police force would be there?" I asked.

"Unofficially. But officially they're duty bound to shut it down. So it has to be at a secret location."

"And you know where that is?"

"I just happen to know where that is," he said with a smile.

The streets of Brooklyn were congested with Sunday evening activity as families enjoyed an hour or two of leisure on the stoop. We were reduced to crawling past children's games and ice cream barrows. We couldn't have been more than halfway there when there was a shudder, a pop, and we came to a halt.

"Danged, blasted thing," Bert muttered. "What can that be now?"

He opened the hood. "Danged fan belt has broken. Where am I going to find another one on a Sunday evening?"

A crowd gathered around us, the young men pretending expertise and offering suggestions. Since I knew nothing about motor cars, I couldn't tell if they were helpful or not. At last one of them mentioned someone who owned an automobile and might have spare parts. Bert took off with him while we waited, feeling horribly conscious of being objects of curiosity. Some of the remaining young men tried a little flirting, but were driven off by Mrs. Goodwin's frowns. At long last Bert reappeared, his face red and his shirt drenched with sweat. A lot more tinkering went on until finally the motor was cranked and mercifully it turned over.

We set off on our way again. Darkness had all but fallen, and Bert had to go at a snail's pace through poorly lit streets. Then we saw a glow ahead of us, and against that glow the monstrous silhouettes of the giant wheel and the roller coaster. We had finally arrived at Coney Island. Bert left the car at a nearby stable, paying the groom to keep an eye on it. Mrs. Goodwin grimaced as she was helped from her seat.

"You weren't wise to do this," I said.

"I've never been known for being wise," she answered briskly. "If I had been wise, I'd have married a bank clerk and stayed home to keep house. Unfortunately I grew up wanting excitement."

"We really are kindred spirits," I said, "but is there some way we can keep you out of the crowds and not have you walking too much?"

"I'll survive," she said. "I'm more interested in getting the job done."

Bert took her arm and escorted us across Surf Avenue. We had to negotiate a throng of people, heading home after a day at the beach and on their way to the nearest railway station or trolley stop. We pushed past them to plunge into the heart of Coney Island. Sounds came to meet us—the competing music of hurdy-gurdies, organs, drums, screams. The night glowed with electric lights at the bigger establishments and hissing kerosene lamps at the more modest booths.

Bert Goodwin took out his watch from his breast pocket. "Dang it, we're late because of that no-good fan belt," he muttered and strode out ahead of us. "This way."

I noted that he had guided us onto the Bowery itself. I had only seen it by day, when it had been lively enough. Now, at night, it was positively bewildering. Touts were shouting outside all kinds of entertainments from the wholesome to the bawdy. Music spilled from dance halls. From the fun house came the sound of mechanical laughter. I hardly had time to take it all in as Bert swept us forward.

"In here," he said, and stopped outside the entrance to Inman's Casino and Dance Hall.

There was a burly man guarding the entrance. He ignored Bert and tipped his derby to us.

"Are you ladies here for the dance?"

"Dance? I thought this was where the fight was going to take place," Bella Goodwin said.

"Fight? What fight?" The man said innocently. "Oh, no. Fights are prohibited in New York State—didn't you know that? What we're having tonight is a nice little tea dance. But if the gentleman gets restless and decides to go exploring, he might come upon some entertainment more to his liking."

He accompanied this last remark with a wink, and we all understood what he was saying. He wasn't allowed to let anyone in to see a prizefight, but if they happened to discover one after they were inside, then it was all right with him.

"We'll have three tickets for your—dance," Bert said, and paid for us.

We went inside and found ourselves in a modest-sized ballroom. It had a fancy chandelier in the center, lit by hundreds of electric lightbulbs, a row of red plush chairs around the perimeter, as well as little tables on which candles flickered. In one corner, on a dais, a band was playing lively ragtime tunes. One couple was already dancing a two-step. A few women sat listening, or fanning themselves as it was stuffy inside, but apart from that, the room was empty. However, we were instantly aware of the noise that almost drowned out the sound of the orchestra. It was a roar, and it came from a small doorway in the corner. Bert almost dragged us toward it. We went down a dark and dingy hallway and emerged into a much larger room that was already so full, it was hard to even get through the door. The place echoed to shouts and catcalls. It was fierce male shouting, alarming in its intensity, like the heat of a battle; and I stood in that doorway, unwilling to force my way farther into the room. At first all I could see was backs and heads. Some men hadn't even taken their hats off and it was impossible to see over them. But little by little we wormed our way forward.

Then suddenly there was a parting in the crowd enough for me to see the object of all the shouts and catcalls. In the middle of the ballroom a raised platform had been erected, surrounded by ropes. There were several rows of chairs around it, all occupied, I noted. Behind the chairs the crowd was packed in like sardines. Over the boxing ring several electric lights were suspended and the heat from them made the room like a Turkish bath.

At that moment the crowd gave another mighty roar, and I got my first good look at the fight. Two big men were dancing and weaving around the ring, both naked to the waist, their bare torsos already smeared with blood. Suddenly the crowd gave a cheer as a powerful punch was thrown. I heard the sickening thud as it connected. One man's head jerked backward and he staggered against the ropes, while a stream of blood and spittle flew out from his face over the spectators in the front row. It took me awhile to recognize that man as Gentleman Jack. One eye was half-closed and his nose was already a bloody mess. I turned away.

"Follow me," Bert said. "We'll see if we can get a better view."

I looked at Mrs. Goodwin. "Don't worry about us, Bert," she said. "I don't think I'll risk getting poked in the ribs so soon after my injury. I'm quite content to watch from the back here. But you go ahead. We'll meet you when the fight's over."

"That could be awhile," he said. "Apparently they're only on the fourth round. It should go for at least twenty-five."

"You go ahead and enjoy yourself." Mrs. Goodwin almost pushed him into the thick of the crowd.

"Well, that's got rid of him," she said. "Now we can make our retreat. I take it you don't really want to watch any more of this disgraceful spectacle than I do?"

"I think it's truly horrible," I said as another punch landed with a deep thud and the crowd groaned.

"We'll let Bert get himself settled, then we'll push off," Mrs. Goodwin whispered.

I was trying not to look at the boxing ring. My eyes

scanned the crowd. Then I froze. I was looking straight at Detective Quigley, and next to him was Captain Paxton.

"Let's get out of here fast," I whispered. "Quigley's over there."

We fled down the hallway. "I hope he didn't see me," she said. "They think I'm still in bed, recuperating."

"So the righteous Mr. Quigley watches fights," I murmured.

"So it seems."

We came out into the dance hall, where a few more couples were now dancing.

"We have an hour at least, if the fight goes the distance," she said. "Let's get to work. What do you want to do first?"

"Find someone who can tell us about the murdered prostitute," I answered.

"That shouldn't be hard at this time of night," she said, as we came out into the bright lights of the Bowery. As soon as I looked around, I realized she was right. Just out of those bright lights, in the little alleyways that ran off to either side, there were girls waiting, leaning against walls, striking provocative poses, some even smoking cigarettes.

Mrs. Goodwin went up to a cluster of them. They eyed her warily.

"One of the girls here was found murdered under the pier a few weeks ago," she said. "You heard about it, of course."

"Course we did," one of the girls said insolently.

"Did any of you know her personally?"

"That would be Jewel. She was one of Harry the Horse's girls," a tall redhead spoke. "He'd probably know more."

"Have any more girls been attacked or had narrow escapes since then, have you heard?" Mrs. Goodwin asked.

They looked at each other for confirmation. "Not that we've heard," one said. "Mind you, we're more choosy who we go with now, and we keep an eye out for each other."

"So you didn't know this Jewel personally?" I asked.

"We knew what she looked like," one said, "but not to talk to. Harry doesn't like his girls mixing too much."

"So where would we be likely to find Harry the Horse at this time of night?"

"Couldn't say," one said. "Down by the pier, maybe? He likes to sit in Maxwell's saloon there and keep an eye on things. Some of his girls take their customers down under the boardwalk. The cheapskates who don't want to pay for a room."

"Now go on, hop it," the first girl said. "You're keeping the customers away. What are you, anyway, her aunt?"

"Just someone who wants justice for her," Mrs. Goodwin said quietly, and we moved off.

"Down to the pier then, I think," she said to me, and we made our way back along the Bowery.

The pier stretched out like a ghostly arm into the black ocean. The bathing house beside it was already shut and in complete darkness. I looked down to see white lines of waves rushing at the beach and lights along the pier twinkling in the water. It was a festive scene, but I was as taut as a watch spring. The couples who passed us would be finding the darkness romantic, I thought. Then my mind went to two couples in particular. Did Rosa Rosetti and Dilly Lindquist have high hopes of a romantic evening when they strolled arm in arm along the boardwalk? When had they been lured into a carriage? When had they first begun to feel afraid? Not here, surely, where there were always people within earshot.

I looked around me. Here on the boardwalk there was a steady stream of pedestrians, but down those steps, on the beach, or maybe under the boardwalk, it would be completely dark now. A good place to go for a stolen kiss, perhaps, but also complete darkness for more sinister motives. Except—I watched figures going up and down those steps. She would only have to scream and help would be at hand. And if he killed her down there, how in heaven's name did he manage to carry the body to a waiting vehicle?

"This is the bar they mentioned," Mrs. Goodwin said, "and if I'm not mistaken, that's the man we are looking for with one of his girls now."

A flashily dressed young man, in jaunty derby and white spats, was wagging his finger as he shouted at a young girl.

She was scantily dressed and shivered as if it was cold, which it wasn't. Even the thick lipstick and rouge couldn't disguise how young she was.

"You Goddamn well get back to work, you lazy bitch," he was growling, "or you'll feel the back of my hand across your face."

Mrs. Goodwin stepped in with me right behind her.

"Are you Harry?" she asked.

"What if I am?"

"I've a few questions to ask you," she said.

"Oh yeah? And why should I answer your questions?"

"Because of this." She whipped out her badge in a way that made me green with envy. This is what a private investigator lacks, I thought. Each time we talk to someone we have to win them over and make them want to talk to us. We can never force them to, like the police.

He laughed. "Go on. That ain't real. There ain't no women cops."

"Want to test it if I blow my whistle?" she asked.

The bluster subsided a fraction. "You can't do nothing to me. I ain't done nothing wrong."

"You were threatening that young girl. And you know she's underage."

"What young girl? Oh—that's my little sister. I have to keep her in line."

"And I'm a sergeant in the marines," she said, making him chuckle. "Look, Harry. I want to talk to you about the girl who was murdered. Jewel—was that her name?"

"Yeah, Jewel. Pity about that. Nice kid."

"So what can you tell me about her murder?"

"Nothing. It happens sometimes. The guys get carried away. Some of them like it rough. The girls, too. Hazard of the job."

"You don't know who she went with then?"

"If I did, I'd break his face in. He lost me one of my best workers."

"So there's nothing you can tell us to help us catch this

man?" she asked. "You must know that several more prostitutes have been killed since then."

"The girls in the city? Same guy, is it?"

"We think so. It might be only a matter of time before he
comes out here again," she said. "So is there nothing you can
tell us?"

"She was jumpy that night," he said. "She told another
girl that she didn't want to go through with it. 'I can put up
with a lot if they pay well,' she said to the girl, 'but that's a
bit much.'"

"So you think she suspected there would be violence?"

"I don't know. That's all I can tell you. She didn't show
up when she was supposed to and next morning they found
her body."

"Thanks, Harry," she said. "Let's hope we catch him."

"Me, too." His eyes fastened on me. "Don't tell me you're
a lady cop as well?"

"I'm her little sister, the same as she's yours." I indicated
the young girl, who had stopped shivering and was looking
on with interest.

"I could put you to work if you're ever out of a job." His
eyes flirted with me. "Good-looking healthy girl like you."

"Thanks, but I'd rather gut fish at the Fulton market," I said.

He laughed and we parted amicably.

"I suppose we should get back and see how the fight's
progressing," Mrs. Goodwin said. "And I must confess I
could do with a sit down. My side is killing me."

"All right."

We made our way back to the Bowery.

"Look," I said as we walked back at a more leisurely
pace. "There is the Streets of Cairo Pavilion. That's where
the Rosetti girls went and right after that Rosa discovered
the note. I suppose it's too much to expect that our man always operates in the same area?"

"And at the same time?" Mrs. Goodwin shook her head.

"If it's someone from the city, he probably only comes
out here occasionally."

And if it's that innocuous divinity student, I thought, he's now supposedly at a camp in the wilderness. We'd have to have the police check on that.

The Inman Casino loomed ahead of us.

"I truly need to rest," Mrs. Goodwin said, "but I understand that we only have limited time. I'll claim I'm feeling faint and have them bring out a chair into the fresh air for me. That way I can keep an eye on you as you explore."

"Good idea," I said. "Don't worry. I won't go out of sight. I just need to see for myself what attractions lie along this part of the street."

I left her installed outside the casino and crossed to the Cairo Pavilion.

"Closing in ten minutes," the turbaned man outside was shouting. "Only ten minutes to see the glories of the harem."

Some of the food booths were also in the process of shutting down for the night. Only the dance palaces, the beer halls, and dubious-looking clubs were still going strong. I looked into them but didn't risk going inside. The boy could have been a day-tripper and have spotted Rosa anywhere. Finding a needle in a haystack was an easy quest compared to the one I had set myself. And yet I was sure that the other girls had met their killer in the same way. He had dumped the subsequent bodies on the same two streets. Did that mean he was a creature of habit? Did he always frequent the same part of the Bowery? I looked around me for young men standing alone.

Then a midget jumped out in front of me, making me jump out of my skin. "Last chance for the freak show, lady!" he shouted, in a funny high voice. "Ten cents to see the most amazing, most disgusting spectacles you'll ever set eyes on."

I looked up at the frontage of the pavilion. This then was the freak show that the Rosetti sisters had been to before they had entered the Cairo Pavilion. On the wall were painted the various freaks exhibited inside. The snake woman, the world's smallest horse, the bearded lady, the mule-faced boy, the human tree.

I stopped, finding it hard to breathe. Wasn't that what

Rosa Rosetti had murmured before dying? Tree. Tree. And at this very spot she had found the note in her pocket. I turned to go back and fetch Mrs. Goodwin, and instead I found myself staring into Detective Quigley's face.

THIRTY-SEVEN

Good evening, Detective," I managed to say calmly. "Did you tire of the fight?"

"I must confess that I did," he said. "I only came along because Captain Paxton suggested it, and it's good to keep on the right side of the top brass. Frankly I find it a barbaric practice, so I made an excuse to come outside, and then I ran into Mrs. Goodwin. I must say I was surprised to see her. I thought she was still in the hospital. She told me she was keeping an eye on you, that you suspected this area had something to do with the Ripper. If it truly does, aren't you taking an incredible risk?"

"I'm staying within sight of Mrs. Goodwin," I said, "and the casino is crawling with police right now."

"Even so," he looked at me in that supercilious way of his, "this case should be left to professionals. What exactly did you have in mind?"

I pointed at the freak show. "I'd like to go in here and take a look for myself."

"You've got a taste for freaks?" He laughed.

"No, but there's something I'd like to check on. It could be important. Could I ask you to follow at a safe distance behind me, in case I need you?"

"I suppose so," he said. "Will you not tell me what could be so important in a freak show?"

"I'd rather not, until I've checked it out for myself," I said. "I may be quite wrong. And anyway, Mrs. Goodwin will be presenting all our findings to Captain Paxton. I think you'll be surprised at what we've discovered."

"Really?" He raised an eyebrow. "Trying to beat us at our own game?"

"Only trying to help," I said.

Quigley sighed and looked around impatiently. "Okay. Hurry up, if you're going in here then. I can't take too long. Paxton will wonder where I've got to. I don't want him to think I can't stomach prizefights."

"All right, then." I nodded to him and went up to the ticket booth.

"Just closing, missy. You'll have to hurry," the ticket taker said. I paid my ten cents and stepped into a dark hallway. After a few paces it opened into a dimly lit room. A jungle scene had been created and suddenly I spotted the snake woman. She was entwined around the branch of a tree. When she saw me, she eased herself over a rock and slithered toward me. And—she really did have a human torso and the tail of a snake. I stared at her, repulsed, fascinated, as her long tail twitched with a life of its own. Then I remembered the reason I was here and moved on, down the next hall and into a room, this time decorated like a stable yard. Standing in front of one of the stables was a little horse, no bigger than a large dog. Where the snake woman had been somehow frightening, the horse was delightful. And there was no trick about it, either. It was definitely real.

One more hall and the bearded lady. She was fat and repulsive and only invoked my pity. I averted my eyes so that she shouldn't catch me staring at her and hurried down the next passage. And there he was—the human tree. He was a giant of a man, brawny, muscled, but there was something wrong with him. Even in the dim light I could see his disfigured face with great gnarled lumps and bumps protruding from it. A great lump came out of one cheek, half closing one eye. The same scaly lumps grew out of his skin, which was flaking off in other places. His hands had fake twigs and leaves extending from them and there were fake leaves on his head. His feet were apparently hidden in the earth.

As I stared at him in horrified fascination, I noticed that he was staring right back at me, appraising me.

"Last call. Closing in five minutes." I heard the distant shout. "All customers head for the exit."

I glanced back, hoping to catch a reassuring glimpse of Detective Quigley. Had this hideous tree man taken a fancy to certain girls who came to stare at him, managed to slip notes into their pockets, and then lured them back to kill them? I heard a rustling sound and spun around to see the tree man lifting his feet out of the fake earth.

"Show's over for the day," he said, in a deep, rumbling voice. "I can go now. You want to come for a drink with me, little lady?"

"Uh—no thanks," I said.

"Why not?"

"I've got a friend waiting for me." I could hardly make the words come out without my voice trembling.

"Then why are you here alone? Where's your friend? Bring her along, too. Come on. Come for a drink."

He was moving across the painted scenery toward me. I stepped back, shaking my head.

"You don't want to come because I'm so ugly. That's it, isn't it?" he said.

"No, of course not. It's just—my boyfriend—" I was already backing away, hoping that Quigley would emerge from the darkness.

He was still coming toward me. "Go on, admit it. I disgust you. You don't want to be near me. Just like all the others. I see them looking at me. How do you think that feels, huh? Seeing beautiful girls and knowing that I can never touch them because I look like this. Well, I'm a man, and I've got a man's body and a man's desires."

Suddenly he reached out and grabbed me. His strength was enormous. His hand felt as if it was crushing my arm.

"Mr. Quigley!" I shouted. "Help! In here. He's got me."

I heard feet along the passageway and to my relief Detective Quigley came into the room.

"Let go of her at once," he commanded. "I'm a police officer."

The big man looked up in surprise and dropped my arm.

"Are you all right?" Quigley asked me. "He didn't hurt you?"

"Just scared me," I said.

"No harm done then," he said. "Some of these freaks are mentally as well as physically unsound. Let me get you out of here." He took my arm. "And you," he said, wagging a warning finger at the tree man, "you've been warned before, haven't you?"

As soon as we had left the room, I grabbed Officer Quigley's arm. "Wait, Detective. That tree man," I whispered urgently, "don't let him escape. You have to arrest him."

"That man?" Quigley looked back. "Because he made a grab at you?"

"No, because he's the East Side Ripper."

Quigley looked at me in amazement. "What are you talking about?"

"I'm sure of it. It all fits," I said. "Two of the dead girls went to meet a mysterious man on Coney Island."

"Yes, but—do you think any girl would go to Coney Island to meet him?" Quigley looked back in revulsion.

"They received notes from a secret admirer. The notes were slipped into their pockets—easy enough to do in this kind of crowd. So they didn't know who they were going to meet. And listen to this. The one girl who was still alive when they found her—her last words were 'Tree. Tree.' " I shook his arm desperately. "Hurry, please, or he'll get away. You must believe me."

"Oh, I believe you," he said. "I'd better get you out of here before there's any trouble. This way then."

He whisked me along the narrow passage, opened a door, and held it for me to pass through ahead of him. I stepped through it and stopped. I wasn't outside at all. I was in a small room.

"This isn't the way out," I said.

"No, I'm afraid it isn't." Quigley was blocking the doorway and the tree man was right behind him.

"Who have we got here, Carter?" the tree man asked, following Quigley into the room and closing the door behind them.

"She knows about you, Jimmy. She's figured it out," Quigley said. "I'm afraid I'm going to have to arrest you."

"You can't do that. You promised. And if you do, I'll talk. I'll tell them . . ."

Something had just struck me. "Carter?" I interrupted. "Who is Carter?"

"I am," Quigley answered. "That's my name. Carter Quigley."

I stood there, my heart still racing, digesting this fact. "Then you are Letitia's fiancé?" I blurted out.

"How the devil did you know about Letitia?" he exclaimed.

"Arabella Norton asked me to find her. I'm a detective, remember."

"Well done," he said. "Your detective skills are not bad for a woman. Better than that stupid Goodwin female. If you hadn't come along, she'd never have got this far."

"But don't you understand," I exclaimed, looking from one man to the other, "this man killed your fiancée. Those dead girls weren't prostitutes at all. Your fiancée was one of them. That day she came to Coney Island and . . ." My voice drifted into silence. I was watching his face. He was not shocked, not angry. He was, if anything, amused.

"You do know," I said, "you know he killed the woman you were going to marry, and you didn't do anything about it? What sort of man are you? If you knew who the East Side Ripper was, why in God's name didn't you arrest him?"

"I had my reasons," Quigley said.

"He made me do it," the tree man countered.

"Oh, come on, Jimmy. Don't play the martyr. I made you do it?"

"You did. I didn't want to kill her. She was nice. She didn't look at me like the others."

I stared at Quigley. "You had him kill Letitia?"

"What else could I do?" Quigley said calmly. "I asked her to let me out of our engagement, but she refused. There was no other way out."

"You had her killed because she wouldn't release you from your engagement?" I couldn't disguise my disgust.

"You don't know what she was like," Quigley sounded angry now. "She was a hysterical female. She was smothering me. I couldn't see my life trapped with her. And a court case with her whimpering on the witness stand would have wrecked my career."

I looked back at the tree man. "You said he made you kill her. How could he make you do something like that? What kind of hold does he have over you?"

Jimmy looked away. "He found out about something I did wrong," he muttered.

"I found out about the others, didn't I, Jimmy?" Carter Quigley said calmly. "That first girl you strangled under the pier?"

"That was an accident!" Jimmy shouted. "I told you it was an accident. She tried to scream. I had to stop her."

"And the second one? She was an accident, too?"

"No, but she laughed at me. She said, 'What a freak. Can you imagine making love to that?' "

"So you lured her back here alone and killed her," I said. It was hard to take in what I was hearing.

"I found you making a pathetic attempt to hide the body, didn't I, Jimmy?"

"I see." I digested this. "And you let him go free on condition he killed your fiancée? You brought Letitia here to be killed?" I couldn't hide my revulsion as I stared at him. An image of that delicate little face floated into my mind. I imagined her coming here, her arm slipped trustingly through his, and then being left to face that unimaginable horror.

"I told you. He made me do it," Jimmy said angrily.

"But then you got the taste for it, didn't you, Jimmy?" Carter said. "Those other girls? It is time you were stopped."

"Dressing them as prostitutes," I said. "Whose idea was that?"

"Mine, of course," Carter said. "Nobody ever cares about dead prostitutes. If this silly fool hadn't started killing so many of them, nobody would ever have found out. Of course, nobody has found out yet. Paxton is a simpleton who will never get to the truth, and McIver—well, he's a lazy son of a bitch. They rely on me to do the work."

In a blinding flash I saw. "Daniel Sullivan." I could hardly make the words come out. "You were the one."

"He was put in charge of the case. He was too good. I saw him out here at Coney Island, and I knew he must be onto something."

He was looking into a doped racehorse, I thought. All this was for nothing. I realized something else, too. "Nobody has found out," he said. He didn't plan for me to leave this room alive.

"Mrs. Goodwin is just down the street," I said. "If I don't get back to her soon, she'll come looking for me. She'll fetch Captain Paxton."

Quigley smiled. "And I'll run back in distress, telling them that you slipped down an alleyway, and I lost you. I've been hunting everywhere."

"They'll find me."

"Too late, of course. Your body won't show up on a city street, like the others. I rather think we'll take you out to sea."

"I get her first, Carter," Tree man said. "You've brought her here for me."

"Of course, Jimmy. She's all yours. And I'll go back to impart the distressing news to my colleagues."

I looked around the room. It was a dingy little place, lit by one kerosene lamp. There were no windows, but a ladder went up through a hole in the ceiling. Jimmy's hidey hole, where I was about to be taken and where nobody would find me. It was now or never, it seemed. As the tree man came toward me with a monstrous leer on his face, I reached out and yanked at the tablecloth. The lamp went flying and smashed onto the floor. A sheet of flame rushed across the room. The tree man let out a yell of pain and jumped back. I didn't wait to see what damage I had done. I grabbed that doorknob and fled into the dark passage behind.

The passage was in total darkness, lit only by the flickering glow of the flames I had created. I heard Quigley's shout and footsteps behind me, but I raced blindly, like a mad thing. The passage turned a corner and I bumped hard into a wall, bouncing off it like an India rubber ball. Somehow I managed to keep my feet and kept running. There was a door at the end of the passage. I pushed on it. It flew open, and I was out into the night.

I saw instantly that I was not back on the Bowery, as I had hoped, but in one of the narrow alleyways. I wasn't sure whether to run left or right. To my left the alley seemed to be blocked by garbage cans. I turned to my right and ran for all I was worth, just as I heard someone burst out of the door behind me. I kept looking for a pathway to my right, to enable me to double back to the Bowery, to Mrs. Goodwin, and to safety. But there was none. Behind the fence to my right was the amusement park, with the ghostly shapes of merry-go-rounds and scenic railways now shut down for the night. Then the pathway went up a flight of steps. I stumbled up them, stepping on my hem and almost pitching myself onto my face. Somehow I scrambled to my feet and lurched forward as I heard feet on the stairs behind me.

I was on the boardwalk. I could see couples strolling, but none of them close enough to be any use to me. I dashed across the boardwalk and made for the pier. If Harry the Horse was still there, he'd remember me. He might help me. But as I approached the little bar where he had been sitting, I saw that it was closed and shuttered. I glanced back. Quigley was right behind me. There was no sign of Jimmy the tree man, but that didn't mean he wasn't following, too.

I had no other option but to continue onto the pier. I realized this was stupid, as soon as I'd passed through the gateway. Now I'd be well and truly trapped. Instead of running straight ahead, I ducked to one side and melted into the shadows, hoping he'd run past me and I could double back.

But he stayed there, at the pier entrance, his eyes scanning the darkness. He was in no hurry now, of course. I had nowhere to go, except—to my right was another entrance, this one to the bathing pavilion, down below. It was now closed down for the night and in darkness, of course, but then I noticed what looked like an iron ladder, disappearing down the side of the pier. Maybe it was there for people to climb up after they had dived into the water. I didn't stop to think any longer, but scrambled over the railing and started to climb down. I was close to the bottom when I heard feet scrabbling on iron above me. He was coming after me. I glanced down at black water below me, sized up how high I was above it, then let go.

I hit the water with surprising force. It was so cold as I went under that it took my breath away. I came up gasping and was immediately buffeted by an incoming wave. I trod water and looked around me, trying to see where I might be able to swim to shore and escape. Surely the bathing area wasn't completely enclosed, was it? The waves must be able to roll, unhindered, to the shore. I let the next wave sweep me along with it. Then I saw that there was an ironwork grille around the sides of the bathing enclosure. The water went through easily, but not I.

Now I was trapped in here. I swam silently to the side of the pool, and maneuvered myself under the ironwork walkway, which ran all the way around the edge. I could no longer see him, but then the walkway vibrated and I realized that he must be running along it somewhere above me. All he'd have to do was look down and he'd spot me. I ducked as low as possible into the water. When the next wave came in, I let it break over me.

I waited, holding my breath, for what seemed an age. The walkway hadn't vibrated again. I looked around but could see no human shape in the darkness. Then I spotted the steps. They came right down into the water, for bathers to lower themselves into the waves with ease, and they seemed to go up and up, maybe right up to the pier again. If I could sneak up without his seeing me, if I could get a decent lead on him, I'd be safe. I swam over to them and grabbed the railing, until my foot touched the solid iron of a step. I hauled myself out and stood on the platform just above the water level, listening and looking. Nothing moved and any sound was drowned out by the noises coming from the Bowery. Sounds of music floated toward me, and that mechanical laughter from the fun house.

All at once my body was doubled up with cramps, I bent over, gasping for air. As I looked down at my shoes I saw that they were stained black. Then I realized that the liquid running down my legs was not water, it was blood. Another wave of cramps came, and I put my hand over my mouth to stop myself from crying out. How could I escape if I couldn't even move? At first I thought I must have injured myself in the fall into the water. It took a moment before I realized what was really happening to me and another moment before I knew that this had happened before. It was the scene of my nightmare.

THIRTY-EIGHT

Suddenly a bright light shone down into the water.

"Hey you, what are you doing down there?" a voice demanded.

The light had picked out the figure of Detective Quigley, standing on the upper level of walkway.

"I'm a police officer," he shouted back. "I witnessed a young girl fall into the water. I think she must have tried to commit suicide. But I don't see her anymore. Go and get help right away."

"Right you are, sir," the voice shouted back, and there were yells for help. I came slowly up the steps. He was going to let me go. Help was on its way. Almost instantly feet came running along the iron companionways.

"Here she is, down here," someone shouted, and I was grabbed and carried up the steps. The pain had now become overwhelming. I tried to fight it, but it felt as if my whole body was encased in a ring of fire.

"Don't worry, miss, we'll get you to a hospital right away," a kind voice was saying. I opened my eyes to see a constable looking down at me.

"I've got my police wagon parked nearby. Let's get her to that." I heard Quigley's voice. "I'll take her straight to the hospital."

"No. Not with him," I tried to shout. "Fetch Mrs. Goodwin. Captain Paxton, at the fight."

They were carrying me relentlessly, across the board-walk, down the steps toward Surf Avenue.

"Not with him." I managed to get the words out this time. "He'll kill me."

"She's hysterical, poor girl," Quigley's calm voice said. "It's all right, miss. I'm a police officer."

From the Bowery came a loud roar and a crowd swept toward us, laughing and shouting.

"Three cheers for Gentleman Jack, he's the best!" men were chanting.

"Knockout in sixteen rounds," someone volunteered. "He's out stone-cold."

And then, miraculously, I heard a man's voice shout, "Quigley, what's going on here?"

I managed to half-open my eyes. It was Captain Paxton.

"We've just rescued this girl, sir," Quigley answered. "She fell off the pier. I've got a vehicle waiting on Surf Avenue, and I'm taking her to the hospital."

"Good man," Paxton said, and went to move on with the crowd.

I made a supreme effort to take in enough air to speak. "He's the one!" I shouted. "The East Side Ripper. He's just as guilty. Stop him."

"She's right, sir," Quigley shouted over me and over the noise on the street. "I have found the East Side Ripper. At the freak show. Calls himself the human tree. This young woman would have become his next victim if I hadn't intervened. We must get men over there right away. When we left he was trying to burn down the place. And shoot to kill. He's dangerous."

"Don't worry, we'll get him. You take this young lady to the hospital," Paxton said and started to move away again.

"This way, boys," Quigley said to the two men who were carrying me. "Only just over here."

The crowd surged around us, laughing, jubilant, chanting Jack's name.

"Help me," I cried, but they were all intent on celebration

and making too much noise for my feeble voice to be heard. Ahead of us I could see the tall, square shape of a black police wagon.

"In here, boys." Quigley opened the back doors.

"No, please," I begged. "He's going to kill me." They were holding my arms and my legs. I struggled but couldn't move. The pain was so bad that everything was turning blurry.

"He's taking you to the hospital, miss. You'll be taken good care of, don't worry." The constable patted my arm as they lifted me aboard. "Methodist Hospital's the closest," he added. "Do you know the way? I'll come with you, if you like."

"No, you'll be needed here," Quigley said. "This crowd could turn ugly at any moment."

They deposited me on a wooden seat. I bent over again as a wave of nausea came over me.

"She's in a bad way," I heard the constable say, "maybe one of us ought to stay with her."

I grasped at his sleeve. "Yes, don't leave me now, please."

"What's going on here?" a voice demanded and through the haze Sabella Goodwin appeared. "Officer Quigley, where is Miss Murphy? I've been worried sick. There's a fire on the Bowery. Half the freak show has gone up."

"I'm here!" I shouted with all my strength. "I'm here. Help me."

"I'm taking her to the hospital. She's been hurt," Quigley said.

"Then I'll ride along, too." She started to climb up.

"No!" I shouted. I didn't imagine he'd have much trouble disposing of the two of us. "Get Bert."

"Oh, yes, the automobile. Very sensible," she said. "You're in a bad way, my dear. My brother-in-law has an automobile, Officer Quigley. He can take us there so much faster." Then I heard her yelling, "Bert—over here. We've an emergency." And hands were lifting me down from the back of that wagon.

After that I was only dimly aware of things going on

around me. I heard Mrs. Goodwin barking out instructions, and I was carried to Bert's automobile. Then I was being taken through hospital corridors, and a doctor examined me in a way that hurt even more. I think I swore at him and lashed out with my foot. But sometime during the night I lost the baby. I'm not sure whether I felt sad or relieved. After what I had been through, I was too numb to feel anything.

In the morning Mrs. Goodwin came in to see me.

"You had a pretty rough night," she said. "I'm sorry that I lost you. Quigley told me you were in danger and sent me to find Captain Paxton while he went after you. I let him go because he was younger and quicker. Thank God he got to you in time before that monster—is it true it was someone in the freak show? He was the killer?"

I tried to sit up. "Wait a minute," I said. "You said thank God he found me? Quigley? He was the one who was trying to kill me."

"Quigley? No, my dear. He was the one who rescued you from the clutches of that freak."

"Is that what he's telling everyone?"

"Of course. He's taken our men to the den where that depraved creature took the girls to be killed. Some of their clothes were still there."

"And what does the tree man have to say? Hasn't he accused Quigley? Hasn't he told the truth?"

"He's dead," she said. "There was a fire in the building. Presumably he set it himself when he knew the police were closing in on him. He didn't get out in time."

The horrifying reality of this shocked me into silence.

"And Quigley is the hero?" It came out as a whisper.

"So what are you trying to tell me?" she asked.

"Quigley was the driving force behind all this. It's true that the tree man killed the girls, but Quigley found him out. He let that monster continue with his killing spree on condition that he kill Quigley's fiancée."

"Are you sure of this?"

I nodded.

"That's horrible. His fiancée was one of those girls?"

"Letitia Blackwell. The missing girl I'd been looking for."

"Why did he want her killed?"

"An easy way out of the engagement without embarrassment to him. And it was Quigley's idea to dress them up as prostitutes and to get rid of the bodies, and I know how he did it, too—he used a police wagon, like the one he was driving last night. Everybody is used to seeing police wagons patrolling those streets, aren't they? If they remembered seeing a police wagon, they wouldn't remember whether it was there before or after the body was found."

"Cunning," she said. "I always knew he had brains, but . . ."

"There's more," I went on. "He was the one who got Daniel into his current predicament. Quigley was leading the investigation, remember? Then Daniel was put in charge over him, and he saw Daniel go out to Coney Island. He didn't realize it was about another case altogther. He thought Daniel was a threat that had to be removed."

"He confessed all this to you?"

"Some of it I pieced together myself," I said.

"Then he can't risk keeping you alive." Mrs. Goodwin put a hand to her mouth. "Oh, my goodness, now I see what he was hinting at last night as we drove you away."

"What was he saying?" My mouth was so dry the words would hardly come out.

"He claimed that your mind had gone. Your ordeal with the monster had made you insane."

"And he'll have me locked away, and nobody will believe me." I tried to digest these words and saw how easily they could come to fruition. "We'll have to stop him before it's too late."

She nodded, a deep frown creasing her forehead. "We must come up with our own proof of his guilt before he has time to act," she said.

"The first thing we must do is get me out of here," I said. "I don't want to be a sitting duck where he can find me—and already helpless in a hospital bed."

"Are you well enough to be moved?" she asked. "I thought you were badly injured last night. You lost a lot of blood."

"I wasn't injured. I miscarried the baby," I said. "I suppose that jumping off the pier and into the ocean wasn't the wisest thing to do. But I had no choice. He was after me. They were both after me. . . ."

She put a hand on my shoulder. "In many ways it's for the best right now, isn't it?"

"That's right. For the best," I said, and burst into tears.

Mrs. Goodwin was wonderful. With her naturally bossy personality and her police badge she had me out of there and taken home in Bert's automobile.

"Is there anyone who could stay with you?" she asked. "I have things that I should be doing, but I want to make sure you are protected."

Before I could answer, the door across the street opened and Sid and Gus came rushing out.

"Molly, we were sick with worry," Sid exclaimed. "What happened? Where were you?"

"She's been in the hospital," Mrs. Goodwin said. "She got hurt trying to apprehend a desperate man."

"Molly, I do wish you'd take a sensible job and leave this sort of activity to the police," Gus said, helping me from the car. "You look white as a sheet. You're coming to us, and we're putting you to bed and no arguments."

I wasn't about to argue for once.

"Are you all right now?" Sid asked, steering me in through their front door.

"Yes," I said. "I'm all right now."

"I'm so relieved you'll be looking after her," Mrs. Goodwin said. "She's still in danger. It's important nobody knows where she is."

My friends looked from me to Sabella.

"This is my friend Mrs. Sabella Goodwin," I said. "She's a lady policeman."

They laughed at the description.

"And right now I have more work to do," Sabella said. "Take good care of her. Don't let her go with anyone."

"We'll guard her with our lives," Gus said. "Oh dear, Sid. We really should have bought that dog we saw in Macy's window the other day."

"It was a Pekinese, Gus." Sid started to laugh. "As a guard dog I fear it would be sadly lacking."

Mrs. Goodwin was about to go when something occurred to me. "Did Dr. Birnbaum come by while I was away?"

"Yes, he did," Sid said. "He pushed something through your letter box. We were curious."

I handed her my key and soon she was back with the letter.

My dear Miss Murphy.

> *I have conducted the most rigorous inspection of the two hair samples, and I think I would be prepared to stand up in court and testify under oath that they came from the same head.*

I beamed at them. "We've got him. We can prove that one of the bodies is Letitia."

"We'll need more than that," Mrs. Goodwin said. "This just proves that Letitia was killed, not that Quigley had any part in her killing. He can act the bereaved sweetheart. We need to put him at the scene. We need to link him to the transportation of the girls."

"You're with the police," I said. "Can't you search the various police wagons? There must be some evidence left behind—a blood spot, another hair we could match."

"I'll do my best," she said. "In the meantime you rest."

It wasn't easy to rest, knowing what I knew. I saw how easily Carter Quigley could convince the authorities that I was out of my mind and have me removed to an insane asylum where I could no longer present a risk to him. A man who could orchestrate his own fiancée's killing, who could knowingly allow innocent girls to be killed so brutally, had to be stopped at any cost; and it annoyed me to be trapped in bed, powerless to do anything. But then I rationalized that it would not be safe for me to be out at large on the streets, where Carter Quigley could find me.

I expected him to show up at any moment, but I suppose he, too, must have been weighing his options. Perhaps he wasn't going to risk having me committed to an asylum, I decided. Perhaps his plan was to have me killed in a nasty accident, like the one that almost claimed Mrs. Goodwin. I realized that if I didn't act first, I'd never feel safe again.

I got up, dressed rather unsteadily, and asked Sid and Gus to come with me to police headquarters. When I arrived, I asked to speak to Captain Paxton, and we were ushered up the stairs to his office. I told him the whole story. I presented him with Dr. Birnbaum's letter. He nodded gravely then opened his door. "Have Quigley come in here," he said.

That was the last thing I wanted, having to meet him face-to-face. He arrived, looking surprisingly calm.

"Miss Murphy! You are recovered from your ordeal already?" he said. "What a frightful shock it must have been to you." He turned to Captain Paxton. "This is the young lady I managed to rescue from the clutches of that madman on Coney Island last night. Last night she was hysterical and out of her mind. In fact, I feared that the shock of what she went through had deranged her permanently."

"I assure you I am perfectly sane, Mr. Quigley," I said. "I remember every detail of what happened last night. I have now told everything to Captain Paxton."

"This young lady charges that you were part of these killings," Captain Paxton said. "She charges that you plotted to have your fiancée killed."

"My fiancée ran off with another man," he said bitterly. "I am heartbroken, naturally, but I would not wish vengeance."

"Your fiancée is one of those bodies you watched disinterred last Friday," I said, "as you very well know."

"Those bodies were decayed beyond recognition, I'm afraid," he said. "I have no way of knowing if one of them was my dear fiancée or not."

"The hair was not decayed beyond recognition," I said. "I have here a letter from Dr. Birnbaum, whom you know, testifying that the hair matched the strand in a locket belonging to Letitia's mother."

"How awful," he said. "Then you bring me the very worst news possible. Until now I had hope that she'd return to me."

"You knew very well that she wouldn't return to you!" I shouted. "You lured her to Coney Island yourself, then pretended she had never arrived in New York. You went to her home and made it appear as if she had run away."

Quigley smiled sadly. "I'm afraid you are delusional after all. I'm so sorry." He turned to Captain Paxton. "I suggested she would need treatment, sir. A stronger mind than hers would have snapped after what she went through. I might suggest she be examined by a doctor?"

"I'll prove that you were involved in Letitia's death," I said.

"How could you possibly do that?" he asked. "If she really is one of those bodies in the morgue, then the monster who killed her is dead and can no longer testify."

"But other people can," Mrs. Goodwin said, coming into the room. "I've just returned from Coney Island. Several people remember seeing you there with your fiancée."

"Don't be ridiculous," Quigley snapped. "Out of all those thousands of people on Coney Island, no one could possibly remember me."

"Except for those poor souls who have nothing better to do than to observe those who stare at them," Mrs. Goodwin said. "I have interviewed the snake woman and the bearded lady. I showed them your fiancée's picture. They remembered that the man who followed Molly through the exhibit late last night was the same man who came in with that young girl on his arm. The bearded lady remembered particularly because the young girl was crying. 'Don't let's stay here another minute,' she was saying. 'It's too cruel. Making them objects of fun. It's not right.' "

"So I might have taken her to Coney Island once during the last year or so. She did get distressed. I was sensitive to her wishes and brought her straight home. But that was some time ago."

He looked straight at me. You can't touch me, his expression was saying. You'll never prove that I had anything to do with it.

"Now really, sir," he said. "If these women have no more strange accusations to make, I should be back on the job. I don't know why they've taken it into their heads to attack me in this way, when I am in mourning for my fiancée and when I was responsible for saving Miss Murphy's life last night."

There was silence in the room.

Then Mrs. Goodwin stepped forward until she was facing Captain Paxton. "You knew my husband," she said. "You thought he was one of the best. And he was. And you know me. I'm not given to flights of fancy, and neither is this young woman. If she says that Detective Quigley tried to kill her, I believe her. I also believe that she has uncovered the truth about those girls. We now know how they were transported and dumped on city streets."

"We do?" Paxton asked.

She nodded and glanced at me. "They were transported in one of our own police wagons, driven by Detective Quigley."

"This is absolute balderdash," Quigley said. "One accusation after another for which you have no proof and can have no proof."

"Oh, but I do," Mrs. Goodwin said. She placed an envelope on Captain Paxton's desk. "At Miss Murphy's suggestion, I searched various police vehicles. In one of them I came up with this hair. It belongs to Rosa Rosetti."

"Rosa Rosetti? Who the hell is she?" Quigley demanded.

"The last of the girls to be killed by that poor, depraved creature, while you stood by and did nothing to stop him," I said. "An ordinary working girl who left behind parents and three sisters, and who went to Coney Island on her day off to have some fun."

"The police lab has been able to confirm that the hair

found in the police wagon matched Rosa Rosetti's," Mrs. Goodwin said. "She was, beyond a doubt, transported in that wagon. A blood spot was found nearby and I believe they also have ways of identifying blood types these days."

"What do you say to that, Quigley?" Captain Paxton exclaimed. "Byrne, Connelly!"

Two constables came running.

"You're fools, the lot of you." Quigley spat out the words. "Meddling, interfering women. Try and prove it in court, I dare you. No jury will take you seriously."

He let himself be led out of the room.

THIRTY-NINE

I t wasn't exactly the celebration we had hoped for that evening. Quigley was under arrest, for the time being anyway. After leaving police headquarters, I had gone straight to City Hall to face Police Commissioner Partridge and tried to convince him that Daniel should be released. I didn't have high hopes that Quigley would confess to planting the evidence that implicated Daniel, but I put the case before the commissioner.

"May I ask you one thing?" I said. "Whose idea was it that you tour the Lower East Side streets that day?"

The commissioner frowned then nodded. "You're right. It was young Quigley. He wanted to show me exactly where the East Side Ripper had struck."

"So he was with you when you came upon Captain Sullivan?"

"No, he'd left us just before that, but he knew which route we'd be taking."

"So now do you believe that he planted the evidence on Captain Sullivan?"

He sighed. "Unless he confesses or we find the gang member who handed over the letter, I have to believe what I saw with my own eyes. If we can get Monk Eastman to testify that Sullivan had no ties to his gang, then I suppose the jury will believe him. But I can't see Eastman being willing to go to court for anyone."

"So you're still going to let it go to trial?" I asked. "Even after I've told you everything Quigley has done?"

"I have no alternative. I have to follow the course of the law. It is my job."

"And is it also your job to dope racehorses?" I demanded without thinking. It just came blurting out.

"Dope racehorses? My dear young woman, what are you talking about?"

"That day at Brighton Race Track," I said, "the favorite dropped down dead. The horse that won belonged to your syndicate. So I'm wondering if your eagerness to keep Daniel in jail has anything to do with the fact that he was investigating that doping."

"How utterly ridiculous," he said. "It's true I do have a share in a racehorse, but I don't even follow the sport myself. It was merely an investment, as it was for all my partners."

"On the other hand," I said, "the papers will believe that you knew something about it if I tell them. The ordinary people had lots of money riding on that favorite. They won't think very kindly of you and your fellow syndicate members—especially you, with your campaign to clean up the city."

His face went red. "Are you threatening me, young lady?"

"I'm just showing you how easy it is to cast suspicion on an innocent person," I said. "How easy it is to convict someone on circumstance and hearsay."

"You should have been a lawyer," he muttered.

"Maybe I will be someday." I couldn't resist a smile. "Does that mean you'll reconsider Captain Sullivan's release?"

"I'll reconsider it," he said.

"Now?"

"Don't push your luck, young lady," he said.

That was the best I was going to get for now.

As soon as I left City Hall, I turned in the direction of the Hudson. I had another sad task to fulfill. The great white shape of the Cunard liner, *Ivernia,* towered over the West Side docks. I asked if Mrs. and Miss Norton had already boarded and was escorted up the gangplank to their cabin. I found the cabin in a state of disarray. The maid was looking flustered, trying to cram several hatboxes on top of a tiny closet. Arabella jumped up as soon as she saw me. "Miss Murphy, how lovely of you to come and see us off." She took my arm and led me along the passageway.

"You have news for me?" she asked quietly, when we were out of earshot.

"I do, but I'm afraid it's not the news you were hoping for." I looked up at those innocent blue eyes. "The worst, in fact." Then I told her the truth, trying to spare her the most sordid details. "I'm sorry to be sending you on your holiday with such grim tidings," I finished, "but I thought you'd rather know."

She nodded, pressing her lips together to maintain her composure. "Carter Quigley. I can't quite believe it. And all this time he was acting the distraught suitor."

"Oh, it's true right enough," I said. "He tried to kill me, too."

"How terrible. But you escaped unharmed?"

"More or less," I said, and left it at that.

"It was most kind of you to take the time to tell me before I sailed. It would have been on my mind all the time. At least now I know. And, of course, I owe you your fee for finding out the truth so quickly." She fumbled with her purse strings. "Will a check be all right?"

I put my hand over hers. "Miss Norton, I can't take money from you. It wouldn't feel right." Even as I said it, I heard a voice inside my head telling me I was a fool. But I think I already knew that.

"But I asked you to complete a commission for me and you did," she said. "It was a business transaction."

"Then wait until you return," I said. "Who knows, by then you may be a countess or even a princess."

She looked at me for a second in astonishment then she burst out laughing. "I may indeed," she said. "And you may even be Mrs. Daniel Sullivan."

"It's possible," I said. "If he is found innocent at his trial.

Mr. Partridge is not willing to release him from jail even though he knows the truth now."

She frowned. "Then I'll telephone my father," she said. "He might be able to do something. He's a very influential man, you know."

A porter's trolley, loaded with trunks and hatboxes, came toward us, forcing us to step outside onto the deck, where a stiff breeze was blowing. "I should go and leave you to your unpacking."

"I'd rather be out here," she said. "Mama is becoming quite upset by the tiny amount of wardrobe space we seem to have." She took my hand and shook it. "Thank you again, Miss Murphy, for all you have done. I wish you only the very best."

"And I you, Miss Norton."

"Arabella," she said. "And your name is Molly, is it not? A good Irish name. It suits you."

"Have a good time in Europe, Arabella," I said.

She nodded. I turned away.

"You know, I think I always sensed that she was gone," she called after me. "Does that sound strange?"

I looked back at her. "It's your sixth sense. You've probably some Irish in you after all." I smiled as I walked away.

That evening, as I dined with Sid and Gus, there was a forceful knocking on the front door. We froze, looking anxiously at each other, until Sid got to her feet and opened it with some trepidation. I heard her say, "Well, would you believe it. Look who's here."

And Daniel himself stepped into the room. He looked terrible—unkempt, stringy hair, pasty face, and clothes that were now too big for his skinny frame.

I had risen to my feet, but was rooted to the spot. I wanted to go to him, to hug him, but I couldn't make my feet obey me. "Daniel," I said, "the commissioner let you out already?"

"The commissioner?" he said. "I've not heard a peep

from the commissioner. No, it was Gentleman Jack who came and posted bail for me. I'm free on bail until my trial."

"But there won't be a trial, I promise you," I said. "They've arrested Quigley. He was the one who did all this, who plotted your ruin, who covered up the killing of those young girls."

"Quigley? Are you sure? Why?"

"It's a long story," I said. I was finding it hard to talk, overcome with emotion as I stared at him, and yet somehow unable to move my feet to go to him.

"Yes, Daniel. Take a seat and all will be revealed," Sid said. "I'll pour you a glass of wine or would you prefer brandy?"

He glanced back at the door. "I've got Gentleman Jack in the cab. He's taking me home. But I just wanted to stop and see Molly first. And to thank her for what she tried to do for me."

"Ask your friend to come in, too," Sid said. "The more the merrier."

"If you're sure . . ."

"Go and get him. There's plenty of food for everyone."

He smiled then. "All right." He started for the front door, then turned and looked back at me. "Aren't you pleased to see me?"

"Of course I am," I said. "It's just that after so long, after all this, it's just so sudden. I can't really . . ." And I started to cry. As someone who had prided herself on never crying in public, I had certainly done a lot of it lately. This had to stop. Maybe it would now.

Instantly he was beside me, wrapping his arms around me. "Molly, my love," he whispered. "Don't cry, dearest. Everything's going to be all right."

I rested my head against his shoulder, feeling the warmth of his lips against my hair. Maybe everything was going to be all right after all.

HISTORICAL NOTE

This story is fiction. However, two real New Yorkers make appearances in this book. John Partridge was the new police commissioner in 1902. His part ownership of a racehorse is fiction.

Sabella Goodwin was one of the first women hired in 1896 to be police matrons, supervising women after their arrest. She was married to a policeman. When he was killed in the line of duty, she was given undercover assignments for the Police Department. She proved to be so successful at these that she was promoted to full detective by 1910.

Be careful what you wish for."
That was another of my mother's favorite sayings—one of the few in her wealth of warnings that didn't predict a bad end, hellfire, and eternal damnation. It was brought out any time I expressed my childhood ambitions to see Dublin one day, to dance at a ball like a real lady, to own a horse and carriage, or just to free myself from our dreary life in Bally-killin. The end of the sentence was rarely said, but always implied—"or you may get it."

Now it had finally come back to haunt me. My mother would undoubtedly be chuckling her head off in heaven, or wherever she was spending the hereafter. Ever since I'd ar-rived in New York and met Captain Daniel Sullivan, I sup-pose I had secretly nourished a hope that we could be together some day. Although I told myself that this would never happen, also that he was unreliable, two-faced, and all-around bad news, I had never quite managed to put him out of my thoughts or my heart. And now it seemed I was be-ing offered as much of Daniel Sullivan's company as I ever wanted. More, in fact.

Three weeks had gone by since his release from The Tombs on bail, and he was still charged with taking bribes from a gang member, being in the pay of a gang, and setting up an illegal prize fight. Since then he'd received no news on his future or his fate, although we now knew who had so carefully plotted his downfall. It was a horrible way to be

living, to be sure—like walking on eggs—and Daniel wasn't
taking it well. He was used to being cock o' the walk, a powerful man who commanded the respect of his colleagues
among the New York police and who had connections to the
Four Hundred—the highest-born families in town. Those
weeks in The Tombs had taxed him physically and mentally
so that he was now alternately moping or prowling around
like a caged tiger.

And much of his prowling was being done at my house,
which is why I was pacing the floor myself one muggy Sep-
tember afternoon. Daniel had finally managed to engage the
services of a reputable attorney, who was working on his behalf, and had arranged a meeting today with the police commissioner, Mr. John Partridge. And I was left to pace the
floor at home, wondering if he'd return a free man, reinstated at his job. Please let him be freed from this terrible
burden, I found myself praying, even though I was not much
one for chats with the Almighty. And please let him get his
old job back and leave me in peace. I was appalled at myself
immediately. Wasn't I supposed to be in love with Daniel
Sullivan? Hadn't I seriously considered the prospect of marrying him some day? And yet here I was, dreading the
thought of his presence. What about for better or worse,
richer, poorer, in sickness or health? This marriage question
would require some serious rethinking, provided Daniel was
ever in a position to ask for my hand, of course.

While I waited I cleaned the house feverishly, polishing
my few pieces of furniture till I could see my face in them
and still no Daniel. Surely the interview must be over by
now. Surely the commissioner would have no alternative but
to declare him a free man. I paced the house, exactly as
Daniel had done so often these past days. I pulled back the
net curtain, looked down Patchin Place, then let it fall again.
Suddenly I could stand it no longer. I needed company, and I
needed it now. Pleasant company, amusing company. And I
knew exactly where that could be found.

I crossed the street and knocked on the door of the house
on the other side of the alleyway. It was opened by an alarm-

ing vision with a deathly white face and two green circles where eyes should have been. I gasped as the vision removed one of the green circles.

"Sorry about that," she said. "Cucumber. We're trying out skin remedies. Sid just read an article in *Ladies' Home Journal* on the subject of natural health and beauty from the larder."

The white-faced ghost now revealed itself as my dear friend and neighbor, Augusta Mary Walcott, of the Boston Walcotts, but more usually known by her nickname, Gus.

"*Ladies' Home Journal*?" I had to chuckle. "You two are the last creatures on earth I would have suspected of reading ladies' magazines."

"The cover promised interesting tips for decorating the home in the Japanese style, which we were thinking of doing anyway, so we bought the magazine and there was this delicious article on health and beauty, so of course we had to try it for ourselves. Come on in, you're just in time to try our complexion paste." She ushered me in and set off ahead of me down the hall and into their kitchen. "It's egg whites boiled in rose water with alum and oil of sweet almonds, and a dash of honey, all whipped together into a paste, and then left to dry," she called over her shoulder. "I must say, it feels very strange as it hardens, but you can actually sense all the impurities being drawn from the body."

Sid and Gus had added a conservatory onto the back of their kitchen and the doors between the two were open, as were the doors to the little garden beyond, giving the place a delightfully rural feel. As we approached I could see another white-faced specter lying under a white sheet on a garden chair, looking horribly like a corpse until she started fanning herself furiously.

"These damn flies," she muttered. "I suppose they are attracted to egg white, but they won't leave me alone."

"We have company, Sid darling," Gus called. "Molly has come to share in our experiment."

Elena Goldfarb, usually known as Sid, sat up and peeled the cucumber slices from her eyes. "I wanted to send Gus to fetch you, but she said you wouldn't be able to desert Daniel the Deceiver."

"He's not around at the moment, saints be praised," I said.

"That doesn't sound like the voice of a woman in love." Sid attempted to frown, but her mask would not let her.

"I know. It's terrible of me. I should be delighted that he is gracing me with his constant presence, but frankly I'm not. His gloomy, moody behavior is driving me insane. I've come to the conclusion that I won't make a very good wife."

"I'm sure every person on this earth drives his or her partner insane from time to time," Sid said. "I know we do. Now tie back your hair and let me slather some of this mixture onto your face. Madame Vestris is said to have preserved her beauty with this very concoction until late in life."

I had no idea who Madame Vestris was. "Oh, I really don't think—" I began.

"Don't be a spoilsport, Molly." Gus was already gathering back my unruly mop of hair. "Besides, it's supposed to draw out impurities so you may be more saintly and forgiving the next time Daniel comes to call."

I resigned myself to my fate, and was soon laughing with Sid and Gus as they turned me into a meringue. The laughter felt strange. How long since I had laughed and allowed myself to be silly with friends? The whole summer had been one of tension and heartbreak, to say nothing of the constant worry about money. Now I was recovered from my recent ordeal, both physically and mentally, but there were no new cases on the books for my small detective agency.

"So where is the dreadful Daniel this afternoon?" Sid asked. "Sit still, or the cucumber slices will fall off."

"His new attorney has set up a meeting with the police commissioner and is asking to have all the charges against him dropped."

"Well, that's finally good news, isn't it?" Gus said.

"I do hope so," I said. "Daniel's reputation means so much to him. His fellow officers still think he betrayed them, and I know how deeply that has affected him."

"All's well that ends well," Sid said. "Daniel will be exonerated and go back to work, Molly can get on with her life, and peace will reign in Patchin Place."

She was just finishing the sentence when there came a thunderous knocking on their front door. Gus hurried to open it. We heard an explosive, "What the deuce?"

"Beauty treatments." We heard Gus's calm voice. "And if you're looking for Molly, she's with us."

I hastily removed the cucumber slices from my eyes in time to see Daniel striding down the hallway toward me.

"I went to your house and you weren't there," Daniel said petulantly.

"So being a great detective, you deduced she might be over here with us," Sid said calmly. "Would you like a glass of iced tea, Captain Sullivan, or something stronger?"

"I'm not in the mood for socializing, I'm afraid," Daniel said. "I've just had an infuriating meeting with the police commissioner."

"He wouldn't agree to drop all the charges?" I asked.

"No, he damned well wouldn't." He checked himself. "I apologize for the language, ladies, but my patience has been stretched to its limit this afternoon. Molly, would you please remove that ridiculous concoction from your face and let's go home."

I put my hand up to my cheek. "I think it needs to harden first or it will be impossible to remove," I said. "But what was Mr. Partridge's reason for not declaring you innocent on the spot?"

"Because that snake Quigley refuses to confess to anything. So until he is brought to trial and found guilty, I am still officially charged and will still have to stand trial myself."

"But that's ridiculous," I said, rising from my garden chair with difficulty. "We have the proof that Quigley is guilty."

"Of his part in the murders, yes, but there is nothing to prove that he orchestrated my meeting with the gang member; and I have, of course, admitted to my part in setting up the prize fight."

"But they can't punish you for that. Half the New York Police Department was present at that fight. I saw them with my own eyes."

Daniel sighed. "I know none of it makes sense, but I have the feeling that Partridge wants to make an example of me. The only way that he'll let me off is if I can get the gang member in question or Monk Eastman himself to come forward and categorically deny that I was working with them."

"Then that's what you should do," I said.

Daniel gave a bitter chuckle. "Ask Monk Eastman to speak in my defense? I don't think you understand the adversary, my dear. He would like nothing more than my downfall. He'll not say a good word on my behalf nor let any of his gangsters."

"He might, if I asked him for you," I said.

"Under no circumstances, Molly. And that is an order."

"You can't order me around," I said. "I'm not married to you; and even if I were, I'd not take commands like some dog."

He laughed again. "I don't doubt it for a second," he said. "But I'd rather suffer the indignities of a trial than send you to plead with Monk Eastman on my behalf."

"Then send Gentleman Jack to plead for you," I said. "He must be in favor with Monk at the moment. I'm sure he made Monk a good deal of money by winning that prize fight."

"I'm sure he did, but you've met him, Molly. The man is so addlepated that he'd forget his own name if people didn't keep addressing him by it. What good could he do?"

"At least give him a try, Daniel," I said. "Write a letter to Monk and send Jack in a hansom cab to deliver it in person. He could then add his appeal to the letter."

"Molly, I can't go on discussing this in these circumstances," Daniel snapped. "Would you please do as I ask. Remove that ridiculous stuff—it makes you look like an iced cake—and let us continue this conversation in private. I hardly think it appropriate to discuss my current situation in front of those who aren't concerned with it."

"Oh, we are most concerned," Gus said. "It affects us too. If you are unhappy, then Molly is unhappy, and if Molly is unhappy, then we cannot truly enjoy life ourselves. And since it is our aim and pledge to enjoy every moment, the sooner the situation is rectified, the better."

"Hmmph," was all that Daniel could say to that.

"Captain Sullivan, let us pour you a glass of brandy," Gus said in her soothing voice. "I'm sure you have had the most vexing afternoon, and poor Molly was quite distressed when she came to visit. It's not easy for her either, you know."

"I'm sure it's not," Daniel said. He sighed again. "Very well. I accept your kind offer, simply because I refuse to walk across the street until Molly has removed that stuff from her face."

"Replace the cucumber slices, Molly, or your eyes won't feel the true benefit," Gus directed as she disappeared into the drawing room to find the decanter. Feeling stupidly self-conscious with Daniel's eyes on me, I replaced them.

"I think you should stay for dinner over here, don't you, Sid?" Gus said, returning with a generously full brandy snifter. "We could try something Japanese. I've been dying to do things with raw fish."

"I really don't think . . ." Daniel began when there was yet another knock at the front door.

"My, but we are popular this afternoon," Sid said, attempting to rise.

"Perhaps I should answer it," Daniel said. "You ladies present a most alarming appearance."

Almost instantly we heard a man's voice saying in theatrical tones, "What a disappointment. I was expecting to see two lovely ladies. Don't tell me they've hired a butler?"

"The lovely ladies you refer to are unable to receive visitors at this moment," Daniel said. "And I am not the butler."

"Unable? Don't tell me they have succumbed to the horrible grippe that is felling everyone. Oh God, tell me it's not bad news. You're not the doctor, are you?"

"No, I'm not, and may I ask who you are so that I can convey a message?"

"*Moi?* I thought everyone knew me. Tell them that Ryan is pining for them and has to see them immediately. You wouldn't happen to know where the divine Miss Molly is, would you? She's the one I am especially seeking tonight."

"Miss Molly is with the other ladies at the back of the house, but they are in no condition—"

Before he could utter another word there was the sound of some kind of scuffle or commotion, a yell from Daniel, and wicked Irish playwright Ryan O'Hare came flying down the hallway toward us. He was wearing a white peasant shirt, a royal blue cape, and I must say he made a most dramatic entrance.

He stopped short when he saw us then gave a delighted gasp. "It's the complexion paste from *Ladies' Home Journal*. What fun. I'm dying to try it."

"We used up the last on Molly," Sid said.

"Molly, my angel, is that you under there? Yes, it is. I'd know that delicate white hand anywhere. Let me give it a kiss."

"I'm sorry about this, ladies," Daniel said in a tight voice. "I presume you know this gentleman?"

"Oh dear. You two gentlemen obviously haven't been introduced. Ryan O'Hare, playwright extraordinaire. Captain Daniel Sullivan of the New York police."

"Not Daniel the Deceiver?" Ryan exclaimed. "We meet at last. I have heard much about you. We're all so proud that our dear Molly managed to rescue you from prison."

"Well, actually I'm only out on bail," Daniel said dryly. "Of course I'm grateful for what Molly tried to do."

Then it hit me. He didn't know the truth. I had never managed to speak of that night on Coney Island, so he didn't know what I'd been through. And would never know, I decided. That chapter of my life was firmly sealed.

"I think the paste has hardened enough," Sid said, and began to peel it off. We followed suit. Ryan danced between us, stroking our cheeks. "Wonderful," he exclaimed, "deliciously soft, like a baby's bottom."

"Really, Ryan, you'll go too far one day," Gus scolded. "You know you only do it to shock."

"One just wants to have one's little fun," Ryan said, pouting.

"Molly, can we please leave now?" Daniel came over to me and took my arm.

"You haven't drunk your brandy," Sid pointed out.

"Thank you, but in the circumstances—" Daniel said.

"You can't possibly take Molly away. I forbid it," Ryan said. "It was to seek her out that I trudged all this way through the heat and the flies and the dust." Ryan took hold of my other arm. "I'm whisking you away, Molly dearest. I've been instructed to escort you to a party tonight. Someone is dying to meet you."

I glanced at Daniel. His face was like granite.

"I'm afraid that I can't go to a party tonight, Ryan," I said, then my curiosity got the better of me. "Who is dying to meet me?"

"None other than Tommy Burke."

"I'm afraid I don't know Tommy Burke," I said.

"Never heard of Tommy Burke?" Ryan sounded shocked. "My dear girl, he is only the leading theatrical impresario in the city. If Tommy Burke puts on a play, it is always a sensation. Did you not see his version of *Uncle Tom's Cabin*? Not a dry eye in the house. But that's beside the point. Tommy Burke is hosting a fabulous party tonight at the roof cabaret at Madison Square. Now tell me you can't resist that, can you?"

"My, that does sound glamorous," Sid said. "But you're only inviting Molly, so we understand. Gus and I are mortally wounded that we're not to be included."

"Of course you two are included. Our bold police captain too, if he so wishes," Ryan said. "It just happened that Tommy Burke expressed a desire to meet Molly."

"Why?" I asked. "How could he have heard of me?"

"I can't exactly say. Something to do with your detective work, I understand. Anyway, all will be made clear tonight at the roof garden cabaret of Madison Square Garden, while sipping the most delightful champagne. I'll return to escort you at eight. Wear something devastating." He glanced at the clock on the kitchen wall. "Horrors. Is that the time? I'm late for my fitting. Must fly."

And he was gone.

John Quin-Harkin

RHYS BOWEN's novels have garnered an impressive array of awards and nominations, including the Anthony Award for *For the Love of Mike* and the Agatha Award for *Murphy's Law*, the first Molly Murphy mystery. Her books have also won the Bruce Alexander Historical Award and the Herodotus Award, and have been shortlisted for the Agatha Award, the Macavity Award, and the Mary Higgins Clark Award. Rhys Bowen is also the author of the acclaimed Evan Evans mystery series, which was a finalist for the Edgar Award, and several short stories, including the Anthony Award–winning "Doppelganger." Ms. Bowen was born and raised in England and now lives in San Rafael, California. Visit her Web site at jqh.home.netcom.com.

OH DANNY BOY

Irish immigrant Molly Murphy is contemplating giving up PI work for something a little less... exciting. Molly has had quite enough excitement recently, thank you very much. Especially from the handsome but deceptive NYPD captain Daniel Sullivan. She wants him out of her life for good. But when Daniel is accused of accepting bribes and lands himself in the Tombs, the notorious city jail, he begs Molly to help prove he was framed. After everything they've been through together, how can she turn him down? As Molly finds herself drawn further into Daniel's case, she begins to fear that his trouble is related to one of his investigations: catching a serial killer who is targeting prostitutes, known to the locals as the East Side Ripper....

ISBN-13: 978-0-312-99701-4
ISBN-10: 0-312-99701-9

www.minotaurbooks.com

50699

9 780312 997014

EAN

S

U.S. $6.99
CAN. $8.99